About the Author

Kat French lives in the Black Country with her husband and sons. She writes romantic comedy full-time, and also writes paranormal comedy under the pseudonym Kitty French.

You can follow Kat @KFrenchBooks.

The Bed and Breakfast on the Beach

Kat French

avon.

AVON

A division of HarperCollins*Publishers*
1 London Bridge Street,
London SE1 9GF

www.harpercollins.co.uk

A Paperback Original 2017

1

A catalogue record for this book is available from the British Library

ISBN-13: 978-0-00-823675-5

Typeset in Meridien by
Palimpsest Book Production Ltd, Falkirk, Stirlingshire

Printed and bound in Great Britain by Clays Ltd, St Ives plc

MIX
Paper from
responsible sources
FSC® C007454

FSC™ is a non-profit international organisation established to promote
the responsible management of the world's forests. Products carrying the
FSC label are independently certified to assure consumers that they come
from forests that are managed to meet the social, economic and
ecological needs of present and future generations,
and other controlled sources.

Find out more about HarperCollins and the environment at
www.harpercollins.co.uk/green

This book is informed by and written for my beloved
life-long best buddies Debbie and Jane.
This isn't our story, but it is absolutely inspired
by our friendship – there's a little bit of all of each
of us in each of them.
I thank my lucky stars for you both.
Cheers to us, ladies, love you! xxx

PROLOGUE

Forty-eight hours earlier . . .

'It looks like a pink sugar cube.'

Winnie flicked her Havaianas off onto the warm sand and slid her huge sunglasses down her nose to get a better look at Villa Valentina.

'Well, they weren't lying when they said it was on the beach,' Stella murmured, grabbing hold of Winnie's elbow while she bent double to slip her jewelled flip-flops off the backs of her heels.

Beside them, Frankie dropped her oversized shoulder bag on the sand and lifted the brim of the pink floppy sunhat she'd bought at least a decade ago, inspired by the effortlessly chic Kristin Scott Thomas in *Four Weddings*.

'What it looks like to me, ladies, is heaven.'

For a second, all three women stood shoulder to shoulder in contemplative silence. Life had dealt each of them an unexpectedly rough hand over recent months, and this weekend was very much needed to take stock, swear like troopers and sink as much ouzo as Skelidos could supply them with.

'Do you think it's too early for a G&T?'

Winnie and Frankie looked at Stella between them in pristine white skinny jeans, her scarlet toe-polish jewel-bright against the pale sand. Her eyes were trained on the faded pink mansion's deserted terrace beach bar, her hands on her hips as if she meant business.

'It's just after nine o'clock in the morning, Stell,' Winnie said, laughing, the bangles on her wrist jangling as she picked at the frayed hem of her denim shorts.

Stella rolled her eyes. 'Says the woman who sank a double brandy on the plane four hours ago.'

'She's a nervous flyer,' Frankie soothed, half-hearted in Winnie's defence.

'You're telling me,' Stella said, flicking her fringe out of her eyes. 'The poor bugger in the seat the other side of her is probably in A&E now with crushed fingers.'

Winnie wriggled her toes blissfully in the powder-soft sand, wandering forward slowly. 'Well, if you'd have put your drink down for more than five minutes I'd have been able to hold your hand instead of his. I'm sitting by Frankie on the flight home, she's more sympathetic.'

Frankie caught Stella's eye behind Winnie's back and shook her head frantically. Stella nodded and pointed first at Winnie and then at Frankie: a clear signal that her friend was on her own when it came to keeping Winnie calm on the homebound journey.

Winnie knew what they were up to behind her, of course; she'd known Stella and Frankie for as far back as sentient memory allowed. Born within four weeks of each other a stone's throw apart on the same street, the three of them had been united by both age and the fact that they were the only girls amongst the rowdy rabble of neighbourhood boys. It was a happy coincidence that they'd turned out to be similar in far more than birthdays; they shared a sharp sense of humour and a strong, abiding loyalty that bound them closer than sisters, albeit all very different in looks and temperament.

'Is that an actual tattoo, Win?'

Frankie leaned forward to get a closer look at the flowers circling Winnie's ankle.

Winnie paused and turned back.

'Temporary. I'm trying it on for size.'

'Shame you couldn't have done the same thing with your husband,' Stella said, throwing in a gentle wink to soften her words. In truth the comment didn't sting, because, in point of fact, it was pretty darn accurate. Rory, he of the wild dark curls and sparkly eyes, the man who'd pursued her endlessly and showered her with his ardent love, had turned out to be the very same guy who'd abruptly turned the shower off to an icy water-torture trickle once the chase down the aisle in front of all of their friends was over. Winnie was a different woman because of him. She'd spent the first thirty-three years of her life merrily believing the schmaltzy songs on the radio; these days she flicked stations at the opening bars of a slow song, tossing the radio an accusatory look, as if it were person- ally responsible for Rory's flimsy heart. She favoured girl-power Little Mix anthems now, belted out at the top of her lungs with the hard-won knowledge that there was no such thing as forever when it comes to love.

'Let that be the last mention of him this weekend,' Winnie said, lifting her face to the already warm morning sunshine. 'As of now, his name is on the banned list, along with Gavin.' She glanced at Frankie as she mentioned her friend's soon-to-be-ex-husband. 'And Jones & Bow, too, for that matter,' she added for good measure, looking the other way towards Stella. Jones & Bow had been Stella's employers and pretty much her home for the last decade or more, and they'd recently repaid her loyalty with an out-of-the-blue redundancy notice and a box to put her things in. The fat redundancy cheque hadn't even been a plaster on the near-fatal wound they'd inflicted on her pride, not to mention that it wouldn't last for ever given Stella's love of designer labels, far-flung holidays and the best new restaurants with waiting lists as long as Dudley Dursley's Christmas list.

'Deal.' Frankie nodded, resolute.

'Come on then.' Stella linked arms with her friends. 'Let's get checked into the sugar cube. We've got forty-eight hours of serious drinking and plate-smashing to get through.'

'I don't plan on smashing any plates,' Winnie said with a frown.

'You're in Greece. It's the rules,' Frankie said. 'Just don't do it until you've eaten your dinner. They'd consider that the height of bad manners.'

'I love Greek salad,' Winnie said, imagining colourful plates laden with fat ruby tomatoes ripened beneath the Greek sun, and huge, creamy chunks of feta.

'I love Greek men more.' Stella grinned as on cue a shirtless Adonis emerged from the sugar cube, all oiled chest and mirrored sunglasses.

'Do you think he'd be offended if I asked him to sing "Careless Whisper" to me?' Frankie murmured. Her enduring love for George Michael had seen her through many a dark time. There were several times in her life when she wished she'd turned a different corner.

'Probably.' Stella rolled her eyes. 'Think he'd be offended if I asked him to slather me with baby oil?'

A second, equally gorgeous guy in DayGlo neon shorts joined the Adonis and kissed the back of his neck.

'Fuck,' Stella sighed. 'All the best men are gay. Look at Matt Bomer.'

'And George Michael,' Frankie added.

'You really need to get over the George thing. He was always too old for you anyway.'

Frankie looked horrified, as if she'd been asked to get over the loss of a limb or broker world peace.

'I think he's staring at us,' Winnie murmured, as Adonis checked his watch then studied them intently. Throwing a few words over his shoulder towards his lover, he broke into a *Baywatch*-worthy jog across the sand and came to a halt in front of them.

'Ladies, welcome,' he said, his accent only adding to his allure. 'You must be the three new guests due this morning?'

Winnie glanced at the other two and nodded, pulling her paperwork from the side of her weekend bag and scanning it quickly.

'Are you . . . Ajax?'

He nodded with a slight bow. 'And one of you is Winifred?'

Frankie and Stella both laughed under their breath at the use of Winnie's much-detested full name. She'd been sentimentally named after a great aunt who'd died a few days before her birth; even her mother had gone off it within a month and everyone had called her Winnie from thereon in.

'That would be me.' She stepped forward and held out her hand, smiling uncertainly at Ajax. 'And this is Frankie and Stella.' She glanced behind him at the B&B. 'Are we too early to check in?'

5

He laughed good-naturedly. 'I make exception for three beautiful ladies. Come.'

He collected each of their weekend bags from where they'd dropped them in the sand and then turned and strode away towards the villa, leaving the three women to exchange speculative glances and then break into a trot to keep up behind him.

Ajax led them through the little beach bar, all white-washed chairs and driftwood tables set with jam-jars of fuchsia-pink wildflowers. The bleached, sand-covered crazy-paved terrace lay warm and smooth beneath Winnie's feet, changing to cool stone flags as they entered Villa Valentina's shady, deserted reception. There was an air of faded splendour to the old mansion house, as if it might once have been home to Greek glitterati and had fallen on hard times. The peeling paint was sort of shabby chic and sort of just shabby, but the high ceilings and grand proportions kind of made up for it and let the villa get away with it. Just.

Ajax slid behind the wooden desk, reached for a huge red diary and leafed through it to today's date. He was quick, but not fast enough for Winnie to miss the fact that the pages he flicked past were emptier than you might expect for a bookings diary.

'OK, so it's your lucky day!' he announced. 'You've been allocated the most splendid rooms up on the top floor.' He tapped his pen against the page. 'Best views in the house.'

'Fantastic,' Frankie said, fanning herself with her pink hat. 'Are they ready, or do you need us to wait?'

Ajax looked slightly wrong-footed before his expression cleared to sunshine again. 'No need to wait. Our cleaners come to work very early to make your rooms ready especially for you.'

'Well, that's very kind,' Winnie said, smiling, grateful for their forethought. Already there was something about Villa Valentina that felt magical; the weight on her shoulders was a little lighter, the melancholy in her heart a little less oppressive. Even though the effects would most likely wear off as soon as they touched down back in the UK, she'd be stronger and tougher for a couple of days off from feeling like a fool.

The three women trooped up the grand central staircase behind Ajax, who skipped his way up the winding flights of steps even though he'd insisted on carrying all of their weekend bags slung over one shoulder. On the top landing he made a ceremony of studying each of them in silence for a few contemplative moments before handing out three ornate keys, as if first deciding which of the rooms best suited each of the women.

'For you, the Seaview Suite,' he said, pressing a key into Stella's palm. 'Because it is grand and has the finest view.'

He moved along the line to Frankie. 'For you,' he said, handing her her key. 'The Cleopatra Rooms, because the bathtub is the deepest. You have the face of a lady who needs to relax.'

Frankie looked almost as if she might burst into tears; it had been a long time since a man had taken the time to notice how worn down she was.

Ajax stepped sideways to look at Winnie. 'And for you, Winifred, I think the Bohemian Suite.' He passed her an old, blackened key. 'Many artists have chosen to stay in here over the years because of the light. I think you will especially like the paintings.'

Winnie took the key, wide-eyed, wondering if Ajax had sneakily researched them all on Google because he seemed to have taken one look at them and seen right into their hearts. He couldn't have, not really; they'd only booked the break two days ago on a last-minute whim and none of them were prolific enough for Google to provide much in the way of interesting gossip. He must just be one of those rare beasts, a genuinely thoughtful, empathetic man. Winnie recognised that her worldview on men was more than a little off-kilter just now, but she genuinely wasn't sure if her heart would recover enough to think more charitably about the other half of the human race. For now though, for the sake of sisterhood, she was prepared to give Ajax the benefit of the doubt.

'Please, call me Winnie. Everyone does.'

He smiled widely, as if truly honoured. 'Then because we're friends now, you should come down to the bar when you have settled and I make special cocktails for special ladies. I mix just the right one to make you carefree.'

He gave them one of his little bows and then set off down the stairs two at a time, leaving them all staring at the fancy cast-iron keys in their hands.

'Does anyone else feel a bit like Alice about to tumble down the rabbit hole?' Frankie asked, turning the key to the Cleopatra Rooms over in her hand.

'This is what happens when you book a last-minute break to an island you've never heard of,' Stella said.

Winnie looked at her, surprised. 'What, you end up in a mystical pink B&B with a guy who seems able to read minds?'

Stella plucked at the bottom of her Breton-stripe vest, flapping it away from her body to cool herself down. 'You end up on the top floor of a place with no lifts. There better be a decent shower in there, I'm bloody melting.'

'Well, I might go and take a bubble bath,' Frankie said with a grin. 'Seeing as I have the best one and all.'

'And you should probably go and, er, gaze at the paint-ings on your walls, Win,' Stella said, wafting her hand towards Winnie's door.

Winnie shrugged, undeterred. 'I love that he thinks I'm bohemian.'

'Must have been your tattoo,' Frankie said, slotting her key into her door.

'Or your plaits.' Stella pushed her key into place too as Winnie frowned at her ankle tattoo and wound one of her shoulder-length honey-blonde plaits around her finger.

'What's wrong with my plaits?'

'Nothing,' Stella laughed. 'If you're a Swedish milkmaid.'

'You're only jealous,' Winnie sniffed, flicking her plaits over her shoulders. But she enjoyed her friends' ribbing all the same, because, God, it felt good to relax and laugh about stupid things. Fitting her key into the lock of the Bohemian Suite, she turned, shiny-eyed, to look at the others.

'Three, two . . .' she counted down, and, on one, they all turned their keys.

Bohemian turned out to be Winnie's idea of perfect. The stripped oak floorboards were warm beneath her feet, and the room seemed vast and airy thanks to the tall, ornate French doors, which had been opened to allow the hint of a cooling breeze to flutter the gauzy white muslin curtains. The walls had been painted deep oxblood, a rich, evocative colour that, coupled with the huge cast-iron bed, certainly conjured up bohemian. An eclectic mix of jewel-coloured cushions topped the crisp white cotton bed linen, and a huge emerald-green velvet chaise longue sat in front of ceiling-high bookcases stuffed with hundreds of books in all sizes and colours. Two glass chandeliers hung overhead, adding opulence to the already dramatic room; it was clearly a space designed for reclining, relaxing and recharging. Winnie had no clue what the other girls' rooms were like, but she knew instinctively that this was the right one for her. Stripes of sunlight streamed through the doors and windows, and when she stepped out of the French doors, she found herself on a wide balcony set with a tiny table and chairs for two beside a 60s-style wicker hanging-egg chair to take in the glittering view over the Med.

'Are you feeling all arty-farty yet?'

She turned and found Stella peering at her from her wraparound balcony at the far end of the villa. She'd already changed into a halter-neck polka-dot bikini top and teeny black denim shorts, and pulled her long red-gold waves back into a swishy ponytail.

Winnie laughed, delighted. 'I think I am! How's the Seaview Suite?'

'I've really no idea why they call it that.' Stella shrugged and rolled her eyes, flopping blissfully down onto the padded wooden steamer chair on her balcony. 'I mean, come on.' Ajax had been right about the view from Stella's room; she had an uninterrupted, picture-postcard-perfect vista out over the gorgeous sugar sand and crystal sea.

Between them, Frankie wandered out onto her balcony, cool as a cucumber in a black linen shift and big Jackie O sunglasses perched on top of her bleached pixie cut.

'Bath's running,' she said. 'It might take a while, it's practically a swimming pool.'

A peaceful, easy feeling washed over Winnie's shoulders, warmer even than the Greek summer sunshine. Frankie would be a while yet, and Stella looked set for some serious sun-worshipping.

'I might just test my bed out for five minutes,' she said,

lifting her hand to wave to her friends. Frankie did a tiny, crazy, happy dance out of pure contentment, and Stella lifted her hand above the balcony balustrade with an indistinct moan of happiness. Wandering back inside, Winnie momentarily paused to wonder how you might climb up onto a mattress higher than your belly button, then taking a bit of a running jump, she threw herself face-down on the bed and spontaneously laughed for the first time in months.

Ajax placed a tray of three tall, fine-stemmed fishbowl glasses on the beach-bar table in front of them an hour or so later.

'You've built our expectations sky-high now, you know that, right?' Frankie said, lifting her eyebrows at him. 'If these cocktails don't make us feel a million dollars we're going to want our money back.'

'Your first drink is always on the house anyways,' Ajax said grandly. 'Villa Valentina house secret mix, guaranteed to make you happy.'

'Free drinks always make me happy,' Stella sighed. 'People used to give me free drinks all over town. Stella! Come in, have a glass of champagne! And another!'

'Ah, get over yourself, superstar. This one's still free and looks amazing.' Frankie reached for one of the glasses and handed it to Stella.

'What is it?' Winnie lifted her sunnies and squinted up at Ajax hovering close by for their verdict.

He shrugged. 'Gin and tonic.'

It wasn't like any gin and tonic Winnie had ever seen before. Peering into the glass as she slid it towards her, she could see rich shades of honeyed nectarine red sparkling with ice and slices of rose-pink grapefruit.

11

'Is this rosemary?' Frankie asked, plucking a herb from her glass and sniffing it.

Ajax preened. 'I grow it myself in the garden at the back of the villa.'

Frankie dunked it back into her cocktail, using it to swirl the ice cubes. All three women looked up as the guy they'd spotted earlier with Ajax wandered over and placed a platter of glistening halved figs scattered with walnuts down on their table.

'Oh. My. God.' Winnie groaned. 'How good does that look? They're the fattest figs I've ever seen in my life.'

'Best in the world. I grow them myself in the garden behind the villa.'

'I'm sensing a theme,' Stella murmured, then took a sip of her drink and gasped. 'Bloody hell! That's amazing. You have to tell me how to make this before I leave.'

Ajax ignored the request, choosing instead to make introductions.

'Ladies, this is my husband, Nikolas.'

Nikolas stuck out his hand. 'Nik, please.'

'Well, thank you, Nik, for this. It looks wonderful,' Winnie said, nodding towards the plate. 'I'm Winnie.'

The others jumped up in turn and shook his hand, and he just nodded politely and excused himself.

'He likes actions, not words,' Ajax sighed, watching his lover wistfully until he'd disappeared back into the villa.

'My kind of man,' Stella laughed, making Ajax scowl theatrically.

'What is it that you English like to say?' he said. 'Not on your nelly.'

He winked and blew them a kiss before threading his way through the tables in the direction of his husband.

'Happy couples make me want to vom right now,' Winnie

said, taking a good gulp of her drink and then almost choking on the rosemary stem.

Stella grabbed for the glass. 'Christ, Winnie, it's too good to splutter all over the floor!'

Frankie lifted her drink so that the sunlight shone through the liquid, bouncing pink crystal shimmers all around them.

'Everything about this place is special,' she said. 'The villa, Ajax, the cocktails, that view . . . it's all blissful.'

Winnie had recovered sufficiently to raise her glass and toast the others.

'To forty-eight hours of secret recipe cocktails and uninterrupted bliss.'

Stella clinked her glass against Winnie's. 'I'll drink to that. And to friendship.'

Frankie nodded solemnly and touched her glass to the others. 'To us.'

Ajax watched the three women carefully from an upstairs window of the villa, observing the way they laughed together, how they toasted each other, that they were relaxed in each other's company.

Maybe.

With enough of his secret cocktails and a fractured kaleidoscope of sun-gilded images laid out to seduce them, just maybe.

CHAPTER ONE

'How the shagging hell did this happen?'

Stella looked from Winnie to Frankie clustered around the breakfast bar in her screamingly cool loft apartment. They'd barely sobered up from landing back in England a few hours ago, and reality was sinking in fast. It wasn't just their hearts that had come home lighter from Skelidos. Their bank accounts were significantly lighter too.

Winnie's half of the profits from the sale of her beloved house, the one she'd imagined her babies would grow up in.

Stella's handsome redundancy from Jones & Bow, a chunk of which she'd already earmarked for a world cruise.

Frankie's nest egg, bequeathed to her by Marcia, the childless elderly neighbour she'd cared for over the last dozen years.

'Marcia told me that she wanted me to have an adventure,' Frankie whispered. 'The very last time we spoke. I didn't realise that she was leaving the house to me until the solicitor called me in, after she'd . . . after she'd gone.'

Her neighbour had been more of a surrogate mum, and she'd been aware of Frankie's deep-seated unhappiness with Gavin for many years. Her gift had been the catalyst for Frankie to finally find the courage to end the marriage her parents had pressured her into as a frightened, pregnant seventeen-year-old. She and Gavin had rubbed along as best they could and the twins had grown up happy and strong as a result, but they were seventeen themselves now and they didn't need her to wipe their noses or hold their hands when they crossed the road any more. They'd been the reason she'd stayed, and their leaving home had been the reason she'd finally left, too; the reality of living all alone with Gavin had been too much to bear. The boys had filled the silence and the space with noise and clutter: hockey sticks in the hall, muddy football boots in the porch, music too loud in their rooms. Who knew the silence they left behind would be even more deafening? Marcia's money had allowed Frankie to rent a tiny place all of her own while she considered her next move, somewhere to lie low and lick her wounds, somewhere to spin the globe with her eyes closed and choose an adventure grand enough to warrant Marcia's approval.

'Looks like adventure got tired of waiting and came looking for you,' Winnie said quietly.

All three of them stared at the large white envelope between them on the breakfast bar, and at the bunch of keys resting on top of it. They'd flown to Skelidos in the expectation of a couple of days' hedonistic escape, and they'd flown home again with the deeds to Villa Valentina in their weekend bag beside the duty-free.

'God knows what he put in those cocktails,' Stella said, frowning. 'He was more hypnotic than Derren sodding Brown.'

Winnie stared at her. 'You don't think he slipped us something illegal, do you?'

15

'Yes,' Stella huffed. 'He slipped us pipedreams and bare bronzed chests and sand between our toes. He slipped us sunshine on our shoulders and lazy, idyllic afternoons, and he slipped us long starlit evenings drinking cocktails beneath fairy lights strung between pine trees. He slipped us the idea of a perfect life, and we reached out and grabbed it in our pale English hands because we had stressed, lonely and gullible stamped on our foreheads.'

As she spoke she pointed from herself to Frankie and then finally to Winnie. Stressed, lonely and gullible.

'Well, that's lovely,' Frankie frowned, wrapping her hands around her mug of steaming coffee. 'Anyone would be lonely going from living with my kids to the silence of an empty flat.'

'At least you got lonely. I got gullible,' Winnie muttered, twisting the slender wedding band she still wore even though her marriage was all over bar the decree absolute.

'Ladies, it wasn't an insult.' Stella shook her head. 'We are where we are. Of *course* you're lonely, Frank, you're recovering from years of being needed by a whole bloody cul-de-sac, and Winnie, the fact that you're still too trusting after what Knobchops did to you is a good thing, not a bad one. And me? I didn't even have a relationship to break. I pinned years of hopes onto Jones & Bow, and I've been left high, dry and stressed to the eyeballs. The truth is that we're all lonely, and we're all stressed, and given that we've just gone thirds on a bed and breakfast on a Greek island I can't even remember the name of, we're all gullible as hell.'

They perched on Stella's uncomfortably high designer saddle stools and stared at the keys in silence.

'Skelidos,' Winnie said, eventually. 'It's called Skelidos.'

'The villa *is* pretty gorgeous, in its own elegantly shabby way,' Frankie said, after a while.

'And the cocktails were world class,' Stella acknowledged.

They lapsed into silence again.

'What else were you planning on doing this summer, anyway?' Winnie asked, the slow tug of a smile lifting the corners of her mouth. She'd made the horrendous decision to move temporarily back home to her parents after her house sold more speedily than anticipated, and she was already heartily sick of her old curfew being unexpectedly back in place because her father liked to lock up before bed at eleven, and of going to sleep staring into the collective soulful eyes of Westlife because her mother refused to allow her to take her old posters down. She loved her parents dearly, but if she didn't get out of there soon she'd give up, buy a cat, take up macramé and join her mother's Catherine Cookson Monday-afternoon reading group.

Frankie looked up from her coffee thoughtfully. 'I honestly don't know.'

'Well, I need a job, a man and a ticket back to normality, asap,' Stella said.

Winnie nodded slowly. 'Will a business, a donkey and a ticket back to an island you can't remember the name of do in the meantime?'

Stella's expression spoke volumes. 'A donkey?'

Winnie nodded. 'It's in the deeds. Seriously, I'm not even joking. The Fonz comes with the villa.'

'Don't tell me. He lives out the back with the rosemary bushes and the fig trees and the fairies at the bottom of the friggin' garden.'

Frankie pulled her laptop from her bag, her wide, copper-flecked eyes flaring with wary anticipation.

'I'll see if I can book us some flights.'

*

17

Winnie stared at her old single bed, which at that moment was barely visible beneath summer clothes, swimsuits, bumper-size bottles of factor 30 and beach towels. How do you pack for a one-way trip to Greece? She wasn't sure if she should pack for a week or throw her entire wardrobe in her suitcase, because she didn't know if they were heading back to Skelidos for a week to try to wriggle out of the contract or for a lifetime to start a new chapter. Thanks to the lethally large cocktails, she also wasn't sure whether Ajax was their fairy godfather or had played them like a crack hot conman. He'd kept them fuelled up on his secret recipe gin and lured them in with tales of his bucolic life on the island, and, their tongues loosened by the alcohol, they'd poured out their woes faster than three leaky jugs.

He hadn't even directly suggested that they buy the villa, at least not at first. He'd talked around it, and let them think it was their idea. It was just damn good fortune that Nikolas happened to be the local property notary and had had the sales paperwork already drawn up in preparation for the planned sale which had just fallen through at the last moment. Convenience, or fate? Either way, he'd had them signing on the dotted line and arranging bank transfers with lightning speed, all buoyed up by Ajax and his constant supply of free drinks and his endless tales of how marvellous life on Skelidos was going to be for the three women. What an adventure they'd have! What a brave and smart move to leave grey old England behind for the idyll of sunny Greece! He'd sealed the deal with big fat tears as they signed, tears of joy tinged with sadness that his wonderful B&B was now in new hands and that he'd forever leave part of his heart there when he and Nikolas moved to Athens in a few days' time. Nik had accepted a high-profile job over on the mainland, and much as they adored their one-long-honeymoon island life, the bright city lights were calling.

Ajax was in no doubt; fate had conspired to bring Winnie, Stella and Frankie to his island at that precise moment because this place was now their destiny, not his. At heart, Winnie was a believer in fate and superstition; the idea that she'd been guided to the island charmed her all the way to the bank. Frankie, of course, felt more guided by Marcia's instruction to find adventure; she'd needed little in the way of persuasion to realise that this would certainly be that. Stella had been perhaps the most hesitant of the three, until Frankie and Winnie had decided that they'd find a way to buy it together even if Stella decided it wasn't for her. The idea of missing out on a potential business opportunity and a life in the sun with her best friends had proved too tempting to pass up, and in the end she'd signed on the understanding that she could always pull out after a year if she wanted to. They each had their own reasons for signing, and for all of them there was an element of running away and an element of looking for a new place to call home.

A text alert vibrated her phone, making it rattle and jump around on the little pine bedside table. Winnie lunged for it before it slid off the edge, momentarily grateful for the distraction until she saw who had sent the message.

Did I really need to hear you're leaving the country from Stella's sister-in-law? What am I supposed to do, send the divorce papers by carrier pigeon? I've never even heard of the fucking place.

Winnie closed her eyes and took a few measured breaths so she didn't text back the response hovering on the tip of her fingers.

Did I really need to hear you were screwing the girl from the canteen from your secretary? What was I supposed to do, make your favourite dinner more often and be more adventurous in the bedroom? You've no fucking right to question me.

God, it was tempting and Rory completely deserved her animosity. She didn't write the message though, because she was slowly coming to realise that the person her anger hurt the most was herself. He'd probably check his phone, roll his eyes and delete the conversation before his precious receptionist realised he'd sent a text to his ex-wife. Winnie, on the other hand, would feel the after-effects of their exchange like a hangover without any of the fun first, miserable and heartsick until she could return the whole sorry situation to its box at the back of her head.

The internet works perfectly well in Skelidos. Please send all solicitors' correspondence via email and I'll make sure it gets back to England without delay.

Bloody man! He wouldn't even have known she wasn't around if Stella's sister-in-law didn't work for the same law firm. Oh, well. What did it matter anyway? As long as he didn't intend on booking a romantic Greek holiday with his lover and wind up at Villa Valentina, then it'd probably be all right. Winnie sat down on the edge of the bed and let herself imagine him booking in unaware, and her inadvertently killing him with a really heavy frying pan then leaving him in the garden for The Fonz to feast on. Were donkeys even carnivores? She doubted it; it'd make seaside donkey rides an insurance nightmare. She'd just have to hire a boat and chuck him overboard with bricks in his pockets instead. Sufficiently bolstered by the fantasy, she pressed *send* on her polite response and chucked as much in her suitcase as was physically possible without breaking the zips. She wasn't going to Skelidos for a week; she was going for as long as she could possibly stay.

*

A few miles away in a small café with insufficient air conditioning, Frankie drew a line down the middle of a blank page of an exercise book and wrote 'for' and 'against' at the top of the two columns. It wasn't exactly a spreadsheet, but its practicality was a comfort nonetheless.

Under 'against', she noted her only real sticking point; or two points, technically. Joshua and Elliott. Her beloved, boisterous boys, the reasons she'd put the last half of her own life on hold. It was hard to imagine that she'd given birth to them at the same age as they were themselves now; they were still her babies and the thought of them as fathers right now was utterly incomprehensible. Please let them have at least another ten years of freedom first, she murmured. Please let them make a million mistakes that don't matter rather than one huge one that changes their lives for ever.

Tapping her pen against her teeth, she considered what to write next. There really wasn't much she could think of to add to the 'against' column, and in truth the boys didn't really need her around at home any more. Josh was living away at a sports academy for the most promising youth footballers in the country, and Elliott had won a hard-fought-for apprenticeship with one of the luxury car brands he coveted and moved into a shared house forty miles away. Fierce pride bloomed bright in her chest at the thought of how well they were doing; if there was one thing she was certain of it was that her sacrifices had been worth it, and that she'd do the same all over again to ensure that her kids were set on the right path.

After a second, she wrote 'Marcia' in the 'for' column, followed by 'find an adventure'. Then she added 'sunshine', 'friendship', 'new start', 'excitement' and 'not lonely any more' to the list in quick succession. Her hand hovered

21

over to the 'against' column to add 'money', but in fact going thirds on the villa had still left her with a decent chunk in the bank, so it really wouldn't be accurate to put it down as an against, exactly. That made seven for, and two against. Quite definitive, really, even though the thought of living in a different country from Josh and Elliott made her feel queasy. Perhaps if she framed it in her mind as an exploratory trip, then it would be less of a wrench. Three months or so, and if she missed the boys too much, she could always come home again. She closed her book, laid her pencil neatly on top and unscrewed the lid from her bottle of water.

If the spreadsheet said it was a good idea, then it had to be right.

In a dressing room in the department store in town, Stella stripped off and jiggled herself into the first of the many bikinis she'd picked out. For such tiny garments, they were a minefield to get right. She wanted uplift without her double Ds being under her chin, pants that gave the illusion of maximum leg length because she was five foot four on a good day, and for God's sake some bum coverage rather than letting it all hang out. Not that it hung out very much; she sweated blood and tears in the gym most mornings to make sure of that.

Stella knew that self-confidence came from feeling good about yourself, and confidence was one of the most important factors in her job. Or else it had been up to now. As marketing and PR manager for Jones & Bow, she'd been the public face of the company, the brand ambassador. Her eyebrows were always immaculately threaded and her designer clothes a perfect fit around her curves; no workout in the world could minimise the fact that she'd inherited the Daniels family boobs. Her mother, her aunts and her grandmother all had the same small-waisted, full-breasted Jessica Rabbit figure and over the years she'd learned to work with it rather than against it. Sexy was no bad thing, in the boardroom or the bedroom.

Turning, she eyed her body critically in the mirror, and then rejected the polka-dot bikini as too kitsch and opted for the sleek red Victoria's Secret instead.

Working her way through the collection of irritatingly tangled hangers she ended up in a muddle of straps and ties, then lost her cool and threw the whole lot in a heap on the floor and flopped down onto the padded stool. What was she doing? This whole scheme to move to Greece had come as a bolt out of the blue, and her stomach had flipped uncertainly even as she'd signed her name on the contracts. She didn't do random things. She didn't do whimsy. Oh, she could be impulsive, but in Stella's world that meant buying a new leather couch or an unneeded pair of Jimmy Choos just because, not committing her entire life to an ailing business in a foreign country. She couldn't even speak Greek! None of them could. God, it was going to be a disaster – what had they been thinking?

Prickles of panic broke out on her forehead at the thought of leaving behind everything she'd worked so hard for. So she'd lost her job; it wasn't the end of the world or an excuse to have a total breakdown and do something as outrageous as flee the country. Another job would turn up soon enough. She was too good to be ignored, too well-known and respected in her field to be left on the career shelf, so why had she just hurled herself off it like Buzz Lightyear flinging himself from the edge of the table? He hadn't been able to fly, not really. It was just a smoke-and-mirrors illusion.

Stella threw her clothes back on, thrust the knot of bikinis at the shop assistant and marched out of the shop. She didn't need new bikinis. She had three perfectly good ones already, and it was highly likely that she wouldn't be staying on Skelidos long enough to need more.

CHAPTER TWO

Winnie checked her cross-body bag for the millionth time to make sure she had the keys to Villa Valentina zipped safely inside the side pocket.

'We'll have to get some more keys cut as soon as we can,' she said, settling her bag into her lap on the hour-long ferry ride from Skiathos across to Skelidos. Now that they were almost back at the villa, her nerves had kicked in hard. Ajax had emailed to let them know that he and Nikolas had left for Athens a couple of days back and the place was locked up and waiting for them. They'd bought it fully furnished with several upcoming reservations already in the book, so for all intents and purposes they could just turn the key, open the windows and be up and running. It sounded quite easy, put like that, until a worrying thought hit her.

'Oh, God! I hope someone has been feeding The Fonz since Ajax left!' She looked from Frankie to Stella sitting on the opposite bench. 'What if he's starving, or dehydrated?'

Stella shook her head. 'Donkeys are like camels, I should think. They retain water.'

Both Frankie and Winnie looked at her, taken aback. 'Surely he'd need a hump for that?' Frankie said, doubtful.

Stella shrugged and dropped her Aviators over her eyes; the donkey was the least of her worries. She'd had a job offer a couple of days ago from old business rivals of Jones & Bow; on the one hand it was reassuring to be head-hunted, but on the other they were offering a pitiful package and hadn't even included a company car. She hated the loss of freedom being without wheels represented, and couldn't help but feel that the derisory job offer had been designed more to put her in her place rather than to genuinely recruit her. It stung, and it rammed home the fact that she wasn't as indispensable as she'd always allowed herself the indulgence of believing. She hadn't replied yet. Her instinct had been to tell them where to shove their pitiful offer, but she was slowly coming around to the horrible realisation that she might not have the luxury of being so hasty. All in all she was thoroughly miserable, and much as the sunshine was welcome, she hated the feeling that she was running away. Stella Daniels didn't run from anything or anyone. She'd take a week or so to recharge, and then decide what to do about the offer.

Frankie's phone bleeped in her hand luggage, and she scrabbled for it in case there was anything wrong at home. The boys had both been unflatteringly thrilled at the idea of her moving to a Mediterranean island. She'd expected a wobbly lip or two, a 'Please don't go, Mum,' but what she'd got from Josh was a 'Go for it, Mum,' and Elliott was already merrily planning his free holiday to Greece later in the summer. Maybe it wouldn't be so bad being apart from them after all; if they came to stay she'd get some proper time with them for a change. Family holidays had always had been British bucket-and-spade affairs when the twins were little, and in later years they hadn't been at all enamoured of the idea of being stuck in a hotel with their olds. Maybe it would have been different if she and Gavin had been more in love; there might have been more laughter and good times. As it was they only really talked about things to do with the kids, and once they'd moved out they'd been left crunching toast in noisy silence at the breakfast table.

'I've got a long-lost uncle in Nigeria who wants my bank details so he can wire me ten million pounds,' she sighed, reading the phishing message on her phone.

'Bugger. If only he'd texted you yesterday, you could have stayed at home and bought a mansion instead,' Stella said.

Winnie fidgeted with excitement in her seat. 'I'd still have come back here today, even if I'd won the lottery. Aren't you dying to get in the villa and have a good nose around without Ajax and Nik?'

Frankie's face relaxed into a smile as she tucked her phone away. 'I'm heading straight for the bath in the Cleopatra Room before I do anything else. I splashed out on Jo Malone bubble bath especially for it.'

Winnie leaned her forehead against the warm window and looked out over the vast, still sea stretching out around them, and then up at the even bluer, cloudless sky overhead. It was the kind of sky that couldn't help but fill you with optimism and hope; imagine a whole summer, or a whole lifetime, like this. With every extra mile she put between herself and Rory, Winnie sat a little taller and breathed a little easier. She dug in her bag again, pulled out her English/Greek dictionary and flicked through it.

'What are you looking for?' Stella asked.

After a pause, Winnie glanced up. 'Evdaimonia,' she said,

faltering over her pronunciation as she closed the book and clutched it against her chest. 'It means bliss.'

'Remind me how to say bliss again?' Stella huffed half an hour later, pushing her sunnies onto the top of her flat, frazzled hair as they all collapsed like a scuttle of red lobsters onto the shaded terrace of Villa Valentina.

Their taxi driver from the port had been in a tearing hurry and they'd assured him that they'd be fine moving their luggage from the roadside to the villa at the far end of the beach. It wasn't all that far, but they hadn't accounted for the fact that it was impossible to drag heavy-wheeled suitcases across deep, fine sand without feeling as if you're hauling a dead horse up a hill. As a consequence, their return to the villa wasn't at all the champagne-cork-popping experience Winnie had envisaged; it was more of a someone-get-me-some-water-before-I-die situation.

'Evdasomething?' she puffed, tipping her bag out on the top of her suitcase and plucking the keys out from amongst the clutter of sun cream, books, lip balm and hair bobbles.

'Evian?' Frankie croaked hopefully, taking off her sunhat and fanning herself with it. Her outfit had survived the journey surprisingly well; her long linen sundress had a certain safari chic to it and her trusty sunhat had done a decent job of keeping the worst of the heat away from her skin. She was one of those gamine girls who could carry off a pixie cut, all long limbs and pale freckled skin. Her mother always liked to claim they had French heritage, and every now and then when he'd had a few drinks Gavin had called her his Audrey Hepburn. It was one of the nicest things he'd ever said.

Winnie hauled herself up and then stretched out her hands to pull the others up.

'Come on. Let's all go in together for the first time.'

Stella brushed sand from the bum of her shorts. 'I'm not carrying either of you over the threshold.'

'Too right,' Winnie snorted. 'I tried that once with Rory and I think it jinxed us from the beginning.'

'Gavin tried it too. I was seven months pregnant at the time and he put his back out for the first month of our marriage.'

'You two are enough to put a girl off marriage for life.' Stella took the keys from Winnie and studied the bewilderingly large collection. 'Any idea which one it is?'

Winnie shook her head. 'Not a clue.' Studying the door, she added, 'Probably something big and old.'

'They're all big and old,' Stella muttered, sliding one after the other into the lock and giving it a hopeful jiggle. Finally, the last but one key slid into place more easily than the others, and it turned with a satisfying clunk. 'Looks like we're in, ladies,' Stella said, turning the doorknob and pushing the door open.

Even though they knew what lay on the other side of the door, it felt completely different stepping inside Villa Valentina knowing it was their new home instead of their temporary reprieve from the daily grind. Frankie closed the door and they all stood in the centre of the high-ceilinged space, gazing around in silence.

'Is it a bit eerie?' Stella said, screwing her nose up at the stale air.

'Don't say that!' Winnie said, frowning. 'It's just empty. It's been waiting for us to arrive.'

'Don't go all hippy on us, Win,' Frankie said, laying her hat down on the reception desk. 'Let's get some windows open and air the place through. It's like a bloody oven in here.'

Frankie's calm, practical approach got them all moving, flinging open windows and doors, then dragging their luggage inside. Winnie spotted an old radio behind reception and switched it on, instantly transported back to their first stay on the island by the familiar Radio Skelidos jingle. The mix of Greek and international pop music added life and movement to the place, wiping away the stillness that had spooked Stella.

'I found the kitchen!' Frankie called, and the others followed her voice down the hallway to the back of the building. Ajax had given them a brief guided tour, but it was a big old place and it was going to take some getting used to before any of them knew it like the back of their hands. Stella and Winnie found Frankie unscrewing a fresh two-litre bottle of water, and she'd magicked up three tall glasses and filled them with ice.

'Ajax left the electricity turned on and a few things in the fridge for us,' she said. 'We have ice, we have water and we have wine. What more could a girl want?'

Winnie's tummy rumbled. 'Food?'

Frankie shook her head. 'We need to go shopping.'

'I don't think I can face the walk,' Stella grumbled, gulping down water. 'The last one nearly killed me. Can I ride the donkey?'

'Who do you think you are, the Virgin Mary?' Frankie grinned, adding slices of lemon to their glasses as Winnie jumped off her stool and crossed to open the wooden shutters covering the windows.

'We need to check on The Fonz,' she said, craning her neck to look in the garden. 'God, it's a bit of a mess out there. I can't see him.' She rattled the back door and found it locked.

'The key's there,' Stella nodded towards a hook on the

wall and watched as Winnie grappled with the old lock and then threw the bolts. 'Watch out for snakes in the long grass,' she said at the last minute.

Winnie turned back, startled. 'Really?'

Stella shrugged then shook her head. 'Pulling your leg.'

Winnie rolled her eyes and stepped gingerly out onto the cracked, crazy-paved patio.

'Donkey,' she called, in an inviting, sing song voice. 'Mr Fonz . . .' She moved to check down the side of the building, and then ventured further across the parched grass. The garden looked to stretch back quite a way and be walled around the edge by a low, pale, rough stone wall. 'I think we've got fruit trees out here,' she called back. 'But I can't see any sign of a donkey.'

Perplexed, she picked her way along a path haphazardly tiled into the grass, making her way down the length of the garden to the wall at the bottom. Along the way she passed bright wildflowers that would be great on the tables out front and several different types of fruit tree, but no donkey in sight. God, what if he'd keeled over somewhere? She cautiously scanned the ground beneath the trees and bushes but to no avail. It was perplexing really, because there was no obvious exit for a donkey, and the waist-high wall seemed much too big for The Fonz to scale. Wandering back towards the villa, she made a makeshift apron from the bottom of her T-shirt, filled it with fruit plucked from the trees and pondered the missing animal.

'Plums, I think,' she said, giving up the search and unloading her haul onto the big, scrubbed kitchen table where the other girls were sitting. 'And cherries.'

Frankie picked up one of the plump apple-green plums and sniffed it. 'Greengages,' she said, then bit it. 'Oh my God!' She rolled her eyes in bliss. 'So sweet.'

The others helped themselves, and for a few moments they all sat around the table eating fruit from their garden and feeling the welcome rush of sugar in their veins.

'I feel like Barbara from *The Good Life*,' Stella said. 'Have we got any chickens I can kill?'

Frankie loaded the rest of the fruit into a wide, shallow ceramic bowl on the table. 'You wouldn't be Barbara. You'd be the what's her name, the neighbour. The posh one.'

Stella considered it for a second, and then laughed. 'You're right. Winnie can be Barbara and kill the chickens, you can be Nigella and roast it, and I'll be the snooty one in the kaftan who drinks G&T.'

Frankie held her hand up and high-fived Stella silently.

'I think I could get into gardening,' Winnie said, warming to the role of Barbara. 'And I have some cut-off dungarees. I can pull it off.'

'Barbara wouldn't lose her donkey though,' Frankie said, shaking her head.

They all jumped as someone knocked on the back door.

'Maybe it's the donkey,' Stella whispered, making them all laugh as Winnie crossed the kitchen and pulled the door wide.

It wasn't the donkey. It was a man, and by the looks of his scowl, an unimpressed one. He looked dressed for farming in breeches, braces and a loose cheesecloth shirt, and if he wasn't scowling he'd probably be quite attractive.

'Kalimera,' Winnie said, hesitantly trying out her rudimentary Greek.

He let forth a torrent of fast, unintelligible Greek. When he'd finished, she frowned and shook her head regretfully.

'Err . . . signomi . . . my Greek is awful.'

He stared at her in irate silence.

'Signomi . . .'

Winnie glanced over her shoulder for help from the others, but found them both wide-eyed and tongue-tied by the arrival of the stranger in their midst.

'Help me out here?' she muttered.

'Feliz navidad?' Stella tried from her seat at the table, and the stranger lifted his eyebrows and sighed heavily.

'You just wished me Merry Christmas in Spanish. It's early May, and this is Greece.'

'You speak English,' Winnie said, thinking that he might have made that clear right away rather than let her struggle for his own amusement.

'Better than you speak Greek, evidently,' he said. 'I take it you're the new owners?'

Frankie came to stand beside Winnie. 'We are. I'm Frankie, and this is Winnie. And you are . . .?' Winnie admired her friend's polite, cool tone.

'I'm the guy who rescued your bloody donkey. Poor darn thing would have died in this heat without any water.' There was an unmissable hint of an Australian twang to his pronunciation. 'He's in my olive grove with Chachi when you can be arsed to fetch him.'

Oh, right. Winnie felt her fists ball until her fingernails dug into her palms. 'Look, Mr . . . I don't know your name because you didn't bother to tell us . . . we only arrived half an hour ago and I've already been out to look for the donkey. It isn't our fault that Ajax didn't make proper arrangements for him.'

The guy looked bored. 'Typical women. Blame someone else and it'll all be all right.'

Winnie drew in a sharp breath. She'd had enough of men pissing her off back home, there was no way some stranger was going to rain on her parade on the first morning of their brand-new life.

33

'Typical man, shooting your mouth off without knowing the facts.' She stuck her chin out at him and crossed her arms across her chest as Stella came to stand on her other side.

He looked at all three of them for a second, and then seemed to lose interest and turned to leave.

'I won't charge you for the olives he's eaten. Consider it a neighbourly welcome-to-the-island gift.'

He didn't even turn around as he spoke, and Stella said 'Rude bastard,' more than loud enough for him to hear as she closed the door with a pointed slam.

'He's our new neighbour?' Frankie said, pulling three wine glasses out of the wall cupboard.

'Sounds that way.' Winnie reached to get the chilled bottle of white out of the fridge.

Stella rooted around in the cutlery drawer until she pulled out a corkscrew and waved it in the air in triumph. Flopping back at the kitchen table, she cracked the wine and filled their glasses. After a pause for them all to take a much-needed first sip, she held her glass out between them in a toast.

'To our first day on Skelidos.'

'And the fact that our donkey isn't dead,' Frankie said, touching her glass to the others.

'And the fact that we have a grotty ass of an Australian neighbour,' Winnie added. 'Bloody man and his generalisations.'

Stella eyed Winnie slyly over her wine glass. 'He was quite hot though. In a grotty-ass kind of way.'

'Was he?' Winnie took a good gulp of wine. 'I didn't notice.'

'You so did,' Frankie laughed. 'All that red-faced, stuttery Greek and Lady Diana eye flutters.'

Winnie rolled her eyes. 'All right, so maybe I thought he was OK until he opened his mouth. Now I just think he's an arrogant gobshite who's kidnapped my donkey.' She shot a look at Stella. 'At least I didn't wish him Merry Christmas. In Spanish.'

Stella shrugged. 'Pity I didn't know how to say piss off instead.'

'I'm going to learn before I go and get The Fonz back.'

Frankie started to laugh. 'His donkey's name is Chachi. Fonzy and Chachi?'

'Someone around here was clearly a *Happy Days* fan.' Stella grinned. 'I wonder where Joanie is?'

Winnie reached for the bottle and topped up their glasses. 'She probably upped and left because she couldn't stand living with a misogynistic pig.'

Stella and Frankie both looked at her levelly across the table. They didn't say as much, but Winnie knew from their eyes that they were hoping that she wasn't going to stay angry for ever.

'Shall we go and burn our bras in his olive orchard?' Stella said.

Frankie nodded. 'Or chain ourselves to his trees until he apologises?'

Winnie shook her head, laughing softly into her wine glass. She might not have much time for men at the moment, but these two crazy, fabulous women restored her faith in the world every damn day.

Pushing her chair back with a satisfying scrape against the stone flags, she stood up and rolled her shoulders.

'Hold my coat, girls. I'm going to get our donkey.'

CHAPTER THREE

Winnie marched out of the villa, buoyed up by a mixture of wine, lingering first-day euphoria and indignation. What happened to welcoming new neighbours with a cup of sugar and a smile? What happened to the famed Greek hospitality? But then he wasn't Greek by the sound of it, and there probably wasn't any sugar in his cupboards either; he didn't strike Winnie as a man with an ounce of sweetness about him. From their first meeting she'd already deduced that he had no manners and even less in the way of small talk. His only redeemable feature seemed to be the fact that he was passably attractive, and if she was pushed, she'd acknowledge that he must have a shred of decency because he'd taken The Fonz in when he wasn't obliged to.

Meandering through the tables out front on the beach-bar terrace, she paused to get her bearings. Where did he live anyway? Right led directly down onto the beach, so she struck out left and followed the sandy path around the villa and into the fields behind. Gosh, it was hot. Winnie made her way along the track, wishing she'd thought to slather on extra sun cream; she could almost feel her skin frying. She was one of those people with a pale and interesting complexion; achieving anything close to a sun-kissed glow required diligent application of factor 30 and short, careful interludes of exposure to the sun. Anything more intensive was likely to turn her into a walking, talking beetroot, and that really wasn't the look she wanted to achieve before sundown on day one. Nothing marks you out as a tourist quite like a classic dose of sunburn, does it?

Lifting her sunglasses, she paused beneath the shade of an olive tree and looked first one way and then the other. Back home, her house had been a semi-detached in a suburban cul-de-sac, and her closest neighbour had probably been sitting three feet away on the other side of the party wall. Out here her nearest neighbour wasn't even in sight, which, given the fact that he was so rude, was probably just as well.

Movement flickered in her peripheral vision, and she squinted between the trees. Bingo. Not just one donkey. Two.

'At bloody last,' Winnie muttered, shaking her leg to flick the irritating grit out of her flip-flop. A low stone wall ran around the perimeter of his olive grove, so she swung herself over it and started picking her way through the gnarled trees towards The Fonz. As she drew nearer, neither of the animals took the remotest bit of notice of her.

'Hello, Fonzy,' she said, in the quiet, polite manner with which she might greet an elderly relative. Nothing. Not so much as the flicker of an ear from either of them.

'Chachi?' she said, more uncertain this time as she moved within a few feet of the donkeys. One of them was pure white and considerably bigger than the other, and he lifted

37

his head and gazed briefly in her direction before returning peacefully to grazing.

'OK,' she said under her breath, walking closer to the smaller, grey donkey. 'If he's Chachi, then I guess that must make you The Fonz.' She reached out a tentative hand and stroked him between the ears. 'I'm Winnie, your new owner, and I've come to take you home.'

He really did seem very indifferent to her. As a non-rider, she'd vaguely imagined that he'd have a saddle on, or a harness at least, something that she'd be able to lead him by, but he didn't. He was, for all intents and purposes, naked.

'How are we going to do this then?' she asked, walking around him slowly. Running an experimental hand over his flank, she tried giving him a little two-handed push from behind but he didn't even seem to register it. She tried a second time, this time with a little more effort, and he swished his tail as if a fly might have landed on his backside.

'Bloody hell, Fonzy,' she grumbled. 'You need to go on a diet, buddy. You weigh a bloody ton.'

'Why are you fondling my donkey?'

Winnie didn't need to turn around to know who was behind her.

She was quite glad that it wasn't The Fonz after all. 'Might have known this one was yours,' she said to the neighbour. 'He seems as stubborn and unwelcoming as his owner.' She moved across to stand behind the larger, white donkey. He really was big, practically a pony, really.

Winnie wiped her sweaty palms on the back of her denim skirt and patted the white donkey on the rump in a way she hoped was friendly enough before attempting the two-handed push on him too. It was hopeless. After a couple of increasingly effortful attempts, she swung around with her hands balled on her hips, first dashing away several beads of sweat running from her hairline into her eyes.

'Would it kill you to help me out here?'

He looked at her levelly with his arms folded across his chest. 'You look like a prawn that's been chucked on the barbie.'

Winnie shook her head and huffed. 'Could you be any more stereotypically Australian?'

'I could call you Sheila. Could you be any more passive-aggressively English?'

Yanking her sunglasses off, she stared at him. 'Trust me, Mr . . . Mr I don't know your name because you couldn't be bothered to introduce yourself, there's nothing passive about my aggression right now; I'm just about ready to beat you to a pulp with my bare hands.'

He didn't look even the smallest bit threatened. 'I'm not surprised the donkey doesn't want to go with you. You give off a negative vibe. You clearly have anger-management issues.'

'Anger-management issues?' she half yelled. 'I didn't until I met you, you condescending asshat!'

'In some countries this passes as foreplay,' he said, and for the first time Winnie caught the faintest trace of humour behind his tone. 'My name's Jesse, seeing as you asked so nicely. Although I quite like "condescending asshat", so you can stick with that if you prefer. I'm easy.'

'Jesse as in the outlaw,' she muttered. 'Or donkey rustler.'

'He was also a bank robbber, a gang leader and a murderer.' He said it tonelessly, leaving Winnie to draw her own conclusions as to whether she was supposed to feel menaced. She didn't.

'Nice namesake.'

'I was named after my father, seeing as you mention it. Wonderful guy, and surprisingly, he's never robbed a bank in his life.'

Great. Now she felt shitty for insulting his dad. How did that happen?

'So, Jesse,' she said, thinking actually he looked like a Jesse, now she'd said it aloud. Jesse suggested bad boys and motorbikes and leather jackets, scowls, cigarettes and bad manners. Not that she'd seen him smoke, but she wouldn't be surprised if he pulled a box out and lit up. 'Would you mind telling me how to make my donkey move, please?'

He scrubbed a hand over the dark stubble along his jaw and gave a non-committal 'huh'. 'Now there's a question.'

Here we go again. 'And does it have an answer?' she asked, sweet as apple pie.

Jesse shrugged. 'Not an obvious one, no.'

Winnie could feel the threads of her temper unravelling. 'So give me the complicated one. It would appear that I have time to listen.'

'Would you like a drink?'

Whoa. That volte-face was so violent it'd be a miracle if he didn't give himself whiplash. In truth, Winnie was gasping for a drink; she hadn't thought to bring any water with her as she'd expected her neighbour to be closer than he was, and the sun overhead was making her feel every inch the barbecued prawn he'd likened her to. Nonetheless, she still considered saying no, because there was every chance he was being sarcastic.

'I don't suppose it'd go amiss,' she said, feigning indifference.

His full mouth turned down as he shrugged. 'It was just a neighbourly offer. Don't force yourself.'

40

Winnie sighed and gave in. 'Some water would be very nice if you wouldn't mind.'

He inclined his head, then turned away and started to stride through the trees. 'This way.'

Was it OK to follow a stranger into his house in a foreign land? It'd seem terribly rude if she didn't now she'd accepted.

He stopped walking and swung around. 'Are you coming or not?'

'You're not going to kill me, are you?'

'Fucking hell, woman. I think I might if you carry on like this.' He rubbed his hand through his dark, slightly too long hair, clearly exasperated. 'I've lived on Skelidos for the last ten years without murdering anyone and I don't plan on that changing today, but if you'd rather stay out here just in case while I fetch you a glass of water, then be my guest.'

They'd reached a low-slung farmhouse, and he gestured towards a table and chairs set out under the shade of a veranda.

Winnie considered her choices and decided that on balance he was unlikely to bump her off; he knew that she wasn't here alone and, technically, she'd been trespassing on his land and inadvertently tried to steal his donkey so she wasn't really in a position to be judgmental. He led the way through a stable door directly into his kitchen. Winnie wasn't sure what she'd been expecting; something rustic and manly, if she'd been pinned down to take a guess. It wasn't rustic. It was sleek and minimalist, a complete contrast to the traditional stone exterior of the building. Cool and uncluttered, his air-con was blessedly fridge-cold and his drinking water, when he passed it over, was as cool and clear as if he'd just dipped the glass in an icy mountain spring.

'Thank you,' she said, taking a seat when he pulled out a chair at the glass dining table.

'It's safe. I'm fresh out of arsenic,' he said, dropping into the seat opposite hers.

Winnie smirked and took a welcome drink as he watched her.

'So what's going on over at the B&B?' he asked. 'Are you three doing a Thelma and Louise?'

God, he was annoying. 'Meaning?'

He lifted one shoulder. 'Bitter women running off together for an ill-advised adventure?'

'Way I remember it, Thelma and Louise were badasses who murdered a man because he behaved like a cock and then killed themselves.'

Jesse cupped his glass between his hands on the table. 'This could be an interesting summer for all of us then.'

'And we're not bitter,' Winnie added, correcting him belatedly. 'We're three modern, perfectly happy women who spotted a shrewd business investment and snapped it up.'

Jesse nodded, then lifted his glass and downed the entire contents. Something about the action disturbed Winnie; for a few brief seconds she found herself noticing the physicality of him, as if she were watching a movie. He could pass for Greek; the sun had burnished his skin that deep bronze that could never be attained on a package holiday, and if his hair wasn't black, it was as near as damn it. He'd changed from the billowy shirt into a faded red T-shirt that had either shrunk in the wash or been given to him by a lover who enjoyed the way it fit him a little too well; either way Winnie couldn't help but be aware of his long, lean biceps and the generous width of his shoulders. All that fresh air and olive farming clearly agreed with him.

42

'Speaking of badasses,' she said, because getting her mind off the fact that he looked hot was a good idea. 'How do I get that bad ass out there to walk back to the B&B with me?'

Jesse shook his head. 'There's no way you're going to win him over in five minutes, or five hours even. Five days, possibly, or five weeks, I'd say it's almost a definite. He has to trust you. To like you, even, before he's going anywhere with you.' He paused. 'Hard work. Bit like a woman, really.'

Winnie curled her lip at him. 'You just don't stop, do you?'

He lifted his hands palms up. 'Just sayin'.'

'I don't know about us being bitter women,' Winnie said. 'It sounds to me as if you're the one with the chip on your shoulder.'

He laughed and rubbed the heel of his palm into his eye socket. 'On the contrary. I love women. You all just drive me fucking crazy with your complications and contradictions.'

'That is so incredibly rude and ignorant,' Winnie said, bridling. 'So what, you hide out on your farm drinking beers with your donkey?'

'I'm not a monk. I fuck sometimes. I even make breakfast afterwards. I'm one of the good guys; I don't promise the moon on a string, because strings strangle relationships.' He made a yanking gesture that clearly indicated a noose being tightened around his neck.

Winnie stared at him. 'Well, say it like it is, why don't you?' she said, taken aback by his frankness.

'What do you want me to say?' He looked thoroughly unapologetic. 'I like a simple life. I don't do hearts and flowers.'

'So what do you do?' Winnie asked, trying to steer the conversation around to life on Skelidos because they'd got really quite deep into relationship talk, and that was weird given that this was their first real conversation.

'With women? I do talking.' He gestured between them to demonstrate man and woman. 'And I do kissing. I do kissing *really* well.' He laughed, as if that was sort of a given for a cool guy like him. 'And I do sex, naturally. I'm pretty darn good at that too.'

Winnie wasn't sure if she wanted to tip her cold water all over her own head or chuck it at him. It was definitely an inappropriate thing for him to say, and yet he said it so flippantly that it came over as cheeky rather than sleazy. He was a rogue; but at least he was upfront about it, and that was actually something of a relief after all of the underhand behaviour that had ended her marriage.

'I wasn't asking about your sexual technique,' she said, drily. 'I was asking what you do here on the island.'

'Ah. My mistake.' The glint in his eye told her that it wasn't necessarily a mistake at all. 'Well, as you so astutely observed, I farm olives and drink beer,' he said. 'And I sculpt.'

Now he'd surprised her. 'You do? Sculpt as in . . .' She made vague pottery movements in the air with her hands. 'Pots and things?'

Jesse nodded. 'I have a wheel for smaller stuff, but I mostly do bigger commission pieces. Animals, people, that sort of thing.'

'Wow.' Winnie was genuinely thrown. He seemed too much of a jock to be an artist, although she was self-aware enough to realise that her sweeping generalisation was small-minded. 'Can I see?'

He huffed under his breath, as if she'd asked a stupid question. 'No.'

She'd expected as much. Back home in the UK, Winnie had been forging a career for herself as a self-taught jewellery designer, and she'd never been keen on showing any of her pieces to people before they were finished. She'd worked alone from her tiny garden workshop, happy with just the radio and next door's cat for company. Her silver and copper wire work didn't cost the earth, but she'd been making a name for herself as a designer with flair and an eye for pretty gemstones. The last couple of summers had been especially busy with bridal commissions, but this year she'd barely touched her tools. Rory had stolen far more than her happiness; he'd tucked her creativity into his holdall alongside the aftershave she loved the smell of on his skin and the cufflinks she'd made for him as a first-anniversary gift.

'One day maybe,' Jesse relented, and Winnie realised that he'd probably misread her silence as having taken offence at his refusal to show her his studio.

'No, it's OK, really.' Casting her eye around the kitchen, she wondered if he actually cooked in here. It didn't look used. She was about to ask when something brushed against her legs, making her jump and glance under the table.

'You have a cat,' she said, laughing as the big black and white moggy bumped her hand when she reached down to fuss it.

'Bandit,' Jesse said, and the animal jumped up on his knees. 'He isn't mine, exactly. He lives a couple of farms across officially, but he spends most his time here.' The cat scrubbed his head against Jesse's five o'clock shadow, purring like a small generator. 'He's no looker, is he?'

Winnie considered the cat; he was missing a chunk of one of his ears and his fur in places seemed to have worn a little threadbare. He looked like he lived up to his name.

'He's characterful,' she said in the end.

Jesse set the cat down. 'I don't mind him. He's thorny and can be cantankerous, but he's a hunter so he gets to stay.'

Winnie didn't ask what Bandit hunted in case she didn't like the answer.

'It sounds to me as if you make a habit of collecting your neighbours' animals.'

'Come on now.' He frowned. 'I literally saved your ass. I can see that you're struggling to say thank you.' He sat back and folded his arms across his chest. 'Take your time.'

In truth, Winnie could see that he *had* sort of saved their donkey, but she still hadn't completely forgiven him for his earlier rudeness. 'Who calls a donkey The Fonz, anyhow?'

'Ah, now that's a story.'

'Another one?'

He looked at her. 'For a different day maybe. You better come back again tomorrow and try to woo him.'

'Do you think he'll come around to the idea?'

Jesse shrugged. 'I imagine he'll come to tolerate you in short bursts.'

Winnie curled her lip, unsure if they were even still talking about the donkey. She pushed herself up onto her feet and dusted her hands down her skirt to smooth it.

'I should go, before they send out a search party.' She slid her hairband out and gripped it between her teeth while she finger-combed her ponytail back into place. 'You didn't make the best first impression.'

'Can't think why,' he said, standing up and putting their empty glasses into the sink.

Winnie headed to the door. 'Is there anything I can bring to encourage him to like me more?'

'I think he likes bikinis and girls who can cook a good steak.'

Winnie shot him a sarcastic look over her shoulder, and he just shrugged and half laughed.

Pausing by the donkeys to give them both a quick fuss of the ears, she looked back towards the house. He hadn't followed her out; she'd have been more surprised if he had.

One way or another, Jesse was going to be trouble.

CHAPTER FOUR

'What, no donkey?'

Stella and Frankie looked up from behind the reception desk when Winnie walked back into the B&B and flopped down onto an armchair by a low coffee table cluttered with excursion leaflets.

'He needs to be wooed, apparently.'

'The donkey, or his irritable owner?' Stella asked.

'Jesse.'

Frankie lifted her eyebrows towards Stella. 'It's *Jesse* now,' she said knowingly.

'You're planning to woo Jesse?' Stella grinned. 'You go, girl. I thought I sensed a spark.'

'Behave, both of you. You know full well I mean the donkey.' Winnie puffed stray hairs out of her eyes. 'He's stubborn.'

'Who knew?' Frankie murmured, earning herself a sarcastic smirk.

'I'll go back tomorrow and try again.'

Stella nodded. 'You should definitely do that.'

'Take him a sugar lump?' Frankie suggested.

'Or a beer,' Stella added, nudging Frankie in the ribs.

Winnie scowled. 'I know what you're doing and it's not going to work.'

The other two looked as innocent as schoolgirls. 'No idea what you mean,' Frankie said, shaking her head as Stella shrugged helplessly.

'Me either.'

Winnie stood up, changing the subject. 'Come on,' she said. 'Let's go and check ourselves into our rooms.'

'This place badly needs a lift,' Stella said, as they practically collapsed on the top-floor landing after hauling their suitcases up three floors. Winnie had fresh appreciation for the way Ajax had sprinted up and down the B&B stairs like a mountain goat; it had all seemed much easier with someone else to carry their bags.

'Maybe we should employ a bellboy?' she said, dragging her case to the door of the Bohemian Suite. They'd instinctively picked up the keys to the same rooms they'd occupied on their previous visit, subconsciously needing something familiar when everything else around them was alien, perhaps.

'Can he be eighteen with a fit bum?' Stella slid her key into the Seaview Suite. 'I'll do the interviews.'

Frankie was the least ruffled by the climb; her twice-weekly yoga classes at the local centre for the last few years had obviously paid off. Back home, those few hours a week had been a necessary respite from the grind of daily life; they were the only time Frankie could find relief from the crushing weight of being the one who held everything together for everyone else's life to run smoothly. On the mat she was free and totally present in the moment; more than just the responsible adult whom everyone depended on to ensure that there was loo roll in the bathroom and dinner on the table and clean socks in the drawer. Much as she loved her boys, being finally freed from the routines that had shaped her entire adult life felt as if someone had opened the door of her cage and liberated her from captivity.

'I might do some yoga on the beach in the morning,' she said as she opened her door and pushed her case in ahead of her.

'Really?' Winnie glanced across from her own threshold.

Frankie nodded, suddenly determined. Back in England yoga had been her escape; here it was one of the few overhangs from her old life that she was happy to bring with her. There wasn't much else on the keeper list; her mobile to stay in touch with Joshua and Elliott, the small photograph album at the bottom of her suitcase holding a dozen or so of her favourite pictures, and the letter Marcia had left with her solicitor. Her fingers absently touched her wedding ring, suspended on a gold trace chain around her neck. Much as the decision to end their marriage had ultimately been hers, untangling herself mentally from Gav was still a work in progress. It wasn't as if she wasn't fond of him; unlike Winnie's husband he'd never have dreamt of having a torrid affair or intentionally hurting her. It was more that the passing of the years had turned them into friends rather than lovers, and it hurt her romantic heart to not be held at night or made love to as if she was the most beautiful woman in the world. The divorce had hurt them both deeply, and she wasn't quite ready yet to let go of her ring completely. It had seemed wrong to keep it on her finger afterwards, so moving it to around her neck was sort of an interim step. Maybe she'd go all dramatic and throw it into the depths of the sea like that woman in

Titanic. More likely she'd take it off because it reacted with some sun cream or else snap the chain whilst changing one of the beds, but for now she was content to keep it close by.

'I'm going to go for a swim in my bathtub for half an hour,' she said. 'See you downstairs in a while?'

The others nodded.

'I'm just about ready for my afternoon siesta,' Stella said. 'Cocktails on the terrace at sundown?'

Laughing, they stepped inside their rooms, clicked their doors shut softly and returned the villa to its peaceful afternoon slumber.

'We really need to buy some food.'

Frankie stood staring into the empty fridge.

'I think there's some shops on the other side of the beach,' Winnie said. They'd barely ventured further than the beach on their last flying visit to Skelidos, but from what she could remember the few shops and restaurants strung out on the far side of the sand counted as the centre of the small resort. The island in general was very low-key; it wasn't on the hen-party radar or likely to appeal to the thrill-seeking crowd. It was left field of the beaten track, and Winnie for one was perfectly happy for it to stay that way.

'That means that whatever we buy needs to be lugged all the way back across the beach,' Stella groaned. 'We're going to have bigger muscles than Olympic shot-putters after a summer here.'

'You know what we need?' Frankie closed the fridge and picked up her purse. 'A donkey.'

Winnie considered it. 'God, yes! How charming would it be for our guests if The Fonz brings their luggage across

51

the beach for them! Not to mention that we can use him to carry our shopping.'

'Can't we just get a car?' Stella frowned.

'Well, we could,' Frankie said. 'But where's the fun in that?'

'I'm worried people might mistake me for the Virgin Mary if I start riding a donkey around town.' Stella made the sign of the cross on her chest. 'They might all fall on their knees and worship me.'

'I reckon you're safe.' Winnie eyed Stella's legs. 'I don't think Mary wore hotpants.'

'I'll have you know that these hotpants were bloody expensive. They deserve a little bit more reverence, thank you very much.' She flicked Winnie a sly look. 'You can borrow them when you go back to woo the donkey, if you like.'

Choosing to rise above Stella's obvious grin, Winnie looked around the big, airy kitchen, taking in the facilities.

'We need food. Milk, sugar and coffee. And water, lots of water.'

'Eggs. Breakfast pastries,' Frankie added to the list. 'And jam.'

'And a big strapping man to carry it all back for us,' Stella said, picking up the keys. 'Come on, ladies. Let's go and introduce ourselves to the locals.'

'Two shops, a bar and one restaurant,' Frankie said. They sat in a line on the low stone wall separating the sand from the beach. 'It's not going to rival Kavos any time soon, is it?'

'Thank God,' Winnie said, although privately even she had to admit that the resort was several steps beyond quiet.

'I'm not surprised Ajax needed out,' Stella said. 'The

52

bright lights of Athens must have been like beacons out there, attracting all the tourists.'

'So. This store?' Winnie looked up at the cherry-red canopies over the tiny local shop. 'Or that one?' She nodded a little way along the road to a similarly small place with yellow and white awnings. Each of them seemed to be a catch-all shop; convenience food, beach lilos and cheap sunglasses on stands outside, fridges full of cold drinks. Great for a day on the beach, not so fabulous to stock up your fridge.

'We really need to find a supermarket,' Stella said. 'What I wouldn't give for my car.'

They all looked up as a guy wondered out of the solitary bar and raised his hand in greeting.

'Ladies, welcome to Skelidos!' he said. 'Gin and tonic?'

'You're so speaking our language,' Stella laughed, jumping to her feet.

'I'm Stella –' she stuck her hand out as the guy drew nearer '– and this is Frankie, and Winnie. We just bought the B&B over on the other side of the beach. The pink one?'

'The only one in the town,' he said, his grin a slash of white teeth against his deeply tanned skin. 'I'm Panos. We wondered when you'd come.'

'Well, we're here now,' Frankie said and smiled.

He looked from one to the other of them. 'Come in, come in. I'll gather people up to come say hi to our newest locals.'

'Now *there's* that Greek charm and neighbourly hospitality we'd hoped for,' Stella said, laughing and linking her arms through Frankie and Winnie's as they followed Panos between the Coca-Cola sunbrellas shading the empty tables outside his bar.

'Island gin?' he asked, holding up a bottle of nectarine blush liquid as they each took a stool at the pine-topped bar.

They watched as he made theatre of pouring them each a long drink over ice, the tonic fizzing over the ice cubes to create the same rose-pink G&T cocktail they'd drunk so many of with Ajax a few weeks back.

'Gin's clear where I come from,' Stella said, holding her drink up curiously.

Panos nodded. 'Ah, but this one is special. Ajax used to make it for us.'

'He did?'

'He didn't tell you?' Panos frowned as they all looked nonplussed. 'This is very bad.' Turning to look over his shoulder, he called out for his mama.

They watched in silence as a small, slight woman dressed in black appeared. Panos let forth a stream of fast Greek smattered with their names, gesticulating across towards Villa Valentina in the distance.

Panos's mother fired back something equally breakneck fast, speaking with her hands as much as her voice. Panos paused for a moment while he decided how to translate what she'd said.

'She say that it's always been brewed at the villa ever since she was a child. If you live in the villa now, you have to do it. It's the law.'

'The law?' Winnie said, alarmed. 'Are you sure?'

Panos's mother nodded vigorously, speaking again, and they all waited for Panos to translate.

'Island law,' Panos shrugged. 'The plants only grow in the garden at the villa. You make it, I sell it.'

'Well, I wouldn't have a clue,' Stella said, deciding that she much preferred drinking the gin to making it.

'Is there even a recipe to follow?' Frankie asked, unsure if they were being wound up, some kind of odd welcome-to-the-island ritual, sort of similar to how she'd been sent to buy a bubble for a spirit level when she was a fifteen-year-old Saturday girl at the jewellers in the local shopping precinct.

Panos asked his mother Frankie's question, but it was clear from her facial expressions and shrugging shoulders that they weren't going to get a clean-cut answer.

Winnie sipped her drink and closed her eyes. God, it was good stuff. 'It isn't right that the world should run out of this,' she said. 'It's possibly the best drink ever.'

It was difficult to say what it was about the gin that made it so delicious. It was rhubarb-pink in colour but not in flavour, and aromatic from the stem of rosemary Panos had pushed through the ice cubes exactly as Ajax had.

'We could try to find out from Ajax?' she offered, although she wasn't entirely certain that they even had his details.

'You must, you must,' Panos urged, opening a wall cupboard behind the bar. 'This is all I have left and I've never run out yet.'

There looked to be a dozen or more bottles in Panos's stash, all bearing a handwritten and illustrated label. They looked like magic potions.

'Well, we'll look into it,' Stella said. 'Maybe we should have another taste just so to be clear.'

Panos looked at her through narrowed eyes, and then started to laugh. 'You will be the troublesome one. I see these things.'

Frankie and Winnie nodded as Panos obligingly topped up their glasses.

'So you're . . . sisters?' He gestured between them.

'No,' Winnie said. 'We're great friends.'

'And you will all stay here? You won't just come for a few weeks and then run back home?'

Winnie nodded, Frankie smiled diplomatically and Stella sighed into her glass without comment.

Panos didn't miss any of their reactions. 'You will stay. Skelidos does that to people.'

'Like Jesse?' Winnie said suddenly, faltering when Panos's eyebrows lifted. 'We met him already. He . . . he looked after our donkey for a while.'

'Jesse came for a summer too.' Panos poured himself a beer. 'But for him it was different. He was . . .' Breaking off, Panos's face relaxed into a wide smile as a woman came into the bar with a clatter of high heels and a cloud of dark curls bouncing on her shoulders.

'So this is the new blood everyone is telling me about!'

'Corinna,' Panos said warmly. 'Word travels fast as usual, I see.'

Winnie thought she detected the hint of an American accent behind the woman's tone. Older than they were, forties at a guess, Corinna was one of the most naturally glamorous women Winnie had ever met. She could pass as Sophia Loren's daughter, all dark eyes, lush lips and legs that went all the way up to her backside. It would have been easy to be intimidated were it not for her warm smile and the way she made a beeline to gather each of them in turn into an excitable, expensively perfumed hug.

'Tell me, what are three gorgeous young women like you girls doing on a sleepy island like this? Are you criminals hiding from the mob?' Her eyes glittered with humour. 'Please say you are!'

As she spoke Panos poured her a drink and slid it over the bar to her.

'Nothing quite that glamorous, I'm afraid,' Frankie said. 'It was just a good time for a change for all of us, for different reasons.'

Good-natured curiosity filled Corinna's eyes. 'Would it be too rude to ask what they were?' she asked, and Panos immediately jumped in.

'Absolutely, yes, it would indeed be very rude,' he chided, shaking his head at them to let them off the hook.

'I left my husband because we didn't love each other any more,' Frankie said suddenly, then took a huge gulp of her drink. 'I've come here for an adventure.'

Some people might have felt uncomfortable at such a candid revelation from a stranger, but not Corinna. She clapped her hands, her gold bracelets jangling on her wrists. 'Bravo for you, my darling! A marriage without love is a dead dodo!'

Stella nodded, a little morose. 'And I got fired from my job. I came here because I don't know what else to do.'

'Ah, now that is interesting,' Corinna said, looking intently at Stella. 'Because you look to me like a woman who always knows what she should do. I think you're here because you know that this is exactly where you need to be.'

In front of Winnie's eyes, Stella's shoulders straightened a little, as if Corinna had applied soothing balm to her injured pride. Winnie decided that she really quite liked Corinna. Emboldened, she threw her hat into the ring.

'My husband was having an affair with the girl in the work canteen, even though we were trying for a baby and he claimed to be perfectly happy.'

The words left her in a rush, because they stung less if she said them quickly. Left to linger in her mouth they grew thorns and cut into her, leaving her raw and sore for days. Hence the fact that she hadn't told anyone new her sorry story – not until now, anyhow. Surprisingly though, this time she found herself unscathed, and on closer reflection she might even feel slightly liberated from the long shadow Rory's infidelity had cast over her.

Behind her, Panos clicked his tongue in disgust and poured an extra shot of gin into her glass.

'Now, that *is* an unfortunate situation.' Corinna shook her head. 'But my darling, how much worse would it have been if you'd had a child *before* you realised that he was a feckless fool?'

Winnie nodded, downhearted. She'd thought the same herself, although she sometimes wondered if she'd pressured him too much about getting pregnant and that had been the reason for his affair. But what would that say about him if so? If the effort of supporting her was too much hard work to bother?

'Pah. I expect he was a man with a little . . .' Corinna crooked her little finger and winked, making them all laugh despite the gravity of Winnie's marital woes. 'And so now you're all three footloose, fancy-free and ready for adventure. How delicious!' Corinna rubbed her hands together and then turned to Panos, sparkly-eyed with mischief. 'Panos here is one of our most eligible bachelors,' she said. 'He has the best bar on the island, and who wouldn't fall in love with that face?'

Right now, that face had turned puce with embarrassment.

'Corinna,' he muttered, slamming clean glasses away onto the shelf above his head.

'And there I was thinking I was the most eligible bachelor on the island,' someone else said, and they all turned to see Jesse had strolled into the bar. Dressed in faded, frayed denim shorts and a lived-in T-shirt, he looked every inch the relaxed holidaymaker rather than the fiery, ill-tempered farmer who'd banged on their door earlier.

If possible, Corinna lit up even more, shimmying her way through the tables to pull Jesse into a hug. If there was one thing this woman did freely, it was hug, Winnie thought. Jesse seemed to take it well, and Frankie and Stella couldn't have looked more surprised if Santa Claus had walked in and ordered a beer. They'd only met Jesse the grouch, and this was a completely different man.

'Ladies,' Corinna said, linking arms with Jesse to lead him across to them. 'This is Jesse Anderson, Skelidos's secret celebrity!'

Jesse rolled his eyes. 'Hardly.'

'Celebrity?' Stella asked.

Corinna nodded, drawing Panos into the conversation. 'Sculptor to the stars, am I not right, Panos?' Placing her perfectly manicured hands on Stella and Frankie's knees, she elaborated on several of Jesse's better-known clients and what he'd been asked to make for them.

'How long had you been there?' Winnie asked quietly as Jesse came to stand beside her stool.

'Long enough to hear that you left your husband because he had a needledick.' Jesse took off his sunglasses and hooked them into the neck of his T-shirt.

Any attempt Winnie might have made to correct Jesse's interpretation of her marital discord was cut short by Corinna.

'Jesse, wasn't it Jennifer Aniston you sculpted in the nude?'

'You know perfectly well that it wasn't,' Jesse said, nodding when Panos offered him a beer. 'And you also know perfectly well that most of my work is private, and

59

usually of very little interest to anyone but the person who has commissioned it.'

Corinna pouted prettily, as if he'd spoiled her game.

'He's always been secretive,' she sighed. 'Although I'm sure I spotted a bust of Barack Obama in his workshop once.'

Jesse just shook his head, and Winnie found herself wondering how close he was with Corinna to have allowed her access to his studio.

'Winnie's an artist,' Stella said out of the blue, making Winnie's cheeks burn as everyone turned to look her way.

'I'm not, not really . . .' She pulled her drink towards her and took a good glug, then struggled not to splutter because the extra gin Panos had added had made it strong enough to strip paint.

'She makes the most beautiful jewellery,' Frankie said, holding her wrist out to show off the bracelet Winnie had given her for her birthday a couple of years ago. Strands of twisted silver and gold wound around pale-green tourmalines and milky-blue moonstones: it was one of Frankie's most prized possessions.

'Oh, my goodness!' Corinna pounced and held Frankie's hand to examine the bracelet. 'You made this?'

Winnie nodded, still feeling foolish because Jesse was clearly an internationally established artist and she'd worked from her garden shed. 'It was more of a hobby, really,' she murmured, although she'd burned with indignation whenever Rory had referred to it as such when they were married. He'd never taken her as seriously as she'd wished, even though her order book had been consistently full and she'd started to make a name for herself.

'Come on, Win,' Stella said. 'Don't do yourself down, it wasn't a hobby. You're bloody good at it.'

Winnie was aware of Jesse watching her reactions closely.

'I haven't done it for a while,' she said eventually.

'But you will do it again now you're here, yes?' Corinna said. 'Because I'd love to see more of what you can do. This kind of line would be perfect for the gallery shop.'

Winnie frowned, not quite following.

'Corinna owns the gallery in Skelidos town,' Panos offered by way of explanation.

'There's a town?' Stella looked hopeful. 'Is there a supermarket there?'

'Two,' Jesse said. 'I need to go into town for a couple of hours tomorrow. I can run one of you in if you like.'

'Winnie,' Frankie and Stella said at the same time.

They both shrugged when she shot them daggers.

'I'm menu planning in the morning,' Frankie said. She was the stand-out cook of the three of them and was dying to put her stamp on the menu revamp at the B&B. She was itching to test out new recipes and make the most of local produce to really ring the changes.

'And I'm ready to make a start on the media package,' Stella said, sliding into business talk because it came as second nature to her. They'd all readily agreed that she was perfectly placed to give the B&B's tired and very basic website a much-needed makeover. She knew all the right people to take their social media profile from non-existent to boutique, to really try to get their name out there. If there was one thing that Stella understood it was marketing and PR, and she was planning to use all of those hard-earned skills that no one else back home seemed to value any more to put their new business on the discerning holidaymaker's map.

Winnie, it had been agreed, was to be their front of house, the face of Villa Valentina, the warm welcome and

61

the winning smile that would have people booking up season on season. But front of house needed guests, so for now, at least, she had some time on her hands.

Time to go into town with Jesse, or so it seemed.

CHAPTER FIVE

Jesse stood at his kitchen window and watched Winnie as she swung her legs over the low wall around his olive grove and made her way over to the donkeys. She seemed a little more sure of herself this morning, less as if she feared The Fonz might bite her hand off when she reached out to fuss his ears. Or had her skittishness yesterday been more about the fact that he'd been so rude to her on their first encounter? He knew he'd been unnecessarily brusque, but her passing similarity to Erin when she'd opened the door at the villa had been a red rag to a bull. On closer inspection she was quite different, but there was something familiar in the curve of her hip and the slender, lithe length of her limbs, in the natural fairness of the waves that fell around her shoulders and the fullness of her mouth. An echo, a reminder to him of a time in his life that he'd closed the door on. Without even realising it, Winnie had managed to disappoint him simply by not being someone else.

It was a disservice, of course; he was big enough and ugly enough to know that, but just watching her again today stirred that same complicated cocktail of emotions again.

He threw a whole glass of cold water down his throat, then lifted his hand in greeting when she turned and caught him looking her way.

'Get a fucking grip,' he muttered. 'She's not even that much like her.'

It had all been such a long time ago, really; a decade almost, more than long enough for him to make his peace with what had happened. And he had, for the most part anyway. He'd have given himself a fairly clean bill of emotional health up to yesterday, when all it had taken was a swish of blonde hair and a flick of a hip to send him off the deep end.

He didn't do blondes any more. He'd nurtured a taste for brunettes with dark eyes and bad attitudes, girls your mama wouldn't approve of, girls who knew what they wanted and who knew the score. The score, in Jesse's case, was open access to his body and absolutely no entry into his heart or his head. Over the years he'd grown to enjoy being so sexually upfront; it was pretty liberating, freeing really. He couldn't actually see why people bothered bending themselves over backwards to be something they weren't in order to accommodate someone else's needs. It wasn't healthy.

'Am I too early?'

Winnie leaned in through the half-open stable door, cutting off his train of thought. Pink skinny-rib T-shirt. White denim mini. Canvas sneakers. Her face looked free of makeup and she'd tied her hair back in a ponytail; Jesus, if she told him she was eighteen he'd believe her, which pretty much made him a dirty old man at thirty-nine. Brilliant. Another negative emotion to attach to her; she really was pushing all of his buttons without even trying.

Shoving his sunglasses on and sweeping his keys up out of the bowl on the dining table, he shook his head.

'Nope. Right on time. Let's go.'

Jesse's dusty black VW Golf was nothing like Rory's beloved sports car back home, and Winnie decided she much preferred its simple unpretentiousness. The air-con was icebox cool, and that was a much more valuable prize out here than hand-stitched leather bucket seats or tinted glass. The low-slung red Alfa would have been an entirely unsuitable car for a baby; Winnie sometimes wondered if the idea of losing it had been one of the contributory factors to Rory's infidelity.

'I have a couple of errands to run, so I'll drop you at Carrefour and come back in an hour or so,' Jesse said, turning left out of the lane onto the main road.

Winnie nodded, taking in the scenery as it whipped past her window. Olive groves, mellow fields and always the still, glittering Mediterranean in view too.

'This is the island's only main road,' Jesse said. 'It follows the coast all the way around, and the lanes that lead off it all run in towards Skelidos town at the centre. It's a blessedly simple layout, unlike the crazy one-way systems you're no doubt used to back home.'

'Sounds straightforward,' Winnie murmured.

'You'll find that much about Skelidos is like that. Uncomplicated.' Jesse indicated to turn off the main road, leaving the sparkling sea behind them. 'It's one of the big things that I love about the place.'

'Can I ask how you came to live here?' she asked, curious and unguarded.

He flicked his dark eyes towards her over his sunglasses. 'You can ask, but I'll lie about the answer.'

Winnie held his gaze for a second before he looked back towards the quiet lane, and she saw there that although his answer had been delivered in an off-the-cuff tone, he wasn't joking. God, he was a prickly fish.

'Just don't answer at all then,' she said. 'Lies are one thing I've had more than my fill of.'

This time when he glanced her way he didn't look flippant. 'I'll bear that in mind.'

They lapsed into silence for the rest of the ride, Jesse concentrating on the bumpy, dusty lane and Winnie taking the chance to see the more agricultural heart of the island away from the coast.

'Is it mostly olive farms on the island?'

Jesse nodded. 'Olives. Cattle for dairy produce, and vegetables in season of course. I wasn't exaggerating about the simple pace of life here. Farmland has stayed in the same families for generations and property rarely comes up for sale. You guys are about the only new people here in as long as I can recall.'

'Wow,' she said, taken aback. No wonder Corinna had been so eager to get a look at them. Life in England had been so entirely different; neighbours came and went and people did any number of things to make their living. Here there was an actual community, a sense of family and of history. Even in the short time she'd spent on Skelidos so far, Winnie was already starting to feel that it suited her bones more than the complicated, fractured society back home in the UK.

Home. It was a word that didn't seem to apply to anywhere for Winnie right now. Her parents' house would always be her childhood home, but living there again for even a short time had proved glaringly that it was no longer her home these days. Her home had been the house she'd bought with her husband and built into their love nest, but also the place where she'd discovered his infidelity, and so it was no longer somewhere that she held any keys or affection for.

It was too soon to confidently refer to Skelidos as home either though. She hoped that one day it would be in her blood and her heart, but at the moment it felt more like they were visiting the island than emigrating to it. Perhaps it was because the others, Stella in particular, seemed to view this as an experiment, a short-term stopgap to get them all out of crisis points at home. They'd all been in need of something and Villa Valentina had practically fallen into their laps.

They hadn't realised at the time how rare it was for property to become available on the island; they certainly hadn't counted on being the only newcomers in the last decade.

'Is tourism fairly new here?' Winnie asked.

Jesse nodded. 'Very much so. None of the tour operators come here, thankfully. We're happy to leave the crowds over on Skiathos, and on Skopelos too now thanks to *Mamma Mia!*'

'They filmed it there?'

'Sure did, and their tourism shot off the scale as a result. I'm just glad they didn't glance our way instead.'

Winnie had seen the movie several times over. Her mother had even mentioned it when she'd broken the news about the B&B, in order to fret that life wasn't like the movies and they were asking for trouble buying a slice of some unknown island. Winnie's parents valued routine and order; the concept of their daughter upping sticks across the globe to somewhere they'd never even heard of had filled them with unease.

Skelidos did share some of its bigger sisters' beautiful traits, though. Lush green pine-forest-clad hills surrounded by sleepy agricultural lands, all fringed with pale, sugar-soft sands sliding seamlessly into the gleaming turquoise sea. Given the ever-present overhead sun, it was a surprisingly verdant place, with creamy wildflowers awash through the hedgerows and the familiar, abundant ramble of bright cerise bougainvillea in evidence everywhere. For a small island, it certainly packed a visual punch; it was picture-postcard Greece without the crowds or the neon bars, an off-the-beaten-track paradise that few people seemed to have discovered as yet.

'This is you,' Jesse said, turning into the car park of a more sizeable Carrefour than Winnie had expected. 'What?' He slid his glasses off and turned to look at her when she didn't move.

'Nothing,' Winnie said. 'It's just bigger than I thought.'

'Just because we're quiet it doesn't mean we're uncivilised. You're perfectly safe,' he said. 'We like our exorbitantly priced English teabags and imported bacon just as much as the bigger islands.'

Winnie rolled her eyes. 'You think we won't cut it here, don't you?'

'It's not for everyone,' he said. 'You might find it too quiet.'

'Maybe. I don't think so though, somehow. And anyway, quiet is good right now.'

He tapped his fingers on the wheel. 'And what about when you're all done hiding? What will you do then?'

Winnie frowned. 'We're not hiding,' she said. 'Just because you overheard snapshots of our lives in the bar yesterday, it doesn't mean you get to make judgments on our staying power.'

He looked unabashed. 'I'm just sayin' it the way I see it, Legs.'

'Legs? Did you just call me Legs?'

'You've got them.' He nodded down towards her knees. 'Everyone does.'

'Yeah, but yours go all the way up to your ass.'

'Yes, but . . .' She trailed off, blushing a litle. There really wasn't much she could say to that.

'I'll be back in half an hour or so. I'll come and find you.'

Winnie nodded and scarpered out of his car, muttering thanks as she slammed the door, pulling her skirt down her thighs as she went.

Winding his window down, he shot her a grin. 'I can still see them.'

'So stop looking then.'

Winnie turned and walked away, turning at the supermarket to find him still blatantly watching her.

'You're so predictable, caveman,' she half shouted, making a woman pushing a trolley past her turn to look at her in alarm.

'Signomi! Sorry!' Jesse called, raising his hand in greeting as he used both Greek and English for clarity. 'She's new around here.'

It seemed to do the trick, for the woman at least, who shrugged and moved on. It had a far less relaxing effect on Winnie, who felt more like throwing tomatoes from the display outside the store at Jesse's smug grin as he tapped his watch face and threw his arm across the back of the passenger seat to reverse out of the car park.

'Legs,' she muttered, watching him pull away in a cloud

of dust before heading inside the thankfully cool super-market.

'Get everything you need?'

Winnie turned away from the baffling display of cleaning products at the sound of Jesse's voice behind her.

'Has it been that long already?' She frowned down into her half-filled trolley. Her shopping so far had been hit and miss from the list they'd all cobbled together around the breakfast table that morning. There were ingredients for dishes Frankie wanted to test out, and vague things like 'buy dinner' and then a few requests for tastes of home if they were available.

'I'm looking for bathroom cleaner. For the loos and things.'

He scanned the shelves, plucked a spray bottle down and briefly read the back before handing it to her.

'This one. It actually specifies that it's best for delicate-stomached tourists who insist on a full English breakfast washed down with builder's tea.'

'Ha ha.' Winnie grabbed it from him and put it as far away from the bacon and eggs in her trolley as possible.

'What else do you need?'

Surveying the list, Winnie said, 'Dinner.'

'Eat at Panos's place.'

'We *live* here, Jesse. We want to cook for ourselves.'

'*I* live here, and Panos cooks my dinner more than I do.'

'You're a man.'

'Now who's being stereotypical?'

She pulled a face at his back as he wandered away towards the deli counter. Following him, she listened as he chatted easily with the girl behind the display, speaking in fast, fluent Greek that she couldn't follow. He made the girl laugh though, so evidently he was more charming in his second language than his native tongue.

'Not vegetarians, no?'

'Frankie is.' Winnie didn't miss the pained look on Jesse's face as he turned back and ordered more things from the counter.

'Olives,' he said when he turned back around with his hands full. 'And feta.'

Winnie watched him lay the clear containers of gleaming green olives and big creamy chunks of cheese alongside the salad ingredients already in her trolley.

'Spanakopita. It's spinach pie.'

Frankie would approve of that.

'Keftethes. Meatballs. Tell your vegetarian to steer clear.'

'I think she could work that much out for herself,' Winnie said. The balls were huge and clearly strictly for carnivores.

Jesse added a tub of tzatziki and slices of locally cured ham, before moving over to the bakery to order a bag of fresh triangles of pita straight from the ovens.

'Dinner,' he said, waving his hand grandly over the trolley as if he'd been out and hunted the meat himself.

'Thank you.'

They wandered back towards the tills, and once there he automatically unloaded and packed her shopping into brown paper carriers without her needing to ask as she carefully counted out the unfamiliar money. It was a moment of simple harmony, and she had the grace to thank him as they left the store and filled the boot of his Golf with her shopping bags.

'Do you need to go straight back?' he asked as she slipped into the passenger seat.

71

She looked at him for a long moment, wondering what he had in mind. 'I don't think it matters too much. Why?'

He winked at her before sliding his glasses over his eyes and gunning the engine.

'In that case I'll show you something special.'

He threw his arm across the back of her seat to glance over his shoulder and reverse in that sexy way that only men on movies ever truly do, and Winnie tried not to notice the inadvertent graze of his fingertips against the back of her neck as they left the supermarket behind them in the distance and drove up into the hills.

Reaching across Winnie's knees to grab a bottle of chilled water from the glove box, Jesse tried not to notice the fact that she smelled like fresh flowers or that her skin was so double-cream pale against his own sun-weathered arm.

'Come on, it's up on foot from here.'

'What is?'

Winnie slammed her door and gazed around the deserted hillside.

He didn't explain, just headed towards a dusty track leading up through the pine trees. 'This way. It's not far.'

Following the familiar route, he turned back after a few minutes. 'Watch your footing here, the grit can be a bit loose underfoot.'

On cue, Winnie's foot slid sideways, and he held out his hand to steady her.

'OK?' he said, holding on to her fingers.

'Think so.' She half laughed, gripping him.

'We're nearly at the top,' he said, keeping hold of her hand to help her take the last few steepest strides. He resolutely ignored the warmth of her fingers, and the way the exertion made her breasts rise and fall beneath her pink T-shirt. Jesus, did they not make it in her size? It looked as if it had been designed for a twelve-year-old and inadvertently found itself wrapped around the curves and hollows of a fully formed woman.

They reached the summit with a final tug, and he gave her a few seconds to get her breath back and appreciate why the hike was worth the effort.

'Wow,' she murmured, her hands on her hips as she looked down.

'This is the highest point of the island,' he explained, leading her across to a bench that had been placed there to take advantage of the stunning views. They'd crested the hill into a clearing, and from there there was a direct, panoramic view down across the island and the Mediterranean. Skelidos lay before them, a patchwork of fields and forests snaked through with twisting roads, a smattering of houses closer to the coast, jewel-green vegetation against impossibly periwinkle skies and vivid turquoise waters.

'If it were a postcard, you wouldn't believe it wasn't photo-shopped,' Winnie said, lifting her sunglasses onto her head as she perched gratefully beside him on the driftwood bench.

'I know. I could never tire of it.'

It wasn't a lie. Skelidos represented far more than just home to Jesse. The place had literally saved his life ten times over back in the early days when he couldn't have cared less if he lived or died. But Winnie didn't need to know that.

'Does it ever get lonely?' she said, turning her blue eyes to his. 'In the winter?'

'I guess that depends on what you look for in life,' he said. 'It's hardly busy anyway, so we feel the absence of the tourists far less than the bigger islands.'

She nodded, her gaze back on that spectacular view.

'Was it an impulse buy? The villa?' He watched her profile as she considered his question, saw the fleeting conflicting emotions pass across her face.

'In a way,' she sighed. 'It just . . . it just felt like a good time to be somewhere else.'

He identified with that more that she knew. 'Because of your divorce from Needledick?'

She laughed softly and shook her head. 'Rory. His name is Rory.'

There was a vulnerability behind her voice when she said her ex-husband's name that grated on him.

'Why do you do that?'

She looked at him, surprised. 'Do what?'

'Sigh his name with a reverence it doesn't deserve. It sounds to me as if Needledick suits him a whole lot more.'

Her mouth twisted to the side as she scuffed the toe of her sneaker in the dusty earth beneath the bench. 'He asked me out on my fifteenth birthday. He was my first love.' She picked at a loose splinter of wood on the bench. 'My only one.'

'Christ, you're not telling me that he's the only man you've ever kissed in your entire life? How old are you?'

Her chin came up, defensive. 'Thirty-four. And yes, he is the only man I've ever kissed, if you must know.'

Thank God she was over thirty. 'Well, thank fuck he nobbed off in that case.'

'What?' She stared at him, almost gasping in shock. If she'd been expecting sympathy, she was looking at the wrong man.

'Come on, Legs. No one should go through life having only ever kissed one other person. It's not natural.'

Everything about her body language told him she was

offended, from her braced shoulders to her balled fists beside her on the bench.

'I always thought it was romantic, actually. Not everyone has to put themselves about like a . . .' She flicked her hand towards him to encompass all that he was. 'Like a tomcat, snogging anyone and everyone who is even halfway interested.'

Jesse laughed. 'I like kissing, Winnie. There's nothing wrong with that.' He refused to be anything but blasé. 'I like screwing, too. I like it a lot.'

'Well, there's a surprise. No doubt you've lost count of how many women you've . . .' She flicked her hand at him again rather than repeat the word.

'Does it matter?' He shrugged. 'I don't lie. I don't cheat. I don't fall in love either, but we have a damn good time and we respect each other in the morning.'

She spread her fingers flat on the bench and studied them.

'Maybe you've got it right. At least no one gets hurt.'

'Things are only ever as complicated as you make them, Winnie,' he said softly.

'But that's what love is, Jesse. It's complicated, and it's messy.'

'I'm not talking about love. I'm talking about kissing, and about screwing, and about honesty. This thing in here –' he tapped two fingers against his heart '– it doesn't need to get involved.' Reaching over, he drew a cross over her heart with one fingertip. 'No entry,' he whispered. 'It's better that way, trust me. You don't need to involve your internal organs when it comes to sex. All the good stuff happens on the outside.'

She didn't look convinced by his philosophy. 'So to be clear, you're saying I need to exercise my external pleasure organs more and my internal emotional organs less. Is that your actual advice?'

He swallowed. She was wide-eyed and actually looked as if she was seriously considering his life advice.

'Did you know that your skin is the biggest organ of your body?' he asked, letting his arm fall across the back of the bench until his fingertips brushed her upper arm. Her blue eyes widened a fraction as she registered his touch. 'See?'

'No, I don't see,' she said, pulling away a little until he was no longer touching her.

'Then let me show you. Call it an experiment.'

She shuffled further away from him along the bench, her eyes nailed on the view. 'Stop being so ridiculous.'

She was so very, very tense. It emanated from her every pore, and it frustrated the hell out of him that she clearly lived her life as buttoned up as if she were wearing an invisible straitjacket. He'd been there, and he'd learned that flinging off the shackles and sticking two fingers up to romantic notions and expectations was the most liberating thing you could ever do.

'Turn your brain off. Stop thinking about anything and concentrate on that ridiculously fabulous view,' he said quietly, and then trailed the back of his fingers slowly down her arm from her shoulder all the way to her spread fingertips on the bench between them.

'Now do you see?'

She pulled her bottom lip between her teeth and her nostrils flared slightly.

'What I see is you trying to make a point,' she said, turning to look at him with those big, trouble-filled eyes.

'Damn right I am,' he said, stroking his fingertips along her jawline from beneath her ear to her chin. 'If showing

you that it's OK to let someone make you feel good physically without risking your sanity is making a point.' As
he spoke, he let his thumb skim lightly across the fullness
of her bottom lip. Jesus, it was soft.

'And what was that supposed to show me?' she breathed,
as still as if they were playing statues.

'That the mouth has more touch receptors than any
other part of your body.' He paused to stroke his thumb
the other way across her mouth, and looked away for a
second when her lips parted in a tiny, involuntary sigh.
'Even more than . . .' He lowered his gaze to her lap for
a second and lifted a knowing eyebrow.

'Are you blushing?' he said, leaning slightly back to
study her face better. 'Man. You're something else.'

'I'm hot,' she shot back, defensive.

'You are,' he agreed, and then slid his hand around to
cup the back of her neck.

Anxiety clouded her pretty eyes.

'I get it, Winnie,' he said softly, massaging the tense
muscles beneath her hairline. 'You've never let anyone
except Needledick try to make you feel good.' Unshed tears
pooled in her eyes, making him feel like a prize cock for
pushing her like this. In truth, he didn't know why it
suddenly felt important, but he couldn't hold it in.

'I can't separate love from sex,' she said. 'They go
together like a package deal.'

He shook his head, his fingers sliding her hairband out
until he could muss her hair down around her shoulders
and her jaw.

'You have real pretty hair,' he said, and then wished he
hadn't because it was a physicality of hers he didn't care
to acknowledge. 'I'm gonna kiss you now,' he said, and
her eyes widened in alarm. 'I'm going to show you how

a kiss can just be about your mouth and mine, and about pleasure, and hedonism, and nothing whatsoever to do with love, or your heart, or even your brain.' He slid closer until her body was almost but not quite pressing his. He'd never seen a woman look more like she was staring down the barrel of a gun. 'Are you OK with this?' he asked, stroking his hand over her hair once, and then again when she gave him the tiniest of nods. 'Good girl,' he said. 'You can say stop whenever you want.'

What in God's name was he doing? This wasn't his plan. He was way off track and somewhere in the back of his mind an alarm sounded, but the bell was drowned out by the loud drum of his heartbeat and the soft sound of Winnie's shallow breathing. Was she trembling? Jesus, she was. Had he pushed her too far?

'Do it,' she murmured, like a determined sixth-former telling her first love to take her virginity on the back seat of his car. It was enough to make him tip his head to hers until their lips touched and her eyelids drifted down. He didn't close his eyes. He couldn't, because the pure crack of electricity that flowed from his mouth to his groin wouldn't let him. He watched her instead, saw the single tear slide down her cheek at the same time as her lips began to move tentatively against his, the smallest of movements, parting to let her sigh slide into his mouth. *Christ.* It really was like kissing Sleeping Beauty, as if she'd spent a lifetime waiting and this was the moment he woke her up. And then she snaked the tip of her tongue along his top lip, and she stopped being a fairytale princess and turned into a siren instead, and he lost all sense of sentient thought and slid his hands into her hair and kissed her mouth hard and open. He heard her gasp, and then her arms moved around him and pulled him into her, both of her hands sliding into up his hair at the back of his neck.

'Holy God,' he muttered, ragged against her mouth, and then he stopped thinking and took his own advice to shut the hell up and just enjoy it. God, she was too responsive, he couldn't control himself or her. He licked his tongue inside her mouth and felt himself spiral, the sensual kick of her intimate reaction pulsing all the way through his body. Could you kiss someone for ever? Because he wanted to. He wanted to spend the rest of his life right there on that bench without even coming up for air, because this was the most sensational, mind-bending, unexpectedly better-than-any-sex-he'd-ever-had kiss he'd known in his entire life.

'Jesse,' she gasped when he broke the kiss to tilt her head back and slide his open mouth down the centre of her neck, licking her skin, inhaling the scent of her into his lungs. Her clothes were in his way. His clothes were in his way.

'Jesse,' she said again, a little louder, her fingers tightening in his hair so she could hold his head and lower her gaze level with his. 'Stop.'

He nodded, both of them breathing harder than if they'd sprinted a hundred metres, staring into each other's wide eyes, speaking without words.

What the hell was that?

Did you feel it?

Did you know that would happen?

Winnie pressed her still trembling fingertips against her lips, and Jesse wiped the back of his hand across his mouth.

'Well?' he asked, and she half laughed shakily.

'Well what?'

Jesse concentrated on counting his own heartbeats to

slow them down. 'Do you see now how a kiss can be a physical pleasure in its own right?'

She shook her head slowly. 'No. No, I don't think I do.' Picking his hand up, she laid it flat over her heart. 'Here, feel how fast my heart is beating.' He could feel it racing, but he could also the feel the swell of her breast and it made his own heartbeat quicken again too. 'And in here,' she tapped her finger to her temple, 'my brain felt as if someone was letting off party poppers. So no, I can't kiss for physical pleasure alone, and for the record, I don't think you can either.'

Oh, she was wrong there. He shoved his hands through his hair and concentrated on tracking the lanes criss-crossing the island while he marshalled his thoughts.

'I'll level with you, Legs, you caught me off guard. I expected that kiss to be a little more . . . well, chaste, shall we say. You blindsided me when you put your tongue in my mouth.'

She sucked in air, affronted. 'I did not.'

'You so did. It was meant to be five seconds max, not a full-on pash.'

'Pash?'

He flicked his eyes to the side like a teenager caught smoking. 'Call it what you like. Point is, it wasn't supposed to give you a heart attack or me blue balls.'

Winnie's eyes dropped momentarily to his crotch, and he scowled and fired her a tiny sarcastic smile.

'I think we can safely conclude that you just proved yourself wrong with your own experiment,' she said, prim and just a teeny bit superior.

'Not exactly.' He jerked his chin towards his lap. 'My junk is on the outside, strictly speaking.'

'Junk?'

'Do you have to keep repeating my words?'

They both stared dead ahead. For his part, Jesse was confused how to play it. On the one hand, Jesus bloody Christ, that had been one hell of a kiss and a big part of him wanted to take her home, fling her on his bed and rip her clothes off, because if that was how they kissed, what would sex be like? On the other hand, Winnie didn't conform to any of his rules. She wasn't passing through. She was his new neighbour, and she'd come here to recover from a crapshoot of a relationship, and if he really, truly examined his feelings, there was an element of nostalgia in play here. She reminded him of Erin. That hair . . . those eyes . . . she was different but cast from the same mould, and it was a mould he'd deliberately denied himself any right or access to. He should never have kissed her.

'I'm sorry,' he said, and he found that he meant it. She'd cried, for fuck's sake. Was he such a selfish man as to let his own desire override common decency? Had he kissed her against her will? 'I shouldn't have kissed you.'

She sighed and crossed her arms, leaning back against the bench.

'Don't apologise, Jesse. I enjoyed it.'

OK, so that surprised him. Not surprised because it had been fairly bloody obvious that she was into it, but that she had the balls to say she'd enjoyed it rather than let him feel shoddy was unexpected.

'I need a beer.'

'I need to get back to the villa.'

It seemed that they both needed to get off that bench. He stood up and she did the same, following him carefully down the uneven path through the pine trees to his car.

'Thanks for showing me the view,' she said, after he'd

been driving for a couple of minutes. He glanced sideways towards her, but she didn't look at him.

'I can show you around the rest of the island, if you like. I know it like the back of my hand.' Shit. Why did he say that? He was so obviously suggesting that they have wild animal sex because he knew women's bodies like the back of his hand. He might as well have said, 'I'm a gigolo and you're a desperate fair maiden, let me deflower you in my olive grove while the donkeys watch.'

Winnie tipped her head back against the headrest and closed her eyes.

'I think I should probably take my time to discover it on my own,' she said eventually.

'For the best.'

They didn't speak again until he pulled the Golf back through the gap in the stone wall onto his property.

'Go on home,' he said, slamming his door. 'I'll bring your shopping over in the cart. The car won't fit down the far end of the lane.'

'I can take the cart myself, if you want?'

He huffed. 'Winnie, what kind of man would that make me to let you haul all of that stuff yourself?'

She frowned. 'A normal one, in my world.'

Jeez, what sort of men had she surrounded herself with? He reached into the car and tossed her a fresh bottle of water.

'Go home.'

She nodded just once, and then turned and half walked, half ran across the olive grove and disappeared over the wall. He stood still for a few deep breaths, and then banged his fist down on the roof before heading into the house.

Down the lane, Winnie kept going until she was well out of sight of Jesse's place and then dropped down onto a

82

boulder beneath the shade of an olive tree, holding her head in her hands. Tears came easy, soaking through her fingers, her shoulders shaking. She was such a long way from home, a lifetime away from all that was familiar, and she'd just been kissed stupid by someone who wasn't Rory. She felt right and all wrong, unfaithful and mad with herself for feeling that way because she hadn't done anything out of line, but whichever way you shook it down she'd complicated things in a way she wasn't ready for. They'd all come here looking for escape, and she'd somehow walked out of one romantic mess and straight into the arms of the nearest stranger. What a stupid, stupid thing to do.

CHAPTER SIX

Their first week on the island passed them by in a haze of sun-warmed shoulders and tentative plans. The three women fell into a pattern of spending their days acquainting themselves with Villa Valentina's charms and secrets, its nooks and crannies, the rickety staircase up to the dusty attic filled with intriguing old boxes and trunks. They were long, sun-drenched days, and invariably ended with a sundowner on the terrace watching the sun sizzle down into the sea.

'I'm going to investigate the cellar,' Stella said, as they sat around the kitchen table drinking strong coffee on their seventh morning. The back door stood propped open to let the light morning breeze in, and they'd just breakfasted on toast slathered with heavenly greengage jam Frankie had made the day before and bowls of thick creamy Greek yoghurt given to them as a welcome gift by one of the neighbouring farms. The locals had been calling thick and fast, everyone keen to get a look at the mysterious trio of English women who'd unexpectedly come to their island. They'd ended up with a fridge stuffed with all kinds of produce and a table overflowing with wine and sweet pastries, and with their hearts warmed and well and truly welcomed.

'There's a torch underneath the sink,' Frankie said, dragging a huge, battered old brown cookbook towards her across the table. It had come with the villa, and she'd read it from back to front already, deciphering the Greek family recipes from the pictures and Google translate and then adapting them in her notebook to make them her own. She was an intuitive cook with a natural flair for flavour and a taste for the simple and delicious; she was in her element on Skelidos surrounded by nature's bounty.

'I'm going to try to make this for dinner tonight,' she said, tapping an image of fat, ruby stuffed tomatoes.

Stella leaned over to look. 'It's a good job we've got you, Frank,' she said. 'If it was left to me to do the cooking, we'd live on halloumi on toast.'

'Or crisp sandwiches,' Winnie said, thinking back to Stella's favourite TV snack as a teenager.

'Don't knock it till you've tried it,' Stella said. 'Nothing better than cheese and onion crisps and mayonnaise.'

'I hope I never fall ill and have to leave you in charge of the kitchen,' Frankie said. 'Our guests would be in for a shock.'

'I'd just get them all drunk on gin so they couldn't remember anything,' Stella said with a grin, scraping her chair back on the flagstones and gathering the dishes into the sink. She opened the cupboard underneath, bent down and came up brandishing a long black torch. 'Wish me luck. If I'm not back up in an hour, send out the search party.'

'Do you want me to come down there with you?' Winnie asked, relieved when Stella shook her head.

'We all know you're rubbish in the dark. I haven't forgotten when we went into that haunted house at the Pleasure Beach in Blackpool.'

'I thought I was very brave,' Winnie sniffed, refilling her coffee from the cafetière and avoiding Stella's laughing gaze because they all knew she'd screamed like a baby and almost got herself arrested for assaulting one of the zombie staff who jumped out on her.

'Poor guy was only doing his job. You nearly broke his nose.'

'God, yes. There was blood all down his shirt,' Frankie laughed.

'It was fake!' Winnie protested.

'Just stay up here in the daylight unless I shout,' Stella said, turning the knob on the creaking cellar door beside the walk-in pantry. 'Wish me luck. I'm going down.'

Stella reappeared in the kitchen half an hour later, considerably dustier than when she'd descended and carrying half a dozen bottles of island gin under her arms.

'Look what I found,' she said, as Frankie wandered back inside carrying a bowl of huge ripe tomatoes.

'A whole load of island gin!' Frankie raised her eyebrows in surprise.

Stella nodded, then stuck her head out of the kitchen and called Winnie's name loudly down the hallway.

'I've started cataloguing all of the linen,' Winnie said as she came back into the kitchen carrying a pile of sheets and deposited them on the side. 'There's heaps of it in those huge cupboards on the first-floor landing.' Her eyes moved to take in the bottles of gin that Stella had lined up on the kitchen table. 'Where did that lot come from?'

'That's why I called you,' Stella said. 'You two have to

see this.' She led them across to the cellar, then turned back and looked at Winnie. 'Don't worry, you're safe. There's a light down there.'

They all trooped down the stone steps into the cool cellar. About the same size as the kitchen overhead, the bare earth-floored room was lit by a single bulb hanging from a wire in the centre of the ceiling.

'I know where to come if I need to cool off,' Frankie murmured, as they all stood and surveyed the long wooden bench loaded with glass jars and bottles. One side of the room had been lined with deep wooden shelves, and they were filled with row upon row of island gin.

'One hundred and twenty-seven bottles of the stuff, to be exact,' Stella said.

'Wow.' Winnie crossed to study them, admiring their *Alice in Wonderland* style handwritten labels all individually numbered in flowing black script. 'Looks like the gin really is part of the villa's history.'

Frankie was at the bench examining the jars and bottles.

'Juniper berries,' she said, pulling the lid off a big jar of tiny dried berries to sniff the contents.

'And coriander seeds.' She twisted another jar around to read the hand-inked label.

Stella joined her by the bench and steered her to the other end.

'Look at this.'

Winnie joined them, and they all gazed down at the words etched into the surface of the wood.

'It's a recipe, I think?' Frankie traced her finger over the inscriptions. It was difficult to make out in places, worn almost away by hands and time.

Stella reached down to the shelf beneath the bench. 'I found this too.'

87

She laid an envelope down on the surface so they could all see that it bore each of their names.

Winnie. Stella. Frankie.

'What does it say?' Winnie asked, lifting her eyes to Stella's.

'I don't know, I didn't look. I thought we should read it together.'

For a minute they all stared at it in silence.

'You do it, Frank,' Stella said. Winnie swallowed and nodded, and Frankie sighed and picked it up.

'Just because I'm a mother, it doesn't mean I'm always the most responsible adult.'

'Of course it does,' Stella laughed. 'You kept two actual people alive. I couldn't even keep a goldfish going.'

With a roll of her eyes, Frankie picked the envelope open and pulled out the sheaf of papers, smoothing the sheets out on the bench to read them aloud.

Hello ladies,
  I hope that by now you've settled into Villa Valentina and have realised that you've landed in paradise.

All three of them nodded slowly. They couldn't disagree so far.

  You may or may not have heard talk of the island gin being linked to the Villa. It isn't a myth; as custodians of the place, you've also taken on responsibility for running the island's distillery, such as it is. (You're standing in it.)

Frankie broke off to look incredulously at Winnie and Stella, then dropped her gaze to carry on.

I expect you're wondering why I didn't mention this before the sale. In truth, I was worried it might give you pause for thought, but there's really no need to feel overly concerned. You have all of the necessary botanical ingredients readily available in Valentina's garden, and you'll find a supply already dried out in the jars on the bench, enough to make a couple of batches while you get the hang of preparing the ingredients yourselves.

Please don't think badly of me. You might even enjoy it! I know I did. The recipe is engraved on the bench. I don't know who wrote it, it's been that way for as long as anyone on the island can remember. I've taken the liberty of translating it into English for you here, because the locals take the spirit of the island seriously and won't appreciate it if you get it wrong! No pressure, ha!

Anyway, I found that distilling around fifty bottles a month keeps the island from running dry, plus enough for Hero. It's only supplied to the bars and restaurants and any locals who want to buy it directly, it doesn't leave Skelidos. Panos will supply you with the base spirit, and you'll see the record book on the bench so you can number the bottles. It's all sold through Panos's bar, he'll clue you in on the arrangements.

Each new owner gets to design their own label. You can see that I went for a strong italic. I'm looking forward to seeing what three English adventurers come up with when I come back to visit!

Love and luck,

Ajax

PS . . . it's all sort of a bit of a secret. No one else knows the recipe. I've deliberately forgotten it already. Gin? What gin?

Frankie lifted the top sheet to reveal the recipe written out on the page below, and rubbed her hand over her cheek thoughtfully.

'We've bought a gin distillery,' Winnie said slowly.

'Is it even legal?' Frankie asked, wary-eyed.

'Well, it wouldn't pass any health and safety checks, that's for sure,' Stella said, looking at the bare earth floor and then towards the shelves on the wall. 'Going on Ajax's calculations, there's roughly three months' supply on the shelves already. And Hero? What does he mean by that?'

'Perhaps we're to give free gin to anyone who does something heroic,' Winnie shrugged, knowing it was a reach.

'It takes about a week to make it, looking at this.' Frankie was reading the recipe and turning the jars on the bench to check the contents.

'You're the chef amongst us, Frank,' Winnie said, nodding towards the recipe. 'Do you think we can do it?'

Frankie lifted one unsure shoulder. 'Well, it doesn't look especially complicated. I think a lot of it is making sure that we keep the botanical stocks replenished. We'd need to get a system going for picking, drying out, all that stuff. I don't know much about it, to be honest.'

'But between us . . . we've got this, right? If Ajax could do it, then surely we can?'

Stella looked from one to the other, then threw her hands in the air and laughed. 'In for a penny, in for a pound. This adventure just got even weirder.'

Winnie met Frankie's warily excited, shiny gaze. Unscrewing the lid from the nearest bottle of gin, she took a heady swig. 'The secret gin fairies it is then,' she said, her throat still burning from the spirit as she handed it along.

Frankie took a swig and then spluttered gently. 'I quite like the idea of us as bad fairies. Can we have that on the label?'

Stella took her turn drinking from the bottle and then raised it towards her friends. 'To the Secret Gin Fairies of Skelidos.'

'I think I've got a headache,' Frankie said as they all lay out on the terrace later that afternoon. They'd abandoned any pretence of work after discovering the distillery in the cellar and spent the day sunbathing, snacking and drinking the rest of the bottle of gin they'd opened.

'You need another drink then. We need to make sure we list the number of the bottle we've drunk in the book,' Stella said. 'Your job, Win.'

'Is it?' Winnie said, sitting up to adjust her bandeau bikini top. 'Okey-doke.' She raised her glass, totally unfazed. It was amazing how much more brave yet relaxed she felt after a day playing hooky and a few heavy-handed G&Ts.

They'd applied themselves wholeheartedly to work since they'd arrived, so the snap decision to down tools and soak up some rays had been a welcome one all round. They lay toasting themselves in a row, facing the sea, floppy sunhats over their eyes and painted toes pointing towards the beach.

'Do you think we look like one of those "wish you were here" pictures that people in England would have as their screensavers at work and die of jealousy?' Stella circled her ankle one way in the air and then the other.

'Abso-bloody-lutely,' Winnie said. 'I'd totally choose us.'

'I always had the boys as my screensaver.' Frankie sat up, suddenly morose.

Winnie reached out and patted Frankie's arm. 'They're coming over in a few weeks, you'll see them soon.'

'And just think how cool they're going to think their mum is, doing yoga on the beach at dawn and running a secret distillery,' Stella said, struggling to drink from her glass without sitting up. 'Balls, I've spilt gin between my boobs.' She rang an imaginary bell then huffed impatiently. 'Where's that sodding bellboy got to? I need him to mop me.'

'Will they really think I'm cool, do you think?' Frankie said, tossing a hand towel towards Stella as she pulled her knees into her chest and wrapped her arms around them to gaze out towards the horizon. 'I'd like that.'

'You're a frickin' fairy, Frank,' Winnie said, in the same tone she might have said, 'You're a millionaire supermodel.' 'Fairy,' she said, determined, pointing at her friend. 'Fairy.' She jabbed her finger at herself. 'Fairy.' She poked Stella in the arm.

'Fairy with sticky boobs,' Stella grumbled.

'And a bit badass,' Winnie added. 'We can be fairies, but we have to be badass ones.'

All three of them nodded and lay back on their loungers.

'So, Win . . .' Stella said. 'How's the donkey bothering going?'

Winnie had been over to Jesse's property every morning since their shopping trip to spend a little time attempting to charm The Fonz, and so far it had to be said that he remained completely indifferent to her overtures. He was more than happy to take her offerings, but in terms of reciprocal affection she'd yet to reap even an iota of benefit.

'I don't think he likes me very much yet.'

'Typical man.'

'He is,' Winnie agreed. 'He just does his own thing and flicks his eyes at me every now and then to throw me a crumb.'

'Are we still talking about the donkey?' Frankie asked.

'Haha,' Winnie said. 'Although actually we could be talking about either of them. Jesse is equally bloody awkward.'

'Surely you knew that much already?' Stella said. 'Given that he rocked up here on our first day all moody and floppy shirt, like Heathcliff in a rage? If he calls you Cathy, run.'

Winnie had barely seen Jesse in the days that had passed since their kiss up at the lookout point. She was more than half relieved; things between them were a tiny bit massively awkward. She hadn't found the right moment to mention what had happened to Stella or Frankie either; she'd wound up feeling as if she'd done something wrong or stupid, which was ridiculous given that she was a free agent and could kiss whoever the hell she wanted to. It was a little bit to do with Rory, because she was still emotionally tied to him and those strings were going to have to fray and snap in their own time. But it was as much to do with the fact that the three of them had come all this way for a fresh start, a clean new sheet of paper, which they could fill with only good things. To rush headlong into the arms of the nearest man felt a bit weak, if that was the right word. They were supposed to be adventurers, brave badass fairies, Thelma and Louise with a happier ending. Although, to give Thelma her dues, she did get to boff Brad Pitt, so it wasn't all doom and gloom.

'Maybe he's my Brad Pitt,' Winnie said.

Both Frankie and Stella turned to stare at her and she realised that only the last bit of her train of thought had made it out of her mouth. 'It's too complicated to explain,' she said, batting the air.

'Your Brad Pitt?' Stella said, ignoring her.

Winnie pulled her hat down over her eyes.

'He kissed me.'

Frankie reached over and pulled Winnie's hat back up again so they could see her face.

'Jesse the grumpy neighbour kissed you?'

Winnie wondered why in God's name she'd said it, and then in the same breath she was glad she had, because it had confused the hell out of her and these two women were her confidantes and her sisters. So she nodded, sitting up and crossing her legs, her drink cradled between her hands.

'When? Where?'

'The day he took me shopping.'

Stella frowned. 'He kissed you a whole week ago and you're only mentioning it now?'

'I know,' Winnie sighed. 'It came out of the blue. Well, no, actually that's not true. He told me he was going to do it first.'

Frankie leaned around Winnie to share a private 'we need to keep an eye on this because she isn't up to having her heart broken' look with Stella.

Stella threw back a quick and equally protective 'I'll drown him in a bucket of island gin and pickle his genitals if she cries even one tear' look, and then turned back to Winnie.

'Come on then, spill. What happened?'

'Well, we went shopping, obviously.' Winnie picked at a piece of loose cotton on the sun lounger's deeply padded ivory cushion. 'And he was showing me bits of the island as we drove, and then he took me to see the highest point of the island because the view is amazing. There's a bench and everything.'

'And you sat on the bench?' Frankie said, encouraging the story along.

Winnie nodded. 'I did. And he did. And I somehow told him that Rory is the only man I've ever kissed and he was like, oh my God, you're practically a nun, I'm going to have to snog you right now to save you from a lifetime in a wimple.'

They all laughed.

'He didn't really say that, did he?' Stella laughed.

Winnie rolled her eyes. 'No. He called Rory Needledick and told me that pleasure is all about the external bodily organs, then stroked my arm to demonstrate.'

'It sounds like a biology class,' Frankie said.

'It didn't feel like one,' Winnie said. 'He wanted to show me that you can enjoy physical pleasure without involving your heart or your head.'

They fell silent. Stella was thinking that he was bang on the money, and Frankie was wondering how it would feel to be kissed by someone if it *did* involve your heart or your head. She and Gav must have had a spark back in the early days, but they'd been little more than children themselves really and their relationship would probably never have made it beyond a few months if she hadn't fallen pregnant. Melancholy thoughts of what her life might have been like started to seep in, and she took a good glug of gin and pushed all of the negativity back across the sea in her head towards England. She'd left it there in that soulless rented flat. It wasn't allowed to follow her here.

'And then he said he was going to kiss me.'

'Wow. I mean, he's grumpy but he's *hot*, Win. Was it good?' Stella swung her legs around to put her feet on the floor and face Winnie.

'It was . . . it was . . .' Words genuinely failed her.

'What? Good? Hideous?' Frankie said, impatient.

'Oh no,' Stella muttered. 'He wasn't terrible, was he?

Did he slobber all over you like one of those dogs with ten chins?'

Winnie laughed softly, her cheeks warm from the sun, the cocktails and the memory of Jesse's kiss.

'No, he wasn't awful, and he didn't slobber. He was . . . God, it was shockingly good.' And then she said, 'Very different to Rory,' and felt like a terrible person for comparing them.

Both Frankie and Stella sighed in half relief, half envy.

'He was gentle, and then he wasn't. It started out sort of subtle, but then it wasn't subtle at all, it was like three minutes of dynamite sex with your clothes on!' Her voice escalated, giddy with too much gin and the relief of finally sharing the story.

'Shit,' Stella said, with a low whistle.

'Winnie!' Frankie laughed. 'No wonder you've been going round every day to visit the donkey.'

'Have you two been shagging like goats under the olive groves?' Stella said suddenly, raising her eyebrows.

'Goats?' Winnie said. 'Do goats have lots of sex?'

'I don't bloody know! Are you?'

'No. I've barely even seen him since. I think he's avoiding me.'

They all slumped back onto their sunbeds with the cocktails on their bellies.

'My advice?' Stella said. 'Have fun, but stick to those outside feels only.'

Frankie made sounds of approval. 'Because your heart isn't ready for any action.'

'I guess that's the beauty of him, then,' Winnie said. 'His heart belongs to the island, and his work, and his home, and cold beer. He neither needs nor wants a woman for anything other than carnal pleasures.'

'If you don't want him, can I have him?' Stella sighed. 'That sounds like my ideal man. If he were blonde I'd be shoving you off a cliff to get to him.'

Nordic men were Stella's weakness; it had been a long-standing joke that she hung around in Ikea in eternal hope of bumping into Alexander Skarsgard. She'd have moved to the Arctic Circle long ago if there was a beach and it wasn't freezing. Salopettes were so not her thing.

They lapsed into companionable silence, looking out over the glittering Med, each of them lost in thought.

Frankie imagined the twins strolling down the deserted beach in front of her, and idly wondered if there was someone out there who might save his dynamite kisses all for her one day. The very idea came as a surprise; she'd had so little time for romance in her life for a long time, she'd almost written herself off.

Stella felt encouraged by the fact that at least one of them had already found a little heat, though she wouldn't have put money on Winnie being first to break cover. Her mind wandered back to her apartment back in England, the scene of many of her easy come, easy go romances, and she was surprised to find that, for now at least, she wasn't missing the slick, sophisticated trappings of success.

Winnie closed her eyes and slid into a daydream, a daydream of capable male hands rubbing sun cream into her shoulders, of a man bending to kiss her neck. She twisted around to try to catch a glimpse of his face, and in doing so jolted herself awake and sloshed her cocktail all over her navel.

'Balls.'

She jerked up, annoyed with herself.

Now she'd never get to see who'd been kissing her neck.

CHAPTER SEVEN

'Ladies, I need some help.'

Stella and Frankie were in organisation mode behind the reception desk a few mornings later, and Winnie was halfway up a stepladder putting a fresh coat of white paint on the window shutters. All three of them turned to look at Corinna as she came through their open front door on a waft of Chanel and a clatter of tan high-heeled sandals. She looked spectacular in an orange silk shift, her long hair in a businesslike chignon and her lipstick a perfect match with her dress.

'What can we help with?' Frankie smiled and closed the ledger.

Stella poured Corinna a glass of water from the iced jug on the counter and handed it over. 'Too early for a shot of island gin in it?' she said, knowing that a little after ten in the morning was hardcore even for a Skelidos native.

'You might all need a shot when you've heard what I've come to ask,' Corinna said. 'It's my brother.'

Winnie frowned, wondering what Corinna's brother could have to do with them.

'Have we met him?' Stella asked, doubtful.

God, Winnie thought. I hope she's not about to ask one of us to go on a blind date with him. If she does, it's definitely not going to be me.

Corinna shook her head. 'Oh, believe me, you'd know if you'd met him. He lives over on the mainland, but he's broken his collarbone in an accident a couple of weeks back and wants to come over and spend some time on the island to recuperate.'

'Oh, I'm sorry,' Frankie said, instantly sympathetic.

'Not as sorry as I am,' Corinna said. 'I adore him of course, but if I have to have him in my house for six weeks I'll go crazy. It's a small house and he's a big man with even bigger opinions.'

'Ah,' Frankie said, starting to see where the conversation was headed.

'So you're thinking . . .' Winnie said, climbing down the ladder and placing her paintbrush on the top of the paint pot.

'Well, you have all of these rooms available, and you need guests to stay afloat.' Corinna waved her hand in the general direction of the staircase and looked from one to the other of them, nodding as she spoke. 'A nice six-week booking to get the ball rolling? You'll hardly know he's here, I promise. He's always on his phone doing one business deal or another. Give him the Internet and he'll be no trouble at all.'

'Even though he's a big man with even bigger opinions?' Stella laughed, seeing straight through Corinna's words.

'Did I say big? I meant . . . gregarious.'

Winnie didn't doubt it; any brother of Corinna's was sure to be a force of nature.

'I think we can squeeze him in,' Frankie said, looking at Stella and Winnie for confirmation as she spoke.

They both nodded; much as they were enjoying having the place to themselves, they couldn't call themselves a B&B if they didn't take in guests.

Relieved, Corinna banged her hand down flat on the reception desk and laughed. 'Ladies, you're marvels. He's going to love staying with you all, I know it. He'll be here on the morning ferry tomorrow.'

'Oh!' Winnie said. 'So soon.'

'Is that OK? I expect I could manage him for a couple of nights if you need me to?' Corinna looked as if she'd rather put Darth Vader up than her own brother.

'No, no need,' Stella said. 'We're as ready as we need to be, aren't we, ladies?'

Ajax had left them a couple of reservations in the book, the first of which wasn't until the end of the following week. They'd been busy preparing for them, but in truth the place was ready. There was still lots of internal cosmetic work they wanted to do, but the B&B needed to thrive and grow in order to build an improvement nest egg. Besides, Villa Valentina's shabby grandeur was kind of part of its appeal. Their job was to maintain it with a subtle hand, and to wow their guests with great service, island gin and a warm welcome. A six-week booking was just what they needed. Frankie opened the reservations ledger and clicked her pen.

'So, what's your brother's name, Corinna? I think we should put him in the Captain's Suite.'

'Angelo.'

Winnie nodded. 'Captain Angelo it is then. Looks we've got ourselves our first guest, ladies.'

'What time does the boat arrive?'

Winnie straightened the reservations book and laid the

100

pen on top, and then changed her mind and laid it along-side it.

'Eleven. Will you stop fiddling? You're making me nervous,' Stella said, putting the pen back where it had been in the first place.

Frankie came through with a big ceramic painted bowl full of fresh fruit from the garden and set it on the low table in the seating area.

'If he eats all of that, I'm not going to be the one who cleans his loo,' Stella said.

Frankie frowned. 'Too much?'

'Unless he brings everyone else off the boat with him too and they haven't eaten for a week, yes,' Winnie said. 'It looks welcoming though, so leave it for now.'

'It makes us look as if we're expecting hordes of guests, I thought,' Frankie said, studying the bowl to see if it was in the centre of the table, and moving it an inch to the left.

Winnie glanced up at the clock, thinking that the boat should dock in about an hour, so allowing for Corinna collecting her brother and getting him to the villa, that gave them about ninety minutes with the place to them-selves before they were officially open for business.

'I'm nervous,' she said, moving the pen to one side of the ledger again. 'Are you?'

'Well, I'm definitely nervous about the food side of things,' Frankie said. Officially they only offered breakfast, but Frankie had put together an interesting choice of home-made dishes and also planned to offer different cakes and pastries in the afternoons. If nothing else, Corinna's brother would breakfast like a king in the mornings.

'Nope. Not nervous,' Stella said. 'It's exciting. This is what we came for.'

Winnie swallowed. Stella was right, of course; without guests they'd be packing their bags and going home to England. The thought had her reaching for the pen again until Stella smacked her fingers away.

'Go and have a gin or something, will you? You're making me twitchy.'

'Kalimera?'

They looked up as a woman walked in and gazed at them enquiringly.

'Kalimera,' Frankie tried, and the woman let forth a long string of Greek that none of them had a prayer of understanding. Winnie watched her, trying to guess what she might be saying from her body language. She was in her late fifties or sixties at a guess, and dressed in a black dress with a kitchen apron around her waist. Her greying hair was fastened at her nape, and her lined face was free of makeup. She gestured around at the villa as she spoke, and then stared at them as if they ought to know exactly what she meant.

When they stared back, mystified, she huffed with frustration, fell to her knees and made motions as if she was scrubbing the floor.

'Does she think our floor is dirty?' Frankie asked, affronted after scrubbing it herself the previous day. After a few seconds of charades she got off her knees and crossed behind the reception desk and started to rummage in the cupboard behind there.

'How do we stop her?' Stella whispered. 'She might be about to rob us.'

'No clue,' Winnie said, watching the woman as she pulled an annoyed face and shut the doors again. They'd emptied out the cupboard last week, moving the contents under the sink. As they watched, the woman pulled a large cotton hankie from her apron pocket, spat on it, and started to clean the reception desk with gusto, shoving the ledger and pen aside as she went.

'Ah! Stella, do something!' Winnie spluttered. 'She's wiping her saliva all over the ledger!'

'Do you think she wants to do the cleaning?' Frankie said. The cupboard had housed all of the cleaning products, which presumably was what the woman had expected to find when she flung open the doors.

'Not if she's going to spit on everything, she isn't,' Stella said. 'Do we even need a cleaner?'

Winnie reached for the phone on the desk. Flipping open the diary to the small list of numbers she'd amassed, she dialled Panos and quickly asked him if he'd mind chatting to the woman on their behalf.

The woman looked at the receiver suspiciously for a moment before taking it, and then at Winnie through narrowed eyes.

'Panos?' Winnie said, and the woman's face cleared as she lifted the receiver to her ear and started a rapid-fire exchange. After what seemed to be half an hour but probably was more like five minutes, she handed the phone back with a 'you talk now' gesture at Winnie.

'Panos? It's me again, Winnie,' she said.

'Ah, Winnie. I come by for my gin supply later today, yes?'

Winnie frowned. 'Well, yes, OK, but can you tell me what this lady wants from us, please?'

He laughed. 'It's Hero. She work for you.'

'She does?' Bloody Ajax! Was there anything else he 'forgot' to mention when they bought the place?

'Sure she does. You don't know this thing already?'

'Well, no. This is the first time we've met.'

'Right,' Panos said, drawing the word out. 'Hero has worked at the villa for many years, different owners. She come in to help clean, she does the sheets, and washing, you know the things.'

Winnie wasn't certain that she did. 'What do I pay her?'

Panos mentioned a small sum of money, and then added 'and four bottles of island gin on Friday'.

'Four a week?' Winnie said. That seemed a heck of a lot of gin for one small woman.

Hero must understand more than she let on, because at that she nodded, grinned and held up four fingers.

'Thanks, Panos. I'll see you later, OK?'

Winnie hung up the phone and lifted her shoulders at the others.

'Well, this is Hero,' she said. 'And she works here.'

Frankie and Stella looked taken aback.

'She does?' Frankie said.

'Hero? As in action hero?' Stella said. 'Is she going to take us all out if we say we can't afford her?'

Winnie relayed the unusual pay arrangements, and a look of pure admiration flickered through Stella's green eyes.

'Well, at that price, I vote she stays,' she said. 'We could use the help when we get going. Besides, I don't know the Greek for "You're fired."'

'You're not Alan Sugar,' Winnie said.

Hero watched the quick conversation with her dark, interested eyes, nodding along oblivious, then held up four fingers again just to make sure the arrangement was clear.

'Seems like the gin is the most important part of the deal,' Frankie said.

Winnie nodded, clicking the pen. 'The whole island is crazy for the stuff. We need to think about making our first batch, because if we run out they're going to lynch us.'

The others nodded. 'I'll take Hero through to the kitchen and show her the new cleaning cupboard, shall I?' Frankie said, smiling at their newest member of staff and nodding for her to follow. Hero looked over her shoulder to make sure Frankie wasn't speaking to anyone else, and then disappeared off in Frankie's wake.

Having straightened the ledger and moved the pen from one side to the other for the millionth time, Winnie smoothed her hands down her red linen dress. They'd all dressed differently this morning: Winnie in the flippy dress she'd bought for her cousin's wedding the previous summer, Stella all in black from her off-the-shoulder Bardot top to her cropped jeans, Frankie in her flowing safari dress. Cut-off shorts and vest tops just didn't say professional, and they all wanted their inaugural guest to think he'd checked into the best damn B&B in the whole of Greece.

Stella and Winnie stood behind the reception desk watching the open door and, when Winnie turned to open the window behind them, Stella stole the pen and put it in the drawer.

'Is it me or is it hotter today than normal?' Winnie tucked a stray lock of hair behind her ear. She'd plaited her hair in a crown around her head that morning in an effort to look more put together. 'Where did the pen go?'

Stella shrugged. 'No clue. Shall I put the fan on?' They'd hauled a big old fan down from one of the bedrooms to try to encourage air flow through reception.

'It was right here.' Winnie tapped the desk beside the ledger.

'Maybe Hero borrowed it,' Stella said, casually scanning the desk.

'No, it was here, I'm sure it was.' Winnie lifted the ledger to look beneath it. 'Maybe it rolled off.' She stepped back to inspect the tiled floor and found nothing, so got to her knees and crawled around the front to look underneath. 'It must be here somewhere,' she said, her cheek almost skimming the floor as she felt under the desk. It was an unfortunate series of events really; Stella had bent down on one side of the desk to plug the fan in, and Winnie had her backside in the air towards the said fan on the other side when it burst violently into life, blowing her skirt clean over her head.

'You really should get some cream on that sunburn.'

Balls. *Jesse.*

Winnie shot to her feet, fighting with her tangled dress.

'Jesse,' she said, flustered and aware that her face was probably the same colour as her dress.

'Do you flash your knickers at everyone or should I feel honoured?'

'Ha ha,' she said, sarcastic. 'What can we do for you?'

He stepped outside the door. 'I thought you might like this.'

Winnie looked at Stella, and they both trailed out onto the terrace to see what it was.

'Oh my God!' Stella said. 'It's gorgeous.'

Winnie looked at the hand-carved wooden sign Jesse had propped against the wall. 'I don't really work with wood, but I've had that piece lying around for a while looking for a home.'

On a natural slice of tree trunk he'd carved 'Villa Valentina' in perfect script, and beneath in smaller lettering he'd inscribed each of their names as proprietors.

'Thank you,' Stella said, her eyes sliding speculatively from Winnie to Jesse. 'I'll just go and hunt that pen down,

Win.' She slipped past them, her long hair swinging in the sunshine, leaving Winnie still smoothing down her dress and standing on one high-heeled foot and then the other. She'd been attempting to channel Corinna with her leather sandal choice that morning, but was regretting it now that she was stood here with Jesse in washed-out jeans and T-shirt. He looked like a beach bum and she looked like a wedding guest; a wedding guest who'd just shown him her knickers.

'I'd have had you down as a plain white girl. Hot pink lace was a shock.'

Winnie closed her eyes momentarily. The tiny pink knickers were the only ones that didn't give her VPL with the dress. She took the only available option and ignored his comment, clearing her throat and gesturing at the sign. 'It's very nice. You didn't have to.'

'I know that. Call it a welcome gift.'

She nodded, running her hand quickly over her hair to make sure the plait was still wrapped securely around her head.

'Can I have my donkey back soon?' she asked. 'Only I think you might need to bring him. He doesn't seem very keen on me.'

Jesse curled his lip. 'What do you think he is, a holiday romance? You need to put the hours in with The Fonz.'

'I'm starting to think he's moody.'

Jesse laughed softly. 'You know what he likes?'

Winnie shook her head.

'Picnics.'

'Picnics,' she said.

'You're doing that repetition thing again. Come for a picnic with the donkey.'

'Is that an invitation?'

107

Jesse inclined his head. 'I'm just the messenger. Come at seven.' He paused and tipped his head to the side. 'He likes red, too, so you should probably keep that dress on.'

'Should I bring him anything?'

'A carrot?' Jesse shrugged. 'He likes island gin too.'

'Does he now,' Winnie said. 'Like every other man, woman and beast on Skelidos then.'

'We just know what's good for us.'

Winnie studied the cerise bougainvillea growing at the side of the terrace, unsure if she knew what was good for her.

'Sundown,' she said, with the smallest of hesitant nods.

Jesse shoved his hands in his pockets. 'I'll let him know.' As he sauntered away, he turned back. 'I wasn't kidding about that sun cream.'

Winnie shot him in the back with an imaginary gun and then headed inside the villa in search of the after sun.

CHAPTER EIGHT

'Ladies, we're here!' Corinna's voice floated in through the open front door to Stella, Frankie and Winnie all standing like soldiers on their strategically placed spots inside.

'Should we go out to greet them or stay here?' Winnie whispered. 'We should go out, right?'

They'd been playing statues for the last five minutes in anxious readiness, and now they all surged towards the door and spilled out onto the terrace.

'Corinna,' Stella said, kissing their as usual impeccably turned out friend warmly on both cheeks. 'And you must be Angelo.'

She looked up at Corinna's companion and then stepped back to look up again, because he was a good six foot two and towered over her even though she was in heels. It wasn't only that; he struck her as a dead ringer for Don Draper and had the brooding charisma to match. He was as expensively dressed as his sister in tailored dark trousers and a charcoal shirt; the sling for his injury was black and discreet.

He held out his good hand towards her, no nonsense. 'Angelo Vitalis.'

Stella shook it, unfazed by his brusqueness. She'd spent her life dealing with professional business people, and everything about this man screamed business.

Winnie and Frankie moved in to introduce themselves and received the same cool handshake, and Corinna caught Stella's eye behind her brother's back and smiled tightly.

'Shall we?' Stella stepped naturally into the role of leader, ushering them all inside.

'We've put you in the Captain's Suite,' she said, reaching his key down from the board behind the desk. 'It's the biggest room on the first floor with a great view out over the sea.'

Angelo nodded curtly as he accepted his key.

'Would you like breakfast in your room in the morning, or out on the terrace maybe?' Frankie asked. 'It's gorgeous out there first thing.'

'I don't eat breakfast,' he said, in the same immaculate American English as his sister. 'I just need Wi-Fi and peace and quiet.'

'What? No breakfast at all?' Frankie said, her face falling.

He shook his head, and Winnie felt terrible for her friend because she'd put so much time and careful thought into preparing an appetising breakfast menu that would nourish someone recovering from injury.

'This way?' Angelo said, gesticulating towards the stairs, clearly keen to get settled.

'Can I get you some water?' Winnie said, her hand on the full iced jug on the desk.

'To the room, please.' His small, curt smile brooked no argument and came nowhere close to touching his eyes. 'I'd appreciate it if you could arrange to have my luggage sent up within half an hour,' he said, picking up his briefcase and pausing briefly to kiss Corinna on each cheek. 'I'll call you later.'

All four women watched as he strode away and up the staircase.

Corinna wondered if it would have killed her brother to have been slightly more friendly.

Winnie felt deflated, as if their efforts to be hospitable had gone unnoticed.

Frankie thought despondently of the fridge full of carefully chosen food and hoped he'd come around to the idea of breakfast after he'd had a couple of days to unwind.

And Stella thought how hot his backside was as he climbed the stairs, but also that she didn't care one bit for how offhand he'd been with both his sister and her friends just now. She had the measure of Angelo Vitalis after a lifetime around board tables with people just like him. She'd grant him a free pass on account of having just travelled with a no doubt painful injury, but he was going to be in for a shock if he thought he'd get away with being unappreciative for long around here.

'It's odd having someone else but us here, isn't it?' Winnie had kind of got used to the relaxed vibe they'd created at Villa Valentina over the last couple of weeks and she missed it already. They sat around the kitchen table, speaking in hushed voices over lunch even though there wasn't a chance that Angelo could hear them up in his suite.

'I don't like him very much yet,' Frankie said, feeling disloyal to Corinna. 'How can he not eat breakfast?'

'He might warm up a bit once he's settled into the more relaxed pace of life here,' Stella said, even though privately she had her doubts. They'd lugged his cases up the stairs after Corinna had left, and when she'd tapped his door he'd called out that they could leave his cases in the hallway along with a jug of water and he'd prefer not to be disturbed until morning. So far, not so good.

'Maybe a G&T would loosen him up,' Winnie said, even though she was nowhere near brave enough to ask him if he'd like one.

'God, don't let him see the cellar,' Stella said. 'He doesn't seem the kind of man to approve of home-brew.'

Frankie picked a plum from the fruit bowl and polished it on her dress. 'We really need to make time to do our first bottling. I've already started to gather ingredients to dry so our stocks don't run out.'

'Well, not today, that's for sure,' Stella said. 'The last thing we need him to do is find us brewing potions in the cellar like the Witches of Eastwick. Let's get an idea of how he's going to spend his time for a couple of days first.'

'Is that sign out front the one Jesse made?' Frankie asked, changing the subject.

Winnie nodded. 'We should try to get it hung. Which of us is best with a hammer?'

'Don't look at me,' Frankie said, biting the plum. 'Gav was the DIY king. If it needed fixing, he's your man.'

'Yeah, well, he's a long way from here, Frank,' Stella said.

Frankie nodded. Her old life seemed more distant than ever, and she felt disloyal for the second time that day because there wasn't much about her life back in England that she missed. Since Marcia passed and the boys left home, she'd grown lonelier than she'd known how to handle. Life on Skelidos had changed all that in a blink.

'Maybe Jesse would hang it for us,' Winnie said. 'I'll ask him later.'

'Later when?' Stella asked, curious.

'Later when I go over,' Winnie said, slowly, stalling for time because she didn't want to make a big deal of it. 'I've not visited The Fonz yet today. I'll just nip by and take him a carrot.' She suddenly began to find the pattern on the marble floor tiles terribly interesting. 'And have a picnic with Jesse.'

'A picnic?' Stella said loudly.

'With Jesse?' Frankie added, and they both stared at her, waiting for more.

'I don't know,' Winnie said, under pressure. 'It'll probably just be bread, cheese and water while we watch the donkeys eat carrots. That's all. No biggie.'

'I'm locking the doors if you're not home by ten,' Stella said.

'Want to take the smoked salmon quiche out the fridge?' Frankie said. 'Mr Big upstairs is clearly not going to eat it.'

'Mr Big,' Stella said, nodding slowly. 'I thought more Don Draper, but Mr Big works too.'

'I'll take the quiche,' Winnie said. 'But I seriously doubt you'll need to lock me out. I'm going over at seven and will probably be home within the hour.'

She was still wearing that red dress. Jesse watched her swing her legs over his perimeter wall in the late-evening sunshine, her high heels now switched for flats and her arms full of something he couldn't discern across the olive grove.

'What the fuck are you doing asking her for a picnic, Anderson?' Jesse berated himself with the rhetorical question as he went to the half-open door and watched her amble slowly towards the house, pausing to pass the time of day with the donkeys. He saw her pull carrots out of the bag she was carrying, and noted her improved confidence with the animals as she hand-fed them.

113

Retrieving the platter of food he'd prepared from the fridge, and a bottle of wine, he went outside to meet her as she approached.

'I brought quiche.'

No hi, no preamble. She'd brought quiche. Had he made her nervous? The skittish look in her eyes would suggest so.

'I didn't make it. Frankie did,' she said. 'Not for us especially though. She made it for Don Draper, or Mr Big, or Angelo, as his actual name is, but he didn't want it.'

'Frankie made a quiche for Don Draper?' They'd had the odd celeb come to the island in search of escape from the long lens of the press in the past, but surely Winnie and Co. hadn't lured John Hamm to holiday at Villa Valentina within a couple of weeks of moving here?

Winnie fetched a plate from the bag she was awkwardly balancing to show him the deep, salmon-studded quiche with its golden pastry crust.

'Not the actual John Hamm. Corinna's brother, Angelo. He's our first guest at the B&B, but he doesn't want any of the lovely food Frankie had planned for him and it's driving her crazy.'

'Oh,' he said. 'OK. Shall we?' He nodded around the side of the house. 'I thought we'd head round the back, you get a better view of the sunset from there.'

Winnie glanced quickly back towards the donkeys and then chewed her lip and nodded. Surely she hadn't taken him seriously about the invite being given on behalf of The Fonz? Stepping ahead of her, he led the way along the path he'd laid around the side of his house to the spot where he'd already set a big checked blanket down in readiness and left crockery and glasses.

'This is nice,' she said, leaving her shoes at the edge of the blanket and stepping onto it barefoot.

'Sit down,' he said, as if she were taking a seat in his dining room rather than his garden.

She bent to place the quiche down and then lowered herself to sit up straight with her legs stretched out in front of her and her ankles crossed.

'I wouldn't have had you down as a tattoo kind of girl,' he said, nodding towards the slightly faded circlet of flowers around her ankle as he put the food down and flopped beside her.

She put her hands behind her as a brace and leant back a little, her head tipped to one side as she considered her ankle.

'It's not permanent. I wanted to see how I got on with it before I had a real one.'

'And?' he said, pulling the cork out of the chilled bottle of white.

Winnie's mouth twisted. 'Not sure yet.'

'I like it,' he said, and simple as that she blushed redder than the strawberries he'd packed for their dessert. 'Come on,' he said. 'You seriously can't blush this easily. Make it harder for me, for God's sake.'

She swallowed hard. 'I'm sorry.'

He shrugged, exasperated. He'd intended his remark to be flippant, to maybe get a rise out of her, not an apology. 'Winnie, would you please just relax? It's just food on a blanket. We're probably going to be neighbours for a pretty long time, so we need to get along, right?'

She nodded. 'Now I feel stupid.'

'I'm starting to feel stupid for suggesting it,' he said drily, pouring them both a big glass of wine. 'Drink that. I'm going to do the same. I think we might need it.'

Winnie accepted the glass he held out and took a good gulp, hoping the wine might cool down her stupid, hot cheeks. Jesse had a way of putting her on edge; being around him wasn't remotely relaxing. The wine, however, was deliciously crisp and cool, so she held her tongue and watched him pull the food platter up the blanket towards him. Accepting the heavy pottery plate he handed her, she admired its bold cherry-red and ivory design as he dug around for a knife to slice the quiche.

'Yes. I made it,' he said, sensing the question she was about to ask.

'I like it,' she said, wondering if she'd ever get to see anything he'd made besides his crockery.

'I needed plates.'

It was an odd attitude to creating art. Winnie had always found deep satisfaction and pleasure in crafting beautiful jewellery, but she couldn't imagine doing it out of simple necessity; it kind of drained the spontaneity out of it. Not that she could imagine ever feeling creative again. She was relieved to have the B&B filling up every nook and cranny of her life now. Any lingering creativity she had went into painting the shutters and artfully arranging the flowers on the reception desk.

'So, Winnie,' he said, sliding a huge slice of quiche onto her plate. She helped herself to salad from a bowl on the tray, bright green and red tomatoes with creamy crumbled feta. There was chicken too, and thick slices of ham. 'Tell me something about you that I don't know. Surprise me.'

She'd been about to test Frankie's quiche, but her mouth was suddenly bone-dry. 'Umm . . .'

'I'm kidding, I'm kidding,' he said, holding his hand up. 'Unless there's something you're burning to tell me, because I'm all ears if there is.'

She shook her head, feeling out of her depth and gauche. She was sitting in a Greek olive grove having an evening picnic with her enigmatic neighbour, and she had no worldly experience to draw confidence from. She'd never been on a date in her adult life. Not that this was a date, it was food on a blanket with a neighbour. Casual. Keep it casual.

'So, Jesse,' she said. 'Can I ask what you're working on at the moment? Vaguely?'

His 'I'm kidding' face slid into his clammed-up one.

'A commission for a regular client,' he said, non-committal.

'Not plates, I'm guessing?'

He narrowed his eyes. 'I don't make plates for other people.'

Right. So they'd both managed to piss each other off a little bit now. They ate for a few minutes and talked quietly about more mundane things to settle each other down: about the ritual of olive harvesting, about her plans to redecorate one of the bedrooms at the B&B, about Corinna and the gallery. Winnie was surprised to learn that she wasn't an island native; she came from a wealthy family in Athens and the children had spent much of their childhood being educated in the States. That accounted for their immaculate Americanised English, then. Corinna had come here for a summer fifteen years back to recover from a rocky divorce and stayed for a lifetime; that seemed to Winnie to be the case for many who came here.

'And you? Is now a better time to ask you what brought you here?' she asked, digging a little deeper.

He laid his plate down on the blanket beside him, and the twist of his mouth told her that it wasn't a subject he was easy with.

'Same sorry story, more or less.' He shrugged. 'I guess Skelidos is just home to the broken-hearted and dejected.'

'You had your heart broken?' Winnie couldn't imagine anyone less likely to confess to heartbreak.

He took a drink, savouring the wine in his mouth. 'Not exactly, and it was all such a long time ago now. You learn your lessons, you move on. In my case, that meant coming here. Best damn decision I ever made.'

His bare-bones story told her barely anything really, enough to have answered the question but not even scratching the surface of the truth. His dark eyes hinted that there was much more to know, but they also warned her not to ask because his secrets were his to keep.

'I guess that makes it my turn to ask a question,' he said, refilling their glasses.

The wine Winnie had already drunk had eased her nerves a little. 'Shoot.'

'When are you going to get back to work?'

She frowned. 'I *am* working. The B&B is my work now.'

He huffed, clearly not convinced. 'Sure it is.'

'Don't do that,' she said, offended. 'I mean it. Making the B&B a success is top of all of our lists. I'm way too busy for hobbies.'

Jesse laughed softly and shook his head. 'You know, when I first came to Skelidos I said almost the exact same thing. I was going to farm olives and live off my land. No art, no women, and no hassle.'

She let his words settle on her shoulders. For a man who claimed to deal only in pleasure, his line of conversation was turning out to be more than a little painful.

'Yeah, well, that's you,' she said. 'You're a man.'

He let that one slide. 'And you're an artist, Winnie.'

'No. I *was* an artist.' She was already halfway through her second glass of wine. 'Now I'm a badass businesswoman instead. And a fairy.'

118

'A fairy?' He laughed, sceptical.

She nodded. 'Yeah, but not a sickly one from a kids' story. I'm thinking more along the lines of Kylie as Tinkerbell.'

'Hey, I'm Australian. You're talking to the converted.' His gaze touched her mouth as he nodded his approval. 'I reckon you could pull off that green corset.'

This time Winnie didn't blush. The wonders of alcohol. 'I'm far more interested in the wings, actually,' she said.

He watched her take a sip from her glass, and then just carried on looking at her, scrutinising her almost.

'What?' she asked softly.

'I was wishing I could draw you just the way you look right now. Relaxed. Softer.'

'Softer?' She was almost glad if he saw her as tough; it was a new look for her. People back home had regarded her as someone they could walk on, and a big part of coming here had been about being the person on the outside that she was on the inside.

'Less guarded,' he said, assessing her. 'Are you brave, Winnie?'

'Am I brave?' She repeated his question slowly, turning it over and looking at it from every angle. Was she brave? 'I don't think of myself as especially brave all of the time. Maybe I'm like Matt Damon in that movie where he bought a zoo – you know, the one with the famous quote? Every now and then I'm prone to twenty seconds of insane courage.'

'Cool,' he said, getting up and crossing to slide open the glass doors on the back of the house. He disappeared momentarily, and when he sat back down again, he was holding a pencil and a sketchpad. Looking at his watch, he studied the second hand.

119

'I'm going to ask you something now, and then you have twenty seconds to decide whether to be insanely brave.'

She stared at him, almost holding her breath in anticipation.

'Ready?' he asked, and she nodded without blinking.

He nodded too, his dark eyes nailed on hers.

'Take your dress off and let me draw you naked?'

CHAPTER NINE

'What? No!' Winnie stared at him, wide-eyed with shock.

He didn't speak, just stared at his watch.

'Jesse, I can't,' she said, and still he didn't look up.

God, how long was twenty seconds anyway? She should have paraphrased the movie and said five. She couldn't take her dress off, that just wasn't who she was. But then . . . who was she? Wasn't this a chance to redefine herself, not for Jesse, but for her own benefit? A handsome man wanted to draw her naked at sunset; just six months ago this would have seemed beyond the realms of reality for her life.

She'd probably blame it on the wine when she recounted the story to Stella and Frankie later, but right there and then she didn't feel like it was the wine talking as she made her decision and got to her feet.

'Stop the clock,' she said quietly.

Jesse finally looked away from his watch and stood too, waiting for her to make her move. She looked him square in the eyes for a moment, and then turned her back.

'Help me with my zipper?'

She said it so quietly that she wasn't even certain that he'd heard her, but then she heard his breath close to her ear when he stepped in.

'You're insanely brave,' he murmured, and his fingers brushed her neck as he slid the zip slowly down the length of her spine. He let her dress fall to pool around her ankles, leaving her standing in just her underwear.

Closing her eyes, she went for broke. 'Now unhook my bra.'

He stilled. 'You're sure? You don't have to.'

She swallowed hard. 'You can hardly draw me naked if I don't.'

'It's enough that you said yes. You've proved it to yourself,' he said, reading her too easily.

'Just unhook it.'

The sound of his breathing made her heart pound, and then his fingers moved to deal easily with the clips of her bra.

'There,' he said. 'You're undone.'

He had no idea how right he was. She was unravelling right there in front of him, unpicking the stitches of her personality and re-embroidering herself back together a little braver, a little more daring.

Winnie peeled the white cotton and lace from her body and let it join her dress on the floor, and then without giving herself a second to think or panic, she hooked her fingers under her knickers and pushed them down too.

'There,' she said, feeling all kinds of exposed and vulnerable.

'I'm not going to touch you,' he said, and she squeezed her eyes tight shut because this wasn't about sex but it absolutely was too, and because the only man who'd ever seen her naked was Rory, and never like this. Never standing in an olive grove with the sky overhead streaked pink and rose-gold like abstract art.

She sensed him step away, and it only made it all the more intimate because she knew he was studying her. He didn't speak, and she found herself desperate to hear the thoughts running inside his head. Was he analysing her from an artistic viewpoint, or was he looking at her as a man looks at a woman?

'Will you turn to face me?' he asked, and everything about his low, measured voice told her that it was OK if she didn't want to, and somehow that made it OK for her to want to.

Slowly, one heartbeat at a time, she turned around.

He met her gaze, and she didn't recognise the look in his eyes because she hadn't seen it before. He didn't rush to take in her body. His gaze lingered on hers instead, waiting for her to be ready.

'OK?' he said, and she nodded, the tiniest of movements.

'How do you want me to pose?' She had no clue how this was supposed to go.

His gaze slid away from her, considering their surroundings.

'I have this idea of you,' he said. 'Sit here.'

He stepped over the blanket to indicate a large smooth boulder.

She followed him, and then shyly perched on the rock. It was smooth and worn, but none the less it came as a sensory shock to feel the cool granite against her bare skin.

He stepped back a few paces. 'Pull your knees up and then drop them to one side?' he asked, more detached now as he immersed himself in the technicalities of the pose.

She did as he asked, her hands demurely in her lap.

He studied her, and then came closer.

'Can I try something?'

'Yes,' she breathed, trusting him not to do anything she didn't expect.

'It's your hair,' he said, touching his fingertips to the braid wrapped around her crown. 'May I?'

His fingers gently unpicked the grips from her hair and placed them beside her on the rock, and then eased the band from the end of the plait. Winnie closed her eyes against the sudden rush of emotion that thickened her throat. Rory had never taken the clips from her hair, and it was such a simple but sensual thing that she frowned with concentration not to blush or, worse, to cry. His fingers moved to unpick her hair, freeing it into long crinkles as he ran his fingers through it.

'That's better,' he said. 'You *can* open you eyes, you know.'

She smiled, tremulous, and when she opened her eyes she found him waiting, one hand still on her hair as he met her eyes.

'You're impossibly lovely, Winnie,' he said, placing his fingers loosely on her shoulders to straighten them and position them as he wanted. 'Please feel it. Feel the warmth of the sun on your bare skin, and your hair where it brushes over your breasts. Don't shy away from the woman you are, Winnie. Don't blush. Bloom.'

God. He was a man of such contrasts. So many facets. She'd known him barely three weeks, and yet he seemed to see past all of her layers and defences straight through to the woman inside, as if he wanted to drag her out of the shade to sit in the sun. How did he do that? How could he be wise-cracking and sarcastic and then tender, empowering and fierce? It made him difficult to read and a little bit dangerously addictive to be around. She watched him settle himself on the ground against the trunk of a nearby olive tree, his jean-clad knees pulled up to create a rest for his sketchpad.

'Sit up a little straighter and look slightly to your left,' he said, his head on one side as he looked at her. 'We'll do ten minutes like this, no more than that, OK?'

She appreciated his consideration of her comfort, and realised that it must come from his experience of posing others. Did he do this often? Arrange naked women? She wasn't brave enough to ask.

'Like this?'

He nodded, thoughtful. 'Can you sweep your hair over your left shoulder for me?'

It would expose her breast. She'd come this far. Tentatively, she did as he'd asked, running her hand down the rope of her hair.

'That's good. Twist your hair like that again?' He made the motion he wanted with his own hand.

'Like this?' she said.

He shook his head and came over. 'Like this.' He slid his hand beneath the weight of her hair over her shoulder and spiralled it around his hand, laying it down like a twisted rope as he moved his hand down. His fingers were centimetres from her breast, and although he was careful not to touch her, Winnie felt her nipple tighten in response.

'Perfect,' he said, without smiling to lighten the moment. 'It *is* normal for your body to react to being touched, even in a non-sensual way.'

Because it seemed to be his preferred method of communication, she answered him honestly.

'It *is* sensual, Jesse. Being naked with you here, like this. Having your fingers almost touch my breast.'

He watched her face. 'Being turned on is OK too. This is exactly what we talked about up at the lookout point,' he said. 'Pleasure for pleasure's sake. Enjoying a connection with someone. Enjoying someone looking at you, and touching you, and acknowledging that sex and love don't have to be connected.'

'Are you enjoying looking at me now?' She shouldn't have asked, but she needed to know.

'Very much,' he said quietly, retreating to his spot beneath the olive tree.

For a while, she turned her face in the direction he'd asked and looked away into the distance. She ought to feel embarrassed, she told herself so. She should feel weird, she was sure of it. But she didn't feel either of those things. She felt . . . liberated, and brave, and, damn it, she felt sexy. Being naked had gone from terrifying to one hell of an aphrodisiac.

'Light's gone,' he said eventually, placing his pencil down.

Winnie slowly came back from where she'd mentally wandered away to and realised he was right. The sun had dipped below the horizon, throwing the shadows of the trees long and spindly on the ground. 'Can I see?'

'It's not finished.' He flipped the sketchpad shut, brooking no argument as he came to her on the rock and held out his hand to help her up. Much as she wanted to, she didn't push the point. He'd show her when he was ready.

'My legs have gone numb,' she said, unfurling them from beneath her and stretching them out. She was all at sea, a conflicting mix of lingering shyness and insistent boldness churning in her chest as he led her back to the picnic blanket.

'How do you feel now you did that?' he asked.

'Ready to ask you to do something in return.'

Wary surprise flashed through his eyes. 'Go on,' he said.

'I'd like to stay naked for a little while, and I want you to look at me as a man, not an artist, and tell me what you see.'

'I'm not a machine, Winnie. I've been looking at you as a man for the last half an hour.'

She sat down, and when he dropped beside her, she lay back, feeling the stretch of her body against the woollen rug.

'You really want me to look at you,' he said, soft and low, and when she nodded, he lifted her arm above her head and laid it on the blanket.

'OK,' he whispered, lying on his side beside her, propped up on one elbow. 'Your eyes tell me that you're anxious, despite the fact that you're in complete control of the situation.'

'I know I am,' she acknowledged.

'Your shoulders are tense and your fingers are curled into your palms, Winnie. I'd love to see you untense. Let your body relax.'

She tried. Frankie had said something similar to her yesterday when she'd joined her for a little early-morning yoga, but it was a whole lot more difficult now with Jesse watching her unflinchingly.

'Stop thinking so much,' he said. 'It's getting in the way of your pleasure.'

She nodded and closed her eyes, because his eyes had slipped lower. She'd invited him to look at her body, but she hadn't counted on the fact that his gaze would feel like stars on her skin, or that she'd hear his breath hitch in his throat, or that she'd ache for him to touch her.

'What do you want me to say, Winnie?' he said. 'I could

127

tell you that the slopes and curves of your body are pretty damn perfect to me, or that the sweep of your hip makes me want to press my body against yours. I could tell you that I'd die to feel the weight of your breasts in my hands, to run my tongue over your nipples, or to slide my hand down your body because your skin is fucking luminous. Is that what you need from me?'

She didn't speak, because in truth she didn't know what she needed.

'But I think what you *really* need to hear is that I want you. That the fact that Needledick screwed someone else doesn't mean you weren't good enough as a woman, or special enough, or beautiful enough. You're plenty beautiful enough.'

Jesus. Tears slipped down the side of her face, because he was right. Rory's affair had struck at the heart of her femininity and left her feeling second-rate as a woman, and what Jesse had given her tonight had gone a little way towards restoring her battered dignity.

Sitting up, she wiped her hands over her damp face and sighed heavily.

'Come on.' Jesse leaned in and pressed a single, lingering kiss against her shoulder. 'Put your dress back on, Legs. I'll walk you home.'

Walking back down the moonlit lane after safely depositing Winnie back at Villa Valentina, Jesse couldn't believe how the evening had panned out. The fact that he'd even invited her to come over at all had been unintentional, but asking her to pose naked for him? He must be out of his mind. He should have called a halt to it when she agreed, but when she'd turned her back and offered him her zipper he'd lost any ability to call a halt to it. The only thing that truly surprised him was that he'd kept his hands off her, because the woman was spectacular naked. She didn't even seem to realise it; he was unaccustomed to women so lacking in vanity or confidence. Needledick ought to thank his lucky stars that he was in a different country, because he'd crushed Winnie's self-belief like seashells beneath a riptide, and for that he'd earned himself a smack in the mouth.

He let himself into the house through the unlocked kitchen door, grabbed a bottle of brandy and headed back outside to sit on the low-slung chair he liked to use sometimes to look at the vast night sky. It was one of the many things about Skelidos that had beguiled him. Winnie had asked him earlier why he'd come here, and had he been more honest he'd have told her that he'd come here to hide, and that somewhere along the way he'd cut all ties with home and family and cast himself adrift. Not that he imagined anyone missed him; killing the woman you love had a way of making people feel awkward in your company.

Closing his eyes, he let his mind slide back to another place, and another time, and another blonde, and then his heart seemed to shudder in his chest, a timely reminder that he needed to protect it. Jesse traded on being skilled with his hands, but he'd never managed to sculpt his heart back into the exact right shape. It was a bad fit these days, sharp and jagged behind his ribs.

Studying the constellations to distract himself, he took a mouthful of whisky straight from the bottle and wondered whether to ask Panos to punch him in the face tomorrow to knock some sense back in.

Angelo had been at the B&B for two days and they'd barely seen him at all, so when he tapped the kitchen door as they breakfasted on his third morning they all jumped, startled.

'Angelo, hi,' Frankie said. 'I'm so sorry, I didn't realise you were downstairs.'

He held a hand up. 'Is there any coffee going?'

Stella nodded, getting up. 'Why don't I go and open up the front door and you can sit out on the terrace. The morning paper should be here by now. It's a relaxing place to start the day.'

The youngest son of the family in the local store did a newspaper run most mornings, just one of the charmingly old-fashioned things they'd discovered about the island. They locked the villa doors at night out of habit rather than necessity. Crime was pretty much non-existent on the island; it really was like stepping back into the 1950s.

'I'll put some coffee on and bring it out to you,' Frankie said, wondering if he'd be tempted by the idea of food this morning.

Winnie watched Stella leave with Angelo behind her.

'I hope he's more polite this morning or she might clip him around the ear with the newspaper.'

Outside, Stella suggested Angelo take a seat at one of the driftwood tables in the shade and then poured a tall glass of bottled water over ice and lemon from the glass-fronted fridge at the outside bar. She was aware that she didn't know where anything was and hated the idea that she looked anything but in control under Angelo's scrutiny. They'd barely used the outside bar yet save for making themselves a G&T out there in the evenings.

'How's the shoulder?' she asked as she placed the glass down and handed him the newspaper she'd picked up from the front step.

130

'Nothing I can't handle,' he said, flipping the paper out flat with his good hand. Stella wasn't convinced; he moved awkwardly and she saw his jaw tighten as he opened the front page.

'And your room?' she said. 'Do you have everything you need?'

He snapped his sunglasses out of the top pocket of his crisp open-necked shirt. 'The bed isn't exactly world-class hotel standard and the air-con could stand to be improved, but I can work with it.'

Stella wished she hadn't asked now. The bed in his room was perfectly fine; they'd even added an extra mattress topper to ensure that their first guest slept comfortably.

'You can always move to one of the other rooms if you'd prefer?' she suggested. 'We don't have anyone else booked in until next week, so feel free to go and bounce on all the beds on the first floor.'

He glanced down at his sling. 'Do I look in any condition for bouncing, Miss . . .?'

'Stella,' she said. 'No need to stand on ceremony.'

He flicked the page of the newspaper over and slid his sunglasses over his face. 'Perhaps a little ceremony might be professional when it comes to running a professional establishment,' he said. 'Like coffee.'

What the –? Stella opened her mouth and then shut it again, aware that to respond would be discourteous but ready to unceremoniously tip his glass of water over his head.

'Did someone mention coffee?' Frankie said, walking out onto the terrace with a tray carefully balanced in her hands. Angelo watched as she slid it carefully down on the other side of his table.

'Coffee,' she said, placing the unplunged cafetière down

131

on his side of the table and then adding a milk jug and a little bowl of demerara sugar cubes beside it.

'I wasn't sure how you took it,' she said.

'Black.' Angelo placed the sugar and milk back on the tray.

'Oh,' Frankie faltered, and Stella simmered. 'Well, there's fresh juice.' Frankie set a glass down. 'And I don't know if you're hungry, but I baked these just this morning, and the jam is fresh greengage from our garden.'

She lifted out the basket of pastries and laid the small pot of jam beside them with butter and a silver knife.

Angelo looked at them once, and then put them back on Frankie's tray. 'Just coffee is fine.'

'I can make you something different if you'd prefer? Bacon, or some eggs perhaps?'

He closed his eyes and pinched the brow of his nose. 'Please. Just coffee.'

Stella hated the downcast look on her friend's face as she gathered the things back onto the tray and took everything back inside except the coffee.

'I'll leave you to your paper,' she said, stepping away to follow Frankie. She made it as far as the door before her annoyance got the better of her, carrying her back to his table.

Clearing her throat when he didn't look up, she said, 'The bed may not be world-class standard, Mr Vitalis, but that breakfast would have been. Frankie has been diligently testing out recipes and she's a fabulous cook. You could have been kinder.'

He slid his glasses far enough down his nose to look over them.

'I've stayed in many fine hotels, and no one has ever questioned my breakfast choice before.'

132

'This isn't a fine hotel. It's a bed and breakfast on a sleepy backwater island, and so far this morning you've insulted our beds and rejected our breakfast. Corporate mattresses and ice-cold air-con might be in short supply here, but common courtesy certainly isn't.'

'You're doing a fine job of proving yourself wrong with your rudeness.'

'Really? I don't think so,' she said, thoroughly annoyed. 'Enjoy the view with your coffee, Mr Vitalis. It's one thing you certainly can't criticise us on.'

'Man, he's something else!'

Stella stomped into the kitchen, all guns blazing. 'I've a good mind to call Corinna and tell her to come and get him. I don't give a stuff if he's a paying customer, I'd rather have an empty B&B than have him stalking around like a sodding thundercloud. Spike his coffee in the morning, Frank.'

'I think you'll find that's illegal,' Winnie said, tearing apart one of the cinnamon pastries Frankie had made that morning. 'Bloody hell, Frank, this is amazing. He doesn't know what he's missing.'

'He seems over-stressed to me,' Frankie said, storing the rest of the pastries away. 'I wonder if he'd like some chamomile tea or something?'

Stella stared at her. 'Being stressed isn't an excuse to be rude,' she said. 'And he was rude.'

'Don't let him wind you up, Stell,' Frankie said. 'He might chill out yet. How can you spend time on an island as peaceful as this without relaxing?'

'I don't get why he wanted to come here at all,' Winnie said. 'It seems like an inconvenience to him.'

'Can I suggest you ladies keep your voices down if you're going to be indiscreet about your paying guests?'

133

They all turned guiltily to see Angelo standing in the doorway with his empty coffee cup and cafetière in his hand.

'I brought this inside to save you the trip.'

'Thank you.' A flush crept up Frankie's neck. 'I'm sorry if you thought we were talking about you just now.'

'You were.'

She looked at the floor like a scolded child. 'I'm sorry.'

'I'm not,' Stella said. 'I'm afraid the kitchen is private, as is whatever is said in it, Mr Vitalis. There's a bell at reception. In future please ring it if you need anything and someone will always come to help.'

He pushed his good hand through his black hair and looked as if he wanted to give Stella the sharp end of his tongue, but she held his gaze head on and he seemed to decide better of it and stalked out.

'Well,' Stella said, when the other two looked at her. 'He needs to learn some manners.'

Her mouth dropped open, because someone, presumably Angelo, had rung the bell. In fact he must have held his hand pressed down on it, because it was more like an ongoing fire alarm than a polite ding.

'Right.' Stella marched down the hallway and found him leaning with his elbow on the buzzer. 'Can I help you with something?' She rearranged her mouth into a cabin-crew-worthy smile whilst shooting nine-inch nails at him with her eyes.

'I wasn't sure where to leave the newspaper.'

'On the coffee table would be perfectly fine, thank you.'

He placed the newspaper down, and they stared each other down for a few long, hard seconds before he turned on his heel and left the building.

CHAPTER TEN

'Hubble, bubble, toil and trouble,' Stella said, rubbing her hands together. 'So what do we do first, Frank?'

It was their third Monday on the island, and they'd gathered in the cellar for their first ever gin distilling session, hair tied back and aprons on. They'd decided that they'd be best all learning the process together, as much for hand holding and mutual blame purposes as anything else. Frankie stood with her hands on her hips, her eyes scanning the assortment of jars and bottles amassed on the bench.

'I vote we make just five bottles for our first run,' she said. 'It only needs to stand for a week, so we'll know pretty soon if we've ballsed it up and we won't lose too much stock.'

Stella fished out five bottles of spirit from a box on the floor and lined them up on the bench.

'So far, so good.'

Winnie pulled Ajax's letter from her apron pocket and laid his handwritten botanicals recipe out, weighing down the corners of the paper with jars or bottles.

'We're going to need scales,' she said. 'This is all in

weights per bottle. Oh, hang on. He says the scales are in the bench drawer.'

Frankie opened the long drawer, and sure enough, she found an electric scale.

'Rightio,' Winnie said. '"To each bottle, add the following ingredients. Twenty-two grams of dried juniper berries."'

'Shall I unscrew all five and we can do one ingredient at a time?' Stella said, and when the others nodded she went along the line and cracked them all open.

Frankie carefully weighed out twenty-two grams of the tiny, hard berries into the scale.

'How do I get them in the bottle without dropping any?' she said, frowning.

Winnie looked back at the letter. 'There should be a funnel in the drawer too?'

Frankie opened the drawer for a second time, nodded and withdrew a small plastic funnel. Slotting it into the top of the first bottle, she slowly tipped the berries into it. They all watched the inky black dots sink with almost ceremonial grace to the bottom of the bottle.

'That's it then. No going back now, we're gin alchemists,' Winnie said.

Frankie measured out berries for the next bottle, and they worked their way along in a production line.

'What's next on the list, Win?' Frankie puffed her fringe from her eyes, looking slightly less terrified now the first ingredient had gone in.

'"Nine grams of coriander seeds."'

Duly weighed, the small brown husks sank to join the juniper.

'This is sort of like magic, isn't it?' Winnie said.

Frankie glanced around the shady cellar. 'Potions class at Hogwarts?'

'I'd quite like a stern teacher to glower at me like that,' Stella said. 'All brooding and sexy.'

Winnie couldn't imagine a man in the land who could intimidate Stella with a brooding glower. '"Two grams of angelica root,"' she said, nudging the jar towards Frankie to weigh out.

'It looks like something someone swept up from behind the fridge,' Stella said, frowning as she watched Frankie weigh out the dried shreds of root and add them to the bottles.

'"Ten cracked pink peppercorns and a pinch of pine needles."'

'A pinch of pine needles?' Stella said. 'Really? It'll end up tasting like toilet bleach at this rate.'

'Really,' Frankie said, showing Stella the small hand-marked tub. 'Here. You can be in charge of that bit.'

Winnie counted out the peppercorns as Stella added a sprinkle of needles, and Frankie followed along with three curly strips of dried lemon peel.

'Is there anything else?' Stella asked.

Winnie ran her finger down the list. '"And now for the final and most secret ingredient of all,"' she read. '"Eleven arbutus berries*. Count carefully, as they give the gin both its colour and its sweetness." Why has he put a star next to that, I wonder?' She turned the page over and found her answer. 'Ah, here we go. "The English name for the arbutus is the strawberry tree, because the fruits are similarly red and sweet. However, it is much rarer and more prized, because it's thought to possess magical qualities for good luck, love and respect. Many believe that the presence of the arbutus berry in the island gin is responsible for the island's tranquillity and continued good fortune – perhaps because everyone drinks so much of it! The bush at the villa is the only source of arbutus on Skelidos, so be sure to tend it carefully and harvest it when the berries are fat in autumn."'

Winnie read the last line of Ajax's recipe with increasing trepidation, and when she raised her eyes it was clear that Stella and Frankie shared her anxiety.

'The only bush on the entire island?' Frankie squeaked high enough to sound as if she'd taken a shot of helium.

'Fuck,' Stella said, sitting down hard on an upturned crate. 'Just when we thought we'd got it sussed, he goes and drops that bombshell in at the end. So we're running a bed and breakfast, a donkey sanctuary, operating a secret and no doubt illegal gin distillery, employing staff we didn't know we had, and now we have to tend a bloody sacred bush in the garden as well!' She ticked them off on her fingers. 'What's next? An orphanage in the attic?'

Put like that, it did seem like rather a lot of hidden extras had been included in the sale of Villa Valentina.

'A moody injured Greek whose own sister doesn't like him enough to put him up?' Winnie said, catching Stella's eye.

'And more new guests arriving at the end of the week,' Frankie added. 'I just hope they're the kind that eat breakfast this time.'

They lapsed into silence, all looking at the five bottles of freshly spiked gin on the bench. Winnie glanced at Ajax's letter for a final time.

'"Replace the bottle tops, screwing them tightly, turn each bottle three times and then store upright in the cellar. Turn daily for five days, strain, and then rebottle and label, remembering to add the date and serial number."'

She turned the letter again. 'That's it.'

One by one they screwed the tops back on the bottles.

'We should all turn each bottle once to celebrate our first batch,' Frankie said.

Winnie nodded. 'A gin ritual?'

'Only if we can go upstairs and finish the ritual with a big G&T,' Stella said.

They took their time turning each bottle, counting aloud as if casting a spell.

'They're already changing colour,' Frankie whispered.

'I think we might have just performed actual magic,' Winnie said.

Stella lined the bottles up on an empty shelf in the racks by the wall. 'Come on. Let's go upstairs. We better go and check if that bloody bush needs some water.'

'I've come to hang the sign.'

Winnie looked up from the sketchbook open in front of her on the reception desk when Jesse tapped on the open front door, a battered toolbox in his hand.

'Oh, right,' she said, trying not to flush. She hadn't seen him since their picnic; her daily visits to The Fonz had suffered for her wine-induced bold nakedness. 'Thanks for remembering.'

Stella and Frankie had headed over to the other side of the island with Panos to look at a car he knew was for sale, leaving Winnie alone for the afternoon manning reception. She'd waited until they'd gone to lay out her sketchbook and pencils, opening the book with nervous fingers as she deliberately skimmed past the drawings already in there. Or designs, to describe them more accurately. Bracelets, necklaces, jewelled slides and tiaras, pretty things that seemed so tied up with her old life that she couldn't bring herself to look at them here in her new one. She hadn't wanted the job of label designer at all, but neither Stella nor Frankie were artistically inclined and they'd firmly declared it within her remit. She knew what they were doing, of course; their attempts to reignite her creativity were not exactly subtle. Art of one form or another had defined Winnie's life since they'd been children, and they clearly thought that she'd closed herself off from it as a result of her divorce. She hadn't; she just wasn't inclined that way any more, and she didn't see why it needed to concern anyone else if it wasn't worrying her. Except now that she had the pencils in her hand and the blank page in front of her, she'd stalled like a frightened pony faced with an oncoming tractor in a country lane.

'What are you up to?' Jesse nodded towards her sketchbook.

She lifted one shoulder as she closed the book. 'Not a lot. Doodling.'

He nodded, twisting his mouth to the side. 'Can I see?'

'There's nothing to see, I hadn't started,' she said. 'We need to design our own custodian label for the gin. A rite of passage for whoever owns this place, apparently.'

'Ah, I remember when it changed to Ajax,' he said. 'It's true then, the story about the villa and the gin being entwined?'

'So the story goes.' Winnie wasn't sure how much the islanders were allowed to know about their beloved tipple. 'Would you like a beer while you work? The sign is still propped where you left it against the wall outside.'

'Is that your subtle-as-a-brick way of telling me to shut up and get on with the job?'

She held her hands up and smiled. 'You caught me.'

Jesse tugged his forelock. 'I'll get on then.'

'Help yourself to a beer from the fridge under the bar outside,' she said, staying firmly in her spot rather than following him out. Her eyes followed him anyway though, taking in the generous width of his shoulders beneath his T-shirt and the deeply bronzed colour of his shins below his shorts. He looked as if he belonged here, and it was clear from the warm way the locals spoke of him that he was accepted as one of them.

She wouldn't have had him down as a whistler. She listened to him as he unpacked his tools, whistling almost tunefully.

'Same place as the old sign?' he called, sticking his head around the door frame.

Winnie nodded, leaving him to it. She couldn't see him, but she could hear him whistling and the sound of his hammer banging, and found herself with a choice of going outside or reaching for her sketchbook again. The sketch-book turned out to be the least nerve-inducing of the two, which said much about her feelings towards Jesse.

She flipped her book open to the first clean page, picked up her pencil and touched it against the paper.

'All done,' said Jesse as he wandered back into reception a little later. 'Looks pretty good. Want to come and see?'

Winnie nodded, following him outside to stand back and take a look.

'I love it,' she said, genuinely thrilled. Jesse's sign was in perfect keeping with the place; slightly unconventional and unique. He'd picked out the letters in white against the mellow wood, simple and effective in the sunlight.

'Good. I reckon I've earned that beer now then,' he said, snagging one from the fridge. 'You gonna join me, or keep on avoiding me? Because that's gonna be pretty tough to keep up on an island like this one.'

He was right, of course, and Winnie was about to answer

141

him when her mobile buzzed loudly on the reception desk and saved her the trouble.

'I should get that,' she said, practically running back inside.

Jesse ambled in a minute or two later as she hung up on Stella.

'Saved by the bell?' he said, handing her a beer.

'Not exactly,' she said. 'It was Stella to say they've just bought a car.'

'Something to drink to then,' he said, touching his bottle neck against hers before taking a long slug.

Winnie hadn't thought to close her sketchbook, and his eyes fell on the label sketches she'd made while he hung the sign. She'd had a strong idea of what might work and tried out several variations on the bad fairy theme, looking for a vintage parchment feel, something tongue in cheek and distinctly English.

'Wow,' he said, twisting his head to look. 'I love this one.' He touched the one that Winnie preferred. 'That's one sexy fairy.' He reached for her pencil. 'Except . . . may I?'

It was only pencil. She could always put it back again. 'Sure.'

Jesse paused, studying her drawing before changing it subtly with a few deft strokes of the pencil. There was no denying it; it was better. The fairy had a little more of a glint in her eye, her hip a touch more curved, her brow raised as if she knew something no one else did.

'You can always change it back,' he said casually, laying the pencil down.

'Hey, you're the artist,' she said. 'I like her better.'

'Don't do that,' he said softly. 'You're an artist in your own right, Winnie. It was a couple of tweaks, that's all.'

'I'm not mad at you,' she said, putting her bottle down.

He ran his hand through his hair, agitated. 'I shouldn't have touched it. It was perfect as it was.'

'Jesse, I'm not mad,' she said again, more insistent.

He drained his bottle and banged it down harder than necessary. 'I need to get back.'

He turned and strode out, leaving Winnie confused as to what she'd done wrong.

Back at his place after a ten-minute march, Jesse banged straight through to the back of the house, grabbed the bottle of brandy from the kitchen cupboard and dragged the loft ladder down. Up there, he shoved things randomly aside until he reached the sturdy cardboard box he'd gone in search of. He'd put it up here years previously, tucked right at the back to make getting to it a trial, a self-checking mechanism to make sure he only opened it when he really needed to. He didn't let himself stop or pause for thought, just ripped the packing tape from it in harsh strips as if he were tearing off the sticking plasters that had held his heart together for the last decade.

Opening the flaps, he slid down the wall and sat next to it, knees bent and the brandy bottle in his hands. It wasn't too late; he still didn't have to do this. Closing his eyes, he banged the back of his head slowly against the wall. *Bang*. A mouthful of harsh spirits. *Bang*. A head full of buried memories. *Bang*. Another blonde girl with dancing eyes and glitter in her fingertips.

He screwed the top back onto the brandy and lifted the protective tissue paper inside the box and pulled out his wedding album.

CHAPTER ELEVEN

'Jesus. You bought the Karate Kid's car.'

As instructed, Winnie had opened up Villa Valentina's street-side wooden gates so that Stella and Frankie could pull the newly acquired car onto the patch of earth that counted as the B&B's driveway.

Frankie covered her mouth to hold her laugh in at Stella's offended face as they climbed out of the car.

'I'll have you know it's a Ford Super Deluxe,' Stella said, bending backwards to read the words off the back of the car.

Winnie nodded. 'And I love it, but is it going to be, well, you know . . . reliable?' she said, running her hand over the curve of the huge Tiffany-blue American convertible. It looked as if it ought to be parked up outside an ice-cream parlour in a 50s movie, and exuded the same shabby air of faded grandeur as the villa itself.

Frankie nodded. 'Never given Mr P a day's trouble in twenty-five years, his wife said.'

'What happened to Mr P?' Winnie had a bad feeling.

Frankie and Stella exchanged glances, and Winnie sighed.

'He died in this car, didn't he?'

'Sort of,' Frankie muttered at the same time as Stella shook her head.

'Sort of?'

'They were at the drive-in movie on the beach for their wedding anniversary,' Frankie said.

'There's a drive-in on the island?' Winnie interrupted, utterly beguiled.

'Yes, but that isn't the point,' Frankie said. 'The point is that they were watching a movie, and she went to lay her hand on his knee and he moved at the same time, and she mistakenly fondled his crotch for the first time in ten years and his heart gave out from the shock of it.'

'She told you all this?' Winnie said, wide-eyed.

'Well, strictly speaking, Panos did,' Stella said. 'Mrs P is ninety-three and can't speak a word of English. We thought it'd be cool to pick up our guests from the ferry in it, get their holiday started in style.'

Winnie regarded the cherry leather interior and huge ivory and chrome steering wheel. It really was rather fabulous, and given everything else that had been included in their purchase of the villa, it was actually a perfect match.

'Lots of room in here for luggage.' Winnie knocked her knuckles on the boot for emphasis. 'I'm sold,' she said. 'Space for shopping bags.'

Privately she was just relieved not to have to rely on a lift to the supermarket from Jesse again.

'Cool,' Stella said. 'Wax on . . .' She made the infamous gesture with one hand.

'Wax off,' Frankie and Winnie both said, waxing off with their other hand, and then they all fell about laughing, because they'd just bought the car from the Karate Kid

145

and it was entirely in keeping with their overseas oddball adventure.

'Two more bookings for July,' Stella said, grinning as she clicked through the reservations panel on the shiny new website they'd launched a few days ago. Lots of favours had been called in from Stella's friends and old colleagues back in the UK, and as a result Villa Valentina now had a charming website that showed the B&B off at its enchanting best and a simple interface for them to take and track bookings. Coupled with Stella's killer instinct for marketing and PR, the B&B was starting to pick up mentions on selected boutique websites across the Internet and the bookings were already coming in. It was thrilling and terrifying in equal measures.

'We're going to have to move into the owners' apartment at the weekend,' Winnie said, plunging their breakfast coffee. They were still using the guest rooms on the top floor, but the influx of guests meant that they'd need to decamp into the small two-bedroom owners' accommodation on the ground floor behind the kitchen. It was nothing special, functional at best; a small lounge and bathroom with a galley kitchen and two plain, simple bedrooms.

'We don't really need it as living accommodation, do we? We spend all of our spare time outside or in here anyway.' Frankie gestured around at the kitchen. 'If we use the lounge in there as a third bedroom instead, it could work.'

The others nodded. They were all wistfully reluctant to let go of the rooms that Ajax had so perceptively allocated to them on first arrival. Stella had lost count of the number of hours she'd spent sunbathing on that spectacular balcony in the Seaview Suite, and Frankie was addicted to her deep, relaxing bathtub. Winnie had come to think of the Bohemian Suite as her sanctuary, the only place she could truly let her game face slip and feel like crap about her failed marriage, her lost creativity and her confused feelings towards Jesse. She knew what was happening, of course. She'd needed someone to make her feel better and he was the first man to look her way since Rory; she was like a baby duckling imprinting on first contact. It didn't mean anything, in fact it meant only inconvenience and awkwardness long term, because they were going to be neighbours for a long time and he'd seen her naked, kissed her stupid and now seemed to have the hump with her for no discernible reason. Platonic would have been far more sensible under the circumstances, and Winnie needed complications like a hole in the head.

'Croissant?' Frankie said, wafting the still hot pastries with a magazine.

Stella was about to reply when someone banged repeatedly down on the bell in reception. Rolling her eyes, she scraped her chair back and stood up. 'I'll go.'

It'd be Angelo. It always was. He'd made a point of leaning on the bell for a myriad tiny things since Stella had given him his orders. Coffee? He belled. Jug of iced water? He belled. Where to leave his used towel even though Hero cleaned his room daily? He belled. What the weather forecast for the day was, even though it was twenty-four-seven wall-to-wall sunshine? He belled. And always Stella responded with that big smile on her face and one fist clenched ready to smack his jawline. Today was no exception.

'How can I help you this morning?' she said, noticing that he looked a little different today. Over the couple of weeks he'd spent at the villa he'd relaxed his dress code into deck shorts and polo shirts; he was never going to be a beach bum, and this was probably as close to laid back as he knew how to be. Not this morning though: Don Draper was back in the building. Sharp shirt and tie, discreet cufflinks, and his black hair totally on point.

'Coffee please, Stella,' he said. 'And breakfast, perhaps?'

She tried not to do a double-take. He'd avoided eating at the villa up to now, and Frankie had all but given up on the notion of feeding him up.

'There's warm croissants just from the oven,' she said. 'I'll bring you something with your coffee.'

He nodded, already heading outside. As he bent to pick up the morning paper, he looked her way again.

'And Stella? Coffee for two this morning, please.'

'Coffee for two this morning, please,' she muttered, back in the kitchen. 'He's out there dressed like he's going to a funeral and making demands again. He wants food this morning, Frank.'

Delighted, Frankie sprang into action, making him a tray up while Stella prepared his coffee.

'Who's the second person?' Winnie asked, scraping the last of the jam from the pot.

'Beats me.' Stella added a second coffee cup to the tray and headed for the door. 'Someone he wants to impress, by the looks of him.'

He was at his usual table, and as Stella approached him he snapped the paper closed, laid it down and weighted it with the jug of flowers because there was an unusually strong breeze around.

'Are you expecting company this morning?' she asked,

light and conversational to hide the fact that really she was just being nosey.

'Yes,' he said, businesslike. 'You.'

Stella's hands stilled on the cafetière. 'I'm sorry?'

'I'm requesting your company for breakfast, Stella.'

There had been very few moments in Stella's life when anyone had surprised her more.

'Are you joking?' she said, forgetting her manners.

He shook his head. 'Unless you're too busy?'

Wordlessly, she shook her head, and then slowly took a seat opposite him.

'So how are you finding life in Greece?' He looked at her enquiringly. 'It must be quite the change from England.'

She nodded, transferring the food from the breakfast tray to the table. Warm fluffy croissants, ham and cheese, Frankie's jam and huge, fragrant velvet peaches from their garden. 'It is. The weather's certainly warmer.'

Angelo plunged the coffee. 'A predictable answer. British people, always they comment on the weather.'

Stella frowned. Had he invited her to breakfast just to wind her up? 'If you'd lived your whole life beneath grey skies, you'd notice the difference too.'

'Perhaps,' he said, laying a slice of Gouda on a croissant and then a slice of farmer's ham.

Stella stirred milk into her coffee, still curious about his motives. It couldn't be because he wanted her company.

'Are you working today?' she asked, touching her fingers to her throat to indicate his tie.

'Too much?' he asked.

'It depends what you've dressed for,' she said. 'It's too much for the beach and perfect for the boardroom.'

'And for breakfast with an irritating English woman? Is it too much for that?'

149

'You've dressed just for this?'

'No.'

Thoroughly pissed off with him, she decided against breakfast. 'Scintillating as this has been, I need to get on. If you enjoy your breakfast, perhaps you could go so far as to mention it to Frankie.'

She got up abruptly and stalked back inside, furious. When he leaned on the bell half an hour later, she ignored it.

'Can we open it to sniff it?' Winnie asked. They were all in the cellar for the mid-morning bottle-turning ritual. Their first batch of island gin had stood for four days so far, and had already turned that distinctive strawberry blush.

'No!' Frankie said, putting the bottles back on the shelf. 'You'll mess with the magic.'

Winnie laid her sketchbook on the bench. 'I've been playing around with label ideas,' she said, flicking through to the right page. 'What do you think?'

Stella and Frankie came to stand either side of her.

'This one for sure,' Stella grinned, tapping her finger on the one Jesse had tinkered with. 'She looks up to no good.'

Frankie nodded. 'Agreed.'

Winnie had expected as much. 'I'll draw some up,' she said, and then they all looked up, distracted by the bang of the cellar door. They were shut in.

'What the . . .?' Frankie took the stone steps at a fast jog. Rattling the brass knob, she turned back to look down at the others. 'The handle on this side doesn't work. It won't open.'

'Of course it will,' Stella said, following her up and barging the door with her shoulder to no avail.

'Oh no,' Winnie whispered. 'Oh no.' She really wasn't a fan of cellars, and only tolerated this one because it was well lit and they had a secret mission down here.

'Don't panic, Win,' Stella said. 'It's only wedged. It'll come loose.'

But it didn't. All three of them tried it individually and then as a collective, but the damn thing wouldn't budge an inch.

'OK,' Frankie said, cool and practical as ever. 'The new guests don't arrive until tomorrow, so that's not a problem.'

'And Angelo is out, presumably on business,' Stella said, curling her lip at the recollection of their brief exchange earlier in the day.

'Hero! She can live up to her name!' Winnie said, suddenly animated.

'When she comes to work tomorrow,' Frankie said, grimacing. 'Sorry, she had things to do today so I said she could take the day off.'

'So there's nobody to rescue us or hear us scream, and we're going to die a hideous death down here and they'll find our skeletons in twenty years' time.' Winnie sat down on the steps, dramatic.

'Or alternatively I could call Corinna?' Stella said, pulling her mobile from her shorts pocket and stabbing at it. 'Bugger, no signal.'

'Hold it up in the air?' Winnie said.

'You could call Corinna.' Frankie nodded vigorously. 'Or Panos? He's closer.'

'I don't have his number in my phone,' Stella said standing on the top step with her arm held above her head to dial Corinna. They could all hear it click through and start to ring, and then the dreaded sound of it going through to answerphone a few rings later.

'Shit,' Stella muttered, and then left a garbled message for Corinna, explaining the mess they were in and asking her to contact Panos and get him to come and let them out as soon as possible.

'And now we wait,' Frankie said, taking the step up from Winnie's.

'Won't be long,' Stella said, sitting down by the door. 'I wish I hadn't been so hasty about refusing breakfast with Mr Big-shot now though. I'm sodding starving. There's only one thing for it.'

'Are you going to turn cannibal and eat us?' Winnie said.

Stella rolled her eyes. 'Ask me again if we're still down here in the morning. For now though?' She skipped down the steps and pulled a bottle from the shelf. 'There's gin.'

They hadn't intended to drink very much of it. The first swig had been for fortification, the second for courage, and the third for good luck. By the fourth pass, they'd been locked in for over an hour and a half and given up checking Stella's phone in favour of talking.

'And then he asked me to take my dress off so he could draw me naked,' Winnie finished, having been probed by the others on how her picnic with Jesse had really gone. She'd glossed over it every time they'd asked up to now, still turning what had happened over in her head to try to make sense of it. A few gins and a lock-in later, and unloading onto Frankie and Stella seemed like the best idea in the world.

'You're shitting me!' Stella banged her fist down on the bench and then pointed at Winnie. 'You better be about to tell me that you stripped off, girly, or I'm sticking a stamp on your head and posting you back to England.'

152

Frankie laughed into her gin. 'Course she didn't.' When Winnie didn't answer, she looked at her curiously. 'Did you?'

Winnie twisted her gold feather pendant. 'I wasn't going to, but then a little voice in my head told me to be brave.'

'It was me,' Stella smirked, gesturing between herself and Winnie. 'You could hear me. Thank God for you that you've got me in there. To be honest, you'd be rubbish on your own.' She tapped Winnie on the head with her fingertip, nodding sagely.

Frankie placed the bottle down. 'You did it? You actually took your dress off?'

'Everything off.'

'Holy shit, Win.' Stella high-fived her.

'I don't know what came over me,' Winnie said. 'One minute I was shocked, the next I was starkers.'

'And then he drew you?'

Winnie nodded. 'He asked me to sit on a boulder in his garden, and then he sat under an olive tree and drew me.'

'Bloody hell.' Stella sighed. 'And then what? Don't tell us that nothing happened, because that is scientifically impossible.'

Frankie cupped her chin in her hands. 'I think I want someone to draw me naked. Gavin was useless with a pencil.'

'No lead in it?' Winnie bumped shoulders with her friend.

'I wouldn't know,' Frankie sighed. 'We didn't sleep in the same bed for the last five years of our marriage.'

'Jesus, Frank,' Stella said. 'You've been celibate for more than five years?'

'I know.' Frankie shrugged. 'We just got out of the habit,

153

plus he was working nights for a while . . . It was just, I don't know, easier.'

'We need to find you a hot Greek lover,' Winnie said.

Frankie shook her head. 'I'll just live through you for a while.'

'Nothing doing,' Winnie said, throwing her hands up at their incredulous faces. 'Honestly, I promise. He drew me, we chatted and then I put my dress back on and he walked me home.'

'Fucking hell,' Stella muttered. 'Is he gay?'

Winnie laughed. 'Stereotypical, much?'

'Well,' Stella said, sourly, 'he's as bad as Don Draper. He had me sit with him for breakfast this morning just so he could toss a few insults my way.'

'He joined me for yoga on the beach this morning,' Frankie said.

'Did he really?' Winnie said, surprised. He was the least likely person on the island she'd have expected to practise yoga.

Frankie nodded. 'He's a beginner, but thought it might help his shoulder.'

'Well, he could certainly do with the inner peace.' Stella sniffed. 'Might make him a bit more pleasant.'

'Actually, he was very complimentary about my croissants this morning when I collected his tray.'

'So he should be. You're the best cook on the island.'

Frankie laughed softly. 'And you're drunk. You don't know any other cooks on the island.'

'Not drunk,' Stella sighed, laying her cheek on the bench. 'Just tired.'

Winnie patted her hair. 'Have a little snooze, Stell. We're probably going to be down here for the next hundred years, you might as well.'

154

As it turned out, Winnie had overestimated. Forty minutes later someone wrenched the door open from the other side and came down the steps to find three snoozing English women, a half-empty bottle of gin and a secret distillery.

CHAPTER TWELVE

'Ladies? Stella?'

Winnie reared up as Angelo appeared in the cellar, his tie loosened to accommodate his popped top button, his shirt sleeves rolled back.

'Can I help you?' she said, still half asleep.

'I think it's the other way around, Win,' Frankie mumbled, straightening up. They hadn't really drunk all that much gin, but the fact that they'd drunk it neat, and in Stella's case on an empty stomach, had sent it straight to their heads.

Winnie elbowed Stella, half laughing. 'Wake up, Stell. Angelo has come to save us.'

Stella mumbled something into the bench, clearly not keen on the idea of waking just yet.

'Stella,' Frankie said, more sharply in an effort to penetrate Stella's haze.

'I'll wake her,' Angelo said. 'There was someone upstairs in reception, perhaps you ladies should head on up and take a look.'

Frankie and Winnie exchanged glances, and decided on

balance that it was probably OK to leave Corinna's brother with Stella.

'I'm going to prop the door open at the top,' Frankie looked at him through narrowed eyes, as if she were warning a teenage boy who was being allowed up to a girl's bedroom.

'Come on, Frank,' Winnie said. 'We need a big glass of water before we go out and face anyone.'

'Stella.'

God, was she back at school being shouted at by the headmaster? Maybe if she just kept her eyes closed Mr Tennyson would go back to his dusty spot at the back of her head.

'Stella, wake up.'

Gah, still here. 'Go away. I'm tired and you're not real.'

That seemed to have done the trick. Oh shit! No, it hadn't! He was touching her! Ew, that wasn't all right. Opening her eyes to give him a piece of her mind, she sat up and looked straight into the dark, brooding eyes of Angelo Vitalis.

'You're not Mr Tennyson.'

He crossed his arms and stared at her. 'Sorry to disappoint you.'

She frowned, still not completely with it. 'Not disappointed. He always smelt of cigarettes and liked to hang around the changing rooms.'

'Are you drunk?'

Was she? Shaking her head experimentally, she found that actually she wasn't too bad now she'd had forty winks.

'Don't think so.'

'Stand up.'

She didn't care for his tone but slithered to her feet all

157

the same, straightening her strapless black jersey dress as she went.

'Would you like me to walk in a straight line and recite the alphabet backwards too?'

'Can you?'

She shot him a sarcastic smirk, and then focused on him properly for the first time since she'd realised he wasn't Mr Tennyson. 'You look like you've just come back from a club.'

'I haven't.'

God, was he always this uptight?

'Can I ask you something, Angelo?' she said. 'Are you always this uptight?'

WTF? How did that happen? The words were inside her head, and then they were out of it and hanging in the air between them like little bombs.

He stared at her in complicated silence, then reached for the bottle of gin and took a good glug of it.

'Better?' he asked.

'I don't know,' she said. 'Is it?' It was the first alcoholic drink she'd seen him take.

'Not yet.' He took a second gulp and then held the bottle out to study the label. 'What is this stuff?'

Stella was torn between pride and the need to keep the island's secret. 'Gin.'

His eyes slowly swept the wall of bottles. 'Are you expecting a war?'

She swallowed and shook her head, then held her arms out at shoulder height and started to take toe-to-heel steps, reciting the alphabet backwards with little regard for accuracy. By the time she reached A, she was glad to reach the back wall, laughing.

'Very funny,' he said.

'Your turn,' she said, leaning her back against the cool wall. 'But do it in Greek.'

Had he not had several measures of gin, he'd probably have refused, but as it was he walked towards her with the bottle in his one good outstretched arm.

'Omega,' he said. 'Psi.'

'Christ,' she said. She hadn't heard him speak his mother tongue before, it was actually easy to forget his heritage because his English was so immaculate. Some of his words were familiar, others new and exotic, and all of them were an incredible turn-on.

'Kappa,' he said, more than halfway across the cellar.

Stella watched him, noticing the crinkles around his eyes as he concentrated on going backwards. The closer he came, the faster her heart beat.

'Gamma,' he said, his eyes nailed on hers. 'Beta.'

He was right in front of her now.

'Alpha,' he almost growled, low and much too sexy.

'God, you so are,' she whispered. He was just about the manliest man she'd ever encountered, and right this very second his chiselled lips were slightly parted and his usually unreadable dark eyes were an open book.

'You said I was irritating this morning,' she said.

'You are. Incredibly irritating and incredibly ravishing.' His hand landed on the wall beside her head.

'And you're obnoxious and drop dead alpha frickin' gorgeous,' she said, pulling him closer by his tie until his body pressed hot and oh-so-male against hers. He kissed her, the sort of kiss that went from polite to filthy in ten seconds flat and left them both gasping for more.

'Fuck,' he said, lifting her clean off her feet and pinning her against the wall with his hips.

Stella laughed against his mouth, wrapping her legs

159

around his thighs as her fingers unpicked the buttons of his shirt. 'That, Angelo Vitalis, is music to my ears.'

Upstairs, Frankie and Winnie wandered out to the edge of the terrace and scanned the beach for any sign of their mystery visitors.

'I don't see anyone,' Frankie sighed.

Winnie shook her head. 'I hope we didn't lose customers.'

Frankie shook her head. 'Well, I guess we'll never know unless they come back.' She took Winnie's empty water glass from her hand. 'I need to get back to the kitchen. I'm trying out Panos's mother's baklava recipe ready for the new guests.'

Re-emerging onto the terrace again at a brisk trot a minute or two later, Frankie dropped down beside Winnie on the bench overlooking the sea. 'I don't think there were any visitors at all,' she whispered conspiratorially. 'I think he wanted to get Stella on her own.'

'Does she need rescuing?' Winnie said, ready to go into battle.

Frankie laughed and shook her head. 'Not by the sounds coming from the cellar, no. I had to leave the kitchen.'

Winnie took a second to register what Frankie meant. 'Oh my God!' she mouthed, slapping her hands to her cheeks.

'Well, I just hope they don't break any bottles,' Frankie said. 'How would we record *that* in the log?'

'I'm off to meet the ferry,' Stella said, jangling the car keys. 'Wish me luck.'

Frankie held up her crossed fingers, and Winnie nodded, clicking her pen nervously. 'Have you got the board?' She'd made a board with the guests' names on for Stella to hold up.

'In the car already.'

'And you know their names?'

'Smith, Brown and Williams,' Stella said, even though Winnie had already asked her three times that morning. 'But if I forget, it's on the board. Win, I've got this. I'll bring them back, you can check them in, and Frankie can wow them with baklava. Everything will be fine.'

They'd allocated the guests the three connecting rooms that made up the rest of the first floor beside Angelo's Captain's Suite in the corner. All high-ceilinged and decorated in restful whites, greys and neutrals to make the most of the natural light, they reminded Winnie of artists' studios. Technically, all of the villa's letting rooms were then full, meaning that their move down into the owner's apartment was more urgent than ever.

'Coffee?'

As Stella set off for the port, Frankie came through to reception dressed in chic black cigarette pants and a black polka-dot sleeveless blouse, carrying two steaming mugs. With her knotted silk scarf around her neck and her big dark glasses perched on her head, she looked every inch the cool hotelier, a perfect foil to Winnie's long, flippy ponytail and simple white sundress. In the month they'd been there they'd both been gilded golden by the sun and wore very little makeup aside from mascara and a slick of lip gloss. They didn't even realise how different they already looked from the pale, tired Englishwomen who'd arrived on the island with suitcases full of pipedreams and no real clue what to expect.

'Thanks,' Winnie said. 'You excited?'

Frankie nodded, sparkly-eyed. 'I know we've had Angelo here already, but these are our first actual bookings.'

'Is it a bit odd, do you think? Three English men

travelling here together for three weeks? It's not like we're a party island. God knows how Ajax got the bookings in the first place.'

Frankie glanced at their reservation details. 'Early forties. If they're on a stag do, it's going to be a very reserved one.'

'I hope they like gin,' Winnie said. Their first bottles would be ready to test in a day or two, and they'd all become slightly obsessed with the arbutus bush in the garden. Frankie had researched how to best care for it and posted a bullet-point list up on the cork-board in the kitchen, and they were on a daily rota to pop outside and just look at it for any signs of trouble.

'Who doesn't?' Frankie said. 'Even Angelo seems to have developed a taste for it.'

'Hmm.' Winnie wasn't sure what to make of Stella's sudden change of heart where the current resident of the Captain's Suite was concerned. God knows what he'd said to her in the cellar to make her go from active dislike to insta-lust. Perhaps it was Winnie's own romantic fragility and confusion over Jesse, but she didn't want Corinna's austere brother to leave Villa Valentina with Stella's affections in his back pocket.

Back home in England, she'd worried about moving to an unknown island where she didn't speak the language and she didn't know the customs. She'd been concerned that they wouldn't fit in, or maybe they wouldn't be accepted, or even that they'd be terribly homesick and end up back on the flight home within a few weeks. Just about the only thing that hadn't troubled her had been matters of the heart.

It was kind of funny then that all of her worries had melted like butter on a warm knife, and only their romantic

162

lives seemed determined not to play nice. Thank goodness for cool, calm, unflappable Frankie. She had the right idea; immersing herself into life on Skelidos without having her head turned by the first attractive man to glance her way or have his wicked way with her in the cellar.

Stella practically ran into reception an hour later, darting her eyes around to make sure they were the only three people in the place as she grabbed a hand of each over the reception desk.

'I have to say this really quick because they'll be walking through that door in about two minutes' time. It's not Smith, Brown and Williams. It's Manson, Harte and Miller.'

Frankie gasped and gripped Stella's fingers hard enough to stop her circulation, and Winnie caught up a few seconds later when their new guests strolled in, already looking as if they'd spent the last six months in a five-star resort, thanks to their expensive luggage, metro scarves and leather jewellery.

'Shut your mouth, Frank, you're gaping,' Winnie said through her fixed smile, gazing at the same faces that had adorned their bedroom walls, Frankie's most of all, as teenage girls. There was a time around her fifteenth birthday when she'd seriously considered changing her surname to Manson just so she could tell everyone she was married to Seth, the lead singer of Tryx. The very same Seth Manson who'd just approached the reception desk.

Frankie made a smart grab for the pen right out of Winnie's fingers and nudged her sideways with her hip, greeting Seth with what she probably hoped was a cool-girl smile and weird, tiny wave.

'I'm Frankie,' she said, shoving her hand out. 'Welcome.'

'Seth,' he said, firing Frankie the killer dimpled smile

163

that had had grown women fainting in stadiums around the world. Tryx had split up after six hugely successful years together back in the 90s, but had recently reformed and were riding high in the charts all over again.

'I know who you are,' Frankie blurted, still gripping his hand tightly between both of hers until Winnie jabbed her in the ribs with her elbow.

'Why don't I deal with the booking in while you grab some refreshments?' Winnie suggested, sending Frankie a clear 'go to the kitchen this minute and pull yourself together' glance in case she frightened their fabulous new guests away.

Frankie thankfully seemed to get the message, reluctantly letting go of Seth's hand and glancing at her palms as she walked away as if she was considering how to never wash them again.

'Is it best if I book you in as Smith, Brown and Williams?' she said, looking up into the three familiar faces. If she were to be brutally honest with them, which obviously she wasn't going to be, then she'd been more of a Blur kind of girl herself, but it was undeniably thrilling to think that Tryx had chosen to come here of all places.

'Probably,' Seth said, nodding. 'We'd like to keep a pretty low profile if we can. It's kind of a working holiday, somewhere off the beaten track to write the next album.'

It was more information than Winnie needed or expected; he seemed far more relaxed in person than he did whenever she'd caught him being interviewed on TV.

'Well, I hope you can make time for a little R&R too,' she said, twisting the booking form around and handing him the pen. 'Skelidos is famous for its island gin.'

Seth glanced over his shoulder quickly to make sure the others hadn't heard her, then looked back with a brief but

164

definite shake of his head. Winnie narrowed her eyes, trying to keep up with the silent conversation they'd become involved in as Seth drew his finger across his neck and tipped his head slowly to indicate his bandmates. Winnie followed the nod and found herself watching Mikey Miller and Jamie Harte, the other two thirds of Tryx, laughing over something on Jamie's phone. And then the penny dropped; Mikey Miller was notorious for his wild party lifestyle and drinking habits. Seth Manson clearly didn't want him to get wind of the fact that Skelidos was known for its gin, or no doubt the only thing Mikey would be interested in would be tracking down a supply. Suddenly nervous, Winnie flicked her eyes towards the hallway and the cellar beyond it with its robust stock of gin. Note to self: keep the door locked at all times and under no circumstances was anyone to mention the secret distillery beneath their feet.

'Let me show you where your rooms are,' she said, deciding it was best to get them all upstairs out of sight so she could brief Frankie and Stella.

On that, Frankie reappeared bearing a tray of three sparkling and very large G&Ts.

CHAPTER THIRTEEN

'And now he's sleeping his hangover off and probably going to have a banging headache in the morning,' Winnie finished, having regaled the afternoon's events to The Fonz, who regarded her benignly as he and Chachi ate the apples she'd quartered for them.

'Sounds like someone's had a good time.'

Winnie didn't instantly turn around. She hadn't seen Jesse at all since he'd left the villa so abruptly after hanging their new sign on Monday, even though she'd made the time to come and spend a little time with The Fonz every day and it was now Friday evening.

One large G&T had led to four or five more, in Mikey's case at least, and poor old Frank had been oblivious to the trouble she'd caused as she made a big production about how special Skelidos gin was and that welcome drinks out on the terrace were of course on the house. It wasn't her fault. She was completely wowed by the presence of the object of her teenage affections, and in truth it was kind of intoxicating having three such well-known celebrities all to themselves for the afternoon out on the terrace in the sunshine. Last month The Mall at the Queen's birthday celebrations, last week Wembley with fifty thousand screaming fans, today Villa Valentina with three English women who couldn't quite wrap their heads around it. It was quite a leap.

'Depends on your description of a good time,' Winnie said, scratching The Fonz behind the ears. 'I think Fonzy likes me a bit better lately. I might try to take him home again in a few days.'

When Jesse didn't answer, she turned to look at him. 'Have you been avoiding me?'

If he was surprised by her directness, he didn't show it. 'I work, Winnie. I don't have the luxury of taking a break whenever I feel like it to chat to passing neighbours or to try to seduce a donkey who's perfectly content where he is.'

'By which you mean to say that I clearly don't have enough to fill my time,' she said.

'You have one guest between three of you.' He shrugged. 'I don't expect you're rushed off your feet over there, no.'

Stung, Winnie squared her arms across her chest. 'Four now, actually. And what do you mean, perfectly content? That I should leave him here?'

'He's happy.'

'He's ours.'

'Donkeys are herd animals. He'll be lonely without Chachi.'

It was very difficult to argue a case against his logic, because the thought had crossed Winnie's mind that The Fonz was probably best where he was too.

'Fine,' she said. 'In that case I'll go then. I'd hate to keep you from your work.'

She stamped off across the olive grove, muttering under her breath about rudeness and meanness and suddenly a

167

little bit bereft about the idea of The Fonz never returning to his home.

'Hang on. Winnie, stop.' Jesse caught up and laid a hand on her shoulder. 'I was rude.'

'Yes, you were,' she said, turning back to him.

'Can I show you something?'

Part of her wanted to say no and stomp on home because his rudeness warranted it, but the greater part of her was curious and had her shrugging, ungracious.

'What is it?'

He turned and started walking back towards the house. 'This way.'

She followed him, looking at anything but the way his low-slung jeans cradled his ass. He bypassed the house and led her around the outskirts to a separate outbuilding, a barn, presumably.

'In here.' He unlocked the door and held it open for her to go in ahead of him.

'My studio,' he said, unnecessarily given that it was clearly his workspace. The wall on the other side of the brick and wooden barn had been replaced almost entirely with glass to flood the space with natural sunlight, illuminating the centrally placed work plinth. He was halfway through something large by the looks of the part-finished sculpture currently mounted there, surrounded by tools and tarpaulin. Winnie couldn't help but feel envy at such a fabulous place to work, all of the space and light. Other pieces lay on a long planked workbench off to one side, and a potter's wheel sat in one corner with accompanying stool. It was very much a working space: plaster splatters and dust sheets, buckets of clay, tools, easels, brushes, and the scent of art materials, turps, paint and clay.

'I love it in here,' she said, dropping her angry attitude

168

because she knew what a big deal it was to show someone your work. He'd offered her an olive branch in the form of a peep behind the curtain, in both a professional and a personal sense, because as an artist his work was intensely personal. 'Thank you for showing me.'

He nodded. 'Come on through.'

Winnie followed him across the room to a door behind the potter's wheel. He pushed it open and led her into an equally sunlit but much smaller room, equipped with a desk and chair, a work table and lamp, an armchair and an easel with a cloth protecting the artwork from the glare of the sunshine.

'Is this your planning room?'

'It was,' he murmured, closing the door and leaning against it.

'Was?' she said, suddenly uncertain.

'I can plan in the house or in the main studio.'

Winnie wasn't sure that she followed as he watched her carefully.

'I want you to work in here, Winnie. It's big enough for jewellery design, I think?' His eyes searched hers.

What? 'Jesse, no,' she said, flustered, blindsided by his out-of-the-blue suggestion. 'I don't need a workspace. I've said this already, I left that part of my life behind.'

He huffed. 'I tried that too. It doesn't work. Even if you still think so right now, I guarantee you that within a couple of months your hands will ache to create again.'

She shook her head. 'I'm not you. I'm not some big-shot artist, and I'm not tortured by the need to create. My hands are busy enough here, especially now new guests have started to arrive.'

He laughed humourless and low in his throat. 'Sounded like it out there just now.'

169

Winnie could feel her temper unravelling. 'What is this? You ignore me for days, then you do this.' She gestured around at the room he'd clearly spent time preparing for her. 'And then it's right back to belittling me again.'

'I'm not belittling you,' he shot back. 'I'm trying to help.'

'But I don't *need* help,' she said, frustrated. 'I'm happy as I am, Jesse.'

He pushed a key towards her on the desk. 'It's for the door there,' he said, nodding towards the external door on the far side of the room behind the easel. 'You can have your own entrance to come and go. Lock this one if you like. I won't come in and mess with your stuff.' He tapped the back of his head once against the door behind him.

'You're not listening to me,' she said softly.

'I am. I heard you perfectly. I just don't believe you, even if you do.'

Winnie sighed heavily, deciding how to phrase the mishmash of thoughts in her head. 'When I look back now to when I was married, I see that my husband was pretty fond of telling me what he thought I should do with little regard for my feelings. Now that I'm not married any more, I've decided that making my own decisions is important to me.'

Consternation furrowed his brow. 'I see a problem, I try to fix it.'

'Classic Martian behaviour,' Winnie said, adding, 'Men are from Mars, Women are from Venus?' when Jesse looked nonplussed.

'I'm an Australian man, Winnie. We don't fuck about with self-help bollocks.'

She laughed a little despite herself, wrapping her arms around her midriff. Alpha should be his middle name.

'Take the key,' he said, lower, less insistent, more intimate. 'Please?'

170

She gazed silently at the small silver key. Would it weigh as heavily in her hand as it did on her mind? Was she making too big a thing of it? He'd tried to do something nice for her.

'Would it help if I told you I like having you around?'

Oh, that wasn't fair. He might not read self-help books, but he sure knew how to help himself get what he wanted.

'No complications, you said.'

He shrugged. 'Who mentioned complicated?'

'That key *feels* complicated to me. This *room* feels complicated to me.'

'We're neighbours. I'm just being neighbourly. You're not in England now, Winnie; this is how it goes on small islands like this. We barter, we help each other out.'

'So I should say yes if Panos asks to draw me naked, then?'

Thunderclouds rolled across his dark, expressive eyes. 'He better fucking not.'

They stared at each other, having backed themselves into their respective corners. Jesse cracked first.

'Forget I even suggested it,' he said, short and blunt, then turned and walked out of the room.

'Jesse,' she said, rounding the desk to the doorway, feeling ungrateful. 'I'm sorry . . .'

He moved to the deep butler's sink and threw his brushes in without turning around. 'Don't be. It's just a room.'

Winnie studied the stiff set of his shoulders, and the deep tan on the back of his neck from working in the olive grove. How could someone who went out of their way to keep their life as simple as possible be so stubbornly difficult to understand? She backed into the room again and closed the door with a soft click.

*

171

Shit. He'd handled that like a prize cock. Jesse chucked the brushes in the sink, furious with himself for not seeing how his behaviour was just more of the same old bollocks on repeat. He couldn't help himself, or so it would seem. Show him an artistic blonde, and he'd impose his will on her to the point where she cracked. Hot shame washed through his body at the idea that history could repeat itself, even after a dormant decade of kidding himself that he was past it. Had it been lying in the shadows waiting to catch him out all of that time? When he heard the door click open again a few minutes later, he didn't turn her way.

'Hey, Jesse.'

'Uh-huh?'

She didn't reply, just waited patiently for his attention. He knew he was being rude, but he was pissed with himself, and with her, and with just about every other damn thing he could think of right now.

'I looked at your drawing.'

Christ. He'd put his drawing of her on the easel in there. He'd intended it as a welcome gift, but given how things had panned out it was all kinds of inappropriate.

'I shouldn't have put it there,' he muttered, washing his hands. 'I'll move it later.'

Another protracted silence, and then, 'No . . . I'm glad you did. You see me differently from how I see myself.'

He could hear vulnerability in her quiet words, and, biting down on his lip, he finally turned to look at her.

Fuck.

Fuck.

Fuck.

She was naked.

He rubbed his hand over the two-day stubble on his jaw. 'You've taken your clothes off again.'

172

'Yes.'

She leaned her shoulder against the door frame and crossed her arms lightly beneath her breasts. Frankly, it didn't help him at all.

'I want you to draw me again,' she said. 'I want to feel like the woman on the easel in there.'

'Winnie,' he murmured, walking towards her. God, she was too lovely. His artist's eye saw a study of curves and slopes, and his body reacted to her as a man.

'Don't say no,' she said, watching his face. 'Tell me how to pose for you. Draw me again.' He noticed how tightly her fingers dug into her upper arms, giving her away even though she was trying so hard to look relaxed. 'Please?'

'Don't you already know?' he said, refusing to drop his eyes from hers as he crossed the room, even though there was just a couple of feet between them now and he could practically feel the heat from her skin. 'You *are* her, Winnie. You don't need me or anyone else to validate you.' He took a step closer, within touching distance. 'I'm sorry if I made you feel manipulated. I didn't mean for you to feel that way.'

'I know,' she said. 'I want what you have, Jesse. I want to feel free, to be bohemian and liberated from the complications and strings of conventional romance.'

The light of hope in her eyes lasered into all of his dark corners, a main beam sweeping through his body, finding his secrets, exposing him for the fraud he was. He'd been a fully paid-up member of the 'fake it till you make it' brigade, so much so that he'd believed his own hype. He'd sold Winnie a pup, and now here she was fully invested, out on a limb and exposed, and here he was feeling like a con-artist selling snake oil.

He was close enough to smell the summer scent of sun

173

cream on her skin, her only protection against him. It was nowhere near enough. If she knew the truth, she'd wear chainmail.

'I can't,' he said. His fingers ached to trace the criss-cross of pale strap marks in the gold-dust of her shoulders.

'Yes, you can.' She backed into the room behind her and perched on the desk. 'Like this?' She moved from the desk to the chair, leaning back so her hair trailed down and her breasts rose up.

'Not like that. Christ, Winnie.' He dragged his hands down his face. This was torture.

'How then? Tell me.'

She wasn't going to let this go. He could tell her to put her clothes back on, of course, but he knew her well enough now to know that it would wound her fragile pride, probably enough to send her running and keep her away. She'd taken too many knocks already from Needledick; he wasn't prepared to be the next fool who hurt her.

But to do as she asked compromised him in ways he hadn't imagined possible the first time he'd asked her to let her draw him. In trying to bring her into the sunlight, he'd inadvertently opened up wounds so deep in his own chest that he constantly expected to look down and find his shirt soaked in blood. He was sweating at night, fighting nightmares in his sleep, and his work rate was taking the hit. He'd worked on only one sculpture over the last weeks, and it wasn't even close to the commission he was supposed to be working on for a gallery in Chicago.

'OK,' he said. 'OK.'

Her shoulders relaxed as she sat forward in her chair and rested her head in her cupped hands, elbows on the desk. Behind her on the easel, he could see his drawing of her

174

perched on the rock outside. She surrounded him, and she didn't realise it but she was threatening to engulf him.

'If we're going to do this, I want you to choose your own pose.'

He left the room and slowly gathered the things he needed. Sketchbook. Pencils. His sanity. Swallowing hard, he headed back into the room.

'Is this OK?'

Winnie had tried out the desk, and then the office chair, and eventually she'd decided that if he wanted her to pose herself, then she was going to throw caution to the wind. She wasn't going to hide or pose in a strategic way to minimise exposure. The whole point of this was supposed to be liberation, after all.

Jesse had paused in the doorway, and she turned her eyes to him as she waited for his verdict.

'You have no idea how much I'd love to sculpt you exactly like that.'

His dark eyes travelled across the length of her reclining body, taking in the way she'd draped herself sideways over the armchair, head thrown back, one arm outstretched behind her, her legs tossed carelessly over the other arm as if she were completely relaxed after a long soak in the bath. She'd angled her body slightly into the room, hiding nothing from his gaze or his pencil.

He laid his things down on the desk, came to her and touched her outstretched hand.

'Relax your fingers,' he whispered. 'Imagine you're alone.'

Concentrating, Winnie let her arm drop and go heavy.

'Lift your head up for a second,' he said, sliding his hand under the weight of her hair when she did and trailing it over the arm of the chair.

'Arch your back a tiny bit more?' he whispered, and for the briefest of seconds he slid his hand into the gap between the small of her back and the chair and pressed his finger-tips lightly against her skin to show where. 'That's perfect.'

His gaze moved to her legs, and with the same light touch he eased one knee inwards towards him. 'Like this,' he said. 'It accentuates the curve of your hip.'

Winnie feared that her skin wasn't strong enough to stop her heart from beating out of her chest, and that he must know from the flush on her neck that his quiet words and every feather-light touch set a new fire beneath her skin. She watched him silently retreat to collect his sketchpad and pencils, and then drag the easel around to position it so he could stand and study her.

'You can close your eyes if you want to,' he said as he started to draw. 'Imagine you're alone and completely relaxed.'

Winnie didn't close her eyes. 'I don't want to imagine I'm anywhere but here.'

Jesse paused for a second and swallowed, his pencil hovering over the page.

'Tell me how you feel right now,' he said, changing tack as he resumed drawing.

It was Winnie's turn to stall. 'Womanly,' she said eventually.

'Womanly is good,' he murmured, shading. 'What else?'

'Brave,' she said. 'I feel like I'm braver now than I was when I first came to the island.'

'As I recall it, you were pretty brave coming over to take your donkey back on that first afternoon,' he said drily. Had that really only been a little more than a month ago? So much had happened, it felt like far longer.

'Dutch courage,' she said, smiling a little at the memory.

He nodded absently, studying her and then returning to the easel again.

'So. Womanly and brave,' he said. 'What else?'

He'd reverted to his safe ground, the place where he was the in-charge guy who knew how to be cool, and she the pupil being taught freedom.

'Sexy,' she said quietly. 'I think I feel sexy.'

Jesse laid his pencil down and stared at her.

'You *think* you do?'

She nodded, and he crossed the room, slow and assured, and dropped onto his knees in front of the chair.

'Don't just think it, Winnie. Know it. You were right earlier. You're Venus,' he said. 'So very, incredibly sexy.'

'Jesse?' she said. 'Will you do something for me?'

He nodded, wordless.

'Take off your T-shirt?'

He looked for a moment as if he might refuse, and then he reached down with one hand and pulled the hem up and over his head and chucked it aside. *Jesus bloody God.* They went from artist and model to man and woman in the space of a heartbeat. His skin was drenched in sunshine, and countless hours of sculpting and olive farming had given him fireman-worthy shoulders and lean biceps to match.

The atmosphere in the room had already been charged, but Winnie thought that if someone struck a match right now the whole barn would go up in smoke.

'I want you to teach me,' she said. 'Teach me how to turn my head and my heart off.'

'I'd need to touch you for that,' he said, trouble in his dark gaze.

Winnie stared at him. 'I know.'

For a moment he closed his eyes, and he looked at Winnie like a man on his knees saying his prayers.

177

'It's not a conscious thing,' he said, opening his eyes again. 'You still need to let yourself feel everything, to experience it all, to be in the moment.'

She nodded, otherwise completely still, and then he dipped forward and placed a kiss over her navel. She felt the heat of his mouth, and the brush of his hair on her skin as it fell forwards, and then the skim of his lips as he drifted up over her ribcage.

'Don't move,' he murmured, raising his eyes to hers as his kissed the lower swell of her breasts. She watched his mouth, his slow tenderness, breathing in sharply when he closed his lips over her nipple. His eyelids drifted down, a dark sweep of lashes on his cheek as his tongue slid over her flesh, making her moan lightly because it felt so damn good to be this wanted.

His fingers moved to close over her other breast, giving her more, enjoying her more.

'See?' he said, when he opened his eyes. 'It's OK to feel good, Winnie.'

He held her breasts in his hands as he spoke, his tanned skin stark against hers as he watched her face. He took his time, and suddenly it wasn't enough any more and Winnie swung herself around and dropped to her knees on the floor in front of him. Wordlessly he pulled her up against his bare chest and pressed his mouth into her hair, then filled his fists with it, twisting his fingers in the strands to tip her head back and kiss her, all at once fierce and hot.

'Jesse,' she breathed, loving the hardness and heat of his shoulders and back as she explored him at last with her hands. The press of his naked body against hers had changed everything. From tender to hot, from measured to frenzied, from thinking to feeling, from sensual to sexual. His chest heaved against hers, his hands stroking down the rise and fall of her spine to cup her ass and move her forwards to straddle his thighs.

'I want you,' he whispered, holding her to him with his arm around her waist. 'More than you know. More than I should.'

She knew how much he wanted her; the hard heat of him nestled between her thighs told her so.

And then he kissed her again, changing down through the gears to barely moving and open-mouthed, his sighs on hers, more exquisite and honest and raw than Winnie knew kisses could be.

She wrapped her arms around his head, closing them into a warm, intimate space where only their mouths mattered. It wasn't just kissing. It was giving, and feeling, an intense, overwhelming closeness, all-encompassing and spiritual, the slow slide of his tongue over hers. He spoke her name, stroked her breasts sometimes. She cried a little, but it didn't matter, and when his fingers moved between her legs she rocked with him, biting his lip when he found her rhythm. There wasn't any conscious thought in Winnie's head. Just sensation, just bone-deep pleasure, just heat and need and want and then almost painful need again, because she was so close. He knew, of course, holding her steady, licking into her mouth when her body clenched around his fingers.

Cradling his hand around the nape of her neck, he massaged her as her hips began to jerk.

'Look at me,' he whispered, and when she opened her eyes he met her gaze with deep, abiding understanding of what this was to her. The end, and the beginning. The hint of an incredulous smile tipped his lips, and then hers too, until she almost laughed with the giddy, exhilarated, hell-yes thrill of it all.

'I told you,' he said against her hair, wrapping his arm tightly around her body until there was no space. 'Didn't I tell you that it's better?'

Winnie buried her face in his neck, her mouth moving over the warm crook that smelled of pine needles and picnics at dusk and of him. 'Yes,' she said. 'Yes.'

She said yes because he'd made her feel like a goddess, and because she'd never felt so in touch with her own body before, and because for probably the first time in her life she'd completely let herself go.

The realisation came at a cost; the life she'd thought was perfect with Rory had been only half-lived. And the realisation gave her release, because from here on in she wasn't going to do anything by halves. Life was here, and now, and heady, and goddamn brilliant. It was blue skies and sand beneath her toes, it was an adventure with the best friends she'd been lucky enough to have beside her all her life, and it was embracing life gasp by delicious, exhilarating gasp.

'Thank you,' she murmured, wrapping her arms around the firm, solid breadth of Jesse's deeply tanned shoulders, somewhere between holding him and clinging to him. 'I feel like you should hang a best orgasm medal around my neck.'

Laughter rumbled in his chest as it pressed against hers. 'Solid gold, Legs. Solid gold.'

Bright shafts of moonlight lit the dusty path when Jesse walked Winnie back to Villa Valentina at a little after eleven.

'The skies here seem so much bigger than they are back in England,' she said, looking up at the vast, star-studded velvet overhead.

'Same skies,' he said. 'You just can't see it for all the other crap. Another of the many reasons I stay here.'

She nodded. The list was getting longer every day.

'Can I ask you something?' he asked, shoving his hands deep in the pockets of his jeans.

Winnie nodded. 'Shoot.'

'Do you ever miss your old life?'

She thought about it. 'I don't think it's been long enough for me to answer, really. I don't miss living back with my parents and sleeping in my single bed, but I'm not sure that's what you're asking me, is it?'

He shrugged, kicking a brick along in front of him. 'It's a big thing, being married, that's all. And it's a big thing when you're suddenly not any more.'

Winnie slowed as the familiar outline of the villa came into view, the sound of the sea washing onto the sand a soothing backdrop to their quiet conversation. 'Are you asking me for my thoughts, or telling me yours?'

Jesse looked away, slowing up at the edge of the terrace. 'Just idle conversation, I guess.' He dug his hand in the pocket of his jeans and pulled out the small silver key. 'Will you take it now? If you decide you don't want to use it then that's fine, but keep it anyway, just in case. You never know when you're gonna need a bolthole.' He tucked her hair behind her ear. 'If you ever have to run, run to me.'

Winnie shook her head, looking at the floor. 'Damn it, Jesse. For a man so insistent on keeping things simple, you sure know how to make them feel complicated. Do you even know how romantic that was?'

He dropped his arm around her waist and pulled her close, sliding his hand into her hair. 'I prefer to think of it as practical.'

'It was romantic.'

'Are you still wearing those rose-tinted glasses, Legs?'

He held her face in his hands. 'Take them off and crush them beneath your foot. You don't need romance and sentiment spun around things to make them real.'

He kissed her then, soul-deep, making a lie of everything he'd just said.

'Do you want to come in?' she whispered, sliding her hands inside the back of his T-shirt.

He kissed her again. 'Yes. But I'm not going to.'

'Is that the first rule of living an uncomplicated life? No spooning?'

He shook his head at her, his hand around her nape as he kissed her forehead.

'Go inside.'

She stroked his jaw. 'Can I still come and visit my donkey?'

'I think we both know you were always visiting me.'

'So vain,' she said, backing away. 'So sure of yourself.'

'Goodnight, Legs.' He winked, then turned away and walked down the lane without glancing back.

Winnie watched him until he was out of sight, then wound her way around the side of the villa and saw Frankie flat out on one of the sunbeds facing the beach, with Seth Manson alongside her on another. They were talking, gazing up at the stars and laughing softly. Winnie tiptoed inside, made her way up to the top floor and tapped on Stella's door. She heard footsteps and then it swung open.

'I'm glad you're awa–' Her words dropped off, because it wasn't Stella. It was Angelo who opened the door, dressed only in Stella's badly fitting silk robe. 'I'll just . . . goodnight,' she said, half laughing, almost running for the safety of her own room. She climbed into bed, leaving the French doors open so she could hear the sea, and as she closed her eyes she wondered how they'd all wound up spending their evening with someone so extraordinarily perfect for their individual needs right then.

Stella might think she wanted a Scandinavian puppy, but a big, bad Greek wolf had her in his sights tonight.

Frankie thought romance was a thing of the past for her, yet right at that very moment she was stargazing with one of the most lusted-after men on the planet.

And as for Winnie . . . she was discovering her inner Venus, and how twenty seconds of insane courage really could lead to a whole evening of bone-melting bliss. Thank you, Matt Damon, she muttered. You might have bought a zoo, but we bought our own slice of paradise, and I don't have to wrangle lions as a result.

And that's how it happened that they all took their eye off the ball, and no one noticed Mikey Miller drink himself into a stupor on island gin and then pass out in the garden with a lit cigarette in his hand.

CHAPTER FOURTEEN

'Christ! Winnie, get up!'

Someone was yelling and banging on her door.

Stella was yelling and banging on her door.

'Win! Wake up! Fire!'

Fire? Her feet hit the smooth floorboards before her eyes were even properly open, her heart thumping with panic. Struggling to focus, she squinted at her watch. Half past midnight. She could only have been asleep for half an hour or so.

'What? Where?' she shouted, dragging her robe on over her slip as she half ran, half stumbled across the bedroom and yanked her door open. Stella had already disappeared; Winnie could hear her footsteps receding down the stairs at a pace.

'There's a fire in the garden!' Stella shouted back up. 'Have you seen Frank? She's not in her room.'

'She was outside when I came home. On the loungers by the beach!'

Winnie caught up with Stella at the bottom of the stairs, still barefoot.

'Back garden.' Stella gripped her arm tight for a second and then belted off down the hallway towards the kitchen. 'Angelo's already outside.'

Winnie followed, shoving her feet into her Birkis by the back door, terrified by the bright orange glow on the far side of the garden.

'Buckets!' Stella shouted, panicked. 'We need buckets or something! Anything!'

Behind her, Winnie heard footsteps, and seconds later Frankie and Seth appeared around the side of the building, all of them frantically searching for buckets or anything that might help.

'Call Panos!' Angelo yelled, running back with the only bucket to refill it at the garden tap. 'Hosepipes, we need a lot more water now! The whole damn garden will catch at this rate.'

'I'm here, I'm here,' someone panted, and they turned to see Panos dressed only in Y-fronts and a vest, unravelling a tangled hosepipe and handing the tap end to Angelo. 'I saw the flames from my bedroom window.'

'Thank God,' Winnie said, hugging him fast and hard. 'Thank you for coming so quickly.'

'Mikey!' Seth shouted suddenly, taking off across the garden towards the flames. Angelo ran behind dragging the hose, with all three of the women unravelling it behind him frantically as he went. Winnie's eye's tracked Seth to the body on the grass.

Oh my God, there was a body on the grass.

Seth dropped to his knees beside Mikey at the same moment as Angelo inadvertently doused him with a blast of cold water, waking him from his gin slumber with a violent jerk into sitting position.

'What the . . .?' he mumbled, scrubbing his hands over

his face as he stared at the flames not far from where he'd passed out. 'I'm soaking wet.' He frowned, peeling his damp T-shirt away from his ribs as he squinted around and joined the dots. 'Oh fuck.'

Seth dragged him up onto his feet and deposited him unceremoniously over by the villa. Winnie heard him mutter, 'Stupid drunken bastard,' as he propped him against the wall before running back across to see if he could help. Thankfully, the now plentiful water supply seemed to be doing the trick; Angelo had things mostly under control already, the worst of the flames dying out.

Panos put his arm around Winnie's shoulders. 'Not so bad,' he said, soothingly. 'Could have been much worse.'

Winnie nodded grimly. It could. The whole place could have gone up with them all inside it. Jesus, with the amount of alcohol in the cellar it would have been a fireball in minutes. Angelo gave the whole area an extra drenching just to be certain, and then gave Seth the nod to shut off the water.

'It's out,' he said, stepping backwards to survey the burnt black bushes and shrubs. 'But you've lost pretty much everything on this side of the garden.' He waved his hand along the sodden swathe of land and then unwittingly wiped it over his face, daubing himself with smoky charcoal streaks.

'Thank God you were here,' Stella said, wrapping her arm around his middle. 'Our hero.'

He dropped a kiss on the top of her head and murmured something in Greek that had Panos lifting his eyebrows.

'Well, I think we could all do with a drink,' Winnie said wearily. 'Come in?'

Panos looked down at his underwear. 'I think I should say no.'

'You're sure?' Frankie planted a kiss on his cheek. 'You're our hero too, dashing across the beach to help. We owe you, Panos.'

He shrugged and nodded brusquely, then threw his hose-pipe over his shoulder as he walked away. 'It's the Skelidos way. We look out for our neighbours.'

Winnie wrapped her arms around her midriff, reminded of the fact that Jesse had said something very similar not very long ago.

'Did I miss something?'

Jamie Harte wandered out of the kitchen door, obviously having just woken up. He looked at his bandmate slumped on his backside by the wall, and then over towards Seth.

'Take him up and chuck him in his bed, would you? I might knock his fucking head off his shoulders otherwise,' Seth said.

Jamie sighed heavily, sniffing the acrid air and surveying the soaked, burnt-out half of the garden. 'Mikey?'

Seth nodded. There was an inevitability about the look that passed between them, and Winnie wondered how they'd managed to keep the fact that Mikey Miller was a functioning alcoholic out of the press for so long. It was almost ironic that they'd booked themselves into a secret gin distillery, presumably in the hope of lying low while Mikey cleaned his act up.

They all sat out on the front terrace for an hour or so, too hyped to sleep any time soon after the fire.

'We'll pay to get it all put right, that goes without saying,' Seth said, nursing a tumbler of brandy between his hands. 'But I need to ask you all a favour.'

'You want us to keep Mikey's secret,' Stella guessed, stirring her G&T with the rosemary sprig.

187

Seth nodded, staring into the amber depths of his glass. 'He's been clean for more than seven years now, but these last couple of months have been hard on him. Family stuff. We didn't realise he'd started drinking again. I missed the signs.'

'Come on, man,' Angelo said, his mouth a bitter twist. 'He's a big boy. Every man has to be accountable for himself.'

'Impressive as they are, you don't have to take the weight of everything on your rock-star shoulders,' Stella tried, more gently.

Seth huffed. 'He's always been the kid brother in the band. Old habits die hard, I guess.' For different reasons, his words held resonance with everyone around the table.

'There's something else,' Seth said. 'After tonight, I think we misjudged how long we might need to stay. I'm thinking . . . a couple months, maybe? Time for him to get his shit together again.'

Winnie nodded, thinking about the handful of bookings they'd taken already. 'That's fine. We can do that.'

'Not just our rooms though,' Seth added. 'We'd need to block book the whole place; if word gets out that we're here and he's drinking again the island will be crawling in hours.'

The three women exchanged concerned looks.

'We've taken a handful of bookings for the next few weeks already,' Winnie said. 'Let me look at the diary tomorrow and see what we can do.'

'We'd pay well for the privilege,' Seth said, placing his empty glass down as he stood up and rolled those fabulous rock-star shoulders. 'The privacy here is something pretty special.'

Raising his hand in goodnight, he wandered back inside

the villa, and Angelo took his cue to do the same, planting a kiss on Stella's neck and murmuring something in her ear that made her eyebrows slide into her fringe.

Winnie moved to sit alongside Stella and Frankie on the bench overlooking the dark, moonlit sea. 'That was a close call,' she said. 'We could have lost it all and we've barely got going.'

Frankie nodded, sighing heavily. 'Made me realise how much I already love this place.'

'Mikey bloody Miller,' Stella grumbled, pulling leaves one by one from the rosemary stick and dropping them into her empty glass.

'Thank God the donkey wasn't in the garden,' Frankie said, leaning slightly forward to look at Winnie.

Winnie nodded, philosophical. 'I don't think he's ever coming back.'

Stella looked at her. 'Have you fallen out?'

They all knew that they weren't just talking about the donkey any more.

Winnie shook her head. 'Nothing like that. I just understand him a bit more now. He's perfectly content with his life as it is.'

Frankie frowned. 'But you're still going to visit regularly, right?'

'We seem to have reached an agreement, yes.'

'Does that mean that you're shagging?' Stella said, bumping shoulders with a sly laugh.

'Me and the donkey? That's disgusting, Stell.'

Stella rolled her eyes. 'I'll take that as a yes.'

'Do it, Win,' Frankie said suddenly. 'Just bloody do it. He's the perfect antidote to Rory.'

Both Winnie and Stella looked at her. 'Somebody's fired up.'

Frankie shook her head. 'I'm not especially, but we're thirty-four-year-old women. That's young! We should be able to do whatever we like with whoever we like without feeling bad about it.'

'I know,' Winnie said, thinking as much about Frankie and Seth as herself and Jesse. 'So what's the deal with Seth? You two looked pretty cosy out here when I got back from Jesse's.'

Frankie screwed her nose up. 'Isn't that ridiculous? How can I have been stargazing with Seth Manson tonight?' She paused, scratching her short, deep-red fingernails along the grooves of the driftwood table. 'He nearly kissed me, just before the fire.'

'Christ,' Stella whispered. 'Do you know how many women would literally kill right now to swap places with you?'

Frankie let out a nervous laugh. 'Nothing happened, not really. We were just talking about life, and exes, and complications. Listening to him, I wouldn't want to be famous; everybody around him has an agenda. He likes that I'm just normal, I think,' she said, nodding towards the empty loungers on the edge of the beach. 'We were sitting down there, and I turned to say something at the same time as he did, and suddenly we were nose to nose.'

Winnie clasped her hand over her heart. 'I can't bear that you didn't get to snog your hero. One way or another, you have to do it tomorrow.'

Frankie laughed. 'Maybe I'll have a gin after we've tested out our batch and see where the Dutch courage gets me.'

They fell silent, and then Stella shot up onto her feet.

'Shit! That sodding berry bush was on that side of the garden!'

*

190

It was burnt to a crisp.

'Oh no,' Winnie whispered, her hand over her mouth. 'Ajax said it was sacred to the islanders.'

'We'll just have to grow another one,' Stella said.

'It was the only one on the island.' Frankie huffed and shook her head. 'Crap, this is really bad. They're all going to blame us. It was supposed to be a symbol of good luck.'

'How good is our current supply of berries in the cellar?' Stella asked, quick-thinking as ever.

Frankie's brow furrowed in thought. 'Not great, I don't think. We were supposed to harvest the berries in September, it only fruits once a year.'

'Great.'

'We could try using an alternative?' Winnie said. 'Strawberries are similar? Or blackberries?'

The others didn't look convinced.

'Let's hope it doesn't come to it,' Stella said. 'For now, let's try to keep it under our hats that the bush was a casualty of the fire while we work out what we can do.'

Trooping wearily inside, they locked the doors and headed up to bed.

'Christ, what's that noise?'

Frankie was first through the kitchen door the next morning, throwing the bolt as Winnie and Stella schlepped behind her, not much after six o'clock. The noise sounded like a strangled cat, and was definitely coming from the garden.

'Oh God, what if something was in the fire and we didn't notice it in the dark?' Stella said, cringing.

'Or some*one*,' Winnie said, hardly daring to look.

'Oh crap,' Frankie said, peering around the back door

191

cautiously and then clicking it closed again before she was spotted.

'Good news or bad news?' she said.

'Good?' Winnie said, at the same time as Stella said, 'Bad?'

'Well, the good news is nothing died or got injured, as far as I can see.'

'But . . .?'

Frankie opened the door again, wider this time so that they could all see out into the garden.

'Hero?' Winnie said. 'Hero, what's wrong?'

Their elderly cleaner was on her knees on the grass, wailing at the burnt-out scene before her.

Frankie crouched beside her and put an arm around her shoulders. 'What's the matter?' she asked, trying to convey the question with her eyes and hand gestures. 'Are you OK?'

Hero looked up at them all one by one, and then back at the burnt-out garden, and beat her hands on the floor, starting up the racket again.

'Sshh,' Stella said, touching Hero's shoulder and then pointing at the upstairs bedrooms and making a sleeping gesture with both of her hands pressed together under her ear as a pillow.

Hero seemed to take note. It was as if someone had pressed her mute button; she continued to beat her fists and then raise her head and wail, but silently. If anything, it was odder.

'What do you think she's doing?' Winnie whispered.

'Praying?' Stella suggested.

'Oh jeez, I know what it is,' Frankie said. 'It's the burning bush.'

'Shit. Yes.' Stella gazed at the twiggy black bush. 'I might join her.'

192

'She can't tell anyone else,' Winnie said. 'We need to tell her to keep her mouth shut.'

'Yeah, because that's going to work,' Stella said. 'We can barely string a sentence together between us.'

Someone behind them coughed, and they turned to find Angelo listening to them from the doorway.

'What's so special about the bush?' he asked, seemingly oblivious to the fact that he was wearing Stella's pink and white candy-striped robe. Given his mostly austere appearance, it was comical enough to make Winnie look at the floor to hide her laughter.

'It was the only one on the island. People thought it brought good luck and prosperity.'

He tutted. 'You girls are going to be unpopular then.' He looked at Hero. 'You think this is bad? You wait until there's a queue right across the beach to come and view it. We love a good tragedy.'

'You have to help us,' Stella said, crossing to tug him outside by the hand. 'Please, tell Hero it has to be a secret?'

'Why would I do that?'

'Er, because I asked you to?' Stella said, her hackles up. It was all very well letting him be domineering and kinkily alpha in the bedroom, but she was no shrinking violet. She was a woman who got what she wanted.

'I don't understand,' he said. 'Why can't you just plant a new tree? It'll regrow again in a few years.'

'Years?' Winnie yelped. 'We need the berries in three months!'

Angelo frowned at the same time as Stella tried to surreptitiously draw her finger across her neck to shut Winnie up.

Frankie leaped into the breach. 'For desserts,' she said. 'Cake.'

Angelo looked from one to the other, clearly not convinced. Then he shrugged, and with a sigh, he crossed the grass barefoot to relay their message to Hero.

Frankie, Winnie and Stella stood by the back door in the already warm early sunshine.

'He looks hot in my robe,' Stella said, looking at his long, tanned legs. The robe was knee-length on her, and barely mid-thigh-length on her much taller lover.

'How doesn't he know about the gin?' Winnie asked. 'You had sex in the bloody cellar, for God's sake!'

'He wasn't looking at the walls, trust me,' Stella muttered archly. 'I just said we let Panos use the cellar for storage because he's short on space at the bar.'

'And he believed you?' Frankie checked.

Stella nodded. 'Of course.' She'd asked casually leading questions over the days since to make sure her story hadn't planted any seeds of interest in his head, and so far he didn't seem remotely interested in the contents of the cellar. The Skelidos gin distillery had gone under the radar of the rest of the world for countless decades. She didn't want to be responsible for exposing it because she hadn't been able to resist jumping the bones of a hot-shot businessman from the mainland.

It appeared that Angelo had managed to convey their requests to Hero, because she stopped wailing and drew herself up to her full diminutive height and smoothed her dress and apron. Turning her big, baleful eyes on them as she edged past, she pulled an imaginary zip across her lips for slow, dramatic effect.

'I think she got the message,' Stella said.

'She did,' Angelo said. 'And now I have a message for you too.' He leaned in and murmured something quietly in her ear, making her eyes open wide.

194

'Can you ladies do without me for half an hour?' she grinned. The question was academic. Angelo picked her up and threw her over his good shoulder as he stalked from the kitchen, making her screech and slap him on the ass as he left the room.

Out on the deserted beach an hour later, Frankie unrolled her yoga mat and moved through a series of deliberate stretches, clearing her head of everything but the pattern of her breathing, concentrating on getting her poses right in the hope that they'd grant her some serenity. For Marcia, she'd truly tried to cast herself in the role of brave adventurer since they'd left the familiarity of home shores. She wanted to honour her friend's memory in the best way possible, and that meant chucking away her spreadsheet mentality and stepping outside her comfort zone.

Sensing movement behind her, she sent a small smile to Angelo, who'd clearly concluded his business with Stella and thrown on shorts and a T-shirt for their morning session.

'The range of movement in your joint seems to be increasing,' she observed, as he turned with her to look out over his injured shoulder.

He nodded briefly, not engaging in conversation. Frankie was glad of his quiet company; yoga practice for her was all about peace and harmony, not chatting and competing.

Kneeling on all fours, she walked her hands back to assume the downward dog position, and looking between her legs she spotted a third person laying down a towel to join them. *Seth*. He raised a casual hand when he caught her eye, and Frankie smiled back, small and tight. So much for inner peace and harmony, she thought. How the hell am I supposed to do sun salutations with one of the hottest men on the planet behind me looking at my ass? Does it look huge in these sweatpants? All these thoughts and more whizzed through her suddenly active brain, so much so that she almost felt as if it was pointless to continue. She might have allowed herself to stop, but then she spotted Hero scuttling out of the villa, her shy eyes full of trepidation as she stood at the back of the others and tried to assume the same pose as Frankie.

These people need me. The thought struck her unexpectedly. Angelo was healing, Seth was trying to escape the stresses of his outlandish life, and Hero . . . well, she'd had a traumatic morning and a calming bit of yoga might be just the thing.

'You've got this, Frank,' she whispered. 'You've got this.'

And she had. Hadn't she spent the last eighteen years of her life being an active role model for the boys? Hadn't she spent hundreds of hours on the yoga mat at the local community centre back home, ring-fencing those precious sessions as necessary for her sanity? She'd got this.

Breathing with purpose, she started to move.

A little after lunch, all three of them stood behind the reception desk with the fan on full speed.

'That's it then, I think,' Stella said, crossing the final reservation off the booking sheet. 'All clear for the next two months to accommodate Seth's request for the whole place.'

They'd contacted the handful of holidaymakers who'd already made reservations and explained that unforeseen circumstances meant that they'd have to cancel their bookings, offering them a generous discount on a return visit and hints for other available accommodation over on Skiathos and Skopelos.

'I didn't enjoy that at all,' Winnie said. As it had turned out the people had been generally understanding and appreciative of a personal call rather than an email, but all the same she'd felt shabby for letting them down.

'Maybe we can think of something we can offer them, or send them some island gin as a gift?' Frankie suggested.

'Oh, I like that idea,' Winnie said, and then her face fell. 'The gin doesn't leave the island. Ajax's letter, remember?'

'Did somebody say gin?'

Mikey Miller strolled in from the terrace, fresh as a daisy aside from his bloodshot eyes.

'Mr Miller,' Stella said, cordial given the circumstances. 'You almost burnt our bed and breakfast down last night.'

He looked contrite, as well he might. 'My bad.' He tried out hangdog eyes and got nowhere. 'God, you're a tough crowd.'

He was lucky that Seth and Jamie followed him inside at that moment, because it was highly likely that Stella might have launched herself across reception at him.

'Well?' Seth said, staring at his friend.

Mikey looked at the ceiling.

'Have you done it yet?' Jamie Harte looked equally pissed off with his bandmate. Jamie was known to be the least fame-hungry of the three, a surfer who'd got lucky because he played guitar, could hold a note, and had been in the right place at the right time.

Mikey shuffled his feet and took off his baseball cap, revealing his razor-sharp haircut as he shuffled from foot to foot.

'I'm sorry for causing the fire,' he said, apologising in the manner of a schoolboy dragged back into a sweetshop to apologise for stealing gobstoppers. 'It was an accident and I promise it won't happen again.'

197

'Won't happen again?' Stella said, her voice rising an octave. 'Too right it won't. For the record I was against you staying on for the summer. You're lucky that these guys are kinder than I am.'

Seth brightened. 'We're good for it then?' He leaned across the desk and planted a smacker on Frankie's cheek. 'You're an angel.'

Frankie blushed, and then she froze, because someone new had just walked uncertainly into reception.

Gavin.

CHAPTER FIFTEEN

'Oh my God,' Frankie mouthed, subconsciously touching her face where Seth had kissed it.

'Oh shit me, Frank,' Stella whispered, and Winnie made the kind of sound you might when you stub your toe but are in public so can't swear like a sailor.

Their startled reactions to the newcomer weren't lost on Seth and the others, who all turned to review the new arrival with interest.

'Gav,' Frankie said, floundering as she walked around the desk to meet him halfway across the room. 'What . . .?' She ran out of words, because his presence here was so utterly out of place. 'Oh God! Is it one of the boys? What's happened?' She went from calm to instant heart-attack level in a blink, clutching his forearm like a vice.

'They're fine, the boys are fine,' he said, looking like a fish out of water, uncomfortable and wishing he were back in the safety of his bowl.

Frankie slowly released his arm and placed her hand over her beating heart while she calmed down. 'Thank God for that, you gave me the fright of my life.'

'I should probably have called,' he said, looking down. 'I just . . .' It was his turn to be lost for words to explain what the hell was going on. 'You look . . .' He stopped again, and scrubbed a hand over his dark hair. 'Different.'

Winnie grimaced. It was hideous to watch, so God only knew how Frankie was taking it. Stepping forward, she gave Gav a brief hug and said hello, then turned to Frankie with a 'what can we do?' face.

'Why don't you guys go down to the kitchen?' she suggested, plumping for the only place she could think of that wasn't a public space or Frankie's bedroom.

Frankie looked at her, glazed, and then seemed to see the sense in it and nodded.

'Come through,' she said, leading Gavin away from the others. He walked past the band, then backtracked and stopped, staring at Seth.

'Don't I know you, mate?' he asked, studying his face.

Seth shook his head, glancing quickly at Frankie. 'I don't think we've met, no.' He smiled vaguely.

Gav took another look, and then shook his head. 'It'll come to me,' he muttered, following Frankie down the hallway towards the kitchen.

'Her husband, I take it?' Seth asked thoughtfully, watching them leave.

Winnie nodded, troubled. 'Ex.'

Gavin's arrival was a bolt out of the blue, and for Winnie an unwelcome reminder that however much they thought they'd left their old lives behind, their old lives could turn up unexpectedly on their doorstep. Frank had taken it quite well, to be honest. If Rory arrived on Skelidos, there was every chance he'd go home in a box.

'Hm.'

'Sorry?' She tuned back in and realised that she'd missed whatever Seth had just said.

He shrugged. 'Doesn't matter.' Turning to give his band members the nod to follow him, he headed back upstairs to their rooms.

Down in the cellar a couple of hours later, Stella and Winnie sat Frankie down on the stool and huddled around her. They'd put Gavin in one of the owner's accommodation bedrooms, because now the band had booked the place out they were officially full for the summer. The block booking suited them because it meant that they could stay in their rooms on the top floor, and thankfully it now also meant that Frankie could truthfully tell her ex-husband that he couldn't possibly stay on.

This was the first chance the three of them had had to talk privately since Gav's arrival.

'It comes to something when we have to meet underground to speak freely,' Stella said, looking at Frankie. 'What's going on, Frank?'

Frankie puffed her fringe, shaking her head with an expression that clearly said, 'I don't have a bloody clue.'

'I can't believe he's here,' she said, baffled. 'I could count all the random things Gav's ever done on one hand, and then this? It's just so unlike him.'

'What has he said?' Winnie asked, perplexed.

'Not enough,' Frankie said, twisting her hands in her lap. 'He wanted to see where I was living. Fancied some sunshine. Thought we should stay in touch because of the boys. That sort of thing.'

'Has he not heard of the Internet?' Stella said.

'I know,' Frankie murmured. 'I don't know what to think.'

'Well, I'll tell you what I think.' Stella pulled a bottle of their first attempt at distilling gin out from the shelves and put it down on the workbench. 'I think he's seen where you live now, and you should shake his hand and send him packing to find his sunshine somewhere else. You almost snogged Seth Manson last night, remember?'

'As if I could forget,' Frankie sighed, touching her fingers against her cheek again. 'I *could* do that. I could ask him to leave, and I'm sure he'd go, but I'd feel crap about it. We're still trying to be friends, you know? And we have to stay that way because of the boys.'

Winnie nodded. 'Friends is good.' Friends was something she was never likely to achieve with Rory; it was difficult to think amicable thoughts about him when she was still in the planning-the-perfect-murder stage of healing after his infidelity. Would that ever end? she sometimes wondered. Would she ever reach the fabled acceptance stage? She couldn't imagine it yet. The woman he'd copped off with should think herself lucky too, because she didn't escape Winnie's fantasy cull unscathed. Maybe the car they were shagging in rolled right off the edge of a really high, jagged cliff. Or maybe the ceiling fell in on the seedy pay-by-the-hour motel where they'd rented a room. There had been any number of scenarios, all with the same satisfying outcome.

'I said he could stay for a few days,' Frankie said, looking pained. 'What else was I supposed to do?'

'Bit of a shocker, though, wasn't it?' Winnie read through the distillation instructions and then pulled a funnelled sieve contraption from the shelf beneath the bench. 'I think we need this.'

'What will you do about Seth?' Stella asked.

'Come on.' Frankie's smile was wistful. 'That was never

202

going to be anything. We all know that. He's Seth Manson, and I'm me.'

Stella's brows snapped together. 'Don't do that.'

'It's true, Stell. He's from a different world. In fact he's so different he's practically another species.'

'Everyone's farts are just the same,' Stella pointed out. 'He's just a man.'

'Well, Gav's here now and he's not going anywhere for a few days,' Winnie said, ever the diplomat. 'Maybe just let the dust settle and see how things go. I don't think there's any handy guidance in women's magazines on what to do if your ex-husband and your favourite rock star are vying for your attention.'

'Oh, it's not like that with Gav,' Frankie said. 'That was over years back. You know that.'

Winnie nodded. 'I did. I do. But Frank . . . he's tracked you down on a desert island even though he probably knew that you might not be that thrilled to see him, and if my eyes don't deceive me, I'd say he's been working out.'

It was true. Gavin was a man who'd always enjoyed his food and his beer and he had the dad bod to prove it. Or rather he *had*, but there'd been decidedly less of him when he'd walked into reception that afternoon.

'I didn't notice,' Frankie said.

Winnie found that hard to believe, but didn't say as much. If Frankie wanted to indulge in a spot of selective blindness where her ex-husband was concerned, who was she to judge?

'Right,' she said, looking at Ajax's instructions for this step of the process. 'We have to double filter each bottle through this sieve, once into a bowl and then back into the bottle, and that's it.'

Frankie took a glass mixing bowl from the shelf. 'Hang on while I go upstairs and make sure this is clean.'

They watched her jog up the stairs, and then looked at each other.

'What do you think?' Winnie said.

Stella curled her lip. 'I think she's in trouble. She might think that Gav's visit is a friendship olive branch, but I'm not buying it. He wants something. He has to.'

Winnie knew Gavin quite well, well enough to not think quite as badly of him as Stella did.

'I think he's missed her.'

'He had her under his nose for seventeen years and I bet he still couldn't tell you the colour of her eyes without double-checking.'

Winnie felt almost sorry for him. He wasn't a rock star or a Greek alpha male, or even an Australian sculptor with take-me-to-bed eyes. He was going to find it tough to measure up around here.

'Here we go,' Frankie said, returning with the spotlessly clean bowl. 'Let's crack out our first ever bottle of Bad Fairy Gin.'

'You do it, Win.' Stella pushed the bottle across the bench towards Winnie, uncharacteristically nervous as she lined the funnel up over the bowl Frankie was holding steady on the bench.

Winnie picked the bottle up, turned it a few times for luck, and then twisted the top.

'Sniff it,' Frankie said, almost breathless with anticipation.

Winnie put the bottle under her nose and inhaled once, then went back in again for a second longer sniff.

'Smells OK?' she ventured, not brave enough to call it.

'Gawd, come on, strain it, will you,' Stella said. 'I'm dying here.'

Winnie tipped the bottle slowly, and they all watched the peachy pink spirit slosh into the funnel along with the botanicals.

Lifting the sieve, they all stared down into the now perfectly strained gin in the basin.

'Three straws?' Stella laughed.

'Let's put it back in the bottle and see if it looks like the normal ones.' Frankie placed the funnel into the neck of the bottle and balanced it carefully as Winnie tipped the contents of the bowl through it.

'Oh my God,' Stella laughed, giddy. 'Will you look at that!'

Winnie screwed the cap back on and they all stood back to admire their handiwork.

'We made gin,' Winnie said.

Frankie nodded. 'You know what we need to do now?'

'Taste it?' Stella said, crossing the fingers on both of her hands and screwing her eyes up tight like a kid.

'Yes indeedy,' Frankie laughed. 'Let's take it out onto the terrace and pour three ceremonial G&Ts with all of the trimmings, and mix one extra using the existing island gin so we can compare.'

'I always admire your dedication to a task,' Stella said as they filed up the cellar steps. 'I was all for necking it straight from the bottle.'

'Is this an invitation-only party or can anyone join?'

Winnie shielded her eyes with her hand and squinted up at Jesse as he strolled off the beach, a brown-paper-wrapped parcel under his arm.

'We have been working most of the day,' she said, instantly defensive after his barbs about not using her time constructively.

'And technically, we still are.' Stella gestured at the half-empty G&Ts on the table. 'This is no party, it's serious research.'

'Nice work if you can get it,' he said lightly.

'You can help us, actually,' Frankie said, patting the bench for him to sit.

He flicked a quick glance at Winnie and then dropped down, his long, deeply tanned legs stretched out in front of him.

'At your service,' he said, touching his brow in mock salute as he propped his parcel on the floor against the bench.

He had his beach-bum look on again today, Winnie noted, eyeing his faded Breton T-shirt and cut-offs. His skin was as nut-brown as any of the locals', his eyes as dark and glittering, his lashes almost obscenely long on a man.

At fairgrounds as a child Winnie had always gravitated towards the helter-skelter, and being around Jesse was the closest she'd ever come to that feeling as an adult. He made her stomach dip, her heart swoop and her legs weak. But he also made her a little bit fearful, a tiny bit dizzy, and too much of him made her feel regretful. He made her laugh with pleasure, but you know that last bit at the end of the helter-skelter where you never stop quite as quickly as you hope and bang your back at the end? Jesse had that same sting in the tail sometimes, a sense of unreliability that had her on her guard. She just wasn't sure enough of him to be able to relax.

'I'm guessing from the pale-looking English guy sinking a beer over at Panos's bar that you guys have had a new arrival?'

Frankie frowned across the beach, and Winnie nodded to cover. 'Last minute thing for a few days.'

Stella saved them from the need to elaborate as she returned from the bar and placed two identical glasses down in front of Jesse.

He nodded in approval. 'Why have one G&T when you can have two?'

'You need to test them both and see if there's any difference,' Winnie said. They all sat forward a little; so far they'd decided they were distillery gurus, but they needed an impartial islander's viewpoint to be sure. Jesse would have to do.

'That's it? Just drink them both?'

'Well, you don't have to sink them like it's a drinking competition,' Winnie said.

Jesse inspected both glasses, leaning one way and then the other then lowering his head to look through them and inspect the colour.

'They look the same.'

Stella silently high-fived Frankie and threw a wink at Winnie.

'Does it matter which I try first?'

'Just get on with it,' they all said at once.

He looked perturbed. 'Are all English women this bossy?'

'Yes. Drink or die,' Winnie said. 'You choose.'

He picked up one of the glasses. 'Seeing as you asked so nicely.'

Taking a moment to sniff it, he closed his eyes and sucked the neon-pink straw Stella had supplied.

Sliding the glass back onto the table, he nodded slowly, snapping his eyes open again. 'Spot on.'

Winnie and Frankie looked at Stella, because she was the only one who knew which of Jesse's drinks was which.

'God, you and your poker face,' Winnie sighed, handing Jesse the other glass, this time with a DayGlo-green straw. 'And now this one?'

He did as he was told, most probably because he had very little choice with three pairs of eyes trained intently on him. After a minute of silent drinking and deliberation, he slid the glass back onto the table and looked at each of them knowingly.

'I see what's going on here,' he said. 'You're trying to get me drunk so you can tie me up in the broom cupboard and have your wicked ways with me. Bad form, girls.'

Winnie rolled her eyes. 'You should be so lucky. The gin, Jesse. Better? Worse?'

He frowned. 'Honestly?'

They all nodded, wordless and breathless.

'Exactly the same.'

Stella practically punched the air, Winnie clapped, and Frankie was so thrilled that she whooped and kissed Jesse on the cheek.

'You seem to do that a lot,' someone said, and they all turned to see Gavin had returned from his beer with Panos to find his ex-wife kissing a second stranger in as many days. Yesterday Seth, today Jesse. His words didn't suggest anger or malice; it was more of a melancholy observation followed by a small raise of his hand in greeting as he headed inside the shade of the villa. Robbed of her smile, Frankie excused herself and followed him in.

'That was odd,' Jesse said mildly.

'Stella!' They all squinted up into the sunshine, following the direction of Angelo's voice to the balcony at the top of the villa. He was naked aside from a tiny white towel slung around his hips, and he tapped his expensive watch and lifted his eyebrows. Stella had the grace to turn slightly pink, making a heart sign with her fingers at him until he shook his head and walked back inside.

'Scandalous man,' she muttered, gathering her drink. 'I better go and see what he wants.' Her affected boredom was at complete odds with her gleeful expression as she scarpered back inside.

Jesse handed Winnie one of his G&Ts and flung his arm along the back of the bench, letting his fingertips rest casually on her shoulder.

'Just you and me again, then, Legs,' he said, sliding his sunglasses over his eyes.

Winnie stretched out beside him and settled back with the drink in her hands.

'You're turning native.' He nodded down at her legs and bare feet. Over the weeks she'd turned from pale and interesting to sun-kissed gold, still strikingly different from his deep tan.

Winnie sipped her G&T, unsure if she was drinking their gin or Ajax's. Silently, she tried to decide if she felt awkward or not, given that the last time she was with Jesse she'd stripped off, asked him to draw her naked and then let him have his way with her. Eat your heart out, Kate Winslet, I haven't had to go down on a sinking ship to get this, she thought. But then she thought, I didn't get to shag Leonardo DiCaprio either. And then, most alarmingly of all, she thought that she might prefer Jesse over Leo anyway, so she took a huge gulp of her gin and practically choked herself.

'Are you nervous?' he asked, turning to study her over his glasses. 'You're giving off a nervous vibe.'

'It's because you're so devastatingly handsome,' she said, deadpan. 'I'd even choose you over Leonardo DiCaprio.'

A smirk ghosted his lips. 'You're not the first woman to say that.'

'I *so* am.'

He shrugged, discarding the straw and rosemary from his glass onto the table.

'I've brought you something.' He reached down and picked up the parcel he'd laid against the bench.

Winnie smiled, surprised. 'You have?'

He reached out and stilled her fingers when she started to tug on the strings to open it. Glancing back towards the villa, he cleared his throat. 'It, er . . . it might be better if you opened it in private.'

Realisation dawned as Winnie felt the familiar shape of a picture frame beneath the crisp paper. Caught between embarrassment and sudden, unfurling excitement, she faltered and bit her lip. She could head inside and open it alone, but it was a different option that had her heart banging.

'Will you, I mean, would you like to come up and help me hang it?' God, she could hardly meet his eyes, which was ridiculous given how close they'd been the night before.

'Are you inviting me up to see your etchings, Winnie?' Jesse asked, low and amused. 'I didn't have you down as that sort of girl.'

Winnie decided that embarrassment wasn't part of who she wanted to be any more.

'I think I might be.' She picked up the closest G&T, knocked it straight back and got to her feet. 'Come on.'

Winnie led him through the cool, quiet villa and up the stairs to the top landing.

'This one's mine,' she said, opening her door. 'It's the Bohemian Suite. Ajax thought I'd appreciate the art in here when he first met me.'

'And was he right?' Jesse asked, following her inside.

She closed the door softly behind him. 'Maybe. Or perhaps I'll hang something of my own in here instead.'

210

In answer, he laid the still wrapped picture down on her hastily made bed. 'Maybe you should take a look before you make any decisions,' he said. 'You might not like it.'

Unaccountably nervous, Winnie pulled on the twine and felt for the tape holding the paper together.

'Am I going to be shocked?' she asked, her fingers hovering on the paper.

'I don't know,' he said honestly, watching her hands. She sensed his nervousness too; first and foremost, he was an artist showing someone his work, and she knew from experience that that was never an easy thing to do. Add in the extra layer of intimacy because of the subject matter and what happened between them last night, and right now they were both as skittish as teenagers.

'I'm going to open it now,' she said, balling up the sticky tape between her fingers.

'OK.' He shrugged, aiming for cool and not quite pulling it off.

Slowly, Winnie pulled the paper back, one side first and then the other.

'It's upside down,' he said, stating the obvious as they both looked down at the hessian-backed frame.

She held in the smart answer on the tip of her tongue and carefully turned it over, then laid it down again on the paper. Jesse had framed his pencil and charcoal drawing in an ornate gilt frame, lending his already provocative subject a decadent, rococo air.

'What do you think?' he murmured, frowning. 'A little too heavy on shading here?' He traced his finger in the air over her hip.

She caught hold of his hand and moved it out of the way so she could study his drawing properly. It was from just yesterday; he must have worked for hours to layer in so much life and detail. He seemed to have captured more than her curves and her angles as she'd lounged across the chair with the arm flung above her head; he'd caught the essence of how she'd felt for a few hours with him. Braver. Womanly. In control.

'I think it's the woman I want to be,' she breathed eventually, because she didn't care one bit about the accuracy of his shading on her hip. What took her breath away was the devil-may-care attitude of the girl gazing back at her from the drawing; she had a look in her eyes that said, 'I'm sexy and we both bloody well know it.' She wasn't encumbered by her past or frightened of her future. She was totally in the moment, confident and relaxed in her own skin.

Jesse looked up from the painting to Winnie. 'This *is* who I see when I look at you,' he said softly.

'It's not who I see in the mirror.' She shook her head, staring at the drawing. The woman in Jesse's drawing might closely resemble her physically, but Winnie could only hope to identify with her attitude one day.

Jesse sighed, then caught hold of her hand and tugged her over to the grand cheval mirror standing in one corner of her room. Someone, Ajax maybe, had draped long strings of pearls around its old carved oak frame, a fitting boudoir mirror for the bohemian room.

'What are you doing?' she asked when he positioned her centrally in front of it, his hands lightly on her hips as he stood behind her.

'Showing you what you should see.'

Winnie met his unwavering gaze in the glass.

'Jesse . . .'

He shook his head, determined. 'Here's what's gonna happen next, Legs. You're gonna stop speaking now, and

212

listen to me. If at any point you feel the need to interrupt me, don't.'

'Bolshy,' she muttered, shuffling from one foot to the other, feeling awkward.

He shrugged. 'I'm not kidding. No words except for mine.'

She sighed, pursing her lips and rolling her eyes, but all the same she found that she really wanted to hear his thoughts. She'd asked him what he saw when he looked at her the first time he'd drawn her, but this was altogether different. Then she'd sensed that he told her what he thought she needed to hear. This time he was shooting from the hip.

'Let's see,' he said. placing his hands on her shoulders, his head on one side, considering. 'Without wishing to make this into something it isn't supposed to be, this really would work better without your dress.'

She opened her mouth to say something, but he shook his head. 'No words. You can leave your dress on if you prefer.'

Winnie glanced down and wiggled her pale polished toes against the mellow wooden flooring, feeling the heat of his hands from her shoulders all the way down to the soles of her feet. His thumbs brushed lightly over her shoulder blades, backwards, forwards, until finally she met his eyes in the mirror again.

'You can take it off, if you'd prefer,' she said.

He paused, and then raised his hands to untie her hair from the band holding it up. She watched him take care not to hurt her, working the band out until he could muss her hair with his fingers, snapping the band around his wrist.

'Better.' He smoothed his hand down from the crown of

her head, over the side of her face and further down her neck. 'Your hair is the first thing I noticed about you, Winnie. Probably the first thing most people notice about you. It's sunlight and lazy, salt-tangled days at the beach. It's wind-blown streaks of gold on a cold autumn day. Or it's a tether to hold you captive, if I want to.' He wrapped her hair around his hand several times as he spoke to demonstrate, tugging it just hard enough to lift her chin up. He didn't glance away from her eyes as he spoke, even when he lowered his lips to the curve of her neck. 'You see?'

She saw. Or rather she closed her eyes and felt. She felt the heat of his breath on her skin, and the slow, sure caress of his mouth.

'Open your eyes,' he said, letting go of her hair. Winnie did as he asked, watching his fingers play idly with the shoestring straps of her short summer dress.

'You know what I noticed about you next?' he asked, standing close enough behind her for her to feel the brush of his body. Seeing them together like this highlighted the physicality of him; his height over hers, the breadth of his shoulders, the dark gleam of his hair. They were a contrast in every way; his masculinity served to heighten her femininity. No one had ever really made Winnie feel fragile before, but it was an accurate way to describe how looking at them together in the mirror made her feel.

She shook her head, not prepared to guess what Jesse was going to say.

'Your eyes,' he said, catching hold of her jaw lightly between his thumb and fingers, holding her face steady. 'They lay you bare, Legs. Don't ever try lying, because those eyes of yours will always, always give you away. They told me a million things about you within seconds of meeting you.'

214

'They did?' she whispered, staring at him.

'She's true. She's ballsy. She's hurt. She's soft. She's smart. She's kind.' He dragged his thumb across her bottom lip. 'Your eyes told me all of those things right there on the kitchen doorstep before you even opened your mouth.'

'Careful,' she whispered. 'You're doing that unintentionally romantic thing again.'

Jesse swept her hair over one shoulder and then slipped his arm around her waist, holding her against him, his hand spanned flat over her stomach.

'You're very, very lovely, Winnie. You shouldn't need me to tell you how a man could lose hours just looking at you. Is that sexist?' He shrugged, unrepentant. 'Maybe so and guilty as charged, but it's just human nature. You're the kind of woman who makes a man's mind wander.'

Winnie didn't know what to say, but then hadn't he told her not to say anything at all? He held her close against him as he spoke, watching her eyes as he stroked his free hand from her shoulder to her fingertips.

'You need to understand your own power, Winnie. Because it isn't just about this –' He broke off and nodded towards her reflection. 'It's not just the fact that you're a crazy, sexy cross between angelic and filthy.' He laughed then, low in his chest which was pressed against her spine. 'It's so much more than that. Some people, they just seem to shine. You're one of those people.'

He probably had no idea how much his quietly spoken words mattered to her, or how much strength she drew from his candid, admiring thoughts. Or maybe he did; wasn't that precisely why he was doing this, to build up her pride and her self-confidence? Jesse Anderson was a walking, talking contradiction.

'That's what I've tried to catch in the drawing, the quicksilver of you.'

It was so stripped back and lovely that Winnie felt her heart contract, and she turned slowly in his arms to look at him.

'No one's ever looked at me that way before,' she whispered.

A small half-smile tipped his mouth. 'Yes, they have. Everyone does, Winnie. It's just you that doesn't see it.'

She caught her breath, enjoying the way his hands pressed her close against him.

'You know what I see when I look at you, Jesse?'

He lifted one eyebrow, amused. 'A bloody sexy Aussie?'

She laughed, but shook her head. 'Well, yes, but I see other things too.'

'This was about you,' he said, already mentally closing down in that way he did.

'And now it's about you,' she countered, stroking his cheek. 'I see a man who's hiding behind smoke and mirrors.'

Robbed of his smile, he looked wary and momentarily vulnerable.

'You're wrong,' he said, his light-hearted tone an unintentionally perfect example of those smoke and mirrors. 'What you see is what you get with me, Legs.'

'OK,' she said. 'Well, what I see is a man who wants to believe his own mantra that love is complicated and difficult and counter-productive, but his eyes didn't get the memo because they tell me that he's emotional, and sensitive, and romantic to the core.'

'You've got the wrong guy,' he said, cupping her face tenderly and proving her right.

Winnie turned her face and pressed a kiss into his palm.

'I did have, for a long time.' She hadn't realised how wrong until lately.

'Finally something we can agree on,' he said.

'We should probably stop talking now while we're still friends,' she said, her fingers moving over the warm, firm skin at the back of his neck.

'Friends is good.' He pressed his mouth against her forehead. Winnie closed her eyes and leant into his body, inhaling the scent of him down into her bones. His hands moved in her hair, and it was impossible not to tip her head back into his massaging fingers, and it was nobody's fault when his lips found hers and they kissed. It wasn't the kiss of friends. It was no brief peck or absent-minded see-you-later. It was the culmination of their sensually charged conversation; his affirmation that she was quicksilver in his blood, her confirmation that he was all of the good things he so hotly denied. When he opened her mouth under his to slide his tongue in, his kiss said all of the things he couldn't.

'I can't stay away from you,' he murmured, slipping his hand down to cup her backside and lift her into him. 'I need to, and I can't.'

Winnie wrapped her arms around his shoulders. 'You don't need to,' she whispered, holding him. 'Please don't try.'

His slow, lust-laden kiss told her that he didn't want to. His restless, searching hands all over her body told her that he didn't want to. Yet his stubborn as a damn ox brain wouldn't let him go.

'I have to,' he said, lifting his head. His dark eyes couldn't have been more regretful, or his parting kiss more bittersweet or drenched in longing.

'Come to bed,' she whispered. 'Please, Jesse. I want you to.'

His eyes flickered to the bed behind her, and when he looked back down at her a moment later he looked pained enough to cry tears of blood.

'I should go.'

She shook her head. 'You should stay.'

Jesse slowly slid her hairband from around his wrist, gathered her hair at her nape and tied it loosely back. 'There,' he said. 'Good as new.'

He was leaving. Winnie didn't ask him to stay again; she knew he wouldn't. He might think that she was as good as new, but that wasn't how she felt right at that moment. Jesse was putting her back together again with one hand and pulling her apart with the other.

She shook her head and then opened her door and led him downstairs and back out into the warm island sunshine.

'Bye then,' she said, frustrated, a few minutes later, drawing a pattern in the sand on the terrace with her toe.

He nodded, almost leaving, looking down at her with complicated eyes.

'Will you come on a date with me on Saturday?'

Bloody hell! Hot and cold didn't come close to covering the man.

'God, Jesse. Make your mind up,' she said, nervous now even if she hadn't been before. 'You pretty much knocked me back two minutes ago. Besides, I'm pretty sure bohemian artists don't do anything as pedestrian as date.'

'There's a drive-in cinema on the beach at the weekend,' he said, ignoring her comment. 'Over on Moonlight Bay. I thought it might be your kind of thing.'

'Is it really called Moonlight Bay?' she asked, attracted despite herself.

He nodded. 'They have the open-air cinema there a couple of times a year. English movies usually, with Greek subtitles. I thought we could take your car, being rag-top.'

Her car. The drive-in movies. He sounded like he'd thought this out. 'Oh! Eugh. Well, we could, but the last owner keeled over in the car at the same drive-in movie because his wife touched his . . . er, his knee.'

'I'll control myself if you can,' he said, making light of what had happened between them, retreating behind his favourite safety net, sarcasm.'Can you?' He watched her face over his sunnies.

She looked him in the eye, intending to say something sarcastic, but 'Not sure' came out regardless.

'Saturday it is then.' He kissed her then, hard and out of the blue, taking a second to cup the back of her head in his hand and slide his tongue over hers before he broke away and stood up. 'Oh, and Winnie? Bad news. You're going to need to keep your clothes on this time.'

Jesse let himself into the house and grabbed a beer before heading outside again to his studio. What the fuck had he been thinking of, taking that picture over? What had he expected to happen? He'd wrestled with the idea of asking Winnie to the movies for the exact reason that she'd given when he'd mentioned it: it felt too traditionally date-like, at odds with his no-strings mantra, especially given the charged atmosphere in her bedroom earlier.

But he'd realised something; Winnie wasn't just blowing in and out of his life like a leaf in autumn. He couldn't treat her the way he had up to now because she wasn't one-night-stand material. He'd handled his instant attraction to her badly thus far; he'd allowed her fleeting resemblance to Erin to seduce him into stupidity because he was clearly a lifelong screw-up over leggy, artistic

219

blondes. He'd erotically supercharged his relationship with Winnie on sight because of something and someone she wasn't even aware of, and he'd been cowardly enough to try to flip it back on Winnie, making her feel that her lack of experience was something that she had to remedy for a happier, more fulfilled life.

Who was he to tell people how to live? Just because he thought sentimental romance was a crock of shit, it didn't mean everyone else around him had to subscribe to his viewpoint too.

He'd put all of these thoughts together, and alighted on the realisation that he needed to knock his connection with Winnie back down the scale again towards platonic. Going somewhere public together, getting to know each other properly, was all part of his grand plan to press reset on their relationship, step one in his grand plan to see her less as a desirable woman and more as an islander, as his neighbour, as part of the landscape of his life on Skelidos. He didn't want to hurt her feelings or damage her fragile pride, but little by little he was determined to reverse their relationship down the gears to something altogether less sensual and a damn sight easier to live with.

If he were to give himself marks out of ten for his efforts that afternoon to implement this plan, he'd score himself a three at best. He hadn't planned all of that stuff up in her room; he was supposed to deliver the gift and ask her to the movies. Simple. He should have said no to going upstairs; he could blame only the gin and the fact that the sun had turned her eyes to clear shards of blue-green glass and she'd been so close that he could taste the sweetness of rosemary on her breath. Please, he thought. Please, at some point let me stop being a weak man. It was a work in progress.

220

Winnie was his neighbour. She was too soft and sentimental for his easy come, easy go attitude to sex; she wasn't on the same page, or even in the same book. She was a sappy romance novel with a happy ever after and he was a top-shelf-magazine man, happy for five minutes then even happier to flip the page to the next girl. It had been easy to be lovers, but he suspected that it was going to be a whole lot more difficult to be what he needed to be with Winnie.

Just friends.

CHAPTER SIXTEEN

'I weighed out the remaining arbutus berries in the cellar. We've got enough to make about one hundred and fifty bottles, so a three-month supply going on Ajax's figures,' Frankie said, kneading a ball of dough on the kitchen table a couple of mornings later. 'Add that to the bottles already down there, and I reckon we're likely to run out of gin just in time for Christmas.'

Winnie loaded the sink with breakfast plates from the guests and started to run the hot water. 'Well, that's going to make us about as popular as the Devil at midnight mass,' she sighed. So far, their attempts to source a new arbutus bush on the Internet had come up with a big fat zero, and trying to buy pre-dried berries seemed to be like searching for hens' teeth. Frankie was in the process of drying out a batch of strawberries to test them as an alternative, but none of them were holding out much hope.

'Umm, Frank?' Stella said, looking up from her laptop to watch her friend sprinkle the dough with cinnamon and fresh lemon rind. 'You do know that you've baked enough stuff over the last couple of days to feed a small army, right?'

Frankie paused, her hands covered in flour. 'Just say what you really mean, Stell. You think I'm hiding in the kitchen.'

'I think you're hiding away from Gavin and Seth in the kitchen,' Stella said.

Frankie looked at Winnie. 'Am I?'

Winnie shrugged, unwilling to commit. 'Maybe a bit? Not that I'd blame you.' She dried her hands and picked up a fresh-from-the-oven cheese and rosemary scone. 'Not that I'm – we're – complaining. We're just a bit worried about you, that's all.' She broke the end off the crumbly scone and sat down. 'Do you want me to send Gavin away for you? I can be tactful if you need me to.'

'Meaning I can't?' Stella said archly.

'Er, yes?' Winnie laughed, catching Stella's eye with a wink. 'You're brilliant at just about everything you do, Stell, but tact has never been your strong point.'

'No,' Frankie sighed, rolling the dough up like a Swiss roll and then slicing it through into fat swirls. 'He can stay a while longer. I'm still not even sure why he's really here yet.'

'Free holiday? Because he wants to get back into your knickers?' Stella reeled off, idly Googling Angelo.

'Don't be mean, Stell,' Frankie chided. 'He's the father of my kids.'

'Holy shit,' Stella whispered, completely distracted as she leant in to get a closer look at her screen. 'Oh man.'

Winnie frowned at the disconsolate tone of Stella's voice. 'What is it?'

'I should have known better.' Stella turned her laptop around. Pictures of Angelo with various women and accompanying headlines, all of them salacious.

'Playboy Greek spirits tycoon in danger of drinking all the profits?' Winnie murmured, scrolling down to scan the trashy piece. She screwed her nose up, her opinion

223

of their charismatic Greek guest dimming with every new sentence.

'Bar-room brawl . . . sex addict . . . wines and spirits tycoon . . .'

'Oh,' Frankie said softly, crossing the kitchen to look over Winnie's shoulder.

Stella slammed the lid shut on the laptop and laughed bitterly.

'Doesn't matter,' she said, convincing no one.

Winnie felt wretched. She'd never seen Stella lose her head over a man before, but something about Angelo had slid past all of her usual checkpoints, and Winnie had a sneaking suspicion that he'd unearthed Stella's unused heart and written his name across it.

'He broke his shoulder in a bar-room fight over a woman?' Frankie said, pissed off. She'd wasted countless hours looking up the best recipes for convalescence, and encouraged him each morning in their dawn yoga sessions. She might just throw in a few more taxing moves tomorrow and a couple of extra chilies in his favourite feta and chili morning rolls too.

'Wait,' she said, as a thought suddenly struck her. 'He's a wine and spirits tycoon?'

All three of them looked towards the cellar door, thinking of the tiny, secret distillery that lay beyond.

'I had sex with him down there,' Stella said. 'What if he did notice after all?'

'What difference would it make?' Winnie said, trying to think it through practically. 'It's not like he's going to get us closed down or anything, is he?'

The other two looked at her, perturbed by the revelations too.

'Shouldn't think so,' Frankie said, shrugging. 'We're a

224

tiny two-bit island that hardly anyone knows about. Why would he go to that kind of trouble?'

'Let's not worry about the gin,' Winnie said, rubbing Stella's shoulder. 'I couldn't care less what he does for a living. All I care about is the fact that you've gone and fallen in love with him and he might be a dog.'

Stella turned to look at her as if she'd lost her marbles. 'I'm not in *love* with him,' she said, as if it was the most ridiculous suggestion in the world.

'No?' Frankie said, sliding a warm scone towards Stella, because she was a firm believer in the healing power of good food and they were Stella's favourite. 'You're sure? Only I've never seen you like this with anyone before.'

Stella looked down at the scone for a long, silent moment. 'Stupid holiday romance,' she said. A big fat tear dripped from her face onto the shiny golden top of the scone, and she shoved her stool back, upended her plate into the bin, and marched out of the kitchen.

'It's a pleasure doing business with you.' Seth grinned his trademark heartbreaker smile as he shook hands with each of the three women in turn later that afternoon. They'd just agreed the deal for the exclusive hire of the villa for the remaining weeks of the summer season to Tryx for a sum of money that they wouldn't have dreamt of asking, leaving their books in a healthy state and the future rosy for Villa Valentina.

'Don't worry about the other guest currently staying here,' Stella said, referring to Angelo. 'He'll be leaving in the morning.'

'Angelo?' Seth said. 'Oh, he's cool to stay. I don't think he even knows who we are, and if he did, he doesn't seem like the kind of guy to rat us out to the press.'

The fact that Angelo was leaving in the morning was news to Frankie and Winnie. They'd heard heated voices coming from upstairs after Stella had left the kitchen, but they hadn't had a chance to catch up on any developments as yet.

'Not a chance I'm willing to take,' Stella said smoothly. 'You've asked us for privacy, and God knows you're paying for it, so that's exactly what you're going to get.'

Her no-nonsense tone brooked no argument. They all smiled blandly as Seth left them to it in reception, and when they were alone Stella slammed the diary shut with unnecessary force.

'Yes. He's leaving, before you ask.'

'The villa, or the island?'

Stella hesitated. 'I don't know, and I don't care. I shouldn't think Corinna will be best pleased if he decamps over there.'

Winnie hated seeing Stella so obviously unhappy. 'Did he have anything helpful to say?'

'I didn't care to listen to him.'

Stella was used to being in control of the amount of romance she allowed into her life, but this time she'd well and truly handed over the reins to Angelo. It wasn't so much that he'd lied, because he hadn't, except perhaps by omission. It wasn't even that he'd made false promises, because they were both grown-ups who'd been around the block a few times.

It was much more personal than that. He'd found his way into Stella's soft, vulnerable places, uncharted because no one had ever visited them before. He'd watered the vivid blooms of hope in her chest, chased through the butterfly glasshouse in her gut, and meandered hand in hand with her down the starlit back alleys inside her head.

226

In short, he'd blindsided her, and now, because she felt a fool, she'd come out all guns blazing and given him his marching orders.

'Did he ask you about the amount of gin in the cellar?' Frankie checked quietly.

Stella shook her head. 'He was too busy denying the personal stuff to get around to that.'

'And you didn't tell him about the arbutus bush?' Winnie said.

'Of course I bloody didn't,' Stella said. Ajax's warning to keep the gin's secrets were etched indelibly in all of their heads.

Up until now, their time on the island had been mostly sunshine, new beginnings and excitement; Gavin's arrival and the discovery of the kind of man Angelo really was had interrupted their idyll like a stubborn stone stuck in the tyre of a bicycle when you're freewheeling down a hill on a summer's day. A constant, ticking undercurrent of threat.

'Where is he now?' Frankie asked.

Stella shrugged miserably. 'No clue.'

Over at Panos's bar, a card game and a few beers had led Gavin and Angelo to strike up conversation, and in doing so they unwittingly traded information. Gavin learned that he definitely *did* know that guy's face from back at Villa Valentina, because he'd been plastered all over magazines and TV back home for the last few years. Seth Manson.

Angelo learned that Stella had been made redundant from her job as a ball-breaking businesswoman, and that Gavin had always felt slightly intimidated by her and got the impression that she was a bit of a man-eater.

It was quiet in the bar that afternoon, and Panos pulled

up a chair with a round of beers on the house. Because Angelo was Corinna's brother and Gavin was clearly related to the Englishwomen and would be in their circle of confidence, he felt easy about speaking freely of the fire. He disclosed his private fear that they wouldn't be able to replace that blessed arbutus bush in time to stop the island from running out of gin, and he shook his slightly balding head and shrugged, because the thought of Skelidos without its gin was too bleak a notion to contemplate.

Just after dawn the following morning, Frankie unrolled her yoga mat on the soft, cool sand beyond their terrace then stood looking out to sea. She'd always loved this time of day best of all, but especially since coming here to Skelidos. The morning skies were a calorie-free sweetshop, candy-floss pink tumbled with parma violets and streaks of honey-gold cinder toffee, vivid where it hit the ocean on the horizon. Soon enough the sea would become the star of the show, brilliant turquoise rippled like a slice of agate with aqua and lapis, and Frankie enjoyed watching their battle to be the most beautiful. What a gift, she thought. What a quiet, peaceful joy it was to have a ringside seat to such splendour.

'Morning.'

She turned to see Seth had arrived, as he did most mornings. Her heart considered a flip, a reflex reaction more than a voluntary one.

'Good morning,' she murmured as he shook his towel out. She glanced back towards the villa, wondering if Angelo would come for a last session before he left, but all was quiet. Just as well. It would have been tricky to maintain her inner calm when she felt like planting her foot up his backside.

'Just us this morning,' Seth said, twisting his head from side to side and rolling his shoulders.

'Seems that way,' Frankie murmured, beginning to work through some simple stretches and breathing exercises.

They fell into companionable silence for a couple of minutes, and little by little Frankie felt the tension begin to ebb from her body.

'Would it be all right if I have a go?'

And there was that tension again. She turned and found Gavin hovering uncertainly on the edge of the terrace, a towel under his arm.

'You want to try yoga?'

He was just about the last man on earth likely to opt to voluntarily do yoga.

'Is that OK?' His face was a mask; it was impossible to guess his inner agenda.

Frankie shrugged. What could she say? No? That wasn't very yogic, so despite the fact that it was going to seriously screw with her karma, she nodded and waved her hand for him to lay his towel down.

He seemed momentarily thrown and unsure what to do next, the flare of shy acceptance in his familiar grey eyes reminding her of a child in the playground who hadn't expected to be allowed to join in a game.

'Just lay your towel on the sand and follow my lead,' she sighed, gesturing to a spot just behind her, alongside Seth.

Without turning back, she started from the beginning again for the benefit of her ex-husband. How bizarre was this? If anyone had told her a couple of months previously that she'd be leading Gav and Seth Manson through a yoga session on a beach at dawn, she'd have laughed until tears rolled down her cheeks. Yet here she was.

Twisting smoothly from her waist she looked over her right shoulder at Seth, who, to her relief, followed her movement and looked away over his own shoulder. He really was a fine figure of a man, all hard edges and strong, tanned muscles. But then wasn't it his job to look that way? His face and his sixpack were his fortune.

Twisting the other way, she looked towards Gav, who did as she did, looking away over his shoulder. She took the time to notice that he'd definitely been taking better care of himself lately; his once ever-present beer paunch had all but disappeared, and while he'd probably never have a sixpack, he was easily the leanest and healthiest she'd ever seen him. She'd expected him to huff and puff his way through their session, but he didn't. He was far from an expert, but he'd made a decent fist of copying her moves and followed her quiet breathing instructions.

As they lay on their backs for the cool-down at the end, Frankie's hands moved absently in the sand, letting the grains fall softly through her fingers. Behind her, Seth Manson opened one eye a fraction to look surreptitiously over at Gavin, noting that he still wore his wedding ring. Gav did the same, but his eyes were drawn instead to Frankie's left hand, to the lack of her wedding ring, indisputable evidence of the fact that she'd obviously found moving on easier than he had. Not that that wasn't painfully obvious anyway; she lived here now in this glamorous world of sunshine and rock stars. He'd never have been able to offer her a life like this. He was a regular bloke with a regular job and he'd always been content with his lot. Or, more accurately, he hadn't, he just hadn't known what the hell to do about it; it had taken Frankie walking out to force their hands. He didn't blame her. Their marriage had been mothballed for years, so full of dust and holes it had disintegrated into a pile of solicitor's letters, packing boxes and empty hallways.

For Gav, there had been no future filled with sand, sea and sunshine. There had been only quiet rooms, dinners for one, and occasional pints down the local with his workmate Steve, who had tried to introduce him to online dating a couple of months back with hopeless results. Gav had found himself having dinner in a place he used to take Frankie and the kids on birthdays and holidays, except this time he'd been accompanied by a redhead who kept calling him Kev and had a full sleeve tattoo when she took her cardigan off. Rock bottom had turned out to be a miserable, lonely place, and while there he'd looked around and found there was a Frankie-shaped doorway that he wanted to find the key to again.

He knew it had been a risk coming here. He wasn't fool enough to think that she'd be pleased to see him, but he'd caught the plane anyway, because he had something for Frankie that couldn't be mailed or sent directly.

Rolling his towel up because the others were, he nodded a quick thank you in the direction of the most beautiful woman in the world as Seth abandoned his towel and started off for his morning run along the beach. Did the man never stop exercising? Gav had joined the local slimming club back home, and much as he'd dreaded going in he'd found himself surrounded by a fun bunch of women who'd encouraged him and become his friends. They'd even roped him into going to the gym after group, but it was nothing on the way Seth Manson's body was obviously his temple.

'Gav?'

Her voice stilled him.

'Frank?'

He turned as she caught up with him, more pixie-like than ever in her gym kit with her hair kept from her face by a red band.

'I wondered if you fancied lunch later, if you're free?' she said. 'We could walk over to Panos's bar.'

It was more than he'd hoped for, but there was no softening smile on Frankie's face or sparkle in her eye to turn her suggestion into an invitation. It sounded like more of a summons to the gallows.

'I was kind of planning to go for a hike along the coast-line today,' he said. 'Would you have any objection to making it dinner instead?'

She looked mildly surprised, as well she might. He'd never hiked in his life back home, but things were different here. He was a couple of stone lighter for one, and that view deserved to be looked at.

'Dinner it is, then,' she said, and he nodded and walked away, schooling himself to not look back until he reached the stairs and took them at a jog.

CHAPTER SEVENTEEN

At eleven o'clock sharp on Saturday morning, Winnie, Stella and Frankie met in the cellar to make up their first full batch of gin.

'Let's do it ten at a time to keep things in order,' Winnie said, lining up ten bottles of base spirit on the bench and unscrewing the caps.

Stella lifted the scales out on the surface and wiped them clean. 'Cinema tonight then, Win?'

Winnie nodded. '*Dirty Dancing*, would you believe.'

'Very dirty, if Jesse has anything to do with it, I should think.'

Winnie rolled her eyes. 'It's on a public beach. I hardly think it's going to be X-rated.'

Frankie tipped juniper berries into the scale. 'Just remember what happened to Mr P in that car at that same cinema,' she said. 'Don't put your hand on his knee, for God's sake.'

'Noted.' Winnie screwed the cap on the jar of juniper berries and reached for the coriander seeds. 'So how was your dinner with Gav?'

Frankie's face relaxed into a smile. 'It was fun, actually.'

Stella looked at her, interested. 'Gav was *fun*? Are you sure we're talking about the same man?'

'Don't be unkind,' Frankie admonished her softly. 'He's a good man, Stell. I know you two never hit it off, but he's a gentle soul really.'

Stella frowned. 'Gentle? Frank, you've got Seth "smokin' hot" Manson out there making moony eyes at you over the croissants and you're talking about gentle Gav? Gentle isn't a good word when it comes to men. Try charismatic. Try alpha. Try sexy.'

Frankie looked up. 'Yeah. Because that worked out well for you, didn't it Stell?' She regretted her sharpness as soon as she saw it register in Stella's surprised, hurt eyes. Angelo had been the elephant in the room ever since he'd left the villa earlier in the week; Stella point-blank refused to even acknowledge he'd ever existed.

'We probably shouldn't have left reception unmanned,' Stella said, banging the angelica root jar down on the bench. 'I'll go and watch it. You two can manage this between you I'm sure.'

'Stell–' Frankie said, reaching a hand out to her friend, but she shook it off and huffed out of the cellar.

'Wax on, wax off.'

Winnie tossed the keys across the car to Jesse. 'You know, you're the first person to make that joke,' she lied enthusiastically, opening the passenger door.

'I'm not, am I,' he muttered, sliding into the driver's seat.

'Nope.'

Winnie settled into the big leather seat, crossing her legs.

'Did you mistake *Dirty Dancing* for a spaghetti western?' he said, glancing at her cut-offs and cowboy boots.

She'd thought long and hard about what to wear. A dress felt too formal and jeans would be way too warm. The Lady Antebellum inspired lace top, cut-offs and slightly battered boots combo had won by being kind of dressed up and dressed down at the same time. It was an outfit that she probably wouldn't have been brave enough to wear back in England, but Skelidos had seeped deeper than her sun-kissed skin these days; she'd soaked in some of the island's relaxed confidence, a barefoot, kick-back coolness that she was enjoying very much. She'd left her hair in loose waves around her shoulders and clipped it back with a bohemian flower clip she'd found in the market in town, added a slick of lip gloss and mascara, and she was ready.

'Did you mistake this for dinner with your mother?' she quipped back lightly, casting a deliberately appraising glance over his own attempt at dressing for the occasion. He'd gone for an 'expensive man just stepped off his yacht for dinner at the marina' ensemble of a short-sleeved white shirt that highlighted the depth of his suntan and canvas shorts with his sunnies tucked into his unbuttoned collar. It was a respectable look on him, lending him a sophisticated, worldly air that she wasn't used to.

He narrowed his eyes at her sarcasm as he rumbled the old engine into life. She'd readily agreed when he'd asked to drive; manoeuvring the big old saloon was an artform in itself, but driving it on deep, powdery sand without getting stuck was something else again. She was frankly glad to get out of the villa for the evening; Stella had stayed in her foul mood after her clash with Frankie in the cellar, leaving Frank to test her homemade pizza recipe on Gav and the boys from Tryx out on the terrace with Stella glowering down from her balcony.

'Right then. Now we've customarily insulted each other, shall we get going?' Jesse smiled genially as he pulled out of the gates and headed down the coast road.

She laughed. 'And tell me, Jesse, are you likely to customarily attempt to broaden my sexual horizons later, too? Or am I safe, seeing as we're in public?'

Jesse looked sharply towards Winnie, swerving the wide car dangerously close to the hedgerows on the narrow road, making her instinctively reach out and straighten the wheel.

'Careful,' she said, laughing at his scowl, and watched the countryside slide past, enjoying the warm evening breeze on her skin.

After a while, he huffed, 'Just for the record, I'm not some damn cultish Svengali who's been taking advantage of your delicate heart, OK?'

She studied his profile, trying to judge why he'd taken what she'd intended as a lighthearted comment so personally. 'I never said you were anything of the sort. I was just kidding, Jesse. I took my own clothes off last time, remember?'

'Like I could forget,' he muttered, indicating left to follow the beach signs for Moonlight Bay.

Winnie wasn't certain why the atmosphere between them had lurched towards fraught, but she was glad of the distraction of the crowd on the beach, or as close to a crowd as it got on a sleepy island like Skelidos. Five or six rows of cars had lined themselves up haphazardly pointing towards a large screen that had been erected at one end of the bay, and a couple of teenagers in cut-offs and vests shoved the fee into the aprons tied around their middles and waved them on vaguely to join the pack.

Winnie waited until Jesse had picked his spot and turned off the engine. 'I'm sorry if what I said annoyed you. I didn't mean anything by it.'

He sighed and turned to look her way. 'It didn't. You didn't annoy me, I annoyed myself. I shouldn't have snapped at you.'

'Shall we just forget it and start over?'

The beginnings of a smile tipped the corner of his mouth. 'I like your boots.'

She cast her eyes down, laughing softly. 'My mother calls them my Dallas boots.' Looking up again, she met his gaze. 'I like your shirt. It makes you look respectable.'

He curled his lip and looked down at his torso. 'I was going for handsome and debonair, not bank manager.'

'OK, let me try again. You look handsome and debonair tonight, Jesse, not at all like a bank manager. My bank manager back in England was barely five foot and bald with glasses, bad breath and Dalek cufflinks, so you really are nothing at all like him.'

'Well, I'm glad we cleared that up,' he said, shaking his head slightly, as if to say that, as always, their conversation had veered towards random.

'I brought popcorn,' she said. 'And some pizza Frankie had just pulled out of the oven.'

He nodded his approval. 'I brought wine for you. I even brought a glass,' he said.

'You're a keeper,' she said. 'Until the end of the movie, at least.'

A fizz of excitement sizzled around the beach as dusk slid towards darkness and the huge screen up front blinked into life.

'I love this movie so much,' Winnie said, full of anticipation. 'What's your favourite bit?'

He looked at her as if she'd spoken a language he'd never heard before. 'Ask me again when I've seen it.'

'What?' She stared at him. 'You're not telling me that you've never seen *Dirty Dancing* before. You're not. I don't believe you! Everyone in the entire world has seen this movie.'

Jesse shook his head. 'Not me. Chick shit.'

'*Chick shit?*' She repeated his jock phrase, half laughing. 'This movie is one of the seminal romance movies of modern times. "She carried a watermelon." I mean, who says that?'

He looked nonplussed.

'"Nobody puts Baby in the corner"?'

He shook his head. 'Nope. I got nothing.'

'Oh my God, you're so lucky to see it for the first time somewhere like this,' she breathed, lifting her hands up at their idyllic position beside the sea. He looked like he was going to answer her, but she pre-empted him with a finger against her lips as the opening music struck up. 'Ssh, it's starting.'

Jesse watched Winnie as much as he watched the movie. She was shiny-eyed and rapt, and as it unfolded he could almost get why it was so beloved. Chemistry. For whatever reason, every now and then two people meet and the chemistry between them is off the scale, and if you can catch that on screen then you're in for a box-office smash.

'I carried a watermelon,' Baby said, up on screen.

Winnie looked across at him. 'See? She carried a watermelon. How perfect is that line?'

Jesse reached into the brown paper bag he'd bought with him. 'I carried a box of olives.'

238

Winnie rolled her eyes but took an olive when he opened the box anyway.

'It's a lot smaller than a watermelon,' she said, looking at it.

'You wound me,' he said, laying his hand on his chest as if he'd been shot.

'You'll live,' she whispered, relaxing back into her seat with her wine glass in her hand.

Jesse ate pizza while he watched them gyrate up on screen.

'Do you dance?'

He pretended he needed to think about his answer. 'Never.'

She had that incredulous look on her face again. 'Never, as in not once in your adult life?'

Sometimes it was easier to lie than have to elaborate, so he shook his head. 'Not even once.'

'You're so dancing with me later in that case.'

'I so am not.' He really wanted a beer.

Winnie huffed, a sound that implied that he was going to get little choice in the matter, and returned her attention to the screen. She could huff all she liked, he still wasn't dancing. Glancing around at the other cars on the beach, he found that the couple in the car to the side of him were more heavily engaged in each other than in the movie. Coming here was starting to feel like a mistake, especially when Winnie sighed and laid her hand on his leg and up on screen Baby crawled across the floor towards Patrick Swayze.

'Careful,' he muttered, moving her hand down closer to his knee. 'I don't want the curse of the killer car to strike me down.' Personally, he thought that sounded like a much more entertaining premise for a movie than dancing, dirty or otherwise.

'Have you had many women?' Baby asked, comely and wrapped in a post-coital sheet up on the screen.

Winnie slanted her interested eyes in his direction again.

'Don't even ask me,' he warned, shutting her down. She shrugged and turned her attention back to the screen, and for a few moments he contemplated what his truthful answer would have been. A relatively big number, and most of them since he'd moved here to Skelidos, but then that was one of the side effects of his no-hearts-and-flowers lifestyle. He was neither proud nor ashamed of the fact that he'd slept with more beautiful, interesting women than he had fingers and toes. More than four people's fingers and toes, to be honest. Five even, six at the very outside, but then a decade of one-night stands racks up. And in all that time he'd never felt moved to give any of those women a key to his studio or picnic with them in his olive orchard, and he certainly hadn't taken them to the movies to watch slushy films. He must be going soft in his old age.

Winnie's fingers slipped a little higher on his thigh, light and massaging, and he wasn't going soft at all. *Fuck*. Laying his hand over hers to still it, he laced their fingers and belatedly realised that what he was actually doing, for all intents and purposes, was holding her hand.

'Romantic,' Winnie sighed, as the strains of 'These Arms of Mine' drifted around the beach, and glancing to his right Jesse found that his neighbours had steamed up their windows so badly that he wouldn't be surprised to see a *Titanic*-style handprint appear in the condensation.

'OK?' Winnie leaned his way a little as she whispered, and he nodded and had to look away from the softness in her eyes because she was downright bloody dangerous. Not kissing her was turning into an endurance test. Her lips parted slightly, and the moonlight painted silver streaks in her hair. It wasn't just his arms that were yearning. It was every last fibre of his being.

'Is there any pizza left?' he asked, edging away from her then hating the flicker of confusion in her eyes she wasn't quick enough to hide. He didn't want pizza, he wanted Winnie.

She handed him the bag and sat back again to face the screen, her eyes and attention seemingly nailed on the movie. *Message received and understood,* her rigid shoulders said. *Why bring me here to this most romantic of settings and then make me feel a fool?* her determinedly neutral profile said.

Because the only way I can keep my hands off you is to spend time with you in public places, he sent back telepathically, *and because the only other option is to not spend time with you at all, and I'm too selfish a man to do that.*

Would it have been better to say those things aloud? If Winnie could see inside his black heart, would she understand him better? Or would she run a mile? If she had any sense she'd run until her legs gave out. He just had to hope that his decision to go for a slow, tactful withdrawal of physical contact would leave them with the bare bones of a friendship to salvage.

Up on screen, the movie reached its big climax, the lift that even *he'd* seen despite avoiding the movie for his entire adult life. He risked a look at Winnie when Patrick Swayze uttered his immortal line about no one putting Baby in a corner, and couldn't help but notice that Winnie had put herself as far away from him in her seat as she could. Shit. He closed his eyes, hating himself for the crap way he'd handled this tonight. He'd put Winnie in the corner.

241

'Winnie, I –'

'Shall we go, beat the rush?' she said, over-bright as she gathered up their rubbish from the floor of the car into one bag and screwed it up.

He studied her face, her fierce *don't bother* eyes, and started the engine with a resigned sigh.

Jesse pulled the car into the gates behind Villa Valentina and turned off the engine.

'Thanks for taking me.' Winnie shot him a stiff smile. 'I enjoyed it.' She threw her door wide and climbed out, leaving no time for conversation and saving them from the awkwardness of kissing or not kissing.

'You're welcome. I enjoyed it too,' he said, closing his door and handing the keys back as he joined her behind the car.

Her expression couldn't have been more sceptical. 'Did you?'

Around them, soft night-time sounds offset the silence that hung in the air after her question, crickets and the occasional rustle of movement in the undergrowth.

He shrugged. 'It's not a bad movie. Bit clichéd, maybe.'

'Is that right.'

Jesse wished he could shut the hell up, because everything that came out of his mouth was making the situation more and more awkward. 'Shy girl discovers her inner woman over the course of a summer spent with a guy from the wrong side of the tracks. It's a well-worn plot.'

She leant back against the boot. 'I guess it is,' she said. Only the fast drum of her fingertips against the chrome trim of the car gave away her annoyance. 'Perhaps we should have seen a good horror film instead. Maybe one where the shy heroine discovers her inner woman in the arms of the guy from the wrong side of the tracks, but then she loses it and kills him with a kitchen knife because he's always blowing hot and cold. That sort of thing.'

'Grisly,' he said, yet actually he preferred her being pissed at him than hurt. He could work with that.

'I'll go,' he said quietly. 'Before you invite me in for coffee as a ruse to murder me.'

'I wasn't planning to invite you in.'

'The jury's still out on whether you'd like to murder me though, right?'

She didn't answer and she didn't move, just watched him steadily with those cool, assessing blue eyes. He needed to leave. Her cowgirl look was a confusing crossover of wholesome and sexy, and a good ninety per cent of his brain wanted to haul her up onto the boot of the car and feel her lock those damn boots around his waist. Once in his head, it was an image he couldn't shake, so he nodded goodnight, pushing a hand through his hair as he took a few steps back.

'Goodnight, Winnie,' he said, swallowing.

'Is that it?' she said, crossing her ankles, jutting her chin. 'Not even a kiss on the cheek?'

He willed himself not to look down at her long legs, even though the movement made him ache to, and that angle of her chin broke his heart because it told him that he'd hurt her feelings and she was covering it with bravado. In the movie, Baby had said something about being scared of just about everything, but most of all being scared of walking away from Patrick Swayze and never feeling the same way as she felt about him ever again.

Turning away from Winnie, Jesse walked down the lane towards home, mixed up and angry and frustrated. He'd loved his wife, and he'd spent the last ten years determined to never feel the same way about anyone else.

He'd been deliberately cool with Winnie this evening because she'd found her way under his skin, and despite his promise to himself to turn down the heat on their relationship to friendship, all he'd succeeded in doing was making her feel rejected.

Back at his house, he paced the kitchen, prowled the rooms of the house and knocked back a good measure of brandy before heading out to his studio to pound some clay. Except work turned out to be impossible too, so in the end he threw his tools down, slammed out of the studio and headed back down the lane.

CHAPTER EIGHTEEN

It was a little after two in the morning, and Winnie had finally turned in after a solitary cup of coffee in the kitchen and a fair while spent sitting on her balcony. She'd tried to read but her mind wouldn't settle to her book, and she'd tried to sleep once already but hadn't been able to switch off. And so she lay awake on her back in the middle of her huge bed and gazed at the rafters, wondering why Jesse had even asked her to the movies at all when the thought of being on a date with her was clearly distasteful to him.

Her eyelids had just drifted closed when a noise jolted her wide awake again. What was that? She lay perfectly still, and after a minute or so, it happened again. The tap of pebbles on glass. Propping herself up on her elbows, she flicked on the creamy side lamp and stared at the dark balcony doors, and sure enough it happened for a third time; she saw it as well as heard it this time.

Slipping from between the sheets, she pushed her feet into her cowboy boots beside the bed and crossed to open her balcony doors. Resting her forearms on the edge she leant over and looked down.

Jesse.

'You said you wanted to dance.'

Her bruised ego wanted to tell him to leave, but her tender heart wanted to dance.

'Come down?' he said, when she didn't reply. 'Please?'

If she insisted on having this conversation over the distance of two floors the whole villa would be awake in no time, and given the money that Tryx had handed over for their serenity, that was out of the question.

'Wait there,' she sighed, retreating into her room just long enough to throw her short robe over her slip. She moved quietly through the slumbering villa, opened the front door and stood just inside the frame.

'What are you doing here, Jesse?' she asked softly.

He'd changed from his expensive-yacht-owner gear into his more regular jeans and T-shirt, all faded and worn into the shape of him. He took his time replying, and Winnie sensed that it was because he was choosing his words carefully.

'I'm not a straightforward man, Winnie.'

Tell me something I don't know. She thought it, but she held her tongue.

'There were things . . . people. Someone. A long time ago.'

As explanations went, it was as clear as London fog. Winnie pulled the villa door closed and led him across to the loungers on the edge of the beach. Perching sideways on one, she nodded for him to sit on the other facing her, and then, knee to knee, she studied him, trying to understand what he wanted to say.

'What was a long time ago?'

He shook his head, his eyes turned towards the dark shoreline.

'I came here to escape from my life, Winnie. So much had happened, and Skelidos literally saved me.'

She laid her hands lightly on his knees. 'What was so awful that you needed to move around the world to outrun it?'

His mouth twisted. Whatever it was, it was buried deep and he was having a hard time getting it out.

'You don't have to tell me,' she said quickly.

'What happened . . . it changed me. I don't see life the way I used to. I don't see love the way I used to, either.' He paused. 'In fact, I don't see love at all.'

Winnie shook her head. He was wrong. 'Yes, you do. You love this island. You love the life you've built here. You even seem to love my bloody donkey.'

A smile of appreciation lifted the corner of his mouth at her attempt to lighten the mood.

'Those things are my building blocks,' he said. 'They're my stability, and in truth they're my sanity. They don't go anywhere, even when I fuck up.'

'Unlike women?' she said, perceptive.

'Something like that.' He met her gaze with his troubled, guilty eyes. 'You asked me earlier how many women I've been with.'

Winnie wasn't certain she wanted to hear the answer now but she didn't stop him because this was all leading somewhere, she just wasn't certain where yet.

'I don't know what the number is and it doesn't really matter, but what I do know is that I have nothing to offer, Winnie. I'm a one-night-stand guy. It's who I am.'

She searched his face, unsure what he expected her to say.

'Is this your way of saying that you feel as if we're getting in over our heads?'

He lifted one shoulder, looking lost. 'I don't know what the hell I'm saying. I came here to say I'm sorry, although I don't know if I'm sorry for wanting you or for not kissing you or for taking you to a goddamn romantic movie when I don't do romance.'

Finally, it seemed as if they were starting to be honest with each other.

'I think we've already established that you're more than capable of romance,' she said, loving the warmth of his hands over hers on his knees.

'But I don't want to be,' he said, bereft. 'I don't want to be.'

She closed her fingers around his. 'What *do* you want, Jesse?' she whispered.

He let go of her hands and ran the flat of his palm down her hair, coming to rest around the curve of her neck.

'You,' he breathed, raw. 'I want you so much that it crushes my chest to even look at you.'

For a self-proclaimed unromantic, he'd just stolen the breath from her lungs.

'I'm here wanting you right back,' she said, then turned her face into his wrist and kissed it.

He cupped her face in his hands. 'I can't do it, Winnie. You're too tender for a man like me. You're . . . you're a clear blue sky on the best day of summer. You're straight-forward. You're the most gloriously unfucked-up girl I've ever met, and I'm bent out of shape and bad news.'

She looked at him, really looked at him, exasperated. 'That's probably the loveliest thing anyone has ever said to me in my whole damn life,' she said, her heart uneasy for this complicated man whose opinion of himself was on the floor. What had happened to him to make him take such a dim view?

He dipped his head and she pressed her mouth against his brow. 'If I'm not mistaken, you came here to dance with me,' she whispered.

She felt his grimace crease his skin beneath her lips.

'I kind of hoped you'd have forgotten about that.'

'Then you're fresh out of luck,' she said. As she stood, Jesse's hands skimmed lightly over her hips and down the outside of her bare legs. The simple, intimate gesture said many things neither of them had yet been able to, and Winnie swallowed down the urge to push him back on the lounger and speed their age-old dance up from slow burn to bonfire.

He stepped into the space beside the loungers and caught hold of one of her hands by the fingertips, his eyes hot on hers.

'Come here,' he whispered, drawing her in until she was right in front of him. Winnie could almost hear the strains of 'These Arms of Mine' on the air around them as he dropped his arm low around her waist and splayed his hand flat against the small of her back, swaying her hips slowly into his. His gaze dropped to linger on her mouth, lower again to the V of skin revealed by her robe.

'I like the way you feel in my arms,' he murmured, ghosting his lips over her hair. 'I like it so damn much, Winnie.'

She closed her eyes, moving with him, following his slow, sensual lead, dipping backwards when he trailed his lips down between her collarbones. He made a noise in his throat as the movement pushed her hips closer into his, somewhere between a sigh and a moan that sent a dark thrill spiralling deliciously through the pit of her stomach. She should have known that he'd be as good at dancing as he was at every other thing she'd known him do. He was unhurried, and he held her steady, and he managed to make it both sweet enough to feel old-fashioned and sensual enough to melt her bones. He slid his hand into her hair, rounding his shoulders as he bent to lower his mouth over hers. Winnie wasn't sure if she'd smooched before, but if there was a name for this kiss, that would be it.

The million pin-prick stars overhead were their glitter-ball, the soft rush of the ocean meeting the pebbles on the shore their music.

Her hands found their way under the hem of his T-shirt, and he reached down and tugged it off in one fluid move, seemingly without even breaking the intimacy of their kiss. She revelled in the smooth warmth of his skin, and in the cords and curves of his muscles as he held her, and in the insistent way he opened her lips with his own to let his tongue in.

'Is this what you wanted?' he said, his voice thick in his throat. 'To dance like this?'

'Yes,' she whispered against his mouth. 'But I didn't realise it would be like this.'

'Me neither,' he said. 'I don't know how to stop this thing between us.'

'Then don't. I don't want you to.' She cradled the back of his neck. 'Stay with me tonight?'

'Winnie.' He closed his eyes then, as if trying to hide from what they were doing, what they were feeling.

'Don't run,' she said, sliding her hand down his spine. 'If it has to be just one night, then let it be tonight.'

He opened his eyes, searching hers, as if she were trying to catch him out. She wasn't. She'd listened to him, to his faltering reasons and his attempts to make her feel better and himself worse, and throughout it all she'd been thinking that there was no way in this world that she wasn't going to experience all of the brilliance and beauty of him, even if it was for one night only.

'Do you know what you're saying?' he asked, his mouth moving over her face, making her suck in air when he mouthed her earlobe. 'We're neighbours. We can't not see each other again after this, or pretend it didn't happen.'

'I know that,' she said, her fingers unpicking the belt of her robe. 'But I also know that we'll find a way to deal with it, because we have to. And I know that you're not the terrible guy you pretend to be and I'm not the fragile woman I was when I came here all those weeks ago either.'

'I don't want to hurt you,' he said, but even in the same breath he pushed her robe back on her shoulders and dropped it on the lounger.

'You won't,' she said. 'And I won't hurt you either.'

She didn't miss the flickers of uncertainty and shock in his eyes. It had obviously been a long time since anyone had taken care of Jesse emotionally. He buried his face in her hair and he kissed her again, languid and searching.

'Take me to your bed,' he said, gruff, sliding his hand up her ribs to cover her breast. 'If we're gonna do this, we're gonna do it properly.'

Jesse was way too far over the line to think about tomorrow. He followed Winnie through the quiet villa, pausing to grab hold of her hand on the first landing, pressing her against the wall to kiss her breathless. 'It's been a long time since I've wanted anyone the way I want you tonight.'

'I don't think anyone's ever wanted me this much,' she said, and he made a silent vow to find her husband and plant his fist square in his guts. How? How had he had a woman like Winnie in his life and turned away?

'Come on,' she said, reaching the top landing, leading him inside her room and clicking the door quietly shut behind them. Scanning the room quickly, he lifted her and deposited her on the edge of the huge, high bed.

'I feel like I'm in a fucking fairytale,' he said, taking in the oversized iron bedstead, the cool white linen and the beautiful, sun-kissed girl in just her slip and her cowboy boots.

Winnie caught her bottom lip between her teeth, her blue eyes sparkling in the low, creamy lamplight.

'You should probably know that I'm naked beneath this.' She glanced down at her slip.

'You think I don't know that already?' he all but growled. Christ, she was something. She opened her knees for him to step between them, feeling the pit drop out of his stomach when she flicked her tongue over his lips and popped the top button on his jeans.

God, he needed to be naked, and he needed her to be naked, and he needed the slick press of her warm skin against his more than he knew how to handle. He shucked his clothes and moved onto the bed, taking her with him until she was on her back alongside him.

'Win,' he said, sliding her slip down her arms to her waist. He'd seen her naked before, but never like this, never just for him, never knowing that she was all his until sunrise. Kissing her breasts, he tugged her slip down her hips and let his lips move down with it, making her moan and drag her nails slowly over his shoulders. Fuck.

'Oh God,' he heard her moan under her breath when he lifted her knee outwards, taking the time to slide his tongue into the heat of her folds as her fingers tangled through his hair and her breath caught in her throat.

He wanted to give her more, to linger there and love

her with his mouth but he needed her too damn much, sliding his body up over hers again to kiss her hard and open-mouthed, shocked senseless by the intensity of his own excitement. He burned for her. Leaning over the edge of the bed, he dragged his jeans closer and from his back pocket fished the box of condoms that he'd put there before he'd left the house.

'You're sure?' he managed, ragged as he ripped the silver foil with his teeth, praying she'd say yes because he wasn't sure he could stop.

She nodded, star-bright lust in her eyes, her breathing fast and shallow as she opened her legs to let him settle between them. 'I've never been more sure of anything.'

And then he sank his hips down and pushed into her, taking her gasps into his mouth with his own, knife-hot pleasure so sudden and fierce that he could barely breathe through it. He palmed her breast, feeling her nipple stiffen in his fingers, and screwed his face up to hold on when her hand cupped his ass and pulled him deeper, wrapping her legs around him as they moved and arched. He tried to take it slow, but he was fighting a losing battle, because every tilt of her hips had him closer until she opened her eyes and let him watch her at her most intimate, her most vulnerable and exposed, and it was so insanely sexy that he let go with her, for her, and because of her.

'We'll take it slower next time,' he murmured against her ear, pulling the sheet over their bodies as he spooned around her a little later. Winnie pressed herself into all of the warm crooks of him, relishing the weight and strength of his limbs wrapped protectively around hers. There would be a next time. Tonight wasn't for sleeping together. It was for being awake together, for giving and taking, for drowning and then resurfacing again just before your lungs burst. Jesse's arm lay beneath her head, his hand hot and assured curved over her breast, his other hand over her hip. They'd danced beneath the stars earlier, and their sex had turned out to be a steady escalation of that dance, a slow grind building towards a hot, frantic beat that had left them both exhausted.

Two things happened at once as Winnie opened her eyes. One, she turned over and realised that Jesse wasn't there any more. The sheets weren't still warm from his body heat and his clothes were no longer strewn over the bedroom's mellow wooden floorboards. He'd gone, just as he'd said he would, and although she'd have been more surprised by his presence than his absence, she felt the loss of him all the same.

The second, more pressing thing was that she'd been woken by some kind of commotion outside.

CHAPTER NINETEEN

'What the blazes . . .?' Winnie muttered, struggling through the stages from sleep to wakefulness, blinking rapidly to adjust to the stream of sunlight through her open balcony doors. Realising she was naked, she paused for a second and pressed her hands against her flushed cheeks, because oh my God. Jesse. One night with him had been so much more than she could've guessed it would be, and she'd already guessed it would be something special. For such a smart-mouthed Australian alpha he'd been unexpectedly tender and then sometimes blissfully not so, setting her skin on fire and making her head spin until she was dizzy, euphoric, drunk on him.

'Win? Are you awake in there?' Stella's voice carried through the door. 'We've got a bit of a situation.'

'I'm coming,' she called, dragging on underwear and shorts. 'What's happening?'

'Not really sure,' Stella said. 'But we seem to have half of the island in the back garden.'

Winnie finger-combed her hair and dragged it back into a band, then pulled a sunshine-yellow vest over her head as she swung the door open.

Stella peered around her for a second.

'What?' Winnie said.

Stella lifted an eyebrow. 'Just checking.'

'What are you, my mother?'

'No, but I will tell your mother unless you give me the lowdown. I heard him chucking bricks last night. If he'd have gone the whole hog and serenaded you he'd have felt my shoe bounce off his head.'

'You old romantic,' Winnie teased.

Stella looked at her pointedly. 'Romance is dead to me.'

She didn't say it anywhere near lightheartedly enough for Winnie to say anything flippant in reply. 'He stayed with me last night,' she whispered instead as they made their way down onto the first landing.

'About bloody time,' Stella huffed, then stopped speaking because Frankie ran up the stairs from the ground floor to meet them.

'I can't work out what the hell is going on here,' she said, her face a mask of controlled panic. 'We need someone who can translate for us quickly.'

'Panos?' Winnie said as they reached the ground floor and hurried quickly down the hallway to the kitchen.

'Tried him, no answer.'

Gav looked up when they came in, already in the kitchen filling any glass he could find with bottled water.

'One of them fainted,' he said, looking terrified. 'I thought water might keep them hydrated, at least.'

'Good thinking,' Frankie said, shooting him a smile. Winnie didn't miss the high spots of colour that appeared in his cheeks as he started moving the glasses onto trays.

She crossed to the kitchen window and peered through the Greek lace that they'd not yet bothered to take down.

256

'Holy shit,' she mumbled. The garden was fuller than if they'd thrown an open invite garden party with free drinks, except everyone was in black and absolutely no one was in a jolly mood. Some of them were kneeling, some were sobbing and others clutched each other. 'Has anyone said anything at all?'

'Not that we can make sense of,' Frankie said. 'I hate to say it but I think it might be about the arbutus bush again.'

Gav looked at them all, perplexed. 'This is all over a garden bush?'

'It's not just any old bush.' Winnie stepped away from the window. 'It's sacred to the islanders.'

Gav's face cleared. 'Ah, that one.'

Stella looked at him sharply. 'What do you mean, *that one*? Who told you about it?'

'Panos mentioned something. I couldn't catch what he meant, but now I see.' He picked up the tray of glasses. 'He said you'd set fire to the berries, and that without it the gin would dry up, I think?'

The women exchanged glances. 'Was anyone else there when he told you this?'

Gav shook his head. 'Quiet day. Only me and Angelo in the place.'

Stella looked decidedly grim. 'I'm going to go and try Panos again.'

Handing water around, Winnie tried and failed to find someone who could speak English, because she didn't have a prayer of understanding the issue in Greek. They'd all been working on the language in their own ways; Winnie knew basic greetings and informational stuff, Stella knew most of the drinks at the bar and some financial terms, and Frankie could haltingly hold her own in the supermarket.

In no way, shape or form did that equip any of the women for the fast-flowing flood of Greek language washing over them all around the garden.

Spotting a familiar face at last, she caught hold of Hero's elbow.

'Winnie,' the old woman cried, throwing her hands up and then hugging her. Winnie patted her back awkwardly, and then stepped away and tried to look deliberately confused in the hope that Hero would help her to understand.

'What's going on?' she said slowly, even though she knew Hero's English was as non-existent as her own Greek. 'Why is everyone here like this?'

Hero threw her hands out towards the twiggy, dead arbutus bush, and then said something else as she looked towards the heavens and crossed herself, and finally she drew a slow finger across her neck and whispered 'Nekros.' Closing her eyes, she let her head fall to one side.

'God,' Winnie muttered. 'Nekros? Someone has hurt their neck?'

Mikey Miller had appeared behind her on the grass. 'Nah. Nekros. It probably means dead.'

Winnie twisted to look at him.

'Why would it mean that?'

'Well, for one, she's just mimed slitting her own throat, and for two, it's probably like necrophilia – you know, that really weird fetish where people shag dead people?'

He said it as if he'd just said something far plainer, and Winnie found herself both nodding at the linguistic logic but also shaking her head with disgust at the way his mind worked.

'Thank you, Mikey,' she muttered. 'Maybe you should head inside while we try to sort this lot out.'

'Still no reply from Panos,' Stella said. 'Win, can you run and fetch Jesse? He's our next best hope.'

Winnie hesitated. How do you approach someone who'd just made you feel like he'd hooked the moon just for you and then disappeared when the sun stole over the horizon?

'I wouldn't ask if I could think of anyone else,' Stella said.

Winnie nodded. 'OK. Give me ten minutes.'

Out of breath from running, she banged hard on Jesse's door. Even still, her heart banged louder on her ribs.

'Jesse, it's me!' she called. 'Open the door? Please?'

Nothing.

She thumped it again, this time using both fists. 'Jesse, for God's sake. I haven't come to talk about last night. We never have to say another word about it if that's the way you want it. Just open the bloody door, will you?'

She waited, but still nothing.

'Jesse!' she shouted. 'You stubborn, stupid man! Why be like this with me? I really need your bloody help and all you can think of is your precious one-night-stand rule! I'm sorry if you wish it hadn't happened, but don't ask me to apologise or wish I could turn the clock back and change things because I wouldn't change one single solitary thing about what happened in my bed last night.'

'You're gonna break the door down if you keep that up much longer.'

She swung around and found him sitting in the easy chair in the shadows, his feet propped on a crate in front of him and a half-empty bottle of brandy in his lap. He was still wearing his clothes from earlier, and by the looks of him he hadn't been to bed at all.

259

'What are you doing sitting out here?' she asked, more softly.

'Watching the sun come up,' he said, placing the brandy down beside his chair and easing his feet down to the floor with a grimace. 'Thinking. Wondering why the hell you're banging my door as if the sky's about to fall in.'

'Because most of the residents of the island seem to think it is,' she said, her mind back on message. 'And they've all gathered in the garden back at the villa to wait for it to happen. Honestly, you should see it. There isn't a bare patch of earth that someone isn't kneeling on and crying, and none of us can make any sense of what in God's name is the matter with everyone. We've tried calling Panos but he seems to have conveniently disappeared off the face of the earth just when we need him most, so I've been sent here as a last resort to see if you'll come and try to shed some light on what's going on.' She paused to draw in a deep breath.

'Well, not last resort, exactly,' she added, since that might have sounded rude. 'As our neighbour.' She stopped again. 'And as our friend.' Another loaded pause. 'And as my –'

'Your what?' he said, still and quiet.

Winnie looked down and sighed. 'My friend who happened to make love to me once.'

He stood up, dusting his hands down his jeans, not quite meeting her eyes when he spoke. 'There's a difference between sex and making love, Winnie. Don't confuse the two.'

Wow. Thanks for pointing *that* distinction out. Embarrassment tried to weave its way like thorny tangled weeds around Winnie's ankles, but she stamped it under the soles of the cowboy boots she'd flung back on to run down the lane.

'Whatever,' she said, offhand. 'It's just a figure of speech. Call it what you like. Call it fucking, if you like. We did it, and we're not going to do it again, so let's both just grow up and get over it. Now will you come and help us, or not?'

She had no clue where those words had come from, and they clearly shocked Jesse as much as they did Winnie.

He opened his mouth to speak and then closed it again. Scrubbing his hands over his face, he shrugged.

'Lead the way.'

Winnie half ran, half power-walked back to the villa with Jesse a few steps behind, her wooden heels banging loudly enough on the path to startle the swallows resting in the olive trees.

'Wait up,' he said, catching hold of her hand just before they reached the villa.

Winnie shook him off, still stung by his remark back at his house.

'Jesse,' Gav called out from the garden and raised his hand in greeting when he spotted them out in the lane.

'I didn't mean to upset you,' he murmured, shooting a wave back in Gav's direction.

'You didn't,' she said shortly. 'Let's go in.'

If anything, there were more people in the garden than when she'd left, and alarmingly there were still others straggling across the beach.

'Jesse.' Frankie rushed at them with a look of desperation in her eyes. 'Help!'

He clicked into his role of helpful neighbour, shooting Frankie a reassuring smile and squeezing her shoulder.

'How long have they all been here?' he asked, scanning the crowd.

Since not long after you stole away just before dawn, probably, Winnie thought, but swallowed her words and let Frankie do the talking.

'Since first light. I was doing yoga on the beach like normal and people started to drift across the sand in small groups. I didn't realise at first that they were actually coming to the villa, I assumed they'd head on past and up the lane.'

'Let me go and see what I can find out,' he said, skimming a glance at Winnie before he melted away.

'Everything all right between you two?' Frankie watched his back as he picked his way towards the group huddled around the remains of the arbutus bush.

'Flippin' marvellous,' Winnie mumbled.

Even in the midst of the chaos, Frankie picked up Winnie's mood. 'I'm not sure if you're sad or mad, but either way I'm guessing it's his fault.'

'I'll tell you later,' Winnie sighed. 'Let's just try to get to the bottom of this for now.'

Gav walked past them with a jug of iced water to refill people's glasses.

'Thanks for helping,' Winnie said. 'We can do without anyone else passing out.'

Gav nodded. 'Shall I bring you both a glass?' he said, noticing their empty hands. 'Or maybe you should stand in the shade?'

'We're fine, honestly,' Frankie said as he moved away. Heroically she didn't add that they'd been living on the island for a while now and had worked out how to live with the weather.

'Frank, Winnie.'

Stella called them from the kitchen doorway, giving them a subtle nod to come inside. Checking that Jesse wasn't already heading back with information, they headed indoors.

'Corinna!' Winnie caught sight of their latest visitor and greeted her warmly, then belatedly registered that like most of the rest of the islanders, Corinna was dressed in black and had a sombre look around her dark eyes.

'What is it?' she asked, stepping back to arm's length.

'Ladies, I came as soon as I heard,' Corinna said, her throaty voice adding gravitas to her words.

Frankie frowned. 'Heard what?'

Stella sighed, clearly already abreast with the news.

'It's our mayor,' Corinna said, bowing her head. 'Mayor Manolis. He passed away unexpectedly late last night.'

'Oh,' Winnie said, flummoxed by the unexpectedness of the statement. She'd heard his name mentioned a few times in passing but wasn't really aware of his significance to the islanders.

'He was so beloved by the island people.' Corinna spoke so quietly that both Frankie and Winnie had to lean in a little to hear her. 'Ninety-seven, but as fit as an ox,' she sniffed. 'Very few people remember a time when he wasn't our mayor. He's always governed us with a strong, peaceful hand.'

'I'm sorry,' Frankie said, glancing at Winnie and then Stella as she reached for a tissue and pressed it into Corinna's hands. 'I can see it's very upsetting for everyone.'

Corinna glanced towards the back door, her hands twisting the tissue. 'The thing you have to understand about the island is that it's steeped in tradition and ritual. We're simple people, with traditional family values and, as I'm sure you know by now, deeply held beliefs.'

A sense of unease crept slowly over Winnie as she listened. It was clear that Corinna was working up to saying why what appeared to be the entire population of the island was gathering in their garden.

On that, Jesse opened the kitchen door and stepped inside.

'Bad news, ladies. The islanders think you killed the mayor.'

CHAPTER TWENTY

'That was the worst day I can remember,' Stella said, her chin propped in her hand as they sat around the kitchen table later that night. The last stragglers had finally gone home, having spent most of the day mourning their mayor and shooting baleful, accusatory looks towards the three Englishwomen who'd blown into the island on an ill wind and burned down their sacred arbutus bush. It had seemed almost ridiculous that people would genuinely lay the blame for the mayor's demise on the fire, but there was no getting away from the fact that that's exactly what pretty much everyone had decided. Frankie, Winnie and Stella had robbed the island of its much-lauded good fortune, starting right at the top with their beloved mayor. What was worse was that the three of them had no choice but to assume responsibility for the fire between them, because they couldn't exactly blame Mikey Miller. One word in the wrong ear would be enough to bring the paparazzi running to Skelidos, their long lenses trained on the villa, hoping to catch a few grainy images of its famous inhabitants. They'd spent the day holed up in their rooms;

Seth had offered to come down and help but Frankie had ushered him back upstairs with his friends and sporadically plied them with food.

'The funeral will be within a couple of days,' Corinna said. Winnie slid the band out of her hastily pulled back hair because it was giving her a headache.

'Oh God,' Stella said suddenly. 'They're going to want to drink gin, aren't they?'

All three of them exchanged panicky looks. The supply of Ajax's gin had dwindled quickly; the need to find a replacement for the arbutus berry had gone from pressing to critical.

'Don't panic,' Frankie said. 'It won't help. We still have enough berries in the jar to make a couple more batches.'

The others nodded, thankful for Frankie's calming personality.

'We need to do a full count up and see how much time we have,' Winnie said, sipping her cup of tea. She'd never been a big tea drinker back home in England, but they'd dug out their supply of teabags and made a pot as soon as they were finally alone. They were English, after all, and in times of trouble they turned to tea.

'Did even one person look at you as if they didn't wish you dead?' Stella asked.

Frankie and Winnie shook their heads. The islanders had been nothing but warm and welcoming before today, but they'd dished out a lifetime of reproachful stares between them as they all came to witness the burnt bush with their own eyes. The three women felt well and truly like unwelcome outsiders.

'Corinna did, to be fair to her,' Winnie said.

Frankie brightened a little. 'And Panos.'

Panos had arrived at Villa Valentina around lunchtime,

having spent the morning at the town hall after being summoned there first thing to discuss the crisis with the island elders. He knew of course about what had really happened in the garden, but they'd sworn him to secrecy and he'd reluctantly agreed.

'I think it's time someone showed me this distillery of yours,' Gav said, appearing in the kitchen doorway.

Stella looked like she might protest, but then shrugged, resigned. 'I guess our secret's out anyway. I don't think I ever want to see another G&T.'

'It must be bad then,' Gav said. Stella narrowed her eyes, and then laughed, easing the tension in the room.

'It was a bloody shrub!' The words exploded from Frankie, followed by hysterical gasps of laughter. Winnie looked at her, and then her own shoulders started to shake too until she was laughing so much that tears rolled down her cheeks. Stella gripped one of each of their hands around the table, and there they sat, laughing until they cried despite the fact that none of them really found it even the slightest bit amusing. They were anxious, and they were over-tired, and they all harboured a tiny, niggling question of doubt over whether there could be any truth in the islanders' unshakable belief in the mythical arbutus bush of good fortune. After all, hadn't they been brought here on a whim? Wasn't there an air of magic and happenstance to the way that all of their lives had aligned to give them the means and the motivation to come here at all? Had fate *really* brought them here to wreak havoc?

'Come on,' Winnie said, looking at Gav. 'Let's show you the distillery.'

'We have fifty-four bottles ready to go on the shelf, another fifty of our own gin steeping which will be ready in a few

267

days, and then enough berries to make up about a hundred more before we run dry,' Frankie said, having weighed their dwindling supply of dried berries carefully. 'On usual calculations we'd scrape by for a few months, but God knows how much we're going to have to supply for the funeral.'

'What if they ask for more than we have?' Winnie said, already knowing the answer.

'We're in trouble,' Stella said.

Gav looked around the cool, gloomy cellar. 'Those shelves look like they could come down at any minute,' he said, eyeing the flimsy shelves that housed their only supply of gin.

'God, don't even say it.' Frankie shuddered. 'I'm already paranoid about that bloody bad luck curse.'

'No such thing as curses,' Gav said, stoic. 'You make your own luck. There is such a thing as crap shelving units and drunken celebrities with cigarettes though, and neither of those things are any of your faults. Let's put the existing stock on the table for safety and I'll see what I can do to shore up those shelves for you.'

Even Stella seemed to draw solace from his steady, practical presence. Frankie and Gav might not be a couple any more, but they were cut from the same calm, determined cloth that made people around them feel instinctively safer.

Working methodically, they spent a quiet quarter of an hour moving the gin onto the more solid workbench and turning the newly distilled bottles of gin as required, admiring its already rose-gold hue.

'It's going to be all right,' Frankie said, when they were done. 'Tight, but all right.'

'Fifty bottles?' Winnie all but whimpered down the phone in reception when Panos called the next morning to place the town hall's funeral order for gin. 'Are you sure they're going to need that much?'

Stella stood beside her shaking her head. 'Too much!' she hissed. 'Talk him down!'

Winnie pulled a helpless shrug. How could she tell Panos that the funeral was likely to wipe out their stock of gin? The islanders were already sure their sole intention was to rid Skelidos of its tranquillity and good fortune. If she let on that they were about to run out of gin too she feared that they'd be tied together and stoned in the old square outside the town hall.

'Fifty bottles,' she said, hanging up the phone.

'We're shagged,' Stella said, looking at the ceiling. 'We'll have four bottles left. We may as well book ourselves onto the next plane home. It's that, or wait for them to come and kill us in our beds.'

'At least we'll have our own bottles ready in a couple of days. That's another fifty. I reckon we should make up the whole stock from the berries we've got left, at least that way we'll have some breathing space.'

Stella didn't look convinced. 'It's a stay of execution at best, Win. We can't find any more dried berries to be shipped here for love nor money, and there seems to be no one selling live plants who's able to get them to us all the way out here.'

The mail system to Skelidos seemed to operate on a wing and a prayer, which was fine if you were attempting to order a new dress or, say, a curling iron, but inconvenient if you needed to obtain something as precious and seemingly essential to life as an arbutus plant.

Winnie stared out of the open villa doorway towards the peaceful beach and further to the glittering turquoise sea. It was such a rich, beautiful palette, jewel-bright and vivid. When they'd arrived here she'd been full of hope and sure this place would become home for ever. Now, though, she couldn't shake the unsettling feeling that her days on the island were numbered.

Frankie sat on the shady bench outside the kitchen door, grabbing a quiet five minutes.

'Penny for them?'

She looked up when Seth strolled through the garden gate, a bottle of water in his hand. She wasn't able to share her inner thoughts for a penny or a million dollars, because she was too uncertain of them herself to voice them articulately.

'Nothing really,' she said, lifting her sunglasses onto her head as he sat down alongside her.

'I wanted to say how sorry I am, how sorry we all are, for what Mikey did,' he said, looking at the blackened, burnt-out part of the garden. 'All of that stuff yesterday was pretty full on, wasn't it?'

Frankie shrugged, trying to be philosophical. 'Tradition is important to the people here.'

He took a long drink and slowly screwed the cap back on the bottle. 'Nothing wrong with that,' he said. 'If there's one thing that life in the band has taught me over the years it's that routine and stability can be hard to come by.'

'And are they always a good thing, do you think?' she asked, because his words were pertinent to the questions rolling around inside her head. 'Routine and stability, I mean?'

Seth laughed softly. 'Can I say something?'

The gravel in his voice made her stomach drop, reminding her that this wasn't just any man, it was Seth Manson. 'Of course,' she said, suddenly nervous out of nowhere.

'My life is always moving, Frankie, and people are always moving in and out of it,' he said. 'Being here . . . being around you . . . I like it. There's something about you that makes me feel, I don't know, relaxed.'

She flushed at the compliment.

'And I might be speaking out of turn,' he went on, 'and you can tell me I'm being a vain cock if so, but I think you like me too.' He sounded for all the world like an awkward teenager.

Frankie wasn't sure what to say. 'I've had a crush on you for twenty years' sounded a bit freaky.

'But here's the other thing,' he said, laying his arm along the back of the bench. 'I think you're still in love with your husband.'

'Ex,' Frankie said, a reflex response, and then she sighed and twisted her fingers in her lap.

'And,' he carried on, 'I'm damn sure that your husband still loves you like crazy. Why else would he be here?'

'Ex,' Frankie said again, surprised by the lump in her throat. Seth had managed to cut right to the heart of the knotty issue she'd been weighing up in her head on the bench before he came. Gav.

'We haven't had sex in over a decade,' she said. 'Stella doesn't think he'd even know what colour my eyes are without checking.'

'Brown,' Seth said, without even looking her way. 'Brown, and wise, and very lovely. I don't believe for a minute that Gavin hasn't noticed that every day for the last decade, even if you weren't setting the sheets on fire.'

A small smile touched Frankie's lips. 'Thank you for noticing me,' she said.

'If I'd met you in a different place at a different time, and if I wasn't too fucking grown up for my own good, I

271

wouldn't say this, but I reckon you should think about giving your marriage another go.'

Frankie looked into his eyes, the same eyes that had smouldered at her from her bedroom wall for so many years, and she sighed with deep, longing regret. 'Bloody love,' she said, shaking her head.

He laughed then, a low, intimate noise in his chest. 'Bloody love.' Reaching out, he stroked the back of his fingers down her cheek. 'Frank?'

She looked at him, waiting.

'Now that we've got that out of the way, can I kiss you? Just once, so we both know?'

Her lips parted slightly of their own accord, because this conversation was the stuff her dreams were made of. In fact, it was the stuff millions of women's dreams were made of.

Seth's hand moved to cradle her neck as he drew her closer and, when he lowered his head to hers and their lips met, Frankie touched her fingers against his jaw too. He was brief, but not so brief that he didn't take the time to let his mouth linger on hers for a little while, gentle and full of wonder. It wasn't passionate so much as it was wistful, a kiss of hello and goodbye, a kiss that said, 'I see you, and in another lifetime I'd choose you in a heartbeat.'

It lasted fifteen seconds, twenty at most, but for Frankie, it was a kiss that set the course for the rest of her life.

From behind the lace that obscured the kitchen window, Gav watched his wife and the rock star smooch and felt his heart break into a million tiny pieces.

They hadn't planned on attending the mayor's funeral in case their presence displeased the locals, but Panos and Corinna had been forthright in their insistence that to stay

272

away would give the islanders the impression that they didn't care.

And so it was that at ten o'clock the next morning they found themselves wearing black and sandwiched tightly on a pew at the back of the packed church in the town square, surrounded by what surely must be every man, woman and child on the island. Corinna had taken the seat beside Winnie, and Panos sat the other end on Stella's left, their presence effectively barricading them from any hostilities.

Winnie recognised some of the faces from their garden yesterday, and it was clear everyone recognised *them* from the sideways looks and heads turning in their direction around the room.

'I still don't think we should have come,' Stella whispered.

'It was the best option in the circumstances,' Frankie said quietly as people jostled for space and greeted each other like long-lost friends even though they'd most likely seen each other only yesterday.

At the front of the church the mayor had been grandly laid in an open casket, and a steady procession of islanders queued down the aisle for their turn to pay their respects.

'We don't need to do that, do we?' Winnie murmured.

'Not on your life,' Stella said, a little too loud, earning herself a shush from the pew across the way.

Winnie glanced over and found a sea of eyes surreptitiously looking at them, then felt a touch on her shoulder and turned to find that Jesse had slipped into the end of the pew behind them. He didn't speak, just squeezed her shoulder for a second, and she was grateful for it even though their last confrontation had been less than pleasant.

Throughout the long service of prayers and hymns, the

273

three Englishwomen sat quietly, bowing their heads when others did, keeping their lashes lowered for most of the hymns as they tried their best to hum along. Many people wanted to speak about Mayor Manolis, from his terribly elderly widow and children to various other friends and colleagues, meaning the service was long and stiflingly warm. By the time the congregation moved out into the square, everyone was hot, bothered and more than a little fractious.

'We're not going to come to the burial,' Winnie said, drawing Corinna aside. 'It feels too personal. We didn't ever get to meet Mayor Manolis, and we think it would be more respectful of us to stay away.'

Corinna nodded. 'As you wish,' she said, her dark eyelashes damp with tears as she kissed Winnie on each cheek. 'You were brave to come today. Panos and I will speak for you.'

Winnie hugged her quickly, grateful for the act of friendship. Their own lack of language skills meant that communicating with the islanders was always a hit and miss affair, so attempting to talk to them about something as important as this was nigh on impossible.

'Come on,' Stella said. 'I've just spotted Gav circling.'

Gavin had driven them into town that morning so that they didn't have to try to find a parking space for the car, or indeed so they didn't draw unnecessary attention to themselves in the grand old soft-top.

'OK?' he asked, as they all climbed gratefully into the car as soon as they'd walked around the corner from the square.

'Not really,' Frankie sighed. 'Bit like yesterday, really. Everyone still thinks we're public enemy numbers one, two and three.'

'Except the mayor was laid out at the front for everyone to see today. *That* much was different to yesterday.' Winnie shivered.

'I've been for a drive up that viewpoint on the hill,' Gav said, pulling away from the kerb. 'Spectacular up there, it is.'

Winnie nodded and turned her face to look out at the passing buildings, glad of the breeze. She couldn't think about the viewpoint without thinking of Jesse, who'd gone and confused her all over again today with his solid, comforting presence in church. Just knowing he was there if she needed him had been enough to steel her nerves. At the end of the day she, Frankie and Stella hadn't actually done anything wrong, but they'd been made to feel hideous nonetheless and his open display of friendship had said as much about him as it had about their bond.

Back at the villa, they piled out of the car and made a beeline for the door.

'I need to get out of these clothes and under a cold shower.' Stella kicked off her high heels as soon as they stepped through the front door onto the cool tiles.

'Me too,' Winnie said. 'I might go and lie on the beach in a while and read a book. We never do that, do we?'

It was true. Their time was always taken up with the villa, the gin, Tryx and a million and one other things that didn't involve lying in the sunshine and enjoying the new life that they were building. Or at least they *had* been building, before the fire. Nothing felt as definite any more.

'Coffee, Gav?' Frankie said, drawing a nod and a shy grin from her ex-husband as he dropped the car keys in the drawer at reception. Winnie didn't miss the lingering look that passed between them, and made a mental note to ask Frankie what, if anything, was happening.

Stella and Winnie made it as far as the top landing before they heard Frankie yell out for them, and the panic in her voice had them taking the stairs two at a time to get to her. The kitchen was ominously empty and the cellar door even more ominously open, and as they headed down the stone steps they could see exactly what had made Frankie shout.

The cellar had been trashed, and Mikey Miller was lying face-down amongst the broken glass.

CHAPTER TWENTY-ONE

'Jesus, I'm so sorry.'

Seth stood in the cellar with them a little while later and surveyed the mess. He and Jamie had been out on a hike into the hills that morning, leaving Mikey snoring like a donkey in bed. They hadn't expected him to even surface before they returned, and they hadn't known that Gav had driven the women to the funeral, leaving Villa Valentina in the unreliable hands of Mikey Miller. He'd probably gone to the kitchen in search of food, and while he was about it he'd evidently ambled down the cellar and realised he'd hit drinkers' paradise.

'It's my fault,' Stella said. 'I don't think I closed the cellar door after Panos came and collected the gin for the wake.'

'It's not your bloody fault at all,' Frankie said, in a rare display of temper. They'd been hanging on to the hope that by some miracle they'd be able to limp through the next couple of months on the gin and berries they had left, and that by further extraordinary good luck they'd strike a new source of berries in time for the island's supply not to dry up altogether. It was a whole lot of maybes and if onlys, but thanks to Mikey Miller's solitary, spectacular piss-up, all of that had gone out of the window in the space of a few short hours. He'd drunk at least one full bottle of gin, opened a second, and stumbled into the rest, sending bottles flying in all directions. The floor was strewn with broken glass and scattered botanicals from the Bad Fairy bottles they'd made up themselves a few days earlier. The only thing missing from the scene was Mikey Miller himself, who'd been blue-lighted across to Skiathos by water ambulance to have the contents of his stomach pumped and his cuts sewn up. He was lucky to be alive.

'I don't know what we're going to do,' Winnie whispered.

'I do,' Gav said. 'Go back upstairs. I'll clean this lot up.'

'Gav, no,' Frankie protested. 'It's all right, between us we can –'

'Gav's right,' Seth interrupted. 'You three go up and have a cup of tea, or a whisky, or whatever you need to make you feel better. We can do this between us.' He nodded towards Gav, and they both looked as if they weren't going to take no for an answer.

Because it would have seemed churlish to refuse, but also because it had been such a trying couple of days and they were worn out, Frankie, Stella and Winnie accepted the offer of help and filed quietly back upstairs to get out of their funeral clothes. It crossed all of their minds that the curse of the arbutus bush might be more real than they'd given it credit for.

In the cellar, the two men swept, mopped, bagged and straightened, clearing up all traces of the disaster.

Every now and then, Gav threw a look at Seth's back, wondering how the hell he was ever supposed to compete with a guy like that.

And every now and then, Seth studied Gav as he swept, wondering if he knew how lucky he was to have someone like Frankie. Gav swept a pile of glass into the dustpan, and Seth held an open bin-liner out for him to tip the shards into.

'Do you know what colour Frankie's eyes are?' he asked suddenly.

Gav paused, the empty dustpan in his hand. 'They're brown,' he said, eventually. 'Coppery brown, like English pennies, and when the sun catches her face you can see shards of gold in them, like tiger stripes.' He stopped short and huffed, embarrassed. 'We can't all be clever with words, can we?'

Seth laid the bag down. 'It sounded pretty clever to me.'

Gav looked as if he might say something more, and then he bent to pick up a jar that had rolled beneath the bench.

'Shit.' He turned the empty jar over in his hands.

'What is it?' Seth asked, but the pained look on his face suggested that he already knew what Gav was about to say.

Gav turned the jar around so Seth could read the hand-written label.

Arbutus berries.

'I'm going home.'

'Stell, no,' Winnie said, her head jerking up as she buttered the toast the next morning.

Frankie looked stricken. 'You can't give up just like that,' she said. 'I know it looks bleak now, but if we all stay and pull together . . .' She trailed off at Stella's set expression.

Finding out that not only had they lost all but seven of their own bottles of gin but all of their precious berries too had been the final straw for them all yesterday.

They'd sat outside and watched the sun sink below the horizon, wondering how their adventure had gone so quickly from sand-between-your-toes paradise to hell in a handcart.

'I'm not a quitter,' Stella said, offended by Frankie's choice of words. 'I just know when enough is enough. I had a job offer a while back from a rival marketing company back at home. It's not great, but I've emailed them and accepted it. I'm booked on the morning ferry back to Skiathos.'

Winnie sat down hard on the nearest stool, utterly dejected. 'I don't want you to go.'

Stella swiped the back of her hand over her eyes, and Frankie crossed the kitchen and hugged her hard.

'Please don't go, Stell. We need you.'

'No, you don't.' Stella pulled in a deep shuddery breath. 'This place . . . this life, it isn't for me. I thought it was, for a while, but I don't belong here in the way you two do.'

'You do,' Winnie said, fierce despite her trembling lip. 'You, me and Frank. We did this together.'

Stella shook her head, downcast but determined. 'My bags are packed and my flights booked. This time tomorrow, I'll be back in England.'

'Is there nothing we can say to change your mind?' Winnie held on to the handle of Stella's suitcase, as if she imagined that not letting go would be enough to make her friend stay.

Stella already looked different. She'd dressed as if she meant business, in dark jeans and a white shirt, glamorous gold jewellery at her throat and wrists, her makeup dinner-date perfect. It was all for show, of course;

carefully chosen armour to deflect the fact that she was going home with her heart in her boots and her tail between her legs.

'No,' she said, swallowing the ball of tears in her throat. She gripped Winnie's and Frankie's hands tightly. 'Make this easy on me, OK? Smile, say we'll talk later, and then walk away without looking back.'

A tear escaped from the corner of Frankie's eye.

'I'm sorry,' she said, swiping it with her fingertips. She hugged Stella quickly, then pushed a brown paper parcel into her friend's shaking hands as she stepped back. 'I made you some food. For the trip.'

Winnie couldn't bear it. Her heart ached with unshed tears, but she held them all in for Stella's sake as she hugged her goodbye.

'Text me when you get to the airport, let us know you're safe,' she whispered, clinging to her.

The ship's horn sounded, and Winnie reluctantly stepped back.

'That's your cue to leave,' Stella said, blowing them each a kiss.

For a moment none of them moved, and then Frankie and Winnie both straightened their shoulders, turned their backs and walked away from the port without looking back.

At the cargo end of the ferry, a battered red flatbed truck rolled onto the dock. The driver jumped out to check that his goods were still all intact, and then hopped back into the cab and set off across the island.

Villa Valentina was too quiet without Stella. The place didn't ring with the clatter of her heels or give off the exotic scent of her perfume, and both Winnie and Frank felt as if a wheel had fallen off their tricycle. It wasn't so much a workload issue; the arrival of the band had changed the shape of their summer anyway. It was much, much more personal than that. The fact that Stella had gone home to England without them meant that she'd be there without them. They wouldn't be there to turn to if she needed them, and she wasn't going to have the security of a familiar job or home to ease herself back into her chilly old life. They were as worried about her being in England alone as they were about being in Skelidos without her.

'We can't even drink gin,' Winnie said sadly, trailing behind Frankie into the kitchen, checking her phone in case Stella had texted to say she'd changed her mind and jumped off the boat at the last minute. She dumped the phone on the side when she saw the stubbornly plain screen. The tiny supply of gin they had left was too precious to touch.

'I don't fancy a drink anyway,' Frankie said, tying her apron around her middle. 'It's not the same without Stell.'

'What are you making?'

Frankie reached the flour down out of the cupboard. 'Cheese and rosemary scones.'

'Stella's favourites,' Winnie sighed.

Frankie sniffed and glanced at the clock. 'She should be at the airport now.'

It had been three hours since they'd deposited Stella at the port, and in four more she was due to catch her flight home.

'Shall I text her?'

Frankie shook her head. 'Let her be. It's hard enough for her already.'

Winnie knew Frankie was right, but it didn't make it

any easier. 'So,' she said, to distract herself. 'What's going on with you and Gav?'

Frankie stripped the leaves from a sprig of rosemary without looking up. 'Nothing really. We're just getting to know each other again, I think.' Her hands stilled as she looked up. 'It's so weird, Win. We lived together for so long, day in, day out, and yet we didn't even see each other, not really. What a waste, eh?'

'Maybe not,' Winnie said. 'At least you have the boys to show for it. It can't have ever been a waste, really, when you stayed together to give them the best chance.'

Frankie's expression softened at the mention of her beloved boys. They checked in with their mum most days, ribbing her about her crush on Seth Manson. What she didn't know is that they also checked in with their dad too, giving him daily pep-talks about not being intimidated by some yesteryear boy-band member and to stick to his workouts like they'd instructed him. It didn't matter how old the boys got, they still held on to the fantasy of their parents reuniting.

'True,' she said. 'But I didn't think there were any feelings left between us. You know, husband and wife feelings.'

Winnie tipped her head on one side.

'And what about now? Do you still think that?'

Frankie opened her mouth to answer, and then closed it again when someone tapped the kitchen door.

'Hero,' she said when she pulled the door open, dusting her hands down on her apron.

Winnie crossed to stand beside Frankie, and they looked out at not only Hero but three strapping men in vests behind her.

'My yioi,' Hero said falteringly, and the men all smiled obligingly when she gestured towards them.

'What do you think she means?' Frankie said out of the corner of her mouth.

'No clue. I hope they're not suitors,' Winnie whispered.

Hero's lips twisted as she considered how to convey her message, then she turned to the side, mimed a huge belly and then rocked an imaginary baby in her arms.

'They're her sons!' Winnie said, giving Hero the double thumbs-up to show they understood.

'Three brides for three brothers?' Frankie wondered quietly. 'Someone should break it to her that Stella has already left.'

Hero, however, just seemed glad to have made herself understood. She said something to her sons, and then sent them out of the garden and back out towards the lane.

For a moment, confusion reigned. Hero didn't try to elaborate any further, just shot them an anticipatory smile and nodded, probably because she had a clue what was going on.

'At least she's talking to us again,' Frankie said. Hero had been at the funeral yesterday, but whenever any of the three women had tried to catch her attention she'd quickly averted her eyes.

'What's that noise?' Winnie said, stepping outside to check out what the rumbling, jangling noise was, just as the first of Hero's sons rounded the corner of the villa pushing a wheelbarrow.

Frankie stepped out too, and they stood in silence as one by one, the three brothers lined up in front of them, each of them with a loaded wheelbarrow.

Frankie's hand moved to cover her mouth at the same time as Winnie said, 'Oh my bloody God!' because the wheelbarrows were all stuffed to brimming with unopened bottles of Skelidos gin. They stared from the barrows to the brothers and finally to their tiny mum, hardly daring to hope.

Hero touched her fingers to her chest, and then threw her hands out towards them.

'You,' she said. 'You.'

'Oh God,' Frankie said quietly, as Hero turned and picked up two bottles and gave them one each, then waved her arm over the barrows to indicate that they were all for them. The brothers began to unload them in ceremonial silence, until there were over a hundred bottles of gin lined up like little soldiers all along the back wall.

'Thank you.' Winnie clutched Hero's hands in hers. 'Efcharisto, Hero.'

Hero nodded, clearly delighted to be able to bestow such a kindness on them. She held up her hand and then paused, obviously gearing up to say something else.

'Sorry.'

She looked at one of her sons for approval, and he nodded to let her know that she'd said the word correctly.

It was one tiny word, but said with such practice and faltering generosity that both Frankie and Winnie were moved to hug her, thanking her in both English and terrible Greek.

They wanted to ask her why, and how, but they knew that there was little point because she wouldn't under-stand the question and they wouldn't understand the answer. For now, it was enough to know that they weren't going to have to face the rest of the islanders and declare the gin distillery bankrupt of stock. Hero and her sons took their leave with deep bows, leaving Frankie and Winnie sitting on the bench staring at their unexpected gin windfall.

'Well, at least we know she isn't a raging alcoholic,' Winnie said.

Frankie nodded. 'I wonder why she was paid with gin if she didn't drink it?'

It was a question that had to hang in the ether, because outside on the road someone pulled a truck up to the back gate and then leant on the horn to get their attention.

CHAPTER TWENTY-TWO

'Angelo?' Winnie squinted at the driver of the red flatbed truck. It was definitely Angelo. The sharp business shirt and tie confirmed it, even though he was driving a pickup that would be more suited to overalls.

Frankie joined her on the footpath. 'Oh,' she said, folding her arms. 'It's you.'

It wasn't Frankie at her most polite, but then he'd kind of earned her coolness.

He looked beyond them, craning his neck into the garden. Winnie didn't need to ask him who he was looking for.

'She isn't here.'

His shoulders slumped. 'When will she be back? I'll wait.'

'You'll wait a long time, then,' Frankie said. 'She's gone back to England.' She didn't add *because of you*, but it was clear from her voice that she thought it.

'No,' he said, urgent and hollow. 'When? I need to see her.'

Winnie looked at her watch. 'Her flight leaves in two hours.'

Hope flared in his dark eyes. 'She hasn't yet flown?' He looked away, clearly thinking.

'Look, Angelo,' Frankie sighed. 'Don't even think about stopping her. You're one of the main reasons she's left.'

'But I have something for her.'

'So mail it.'

He shook his head, frustrated. 'It's not that kind of something.'

Winnie took pity on him. 'Then leave it here, she can have it the next time she visits.'

He rubbed a hand over his jaw, thoughtful, then dropped the van keys into Winnie's hand. 'OK. There you go.' He waved at the truck. 'I can't stay.' He looked at his expensive watch. 'There's somewhere I need to be.'

Throwing his suit jacket down in the dust, he rolled his shirt sleeves back then took off on foot, running full pelt down the road as if there was a hot poker up his ass.

Winnie and Frankie watched him for a moment, completely thrown by his crazy, out-of-character behaviour.

'He wanted to give Stella a second-hand pickup truck?' Winnie said, gazing at the keys in her palm.

Frankie walked around it, and then suddenly scrambled up on the bumper and stood gazing at the contents of the open-back truck.

'Win, get up here,' she gasped, tugging Winnie by the hand until she stood alongside her on the chrome.

They stood shoulder to shoulder and gazed in silent wonder at the haul of at least ten verdant, glossy green arbutus bushes with fat, creamy blooms, all tied up in yellow-ribboned terracotta pots.

'Frank?'

Frankie turned from the sink, drying her hands on her

288

apron at the sound of Gav's voice behind her. Winnie had called across to let Panos know about their change in fortunes, and she'd just finished the calming business of cleaning the big old kitchen. Her only plan was to sit down with her recipe books and earmark potential dishes to test out over the coming weeks, so it was a surprise to find she had company. Company with a bottle of champagne in his hand and a bashful, nervous look in his eyes, at that.

'Wondered if you fancied a drop of the proper stuff, to, you know, celebrate,' he said, holding the bottle out in front of him.

'You always said champagne gave you a headache,' she said, remembering how she'd often wished he'd share a bottle with her on special occasions.

Gav cast his eyes down to the floor tiles and sighed. 'You're not the only one who needed to change,' he said softly, coming into the kitchen and pulling up a stool at the breakfast bar. 'You did the right thing, leaving me.'

'Gav . . . I . . .' Frankie shook her head. 'You don't have to say that just to make me feel less guilty.'

'I'm not,' he said, then laughed sadly. 'Don't get me wrong, Frank, it's taken me a while to get to this point. I wanted to kill you for a while back there, but even then I couldn't blame you, not really. We were in the mother of all ruts, weren't we?'

Frankie reached a couple of glasses from the cupboard, nodding sadly. 'Shopping on a Monday morning, fish and chips on Friday, clean the house every Sunday morning.'

Gav popped the cork quietly. 'You forgot about washing the car on Saturday afternoon.'

Frankie looked at him across the breakfast bar. 'Do you still do it?'

'Wash the car on a Saturday?' he said, pouring a foaming inch into each of the glasses. 'Nah. I sold it and bought myself a dirty great motorbike.'

Frankie's eyes opened saucer-wide. 'You're kidding me?'

Gav shook his head. 'I always fancied one.'

'You never told me that.' Frankie watched him top up their glasses, feeling as if she barely knew this fitter, more relaxed version of her husband at all.

'We had twin sons before I'd even passed my driving test, Frank. Hardly any point in letting myself dream about things I couldn't have, eh? There's a lot of things I never told you,' he said, pushing a condensation-coated glass towards her. 'Probably a lot of things you never told me, either.'

It was an unsettling thought, that he'd cherished quiet hopes and dreams of his own that their circumstances had prevented. Frankie realised that she'd spent so much time dwelling on her own thwarted ambitions that she hadn't taken the time to wonder if there were things on Gav's wish list, too. It'd been far easier to cast him as dull and predictable; had he thought the same of her, she wondered now? And if he had, would he have ever reached breaking point himself if she hadn't? It was both comforting and kind of discomforting to think that their separation had allowed Gavin the space and freedom to put his own needs first. She'd lazily imagined him still queuing for his fish and chips on Friday evening, still sleeping in his indent on the lefthand side of their kingsize bed, still washing the car on Saturday afternoon before heading to his armchair to watch the match. Had he just been settling, too? Making the best of things, all of the while dreaming of the open road on a throbbing motorbike, the wind in his hair, some blonde riding pillion? The very idea had Frankie gulping her champagne, her mind racing. She'd let herself see Gavin as . . . well, maybe she'd let herself stop seeing him very much at all.

'We stopped laughing, Frank,' he said, pouring a little more fizz into her glass. 'It wasn't your fault or mine. We were kids raising kids, and it was bloody difficult, wasn't it?'

Frankie nodded, a sudden rush of tears clogging her throat. 'It was. God, I love them, and I know you do too, but our teenage years were a mire of dirty nappies, second-hand clothes and making do, weren't they?'

Gav looked over her shoulder at the garden out of the window, his eyes miles and years away.

'We did our best,' he said. 'You're a bloody brilliant mum, Frank. The boys adore you.'

A tear escaped, rolling down her cheek. It was the most valued compliment Gav could have paid her; if there was one thing that Frankie felt most guilty about, it was that the twins were now officially from a broken family. No matter that they'd stayed together until the boys no longer needed their roof or support, she still felt like a sad statistic; a failed marriage was hard on your heart and your self-image too.

'You're a great dad too, Gav. The boys are lucky to have you.' Gav met Frankie's gaze, and the raw uncertainty there pulled her up sharp. 'What? Don't you feel it?'

He didn't reply, just sighed heavily and looked down into his champagne glass. Frankie realised that in all of the years they'd lived together, she'd rarely made the time to let Gav know that he was doing a stellar job as a dad; she'd seen only the holes in their own relationship rather than the strong fabric of his personal relationship with his sons.

'You're kidding me, you must be,' she said softly, reaching across the breakfast bar to cover his hands with her own. 'All of those Sunday mornings freezing your ass off on the touchline watching them play, the way they always looked to you for help with their homework, the way you always made sure you made it to parents' evenings and assemblies, even though it meant using up your holiday allowance. All of that stuff mattered, Gav. You taught them how to be the young men we're proud of today. You did that.'

In all of the years Frankie had known Gav, she'd never once seen him cry. To see him well up now was almost more than she could bear; she was around the counter in seconds with her arms around his shoulders.

'Oh Gav,' she said, as he turned on his stool to face her. 'I'm so sorry. I'm sorry for everything.'

'Don't say that,' he said fiercely, blinking the tears away. 'I'm sorry. I let you down, Frankie. All I thought about was putting money in the bank and food on the table. I didn't think about flowers, and compliments, or surprising you just because you deserved it.'

'Jesus, Gav, come on,' Frankie said, more sharply than intended. 'Thank God you had those priorities. You kept a roof over our heads doing a job you've never especially loved. Do you really think our divorce was about lack of flowers or compliments?'

He half laughed, picking up his glass. 'Maybe not. But we lost the art of talking somewhere along the way, didn't we?'

Frankie couldn't deny the truth. 'We did. We lost the art of talking, or laughing, or . . . anything else, for that matter.' She couldn't bring herself to say the words, but they both knew that she was talking about sex.

Gav swallowed most of his champagne. 'I still think of you as my Audrey Hepburn,' he said, fast and embarrassed.

Frankie stared at him, incredulous. 'You do?'

He refilled their glasses. They were both drinking their champagne too quickly, to help oil the wheels of the most intimate conversation they'd had in seventeen years.

'I never stopped thinking you were the prettiest girl in town,' he said, placing his glass down and standing up. 'I just stopped telling you.' Tentatively, he put his hand on her waist and drew her nearer. 'That's why I came here, Frank. To tell you now, and hope it's not too late.'

Back in school, Gav had been the handsome rogue, the cheeky, happy-go-lucky guy whom all the girls fancied and who only had eyes for her. Frankie saw that guy again now; those same sparkling eyes, that same reassuring height, and oh God, that same sudden spiral of excitement unfurling in the pit of her stomach when he paid her a compliment.

'This, Gav. This is what's been missing. I thought it had gone for good, but now . . .' she trailed off, not even understanding what was happening here herself. And then he dipped his head and kissed her, slowly at first and then not slowly at all, tentatively and then passionately and undone. Frankie cried a little, because feelings she thought had disappeared had only been hiding all along, and Gav felt as if the broken pieces of his heart were magnetically pulling themselves back into one complete whole. He led his ex-wife through to his room and laid her on his bed, then closed the door and pulled his T-shirt over his head.

A while later, he wandered into the kitchen to retrieve what was left of the champagne, because, at long last, Frankie and Gav had something precious to celebrate.

*

293

Stella flicked through a copy of *OK!* half-heartedly, looking at the pictures of celebs and their beautiful lives, until she reached the latest star-studded wedding centrespread and unceremoniously dumped the mag in the bin beside her unforgiving metal airport seat.

The huge ticking clock on the wall informed her that she had one more hour to go of her own beautiful sunshine life, and then it was back to England, where the current forecast was grey skies and an unseasonably cold easterly wind.

Whatever. Stella's only plan was to check into the nearest Premier Inn, drink a bottle of wine, and then crawl into bed for a day or two before she set about the grotty business of reality again. She should never have come to Skelidos in the first place. She wasn't a whim and exotic adventures kind of woman. She was a go-getter and a ball-breaker, and she intended to live up to her name when she walked into her new job on Monday. *God. Monday.* Her heart wasn't just in her boots, it was beneath the soles of them, squashed into the tread like old mud and stones. God, she was furious. Furious with herself for being so stupid as to believe in fairytale lives, and even more furious with Angelo for being the real reason she was leaving the island.

'Stella!'

Yeah, there he was again. She wasn't even surprised that every man sounded like him. She heard his voice all of the time in her head, and even though she kept telling him to piss off he seemed insistent on hanging around.

'Stella!'

Right, so that was getting annoying. Piss off, Angelo. You're Greek, I'm English, and I'm leaving you here in this bloody airport when I get on that plane and I'm never

294

going to even say your name again. She drummed her polished nails on the metal armrests as her eyes scanned the boards to see if her gate had come up yet.

'Stella.'

So this was a first. Her ears and her mind had been playing tricks on her for weeks, but up until now she'd been able to rely on her eyes at least to tell her the truth. They seemed to be failing her now though, because they were showing her Angelo Vitalis, and he was on his knees in front of her looking out of breath and relieved and terrified and all kinds of gorgeous. She blinked a few times. Be gone, demon man, be gone.

He didn't go anywhere. He stared at her, real as you like in his pale-blue shirt and tie, and then he put his hands on her knees, warm and heavy, and she realised that her eyes hadn't conjured him up from thin air and dogged longing, he was actually there, flesh, blood and beating heart.

'What the bloody hell do you want?'

She went from shell-shocked to furious in a flash. She'd been less than an hour away from escaping this godforsaken place, this place where every raven-haired man made her heart fleetingly hurt and every broad, suntanned shoulder made her remember being unceremoniously thrown over one and taken to bed. And now he was here. He was here, and she wasn't having it.

'I've come for you,' he said, never taking his eyes from hers. Didn't he realise he sounded like the grim reaper?

She coughed, spluttered in fact. 'You've come for me? Bollocks you have. Why? I didn't ask you to come and I don't want you here, so piss off.'

'I've come to take you home.'

'I don't need an escort. I'm a big girl.'

295

'Your home isn't England. Your home is with me.'

Christ! Stella felt her knicker elastic almost literally twang. It was absolutely ridiculous and outrageous, but all the same, he was here and he was saying things he had no right to say and her traitorous body was reacting in a way that proved it hadn't learnt a single lesson when it came to him.

'All of those things you read about me were true,' he said. 'I was a stupid, lonely man looking for company in all the wrong places, including at the bottom of champagne bottles and at stupid parties with people I didn't even like.'

Stella looked at his big, bronze hands clamped over her knees and felt her determination falter, because he could have been describing her own life before she came to the island.

'And if the truth is all I have left to give you, then here it is.' He pulled his mobile from the breast pocket of his shirt. Clicking through it, he found what he was searching for and turned it towards her to show her the grainy image on the screen. It took Stella a minute to understand what she was looking at, and then she felt her blood slowly start to boil in her veins.

'Why do you have that?'

Angelo shook his head. 'I'm not proud of myself, Stella.'

The image wasn't salacious, or sexy. It was far worse than that in Stella's eyes. It was a recipe carved into an old wooden bench. The secret recipe for Skelidos gin, carved into the bench in the cellar at Villa Valentina.

'It's dynamite stuff. The minute I tasted it I knew I could sell it. If I could bring this back to the mainland I'd be able to recreate it, and everyone would forget about those newspaper spreads because all they'd be able to print about me would be about this remarkable gin, discovered by chance on an even more remarkable island. It had the potential to be huge. Gin is the new black, Stella, you know that, and with a backstory like that? You couldn't make up anything better if you tried, could you?'

All of the uncharitable thoughts she'd ever had about this man had been true. He'd been using her to get information on their gin, and at some point he'd been in the cellar and spotted the recipe. *God*. Her cheeks flushed at the memory of being in the cellar with him. What a fool she was to have imagined he'd been there for her. He'd been looking for that damn recipe all along. He probably took the recipe shot while they were banging away and she was too delirious to notice.

And the worst of it was that she could well understand his drive, because she was a similar animal. She knew what it felt like to be on top in the boardroom, and she knew how shameful it was to be clinging to the edge of that table by your ragged fingernails.

'No,' she said. 'I don't suppose you could have invented a better story.' She was refusing to look at him.

'Oh, but I can,' he breathed. 'I can invent one where I'm sitting in the boardroom with the other stuffed shirts about to hit them with my brilliance, and I realise in the nick of time that I'm about to make the most colossal mistake of my damn life, so I get up and walk out of that office, out of the building and out of my job. And then I drive the truck containing the only stock of arbutus plants in mainland Greece out of the car park without revealing them to everyone as if I'm the gin fucking magician, and I don't stop until I reach the port several hours later.'

Stella wasn't sure if her heart was even still beating. 'What happens next?' she whispered.

'I'd make the ferry by the skin of my teeth, of course, and I'd take the plants where they should have been all along, and then I'd go inside and make wild passionate sex with the woman I love, because she's kind and wise enough to accept me back despite all of my faults and my vanities. She'd accept me exactly as I am, because the man I am with her is the man I want to be.'

'Make wild sex, huh?' she said, half laughing and half tearful, aware that the mostly English package-tour holidaymakers around her had stopped what they were doing to listen in, rapt.

'Except I was too late,' he said, shaking his head. 'She'd gone, and all of my plans would come to nothing because she'd already given up on me.'

Next to them, a woman groaned. Stella couldn't blame her; it wasn't the way fairytales were supposed to end.

'What happens in the end?' she said, looking into his soulful, coal-dark eyes and finding all of her own fears and hopes reflected right back.

'Well, he dashes to the airport and catches her just in the nick of time, and then he falls on his knees and begs her to come home with him, because he doesn't think his heart can stand even one more sunrise without her lying next to him.'

'Oh my God,' someone sitting nearby muttered. 'If you don't want him, I'll have him.' Murmurs of assent came from around the departure lounge.

'This isn't some soppy movie,' Stella said, desperate to overcome her fears and believe him. 'This is real life.'

'I know, my love,' he said. 'I know. There aren't any guarantees here after the credits roll, Stella. I can only stand here and give you my guarantee, my love, and hope that you think I'm worth the risk.' For emphasis, he looked at his phone and then smashed it a few times against the table until it was well and truly out of service.

'Do it, Stella!' someone shouted. Actually *shouted*.

She was going to do it. Of course she was. She'd mentally ripped up her plane ticket the moment his warm hands landed on her kneecaps. Angelo stood up, and when he held out his hand she took it and let him pull her up.

'Kiss! Kiss!' two over-excited little girls screamed, and then Angelo swept her clean off her feet and did exactly that, so much so that the little girls' mothers had to cover their daughters' eyes as the lounge erupted into spontaneous, rowdy applause.

'This is crazy,' Stella laughed, a little bit embarrassed and a whole lot in love.

'Come home and have wild sex with me?' he murmured against her ear, making her shiver.

They broke off when a pensioner in a floral dress and sensible sandals approached them and touched Stella on the shoulder.

'Excuse me, dear,' she said, and the whole lounge strained to hear what she was going to say. 'Have you ever seen *An Officer and a Gentleman*?'

Stella nodded, as did most of the other women in the lounge. Who hadn't given a small slice of their hearts to Richard Gere at one point or another?

'I don't have an officer's hat, but you're welcome to my husband's sun visor. It's barely worn, and the forecast in England is for rain.'

The woman reached up and placed a bright orange plastic 'Skelidos Forever' hat on Stella's head, and Angelo took his cue perfectly to swing her up in his arms and stride across the lounge with her to the exit doors.

'Your shoulder,' she laughed, trying to load her weight onto his uninjured side.

'Is better now. Everything is better now.'

As the doors slid open, a hen party stood on their metal chairs clapping and tunelessly trying to sing 'Love lifts us up where we belong', as the bride-to-be hitched up her fake wedding dress and yelled 'Way to go, Stella! Way to go!'

CHAPTER TWENTY-THREE

Four mornings later, Winnie stepped out onto her balcony and found Frankie doing the same in the next room along, except that her clothes suggested she'd already been out on the beach for yoga practice, and the cup of coffee in her hands smelled appealing.

'Morning,' she said, blinking in the bright sunlight. 'What time is it?'

'A little before eight,' Frankie said.

Winnie nodded. 'No signs of life over there yet?' She nodded towards Stella's balcony at the end with a knowing lift of her brows. Stella and Angelo had barely surfaced from their love nest since their return to the villa.

'Not yet,' Frankie smiled. 'I'll be surprised if she makes it to the gallery with us this afternoon.'

'I really hope she does,' Winnie said. Corinna had hand delivered the stiff ivory and gilt preview invitations a couple of days ago, fizzing about a new exhibition opening there next week. Much as they appreciated Corinna's invitation and understood that she was trying to help them re-integrate, all three women were filled with a healthy dose of trepidation at the idea of mingling with the locals at all.

'Do you think people are ever likely to forgive us?' Frankie asked. 'Because I'm not sure how much longer I can handle being the local pariahs.'

As far as the majority of people on the island knew, they were still guilty of ending the island's run of good fortune by burning down that blessed arbutus bush. Only Corinna, Panos and Hero were privy to the truth; the latter only because Panos had known about her stash of gin and taken her into his confidence.

'Hopefully, in time,' Winnie said. She knew exactly what Frankie meant; she felt the coolness from the islanders whenever she went shopping or across to Panos's bar; people were never rude, exactly, but they kept their smiles for other people and their exclusion hurt. 'At least we're not likely to run out of gin now. That's something, right?'

Frankie sipped her coffee and sighed, and on the balcony below, Seth Manson listened to their conversation and wanted to kill Mikey for the trouble he'd caused.

'Does this dress look all right?'

Frankie turned to look at Winnie outside the gallery. 'It's fine,' she said. 'Will you stop with the nerves, you're making me nervous.'

'I can't help it.' Winnie straightened her white linen dress over her thighs.

'I told you we should have had a drink first,' Stella said, resplendent beside her in killer high heels and a black silk dress painted with red peacocks. She looked sickeningly healthy, with the kind of self-satisfied glow usually reserved for honeymooners.

'Because smelling of gin is always a good way to make

people like you,' Frankie said, laughing and pushing the door open.

'On this island, anyway,' Stella murmured as they stepped into the busy, thankfully air-conditioned room.

'Ladies, you made it!' Corinna made a bee-line for them and enveloped them in perfumed hugs. They each appreciated her no-holds-barred greeting; she made no apology for the fact that they were her friends. 'Smile, my darlings,' she murmured. 'Chins up and boobs out.' She stilled a passing waitress and hooked three glasses of champagne for them, promising to come back and find them for a chat later as she melted back into the throng.

Winnie sipped her drink, and it was only then that her eyes settled to the exhibition, and to the name on the easel by the door welcoming them in.

Jesse Anderson.

Her heart contracted painfully. Predictably, he'd slipped straight back into avoidance mode after their night together – in fact she hadn't seen him at all apart from those fleeting moments at the mayor's funeral. He seemed to have gone to ground; she'd even taken to spending a couple of hours a day in the room he'd given her in the hope that he'd come to her there. Tentatively drawing up fresh jewellery designs based on the flora and fauna of the island, Winnie had discovered peace and solitude, all the time underscored by bittersweet, unrequited longing.

'Shit. We can leave if you like,' Frankie said, following Winnie's gaze.

'Don't run away,' Stella murmured on her other side.

Winnie looked from one to the other. 'Are you two playing devil and angel?'

Her friends caught each other's eyes and shrugged, and Winnie took a good glug of fizz and squared her shoulders.

'Let's just get this over with,' she said, moving to the nearest wall to look at the preliminary sketches that accompanied a nearby sculpture.

'Wow, he's good.' Stella stood admiring the charcoal drawings of a huge black and white cat. Jesse had managed to capture the lithe essence of motion in the animal's movement, while in other images he'd encapsulated the level of relaxation only a lazy feline can hope to reach.

Winnie nodded, recognising the cat in the images as the same one who'd dozed on the armchair in her workroom the day before. 'He is.'

The sculpture itself was equally vivid; more so. He'd chosen to show the cat sleeping in the branches of an olive tree, his chin flat along a branch, his limbs dripping casually down.

Glancing around the room, Winnie thought she caught sight of Jesse himself, but when he turned it was someone different altogether. Surely he'd come to his own exhibition?

'Is that our donkey?'

Winnie followed Stella across to the life-size sculpture. It was, without doubt, The Fonz.

Laughing softly, she nodded. 'Sure is.'

Corinna appeared fleetingly beside them again. 'Recognise anything?' she asked. 'This is Jesse's most personal exhibition to date. Most of the pieces relate to his life here on the island.'

Other pieces followed, every one as lifelike as the last and the little red *sold* stickers were appearing thick and fast, until at the back of the gallery the exhibition took an unexpected turn. A really, really personal one, for Winnie at least, because every last sketch was of her, nude.

He'd made sure that she wasn't identifiable, thankfully,

using her hair to obscure her features in any drawings that included her head. Winnie felt an odd mix of pride, fury and hurt. He should have asked her if she minded this. It was an imposition of the most personal sort.

'Holy fuck,' Stella said, a little too loudly, making Frankie elbow her in the ribs. 'Act natural, Win.'

'It's you, isn't it?' Frankie whispered.

Winnie didn't answer. She didn't have to; her friends knew perfectly well that it was.

'Oh, but Winnie, look at these. They're so beautiful.'

Jesse had made two full-size sculptures of her, both of them loosely based on the seated position he'd asked her to assume the first time he drew her. She was a mermaid on the rocks in the first, her head bowed, her long rope of hair swept over one shoulder, her legs encased by a fantasy scalloped tail. It was whimsical and entirely divine.

The second sculpture transformed her from mermaid to fairy, knees drawn up and ankles crossed, her head dipped forward to rest on her forearms. He'd given her filmy, gossamer wings, rendering her ethereal and enchanting, and he'd entitled the entire collection 'Muse'.

Corinna stood oblivious to them a few steps away, deep in conversation with a woman Winnie didn't recognise.

'Stunning, aren't they? A study of his late wife, I think.' Winnie caught Corinna's confidential tone. 'He never speaks of her, but from photographs I saw when he first moved here these images bear a striking resemblance.'

Corinna's words settled like soft falling snow over Winnie's heart. *His late wife?* Little things he'd said suddenly made sense now. He'd been married, and something tragic had happened to take his wife away. God, no wonder his attitude to love and marriage was so intense. Winnie's heart broke a little for him, and for herself too. Jesse was absolutely entitled to his past and his privacy, but the idea of being so similar in looks to the woman he'd loved held a sudden eerie ring of truth.

'Sold already,' Stella frowned, noticing the red stickers on the base of the two sculptures. 'I don't like the idea of you being displayed in someone else's house, it's not right.'

Winnie had seen and heard enough. 'Can we just get out of here, please?'

They sat outside a café in the pretty town square eating freshly made gelato from bright pink tubs.

'He should pay you to use your image,' Stella said, licking chocolate ice-cream from the back of her small plastic spoon. 'The donkey's one thing, but everyone could see your nipples!'

'People see more on the beach every day,' Frankie said, trying to make less of it. 'He should have asked your permission though.'

Winnie stirred her strawberry gelato listlessly, playing with it more than eating it. 'Did you hear what Corinna said?'

Both of the others shook their heads.

'She said that she thought they were based on his late wife.'

Frankie slid her tub of vanilla onto the table, barely eaten. 'Jesse's a widower?'

'So it would seem,' Winnie said. 'Corinna said that the sculptures bear a striking resemblance to her.'

Both Stella and Frankie seemed unsure what to say to that. Winnie couldn't blame them, she was having a difficult time processing it too. Her ice-cream had turned to slushy milk in the tub, and she stood up sharply and picked up the car keys. 'Let's go home.'

*

All was not as they'd left it when Stella eased the big old car back through the garden gates at Villa Valentina. They clambered out onto the uneven paving stones and found themselves met by a reception committee of Angelo, Gav and Seth, all wearing shorts and looking sweaty and filthy.

'You look like three naughty boys who've been caught doing something that they shouldn't,' Stella said, standing on tiptoe to kiss Angelo square on the mouth. He seemed to lose focus for a second, growling 'I like your dress,' and cupping her ass until she slapped his hand away. 'What have you been up to?'

The men stepped aside to show off the fruits of their afternoon of hard labour. They'd cleared out all of the dead plants wrecked by the fire and replanted the bed with the vibrant arbutus bushes, creating a wall of gorgeous creamy flowers that would turn to their stock of berries come the autumn.

'You did all of this this afternoon?' Frankie whispered. It was as if a garden makeover show had swooped in in their brief absence and worked TV magic.

'Seth's idea,' Gav said generously.

'Panos and Jesse were here too,' Seth said quickly, not wanting to take all of the glory.

'Jesse's here?' Winnie snapped to attention. It seemed bizarre that he'd been here digging her garden while she'd been in town at the opening of his exhibition.

'He left a little while ago,' Angelo said, leading them across the grass to take a closer look at their handiwork. 'Pretty special, eh?'

Stella looked him right in the eye. 'I bloody love you, Angelo Vitalis.'

For a moment, he looked as if he might cry, then he

pushed his hands through his dark hair and threw Stella over his shoulder instead.

'You're going to have to stop doing this,' Stella laughed, but from the way she gaily lifted her hands to wave goodbye as Angelo strode inside the villa, it probably wasn't going to happen any time soon.

'There's one more thing,' Seth said, looking unusually uncertain of himself. 'We've invited a few people over tonight, if that's OK?'

Winnie looked at Frankie, and then shrugged. 'Fine with me.' She couldn't really care less what happened for the rest of the night. She was going upstairs for a soak in the bath, and then she was going to go to sleep and try to forget that today had ever happened.

A few friends turned out to be more than a hundred locals, probably somewhere nearer to two hundred. They came as families and laid their blankets on the beach, and they came as couples with romantic picnics for two. They came as groups of teenagers, and they came as elderly friends who set up sturdy deckchairs in the sand and drank gin from silver hip flasks. Panos had managed to rustle up amplifiers and basic equipment from the high school's music department, and as dusk settled, Seth tapped the microphone to get everyone's attention.

Up in her room at that same moment, Winnie regretted saying she didn't mind Seth's plan to have a few people over, and rolled off her bed to shuffle to the balcony and have a look at what all the noise was about.

'What the . . .' she muttered, trying to take in the scale of what was happening down there. The beach was alive with flickering candle lanterns and crowds of people picnicking, and Seth, a guitar slung over his shoulder, tapped the microphone and greeted everyone loudly in really quite terrible Greek.

Then he handed over the microphone to Angelo, along with a letter of apology to translate on behalf of Mikey and the rest of the band. It explained that the three Englishwomen had done nothing wrong but had accepted the blame anyway, and it asked them to find it in their hearts to forgive them because the women loved the island and wanted to stay for as long as they were welcome.

The crowd applauded and wolf-whistled, and then broke into loud cheers when Seth gave Jamie Harte the nod to strike up the opening notes to one of the band's biggest worldwide hits.

Winnie didn't realise that Frankie and Stella had come to find her until they stood either side of her on the balcony, and for a long, wonderful minute they stood hand in hand and gazed out over the impromptu starlit concert happening right there on their beach.

'Come down?' Frankie asked.

Winnie nodded, squeezing Stella's hand. She'd realised lying in the bath that her time on the island had finally come to its natural end today. She couldn't stay here and be Jesse's neighbour without wishing she was his girl, and she could never be his girl because it was never her that he truly wanted. She understood now why he'd pushed her away and then pulled her close again, why he was sometimes so agonised by their relationship; because it was never really about her at all. Winnie thought she'd glimpsed the future in Jesse, but in her he saw only echoes of the past.

It was time to go home, and she could think of no more fitting way to draw the curtain on her brilliant Greek adventure than to head downstairs and join the party.

*

Frankie flicked the switches beneath the beach bar and the fairy lights wound around its roof struts flickered into life, ramshackle and charming, perfectly in keeping with the villa. They'd taken it in turns manning the bar to look after the locals who hadn't come prepared with their own gin, and to hand out ice lollies to the kids, and finally there was enough of a lull for Frankie to slide onto one of the tall bar stools and watch the show as Seth and Jamie slowed things down.

'Something new now, if you'll indulge us. This one's called "Bloody Love".' Seth turned to catch Frankie's eye momentarily before he started to sing the song he'd written for her, a song about a pixie girl with tiger-striped eyes.

'They're not that bad after all.' Gav came to stand beside her stool, and Frankie found herself winding her arm around his waist and leaning her head on his shoulder. He felt achingly familiar and yet alien, solid, dependable and yet newly sexy too, especially since their unexpected afternoon liaison. Her body reacted to his nearness, and when she looked up at him she found him gazing down at her in a way that made her heartbeat quicken.

'Thank you for coming here,' she said. 'It was brave.'

'Thank you for making me welcome,' he said. 'I wasn't sure you would.' He stopped to look over at the band. 'I'm no rock star, Frank. I'm a normal bloke who's good at DIY and gardening, and I like a beer and the crossword. But I'm not the same man I used to be, either.'

'No, I think you've more than shown me that much,' she said, unaccountably nervous of the man she'd lived more than half her life with. 'I'm not that woman, either. We both made a lot of mistakes over the years, Gav.' She was distracted by the feel of his fingers wrapping around her upper arm, and by the delicious shiver of anticipation that shimmered down her spine when he skimmed the back of his fingers down to her elbow.

'I'm out of practice,' he said, looking for all the world like the nervous boy she remembered from their teens.

'Me too,' she said. 'But that's easily remedied, isn't it?'

He cupped her cheek and lowered his face to hers, kissing her in the intense, territorial way she'd needed him to kiss her for years.

'I love you very much, Frankie,' he said, holding her close. 'I always have and I always will.'

Frankie ran her hand down his back as his familiar aftershave wafted around her. She was deeply affected by his words. Sleeping with Gav had been tender and emotional, but wondrous and incredibly sexy too. They'd talked some more afterwards, quiet, hushed pillow talk; shared memories and soothed hearts. She understood now that their relationship had been lying dormant rather than disappeared, and that although they'd neglected each other, it wasn't beyond repair. Theirs was a love story without end, and right now she felt like her sixteen-year-old self again, dizzy and breathless for the handsome man who'd just handed her his heart, if she wanted it.

Looking up into his beautiful eyes, she curled her fingers around the back of his neck.

'I love you too, Gav. I really, really do.'

A little before midnight, Winnie sat alone, tucked into the bench alcove on the edge of the terrace with her knees pulled into her chest. She smiled at the sight of Angelo and Stella necking over by the bushes, and her heart turned over when she spotted Frankie and Gav close together at the beach bar. As it should be, she realised, watching them. Some people were just meant to be together, even if they needed the extreme push of divorce and foreign adventures to make them see that they'd had what they needed under their noses all along.

Pulling her soft fringed blanket closer around her bare shoulders, Winnie tried to make sense of the summer they'd just shared together on Skelidos. It felt as if magic had pulled them there, and as if fate had finally decided who should stay and who should go. But what an adventure they'd had, what laughter they'd shared, what an unexpectedly wonderful and necessary interlude it had turned out to be in all of their fractured lives. The island seemed to have come looking for them, three birds with injured wings, and little by little they'd been healed, ready to fly home again, if they wished to.

Winnie knew that of the three of them, she was the one they'd all have put money on staying in Greece for ever; it seemed ironic that it had turned out that she should be the one who needed to leave. She wasn't certain what she was going to do yet; definitely not move back to her parents though, that much she was sure of. She'd find a cottage perhaps, somewhere she could work again, make up the island-inspired designs she'd been working on. She might be leaving, but she'd go with a head full of inspiration and a suitcase full of Technicolor memories.

'Hey, you.'

She looked towards the darkness beyond the edge of the terrace, towards the lane leading to Jesse's house. He'd come. She wasn't sure if he would, or if she wanted him to.

'Winnie,' he said, and she laughed when she saw what he had in his arms when he stepped out of the shadows, because he always seemed to know exactly the right thing to do.

'I carried a watermelon.'

She nodded as he laid the huge green fruit on the floor at her feet. 'So you did.'

He looked at her for a long, searching moment. 'Can we talk?' Glancing towards the band, he added, 'Somewhere a bit quieter, maybe?'

She nodded, standing up. 'Let's go inside.'

He followed her through the villa silently to her room up on the top floor, to the bed they'd lain in together. She pulled the patio doors closed, turning the party into a low background hum, and then crossed to lie on her back on one side of the bed.

Jesse stretched out on the other, and for a little while they listened to each other breathing.

'Can I go first?' she said, when she was ready. He rolled onto his side and propped himself on his elbow to look at her.

'OK.'

She faltered, wondering where to start. At the beginning, of course.

'When I came here, I thought my heart was broken. And it was, in a way, because the only man I'd ever known had left me and it felt like the end of the world. And then I came here, and I found that it wasn't the end of the world after all, not exactly. How could it be, when a place like this exists? Even if you *feel* like it's the end of the world, the sun still comes up every morning over the hills, and the sand's still warm beneath your feet, and the birds still sing in the olive trees. There's a gentle insistence to living here, and it seemed to insist that I meet you.'

He listened, watching her eyes, not giving himself away as she marshalled her thoughts and lifted her eyes to the ceiling and carried on.

'You stormed into my life on a flurry of bad temper and beautiful eyes, and you completely, utterly blindsided me. You're unapologetically rude, and then you're so damn thoughtful that you seem to see right inside my head, and then you stubbornly refuse to acknowledge that you have this sentimental, romantic seam running through you like words through Blackpool rock.'

He huffed softly and she ignored him. Closing her eyes, she recalled the last time they were together in her bed.

'And then you touched me and tried to teach me how to not let my head or my heart get involved, but, Jesse, you failed. You failed, because my head *is* involved. I think about you all of the time, and I miss you when you're gone from me, and I dream about you when I go to sleep.'

She opened her eyes and looked into his, clear and direct.

'You failed, because my heart *is* involved too. I thought it was broken when I came here, but I was wrong. It was never his to break, because I never loved him the all-encompassing, sun-moon-and-stars way I love you.'

Slow devastation seeped into Jesse's face, but when he went to speak she shook her head for him to wait.

'But in the most important way of all, you didn't fail. I was afraid when I came here. I wouldn't have said so, but I see now that I was.' She swallowed. 'I'm not afraid any more, and much as I want to stay here, I can't. Corinna mentioned your wife, that the sculptures were of her.'

Again, he opened his mouth to speak, and again she shut him down.

'It's OK, it really is. You don't need to explain. It's time for me to go, that's all. I need to find my own place, just like you did. I need my *own* Skelidos, somewhere to put down roots, to work, to find a life that suits my bones.

You've taught me all of that. You loved me better, Jesse Anderson, even though you never intended to.'

She stopped speaking and drew in a deep, shuddering breath, feeling more naked and exposed to him than she ever had before.

'I'm done,' she said, with a tiny, vulnerable half smile.

He nodded. 'I know. And I want to kiss you until you feel better again and tell you it'll all be all right, but I can't.'

There was a melancholy edge to his voice as he reached into his back pocket and pulled out a photograph folded in half. Opening it, he handed it to her.

'This was Erin. My wife.'

The woman in the photograph was young, early twenties, and she was laughing, her long blonde sea-tangled waves swinging around her suntanned shoulders.

'She was beautiful,' Winnie said.

Jesse nodded slowly. 'She was. We were starving art students intent on changing the world one piece at a time, and she was *that* girl. The one everyone's drawn to because her laugh is the loudest, her wit the sharpest, her talent the brightest. And out of everyone she could have picked, she picked me, and I thought I was the luckiest bastard alive.'

Winnie listened, and even though it was ridiculous, she envied the woman in the photograph that she was loved so much.

'We married in January, and in July she stepped in front of a train.'

'Jesus, Jesse,' Winnie gasped, horrified by the blunt end to the love story.

'She was too much of everything,' he said, closing his eyes, remembering. 'Too talented, too jealous, too effervescent, too emotional. She could be wildly loving and

315

then incredibly mean, generous to a fault and then take my breath away with her selfishness.'

Jesse shook his head. 'My commercial success eroded her confidence in her own ability, even though she was always streets ahead of me. I got lucky and she got furious. She packed away her tools and never touched them again after we married.' He opened his eyes. 'Artists need to make art, Winnie. You have to, or else it builds up inside you like pressure, like a bomb, it makes you irrational and brittle and delusional, and if you don't let it out it makes you step in front of a fast-moving train to escape from it.'

Winnie understood now exactly why he'd given her a key and a room to work, and her heart twisted for him.

'So you came here,' she said, quietly.

He nodded. 'I came here. I didn't plan on staying for ever; it just turned out that way. And I thought it was enough, right up until the moment I knocked on your kitchen door.'

He took the photo from Winnie's hands and looked at it. 'You reminded me of her, like someone kicked me in the guts wearing spiked boots. Something in the shade of your hair, the curve of your hip, the air of special that surrounds you.'

There was a compliment wrapped up in there some-where, but his confirmation of Corinna's suspicion was all Winnie's fragile heart heard.

'I tried to stay away from you. I told myself that it was wrong, that your fleeting similarity to Erin was the reason I felt drawn to you. But still you came to see that damn donkey, and every minute I spent with you I saw a different woman, not her at all. You're soft, and you're kind, but then you have this huge fucking brave streak that shines from you like, I don't know, frickin' She-Ra, and you have the biggest heart of anyone I've ever met in my entire damn life.'

He stopped and stared at Winnie, and she just stared right back, both of them breathing a little too fast.

'I've spent the last ten years feeling guilty that she died, and guilty that there were so many sides to her that I found hard to love. One-night stands, skin-deep sex. It was my way of coping, and it became my way of living. And then there was you, beautiful gorgeous you, and I was all kinds of screwed because I knew one night would never be enough.'

Just as he hadn't interrupted her, Winnie stayed silent to let him speak.

'It was something, wasn't it?' he continued. 'That night, right here in this bed? My God, I've never known it. Not back then, and never since. I wasn't lying when I said that there was a difference between sex and making love, Winnie, and I only knew because you showed me. Those sculptures, the drawings at the gallery. You know, Corinna got that wrong. They're all you. You're a mermaid on the rocks calling me in, and you're the fairy who can change lives with one careless wave of your arm. You couldn't see her face on the sculpture, but it's there. You're there, and that mischievous, devil-may-care light is there in your eyes. The same look you had in my studio when you took your clothes off and asked me to draw you naked.'

Winnie wasn't certain where this conversation was headed, or where their lives were headed.

'Someone bought them,' she said. 'I saw the sold stickers.'

He shook his head, as if she ought to know better.

'They were never for sale. They're mine, and they'll stay here.'

317

'Oh,' she sighed, glad. 'Oh.'

'Will you stay too?' he asked. 'Will you stay with me always?'

A tear slid from her eye to her hairline. 'What about your one-night-stand rule?'

Jesse's arm slid beneath her neck, and they rolled onto their sides and lay forehead to forehead.

'It still stands,' he said, stroking her hair back from her cheek. 'I just want it to be with you, over and over again.'

Outside, Frankie and Gav danced beneath a canopy of a million stars and things got decidedly raunchy for Stella and Angelo behind the newly planted arbutus bushes, and upstairs Winnie and Jesse slid between the sheets for the second of a lifetime of one-night stands.

EPILOGUE

Three years later . . .

'I can't believe they're twenty-one.' Frankie leaned back against Gav's arm as she watched her sons play football down on the beach with a crowd of their friends. They were as suntanned as the locals, but given the fact that they spent as much time on Skelidos as they could these days, that was no great surprise.

'I think Josh has his eye on Almena,' Stella said, slanting mischievous eyes at Corinna across the table as she sat on Angelo's knee and spooned paella onto a plate for him. He shifted her slightly in his lap with a hidden grimace, clearly unwilling to tell her to move because her enormous baby bump was in danger of breaking his legs.

'My daughter is a law entirely unto herself.' Corinna laughed good-naturedly. 'God help him.'

They'd gathered on the beach terrace at Villa Valentina to celebrate the twins' birthday, just as they gathered there for many other occasions these days.

Winnie appeared carrying a tray of glittering rose-pink G&Ts and handed them around for a toast.

'Mayor first, of course,' she said, placing a glass in front of Panos. He took the duties of his office seriously, checking the colour and taste of the gin for accuracy even though there was really no need. Frankie and Gav had the distillery running like clockwork, as indeed they did the whole place. Villa Valentina had earned itself an enviable reputation amongst discerning travellers as an exclusive place to unwind and recharge your batteries surrounded by fresh food, dawn yoga and bedrooms to die for. Gav's DIY skills had slowly and sympathetically pulled the bed and breakfast from shabby to boutique, all whilst retaining its understated grand-old-lady appeal.

'Will you give up work for a while when the baby comes?' Corinna asked Stella, who looked shiftily at Angelo.

'Yes,' he said, replying for her at the same time as she said, 'Maybe.'

Stella grinned at him. 'I might take a week or two off.'

'Vitalis Wine and Spirits can cope without you, my love, much as you hate the idea.'

Stella and Angelo spent their time hopping between their home on the island and Athens, running the company they'd founded together sourcing specialist drinks from around the world and turning them into international brands. The only drink they would never dream of selling was Skelidos gin.

Winnie slid into her place next to Jesse, her wedding ring winking in the sunshine.

'OK?' He kissed her shoulder. 'Did he go down?'

'Out like a light,' Winnie said. She'd just rocked their round-limbed, dark-haired baby boy to sleep in his push-chair in the cool shade of Villa Valentina's now discreetly air-conditioned reception. The baby had arrived in their lives a few months ago, turning their slow idyllic life on the olive farm upside down in the best possible way. These days Jesse was as proud of his wife's blossoming jewellery design business as he was of his own high-flying career in the art world, but their best days of all were the long lazy ones spent lying on their backs in the olive grove with the baby kicking his legs like a frog between them, and the hot, sensual one-night stands tangled together under the cool sheets.

'I know it's self-indulgent,' Frankie said, hushing everyone, 'but I'd like to raise a glass to my boys. Our boys,' she corrected herself, looking at Gav. 'I can't believe how quickly time has passed, and I'm proud to death of the men they've become.'

'To Josh and Elliott,' Gav said, choked up.

Everyone raised their glasses, and then Panos stood and cleared his throat.

'I have something of great importance to say.' A hush fell over the group as he lifted his glass and scrutinised it. 'This gin is absolutely, exactly perfect.'

Everyone laughed.

'Too right. It's my baby,' Frankie said.

'It's my plants,' Angelo said, as if that was clearly the reason.

'It's my labels,' Winnie insisted of her by now well-established Bad Fairy branding.

'It's my rigorous devotion to taste testing,' Stella sighed into her juice.

'Maybe it's a bit of all of us,' Winnie said, gazing fondly over at the villa.

They'd come here years ago in search of adventure, not knowing what form it might take, or how long it would last.

How lucky they were, or perhaps they'd made their own

luck. Either way, the garden full of healthy arbutus plants seemed to have restored the island's tranquillity and good fortune, and Villa Valentina continued to rest easy in the Skelidos sunshine, presiding over the bay, ready to provide safe harbour and escape to those in need.

Acknowledgements

Huge thanks to my clever, very lovely editor Phoebe Morgan at Avon. Working together on this sun-soaked book has been a joy, thank you for being endlessly encouraging and wise.

Thank you also to the whole Avon team for your input and help, I feel very lucky to be part of the family. Wider thanks to all at HarperCollins for everything you do on my behalf, I'm really very grateful.

Thanks to my agent, Jemima Forrester, for your sage advice and for being a strong supportive shoulder whenever I need one. I'm so glad to have your help to steer the ship, preferably with a G&T in our hands!

Many thanks to Emma Rogers for another eye-popping cover. I adore it, it really shouts summer on the beach.

Love and thanks of course to everyone who reads the book, and to the bloggers and reviewers. Thank you, I hope you enjoy escaping to Skelidos as much as I did during the cold winter months as I wrote it. People often ask me if the characters in my books are inspired by anyone in particular. In this case the answer is yes, as far as Jesse is concerned, at least. At the time of writing I was often watching *Hooten and the Lady*, starring the very handsome Michael Landes as the swashbuckling leading man. I'm not saying Jesse *is* Hooten . . . perhaps more like Hooten's wise-cracking, imaginary twin. Fans of the show will understand I'm sure, not least the ever so slightly obsessed Kim Nash!

Last but never least, thank you to my family and friends, who I love and lean on for encouragement. You're a fabulous bunch.

All's fair in love and war...isn't it?

Fall in love with more Kat French this summer – the perfect holiday read!

You never know who you might
end up with...

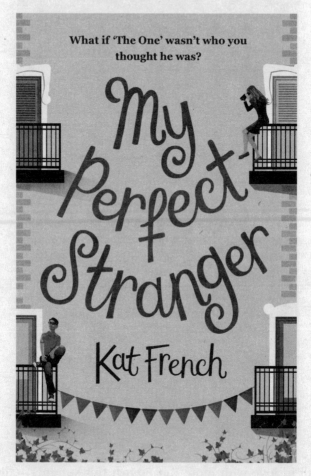

What if 'The One' wasn't who you
thought he was?

My Perfect Stranger

Kat French

Sometimes, the boy next door might just surprise you...

Things are hotting up
this summer...

Kat French is back – and there's a cowboy in town...

If you like Kat French, you'll love Ellen Berry...

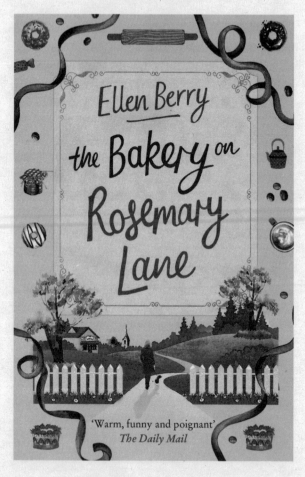

Ellen Berry

the Bakery on Rosemary Lane

'Warm, funny and poignant'
The Daily Mail

Take a trip to Yorkshire this summer
with the bakery queen!